"The insider detail will fascinate you. The action will thrill you. *Shadow Catcher* by James R. Hannibal takes you on a riveting journey into today's U.S. military and CIA in a high-stakes battle against Chinese espionage. Hannibal is the real deal, and *Shadow Catcher* is as authentic as it gets. You won't want to stop reading."

—Gayle Lynds, *New York Times* bestselling author of
The Book of Spies

SHADOW MAKER

JAMES R. HANNIBAL

BERKLEY BOOKS, NEW YORK

THE BERKLEY PUBLISHING GROUP
Published by the Penguin Group
Penguin Group (USA) LLC
375 Hudson Street, New York, New York 10014

USA • Canada • UK • Ireland • Australia • New Zealand • India • South Africa • China

penguin.com

A Penguin Random House Company

SHADOW MAKER

A Berkley Book / published by arrangement with the author

For information, address: The Berkley Publishing Group,
a division of Penguin Group (USA) LLC,
375 Hudson Street, New York, New York 10014.

ISBN: 978-0-425-26690-8

PUBLISHING HISTORY
Berkley trade paperback edition / June 2014
Berkley premium edition / February 2015

PRINTED IN THE UNITED STATES OF AMERICA

10 9 8 7 6 5 4 3 2 1

Cover images: *Flag* © Leonard Zhukovsky / Shutterstock; *Drone*:
HIGH-G Productions / Stocktrek Images / Getty Images; *Landscape*:
From the Heart / Flickr / Getty Images. Cover design by Richard Hasselberger.
Hashashin symbols illustration by John Carroll.
Interior text design by Laura K. Corless.

This is a work of fiction. Names, characters, places, and incidents either are the product
of the author's imagination or are used fictitiously, and any resemblance to actual persons,
living or dead, business establishments, events, or locales is entirely coincidental.

Shadow Maker is dedicated to the outstanding professionals of the 111th Reconnaissance Squadron, whose daily battle to preserve life may never be fully appreciated by the world at large.

ACKNOWLEDGMENTS

There is a long cast of characters that made *Shadow Maker* possible. First and foremost are my wife and our remarkable sons. Without their support and encouragement, there is no way I could keep writing, let alone survive the intense emotional roller coaster that authors ride after publication. I am also thankful for AP, whose generous friendship has kept me sane, though how on earth he manages to do that while denying me sleep and strapping cameras to my head, I'll never know.

Of course, my books would go nowhere without the advice and hard work of my agent, the amazing Harvey Klinger, as well as the team at Berkley—Natalee Rosenstein, Robin, Loren, Erica, and many others behind the scenes. Preceding them in the chain of events is a host of reviewers who see the book and tear it apart (in the most helpful way possible) long before it gets to Berkley. I am extremely grateful to Baron1, Sideshow, Fester, the Millers, Jonathan, the Stanleys, Tawnya and James, and both Nancys. I am also grateful to the rest of my brothers- and sisters-in-arms for the constant flow of ideas, and to London in particular for the use (with permission) of the word *disingenuous*.

There are others who have patiently fielded my research questions. Thank you to Steve Galloway at Heckler & Koch, Noah Durham at the National Archives, Stayne Hoff at Aero-Vironment, and to Skin, the only man I know who must flee from zombies on a regular basis.

Finally, I thank God for His blessings and inspiration, without which I could not write a single word.

PROLOGUE

Yemen
35 kilometers northwest of `Amran
September 2005

Baba, is this the man that is going to kill you?" An adolescent boy lifted a picture from his father's open briefcase and held it up for him to see.

Naseem Kattan crossed the room in three quick strides and slapped the photo from his son's hand. "That is not for your eyes," he growled, slamming the case closed. "And speak the tongue of your fathers. The English language is an offense to your heritage." He glared at the child. He had only been outside for a few moments, and he could swear that the case had been locked.

The boy nursed his hand and looked down at the dirt floor, more surprised and embarrassed than hurt. "But is he, Father?" he asked, obediently switching to Arabic. "Is he going to kill you?"

Kattan's anger subsided as quickly as it had risen. The boy showed no ill intent. He was just curious. How could he not be? Curiosity was a by-product of his intelligence. He reached out with one curled finger and lifted his son's chin. "Let us return to our game, Masih."

The two sat down at a wooden table in the main chamber of their small house. It was more of a hovel, really—a three-chamber structure built of mud. Kattan despised this place, not just the house but the whole village, raised out of the dirt by dirty peasants. Everything here—the air, the water, even the food, tasted of the desert dust, and the desert had long ago ceased to satisfy him.

Over the last two decades, Kattan had developed a taste for the finer things, but the finer things could be tracked, particularly in Yemen, where they were few and far between. He could easily afford to stay in an upscale hotel on the coast in Aden, but there were only two, and the owners were surely on the American payroll. That is why Kattan stayed in this desert hovel whenever he returned to his home country and brought Masih out to see him. With no credit cards to trace, no networks to bug, and no greedy innkeepers or politicians to buy, the Americans could not control this village. The lords of satellites and microprocessors could not control the dust.

Kattan scanned the chessboard, carefully considering his next move. He found a tempting target, checked to be certain there were no threats, and then struck, claiming Masih's bishop. Immediately he caught the faintest hint of a smile on the boy's lips. Masih saw something that he didn't. Unbelievable.

Synagogue bombings in Turkey, the Oasis Compound

massacre in Saudi Arabia, two months of coordinated car-bomb attacks in Baghdad. Kattan had planned the most successful strikes against the infidels and their collaborators in recent history. Large body counts and nothing left behind that could be traced to him or the organizations that hired him. He was a renowned master strategist who could look at a plan and see every outcome, predict the enemies' every move and steer them toward destruction. He nurtured this ability by playing chess, and both his friends and his enemies considered him a master of the game, but Masih . . .

Masih showed signs of *real* genius.

After four moves with a barely contained grin, the boy captured his father's queen. "Check."

Kattan leaned back in his chair and searched the board, trying to see what he had missed. There was a time when he intentionally made mistakes just to prolong their games. Now he wondered if Masih did the same.

"Who is he, Baba?" asked Masih, looking up as he placed the queen next to the rest of his prisoners. "Who is that blond man from the picture?"

Kattan sighed. He could see that the child would not let this go. "He is my persecutor. He has followed me for months, interfering with my holy work, my jihad. But he is only an annoyance, a mosquito to be swatted into oblivion when he comes too close." He positioned his knight to block Masih's next attack.

The child took that piece as well. "Check," he said again. "Will the blond man attack us here?"

"No," said Kattan, offering his son a reassuring smile. "The American cannot attack this house, because it has a special defense."

At this, Masih's eyes began roving the room, searching the drab furnishings and the dirt walls for something extraordinary. Kattan knew he would not find it.

They continued playing in silence. Three moves later, the boy declared checkmate, snatching up his father's king with a wide grin.

Kattan shook his head, but the sting of defeat at the hands of a twelve-year-old was overpowered by the swell of his pride. Look what he had created for the service of Allah: a strategist of unseen brilliance. And Masih already knew the Western mind-set, better than his father, better than any who had come before him. Under Kattan's tutelage, this boy would bring devastation and humiliation to the infidel on a scale that the mujahideen had never dreamed.

"Go get a pail of water from the pump," said Kattan, standing and tousling the boy's hair. "I will make us some tea. Then we will pray."

"But there is a full jug of water by the hearth."

Kattan frowned. "Do as you are told, boy. You may have beaten me at chess, but there is still much that I can teach you. For instance: tea tastes better when we make it with water fresh from the well."

As the boy departed, Kattan went to the hearth to build the fire and cast a furtive glance at the water jug. He had lied. Whether stale or fresh from the well, the state of the water would make no difference in the tea. Like everything else out here, it would taste like dust. He had sent his son to the well for another purpose. The blond American might be watching. Kattan could not be certain he had eluded him at the border. But if he was out there, beyond the edge of the village, the sight of a child near the house would keep him at bay. The infidels did not have the stomach to kill the children of their enemies. That was one of their most exploitable weaknesses.

Kattan had not told Masih the nature of the special defense of this house, because Masih *was* the defense. His own son was his blessed shield.

The terrorist turned from the fire to watch Masih through the open door, pumping water into his pail. The boy was just starting to get some definition in his arms, on the verge of becoming a man, a benefit of letting him live across the sea with his harlot mother. Spared the indignity and starvation of growing up in the desert, Masih had some meat on his bones—much more than Kattan had acquired by that age.

Suddenly, the doorframe and the wall between them evaporated in a blinding flash. Kattan felt flesh ripping from his body as he was slammed into the eastern wall of the house and then dropped onto a pile of rubble. His eyes stung, he choked on a swirling cloud of that cursed desert dust. He could not feel his arms or his legs, yet pain surged through his body.

The cloud thinned. He saw his son, broken, blood staining the mud beneath him black. Masih was still clutching the king in his little hand. He moved his elbow back to his chest and started to rise.

Kattan tried to call out to him, but only a scant whisper escaped his mud-caked lips, "Masih."

The boy did not look up. He collapsed back into the dust and did not move again.

Weakness from blood loss overtook Kattan, and he could not hold his gaze level any longer. His eyes drifted along the ground to the scorched photo of the blond American that lay between him and his son, amid a scattering of burning papers. Then the papers, the rubble, the dirt, all but the photo turned to black. As the terrorist's mind began to fade, one final thought lingered—a name—flickering in the darkness like a dying flame. *Nick Baron.*

PART ONE

OPENINGS

CHAPTER 1

*T*he Christmas decorations are up. That was the first thought that passed through Nick Baron's mind as he walked beneath the grand arched entrance of Washington, D.C.'s Union Station. He was six feet tall and plainly dressed in a brown leather jacket and faded jeans. His wife, Katy, walked next to him, pushing a stroller. She was more elegantly dressed, still resisting the inevitable soccer mom persona. Her auburn hair fell to her shoulders beneath a stylish winter cap. She wore jeans as well, but they were midnight blue and fit her slender form snugly, descending into high-heeled riding boots. Katy was enjoying her afternoon. Nick was not.

His attention to the Christmas decorations did not spring from a yuletide appreciation for the thirty-foot tree in the main hall or the lighted garlands that adorned every horizontal surface, or amusement at the model-train displays stretching across the usually empty floor space. He took notice of the decorations because they cluttered the station, and clutter in public spaces made him uneasy.

They paused in front of the welcome center, a two-story island of cherrywood in the center of the marble hall. While Katy checked the marquee, Nick's steel-blue eyes roamed the crowded station. Smaller versions of the central Christmas tree created shadows in every corner and alcove. Rows of poinsettias and ten-inch riser skirts masked the empty spaces beneath the model trains. All the extra floor displays compressed the heavy holiday traffic into nicely segmented kill zones. What a nightmare.

"You're doing it again," said Katy, letting out a little *oomph* as she thrust Luke's stroller into motion again. "I can see it on your face, the way your eyes are moving. Relax. This is family time. You're off duty."

"We could have had family time waiting in the car at the passenger pickup," he replied, still searching rather than looking at his wife. "You know I hate train stations. They're death traps."

Other terms used by Nick's colleagues in the counter-terrorism community were *low-hanging fruit* and *easy pickin's*. In the post-9/11 world, airports had become ultra-secure, with the latest in screening technology and mountains of rules. In some countries, getting to the aircraft with so much as a toothpick was a challenge. Train stations, on the other hand, remained largely unchanged. Most didn't even use metal detectors. Over the past thirteen years, train lines and their unions worldwide had lobbied hard to keep security lax, in hopes that a public frustrated with being poked and prodded at airports would switch to railways for their domestic travel. Their efforts succeeded in attracting a few extra passengers. They also attracted terrorists in droves.

Since September 11, 2001, eighty-nine people had died in terror attacks against airliners, all of them in a coordinated attack on Russian commuter planes by Chechen Muslims. In the same period, nearly one thousand people had been killed and around five thousand wounded in attacks against railways. Britain, Spain, Russia, no country was immune. Maybe train bombings didn't get the attention they deserved because the body counts weren't high enough, but one day that would change. One day, probably in the United States, some group of radicals would find a way to use the rail system to make a big splash.

Nick quickened his pace and steered Katy toward Platform C, where his father's train was supposed to arrive. As they passed the midconcourse shops, he spied a rolling suitcase sitting by itself, tucked halfway behind one of the little Christmas trees. A security guard a few feet away was too busy gawking at a pair of attractive young window shoppers to notice.

As Nick started toward the bag, a man in a business suit came out of the Starbucks and reclaimed it. He strolled away, oblivious, nursing a venti nonfat sugar bomb.

"There he is," said Katy, tugging Nick back the other way.

Dr. Kurt Baron emerged from Platform C with two small suitcases. He raised one of them in a half wave.

Thanks to strong genes, the older Baron shared Nick's medium build and youthful features, but where Nick's hair was thick and golden blond, his dad's was thin and dark, turning gray. And now it seemed his father had decided to grow a goatee. It looked absurd.

"I told him not to wear that Go Air Force sweatshirt when he travels," he muttered to Katy. "It makes him a target."

"Be nice. You promised no fights."

"He's only wearing it because I told him not to."

"Nick . . ." she warned.

Nick waited impatiently through the obligatory hugs and greetings. He held his tongue while his dad pulled his grandson Luke from the stroller, knowing the effort and time it would take to get the eighteen-month-old strapped back in. He watched the faces in the crowd. None of them seemed threatening or nervous. In fact, most of them looked like they were enjoying themselves. He wondered what that felt like.

Nick took one of his dad's bags and finally got his little group of soft targets moving toward the exit. Miraculously, they made it to the parking garage unscathed.

By the time he pulled Katy's black Jeep Cherokee onto Massachusetts Avenue, a light snow had started falling, adding to the few inches that had already accumulated on the trees and rooftops in the past few days. Streams of tiny flakes ghosted across the street in sidewinding wisps, blown by a light wind. Another front was moving in, this one stronger and colder than the last. Nick sighed. It was going to be a long month.

A delighted squeal erupted from the backseat, and Nick glanced in the rearview mirror to see his dad tickling Luke. At the same time, Katy squeezed Nick's knee—not to say *I love you* but to say *Make an effort to play nice or suffer the consequences.* He frowned at her and then coughed. "Ahem. So, this is very exciting."

"Oh, yes," replied his father, glancing up from his grandson. "I've been waiting for Avi to call me for years. The lecture tour is going splendidly."

"I'm glad you're happy, Dad."

The speaking engagement was a nice distraction, and a necessary one, but Nick did not say that—he didn't need to. They both knew it. Earlier that year, Nick's mom had lost her battle with lymphatic cancer. This would be Kurt's first Christmas without her in forty-three years.

Kurt, a professor of Hebraic studies at Denver Seminary, had received an invitation to speak on Talmudic archaeology at the Hebrew University of Jerusalem, as well as at their satellite campuses in New York and Germany. He started with New York, and with two days to kill before continuing on to Germany, he had taken Amtrak's famous Acela bullet train down to Washington, D.C., to see his grandson. The university's travel office graciously booked his next flight out of Dulles. They booked the return through Dulles too. The older Baron had announced a few days ago that after he came back, he was planning to stay through the New Year.

Nick knew he was supposed to be happy that his dad wanted to spend the holidays with them, but they were both type A personalities, tending to clash when forced together. Since Nick was a teen, his mother had acted as a buffer. Now she was gone.

"You're going to miss the tunnel," said Katy, pointing ahead at the exit for the Third Street Tunnel that ran beneath the National Mall.

"We don't want to take the tunnel." Nick glanced into the rearview mirror with a forced smile. "Dad wants me to drive across the Mall so he can see the sights, right Dad?"

Kurt looked up from his grandson and frowned. "How many times have I told you not to *assume*, Son?" He paused to scratch that ridiculous goatee and watch the exit for the tunnel pass behind them. "However, since you've already missed your turn, I wouldn't mind seeing a bit of your city."

Nick gritted his teeth and jerked the jeep left onto First Street. Yeah, it was going to be a really long month.

CHAPTER 2

The black Jeep Cherokee turned onto Constitution Avenue, entering the National Mall at exactly the predicted time. Standing in the shadow of a tall curtain, a lissome figure lowered his high-powered binoculars and began to dress. Scar tissue covered half of the watcher's back, along with what remained of his right arm. Before donning a shirt, he exchanged the functional prosthetic below his forearm with an aesthetic one, so nicely sculpted that it would fool a casual observer, even if the observer were standing right next to him.

Despite the ugly scars, the man moved with measured grace, taking care to keep the tail of his white linen shirt from brushing the gaudy striped carpet as he lifted it from the bed. His hotel room was adequate, but the institutional-grade carpet offended his bare feet as much as it offended his eyes. He would have much preferred the L'Enfant Plaza Hotel down the road. At least that establishment put pads under their carpets. Unfortunately, their penthouse did not offer the commanding view of the eastern National Mall that today's mission required.

With well-practiced movements, he used his one good hand to button his shirt and then placed a ball cap atop his bald head. He kept it shaven because the scar tissue from his burns prevented his hair from growing normally. This was not vanity. He had learned over the past nine years that appearances played a vital role in achieving one's goals. At times, letting his wounds show suited his purpose. Other situations demanded a more pleasing veneer, and he had acquired the skill and the resources—such as the very expensive prosthetic—to meet that demand.

Like his appearance, the man's name shifted quite often. Sheikh Rahman, Omar Aleem, Mustafa Khan—he traveled and worked under many aliases. But he held only one title. He was the Qaim, the Emissary of the Mahdi, the voice declaring a new age.

The Qaim slipped on a jacket and then returned to the window to check the position of his target. The jeep was now crossing Constitution Avenue. At this range, and from the elevated position of his hotel suite, he could not see the driver through the windshield, but in his mind's eye he saw him quite clearly. He saw the stern expression, those blue eyes searching the road ahead, always searching. He had studied the man for so long that he saw those eyes in every dream, and every nightmare.

The Qaim had studied his target as one should study any opponent, by examining his body of work. That was no easy task, for this man was a ghost and one does not observe a ghost directly—at least, not at first. At the start, one observes the effect a ghost has on its environment, the wreckage it leaves when it passes on. The Qaim had learned to follow the signature his target left behind.

Yemen, Afghanistan, Venezuela, China—the Qaim had traced the blond man's movements across deserts and oceans, digging through the rubble he left in his wake. Capitalizing on the bitterness of survivors and the greed of low-level clerks, he had reconstructed his opponent's previous games one move at a time—pawn, bishop, and king—so that he could understand every maneuver. By now, he knew his opponent better than he knew himself. He knew how this man planned and how he operated. He had learned precisely how the blond man's brain worked.

In his studies, the Qaim had come to know his opponent's family too—his wife and child, his clownish friend, even his boorish, overbearing boss. He wondered how these peripheral players would weather the coming tribulation, and how they would move on in the peace that followed—if any of them survived.

The black Jeep crossed Madison Drive, and the Qaim once again set down his binoculars. With his good hand, he picked up a burner phone and dialed the most recent number. An understandably nervous young voice answered.

"Yes?"

"It is time, Jamal," said the Qaim in a low and comforting voice. "It is time to begin."

————

Jamal dropped his cell phone on the passenger seat. He pulled a tiny ziplock bag from his pocket, dumped the two white pills it contained into his mouth, and forced them down with a gulp from a bottle of water. He set the bottle on the passenger seat as well, without replacing the cap, so that it tipped over and spilled its contents onto the fabric and the phone. Jamal did not notice.

After another moment's hesitation, he carefully got out of the vehicle, struggling to lift the extra thirty-five pounds he carried under his bulky black coat. He had parked in front of the National Museum of the American Indian because it was the only building on this block without metered parking. That allowed him to sit and wait for the Qaim's call without fear of an interruption. At another spot, a meter maid might have noticed the ill-fitting coat and become suspicious.

Despite the cold of the afternoon, there were a number of pedestrians about as Jamal cut diagonally across the street to the Health and Human Services building. A few people sat on the benches in the small park next to the museum. Others huddled under a Lexan shelter near the steps ahead of him, waiting for the next Metrobus. Jamal suddenly wondered if perhaps he should wait for the bus too, but then he dismissed the thought. The Qaim had been very specific about timing.

Most people just hurried by, shoulders hunched against the cold, heading somewhere important. Jamal's eyes fixed upon a particular woman, a blonde in a long black overcoat, her stockinged legs visible from midcalf down to her high heels. She glanced in his direction and caught his gaze. He looked away, feeling the shame he always felt when a woman caught him gawking at her.

Her notice sparked a chain reaction. First the people in the bus shelter, then a couple crossing the street in the opposite direction, then another passing by on the sidewalk. Every eye turned to focus on Jamal. A bead of sweat slowly descended his forehead as he mounted the stacked-concrete platform in front of the building. The drop felt like ice in the cold wind, but he dared not remove a hand from his pocket to wipe it away. He dared not make any move at all beyond crunching up the snow-covered steps. The pills that he had taken were supposed to relax him. Instead, he felt his heart racing, pounding so hard he feared it might explode before he completed his task.

When Jamal reached the top platform and turned to face the street, his pulse settled. All of the terrifying onlookers from a moment ago continued with their former preoccupations. Not a single eye was turned his way. Perhaps they never were. Like every other day of his miserable existence in this cursed country, no one paid him any notice.

That was about to change.

Jamal lifted his head for one last look at the winter sky and snowflakes lighted on his cheeks—the kisses of angels. The blanket of white clouds above glowed with a rosy

CHAPTER 3

As Nick pointed out the National Air and Space Museum to his dad, he heard his wife quietly giggling to herself.

He never got the chance to ask her why.

Katy's laughter became a shriek as an immense blast rocked the Jeep up onto two wheels. The driver-side windows blew completely inward, showering the interior with glass. As the vehicle came crashing down onto four wheels again, it veered left into oncoming traffic. Nick fought the wheel to regain control, swerving back across his own lane and skidding into the curb with his foot jammed on the brakes.

The bomb had exploded ahead and to his left, next to Health and Human Services. The fireball that first flashed in his vision had become a black cloud. Debris rained down around them. Something landed on the roof with a heavy thump.

"Are you okay?" he asked Katy, but she was busy reaching for her son.

"Luke!" she cried.

Nick turned with her and found that the toddler had escaped unscathed. Nick's dad had acted as a shield, taking the brunt of the flying glass.

"Dad, you're bleeding."

"I'm fine."

"Good, then take the wheel."

Kurt Baron furrowed his brow. "What? Where're you going?"

Nick didn't answer. He looked to his wife. She had several small cuts on the left side of her face, but nothing serious. Katy met his gaze and nodded sharply. "I'll be all right. Go."

He popped the rear hatch and climbed out of the Jeep, noting as he stepped around to his father's door that the object that had landed on his Jeep was a severed hand. He brushed it off the roof and into the gray-brown slush beneath the curb. "Dad, get up there and take the wheel. Get them to the hospital in Chapel Point. The closer facilities will be too busy."

"*You* get back in the car and get us out of here yourself."

Nick didn't have time for father-son competition. The Mall was about to fill with first responders and rubberneckers, and soon there would be no exit. Even more pressing, the reaper's relentless clock had started ticking the minute the bomb went off. As the ringing in his ears diminished, Nick was beginning to hear the wails of the dying.

"I can't, Dad. I have a duty to stay and help." He pulled the professor out of the car. "No more argument. Get up there and take the wheel."

Nick continued to the back and uncovered his Beretta Nano micro-compact. He shoved a clip home and slid the weapon into his waistband. Then he grabbed his first aid kit and some blankets. By the time he slammed the hatch closed, his father was in the driver's seat. Nick pounded the side of the jeep with the flat of his hand. "Go!"

As he raced toward the epicenter, the smoke began to clear, revealing a grim scene. In nearly twelve years of special operations, he had seen plenty of blood, but no amount of experience could ever compensate for the shock of a mass-casualty attack. He could swear that he had seen the source, just one man standing atop the puzzle steps outside Health and Human Services, but the casualties looked too widespread for a single suicide vest. It was hard to tell. Maybe the blood stood out more because of the newly fallen snow.

As he reached the outer ring of the carnage, Nick faced the most excruciating question of a first responder: who to treat first? All the wounded were suffering. Some were too far gone to save. He would have to listen to the pleas of the dying while he dedicated himself to saving those who had a chance.

The first of the walking wounded he encountered was a man about his age, dressed in a business suit and still clinging to a briefcase. His other hand covered one of his eyes. Blood seeped through his fingers. He saw Nick and his first aid kit and stumbled toward him.

"Help me! My eye!"

A woman lay mumbling in the snow a few meters beyond the businessman, her abdomen a bloody mess. Nick kept moving toward her, pointing the man toward a nearby bench as he passed. "Sit down over there. Cover both eyes with your scarf and wait for a paramedic to assist you."

The businessman ignored the command. Instead, he dropped his briefcase and turned to follow. He grabbed Nick's arm and jerked him back. "You have to help me!"

"Sir, let go. I need to help this woman."

The wounded man grew more desperate and committed both hands to yanking Nick's first aid kit away. In the instant he let go of his eye, Nick saw that it could not be saved, but he would suffer no other damage either, if only he would be still.

Nick gave into the man's pull for a split second, multiplying his force. Then he struck him full in the chest with an open palm and the businessman fell back on his rear, stunned. Nick quickly turned and continued to the dying woman's side. Amid the dark blood at her midsection, he could see the white of her intestines.

"Jerry," she mumbled, staring with unfocused pupils at the blank sky. "Help Jerry, my husband."

A few feet away, Nick saw a man lying motionless in the street, his head tilted to one side, his eyes open, lifeless. "Someone else is taking care of Jerry," he said. "I'm going to take care of you."

As he opened the first aid kit, he felt a hand on his shoulder. Nick jerked his head around, expecting to see the frenzied businessman. Instead, he found a young man with dark, penetrating eyes. The face was youthful but the expression grave.

"Do you need help?" the young man asked in a commanding tone.

The newcomer had a green duffel marked with a white cross slung under his arm. Despite his obvious youth, he showed no signs of shock or dismay. Nick had to assume from his calm that he had seen combat, or at least worked in a trauma center.

"No," Nick replied. "I've got this one." He pointed toward the epicenter, deeper into the carnage. "Keep moving that way, there are more, lots more."

———

An hour later, Nick sat on the tailgate of an FBI Emergency Response Vehicle, cold, exhausted, and covered in blood. His first aid kit was spent, the bag lying somewhere in the snow. He had laid all of his blankets over victims or folded them under their heads, along with his leather jacket and sweatshirt. Now he wore nothing to guard against the deepening cold but his undershirt and blue jeans.

Washington's army of professional responders had taken over. The severely wounded had been evacuated, and the rest of the living were being treated on-site. The dead lay where they had fallen, surrounded by agents poking them with gloved hands and taking pictures.

Dignity always took a backseat to investigation. The businessman who had tried to take Nick's first aid kit sat on the back bumper of a police car, berating the paramedic who was trying to wrap his head.

When the wounded were taken care of, Nick had turned his attention to the FBI's on-scene commander. He had offered to help with the initial investigation, but the FBI man had tersely directed him to the sidelines. "Get out of the way. You're obstructing our work here."

As he sat there, shivering but too numb to do anything about it, Nick's phone chimed. He checked the screen. He expected to see a text from Katy, asking if he was all right. Instead, he found a black text box with ivory lettering, framed in walnut brown. It came from a chess program that he hardly ever used, one of those game apps that found a random opponent for you if you asked it to. Nick had not. The message in the box sent a chill down his already frozen spine. *The Emissary has initiated a game. Do you want to play?*

CHAPTER 4

"Nick Baron."

A tall black woman with short bobbed hair, dressed in a formfitting gray suit, offered a cold smile and a curt wave from the center of the FBI's crowded Intelligence Coordination Center. Agent Celine Jameson, CJ to Nick, was the head of D.C.'s Joint Terrorism Task Force. She signaled her confused subordinate to back off and allow their bedraggled visitor into the room.

The flustered young agent at Nick's side had given him a lift from the attack site over to the FBI's D.C. Field Office. Nick did not ask for the lift—he was offered a narrow choice by the on-scene commander: hitch a ride to the field office with the rookie and get a cab home from there, or be shoved into the back of a patrol car and be driven six hundred yards to the nearest Metropolitan Police holding cell. Either way, his time at ground zero was over.

Nick had willingly ducked into the back of the black SUV, but that was the extent of his compliance. Instead of catching a cab from the field office as ordered, he had followed the rookie into the building.

The young man had paused halfway through the glass double doors. "I'm sorry, sir, but you can't come through here."

Nick had pushed past him without a word, striding up to the lobby security desk and pressing his Defense Intelligence Agency badge up against the bulletproof glass. Then, at the guard's nod, he drew the Beretta from his waistband.

At the sight of the weapon, the young agent lurched backward, fumbling for his own gun and shouting, "Drop it! Now!"

Again, Nick ignored him. He calmly slid the barrel of his Beretta into a small black cylinder protruding from the security desk. "Oh," he said as he removed the clip and cleared the chamber, "you didn't know I was packing?" He glanced over his shoulder and gave the kid a rueful smile. "I'm sorry. I probably should have advised you that I was armed before I got into your vehicle." He paused long enough to tuck the weapon away again, his thin smile dropping into a stern frown as he turned to face the kid. "Or maybe you should have asked." A loud buzzer punctuated the jibe and the Lexan door to the elevators clicked open.

The kid moved to follow Nick through, but the door slammed closed before he reached it. He rattled it angrily, glaring at the security guard.

The guard glared right back at him. "Identification,

please." He glanced down at the gun still in the rookie's hand. "And you'd better clear that weapon, mister."

The rookie had reappeared a few minutes later, panting at the top of the stairs as Nick stepped off the elevator. From there he clung to Nick's heels all the way to the ICC, protesting loudly, but CJ's dismissive signal served as a final blow. He gave an exasperated shrug and shrank back into the hall as Nick stepped into the room.

On most days, the ICC was a big, eerily empty space with several rows of unoccupied desks. Today it was packed. Scores of people hustled about, representing the FBI, the Secret Service, and a myriad of other agencies and subagencies that never worked well together. Nick stutter-stepped through the crowd, squeezing between desk chairs and forcing the occupants to scoot forward. He earned a number of frustrated scowls. He also earned a few concerned looks. In a brief fit of pity, the on-scene commander had given him an FBI sweatshirt, but the collar of his bloody undershirt still showed at the neck.

CJ stood slightly elevated above the rest of the ICC on a command platform at the center of the room. Behind her were two freestanding boards. One was a touch-screen smartboard with a pair of digital windows showing an aerial photo of the blast site and a live news feed with the sound muted. The other board was clear acrylic with hand-written lists of evidence and a spidery diagram of the agencies that were running down each piece.

"I didn't know the DIA was doing domestic response and cleanup these days," said CJ, glancing pointedly at the badge clipped to the collar of Nick's sweatshirt as he stepped up onto the platform. She smiled as she said it. CJ knew full well that despite his badge, Nick did not work for the Defense Intelligence Agency. She was one of the few outsiders with the clearance to work with Nick's Triple Seven Chase squadron—the last Tier One special mission unit still unspoiled by Wikipedia.

"I was on-site when it happened, CJ," said Nick, ignoring her joke and shaking her outstretched hand.

"So I've heard. The on-scene commander called to complain about a Captain America type hanging around ground zero, barking orders at our people. I figured it was you, so I told him to send you here with the next returning gopher. I also told him to make sure the gopher got you a cab"—she raised her eyebrows—"but I think you know that." She gave him a sly smile. "The OSC told me you offered him a helping hand."

Nick didn't laugh at her joke. "I told him where to find one, anyway. A severed hand landed on my Jeep." He frowned at the agent. "It was the bomber's hand, CJ. Your OSC was looking for remains of a vehicle-borne IED, but the source was just one guy with a vest. I saw him standing up there. I saw him raise his hands to Allah just before the explosion tossed my car and ripped the face off Health and Human Services."

He turned to the aerial photograph on the smartboard. "I understand his confusion," he said, using his finger to draw a white arc on the picture where the debris and the bloodstains began to thin out. "This radius is too big for your average vest made from homemade explosives and tenpenny nails." He drew a line from the epicenter to the arc and tapped it. A distance readout appeared. "Forty meters. That's your fifty-percent kill zone. I've seen car bombs that didn't have half that reach."

"You're saying our bomber used commercial-grade explosives," said CJ. "You're saying he was connected."

"I am. And another thing, the casualties were mostly blast injuries. I don't think there was any shrapnel in the vest itself. It looks like the bomber left it out to make room for more explosives."

CJ shrugged. "Maybe he wanted a bigger boom. You know, Iraq-style shock and awe."

"No way. Even the amateurs know to use shrapnel for the gore effect. That's how insurgents do shock and awe. They don't trade shrapnel for explosives unless they want to bring down a building or blow through a wall."

"So to sum up," said CJ, folding her arms, "you barged into my command center all beat up and bloody just to tell me that this was a suicide vest, that the bomber used the good stuff, and that he made some unconventional choices when it came to shrapnel?"

Nick nodded. "Yeah."

CJ's frown darkened and she turned toward her board. "We already know all of that." Despite the rebuke, she circled Nick's drawing with her finger, double-tapping the screen to take a snapshot that automatically dropped into a folder marked EVIDENCE. "My OSC might not be your biggest fan," she said as she worked, "but he did confirm that the source was a vest instead of a vehicle. His team also tested some residue from the hand you found." She turned back to face him. "You're right about the explosives. The bomber used commercial Semtex. Easy enough to get ahold of. Doesn't necessarily mean he's part of a cell."

"Anybody claim the hit yet?"

"Nothing credible. Right now, the evidence points to a lone nutcase, another loyal reader of *Inspire*." She paused and narrowed her eyes. "Unless there's something more you're not sharing. Was there a reason you happened to be at the scene?"

Nick hesitated, considering the oddly timed chess invitation. His subconscious told him that it could not be separated from the attack, but he refused to accept the resulting conclusion. If the chess invitation and the suicide bombing were connected, then the attack was personal. The implication, the responsibility for all that carnage, was too terrible to acknowledge. "No. I was off duty, just coming from the train station on a personal errand."

CJ nodded. "Then go home. Kiss that beautiful wife of yours and tuck the baby into bed." She looked him up and down, wrinkling her brow. "I'm sure your family is worried sick about you. Call me in a few days when things settle down and we'll do lunch. Until then, I don't want to see you, hear from you, or even hear *about* you." She guided him toward the edge of her platform. "You're not the only game in town, Nick. Let the rest of us do our part."

Nick did not make it home in time to tuck Luke into bed as CJ suggested. The sun had set long before he reached his house in Chapel Point, Maryland, south of D.C. Katy under-stood. She was not happy with his long absence or his refu-gee appearance, but she understood. After suffering through a home invasion and a subsequent kidnapping by Chinese operatives the year before, she had been *read-in* to Nick's unique line of work. She knew why he stayed at the scene of the bombing.

Nick's father did not.

"What makes you so important that you had to aban-don your family in the middle of a terrorist attack?"

"I didn't abandon them. I left them in your care."

"I was wounded." Nick's father raised a hand to touch a wide bandage on the side of his face.

There were also bandages on his neck and his forearm. Nick shuddered to think what all that flying glass would have done to his son if his dad hadn't been there. He was grateful, but he was too busy defending himself to say it. "That's funny," he argued, "because I distinctly remember you telling me that you were fine. You just got a few scratches, Dad. People closer to the blast were dying."

"I have training too, you know. Or did you forget that I spent thirty years in the reserves? I was flying jets before you could spell the word. You could have left me there and focused on your wife and child. At least I would have known when to quit and come home."

Nick clenched his fists and took a breath. "Dad, I . . ." But he couldn't frame the words.

"You what? You had to putter around the aftermath like an amateur detective, bothering the FBI? You don't have the right to do that just because you're military, Nick. A good officer knows to stick to his own job. You're a technical adviser, a pilot flying a desk, not a supersleuth."

Nick did not dare glance over at Katy, who was likely becoming dizzy with the awkwardness of the confrontation. His wife did not know every classified detail, but she knew enough. When his boss finally let him confide in her, she had become his lifeline. Over the last year she had kept him from drowning in the memory of a friend bleeding out in his arms.

Katy was dragged into her clearance by circumstance; she was not made for it. She had no poker face. If Nick met her eyes now, her expression would spill it all. His dad would suspect that they were hiding something and start to dig. The retired colonel would emerge from beneath the archaeology professor and interrogate them both until he got to the truth, the same way he used to get to the truth when Nick came home late after curfew. Nick could withstand drugs and torture, but he couldn't withstand the man who used to change his diapers.

Nick shut down the argument the only way he could. "You're right, Dad. Of course. I'm sorry." All their arguments ended like that, no matter the topic. It was the natural order of things—father over son. They shared a tepid hug. The professor retired to the guest room.

Katy moved into the kitchen and Nick closed himself in his office to check in with his boss, an Army colonel. The old man was at work as he suspected, monitoring the aftermath of the attack. To Nick's frustration, the colonel sounded just like his dad. "Stick to your own job and let the FBI handle it. Let this one go. This is a simple case of wrong place, wrong time."

"Yes, sir," Nick replied, but an insistent voice in the back of his head told him that the colonel was wrong.

CHAPTER 5

Syria
Latakia Military Storage Facility

Footsteps in the hallway—the distinctive clop of boots on polished concrete.

Kateb set his heels on the desktop, leaning precariously back in the rolling chair and placing his hands behind his head. He gave a carefully choreographed indifferent nod to the guard as he passed.

The guard knew little of Kateb, a lowly second-assistant security clerk, but Kateb knew everything about him—Azzam Safri, identification number 5975. Azzam's information was the key to Kateb's financial freedom.

The guard paused long enough to snort derisively at the clerk's lazy pose and then continued on his beat. Kateb resisted the urge to sit forward again. He counted the echoing footsteps as they faded down the hallway, five . . . ten . . . fifteen . . . When the count reached forty-three, he stood up, started the timer on his wristwatch, and quietly peeked out into the hall. Azzam had disappeared around the corner. His normal routine would not bring him back this way for another seven minutes, give or take.

Kateb grabbed a leather satchel from under his desk and hurried down the hall in the opposite direction, the soft rubber soles of his sneakers hardly making a sound. Fifty seconds later, he stood in front of a black door protected by a keycard lock. He passed a blank white card over the sensor and entered the code he had created for it.

Nothing happened.

Kateb cursed his sweaty palms and rubbed the card dry on his shirt, glancing over his shoulder at the empty hall. On his second attempt AZZAM SAFRI passed across the digital screen in green block letters, followed by ACCESS GRANTED. He could have accessed the door with his own card, but his supervisor might notice the entry log and ask him why a second-assistant security clerk had cause to enter the giant storage locker. Azzam, on the other hand, routinely accessed the room as part of his guard duties. No one would notice an additional entry on his account, not even Azzam.

Beyond the door, a short alcove gave way to a large warehouse. The air was cold and dry, the temperature and humidity tightly regulated by an isolated environmental-control system. Kateb descended a short flight of corrugated steel steps to a floor lined with row after row of barrels stacked eight feet high, all made of a roughly polished alloy and all marked with red and yellow warning labels.

The American president's infamous "red line" statement

had created this giant cache. In exchange for a small extension of Syria's current missile-acquisition contract, the Russians had readily agreed to allow Assad to retain a portion of his chemical and biological weapons. Unfortunately, the UN inspectors were not so malleable. Weapons from all over Syria were brought here to be concealed from prying eyes. Speed and secrecy were paramount, and cataloging was less than efficient. That inefficiency would make Kateb's fortune. He checked his watch. Five minutes and eleven seconds remaining. He had to keep moving.

He jogged down the center aisle and turned at the third side lane, trying to remember the digital schematic. He hadn't dared print it out. After making a wrong turn and then backtracking through the maze, he finally found his way to a stock of smaller canisters, set on industrial shelves. These bore yellow-and-black biohazard warning labels. Kateb was tempted to hold his breath in their presence, but he shook off his fears and shoved one into his satchel, rearranging the others to cover the telltale gap.

By the time Azzam passed by the security office again, Kateb was back at his desk, reclining in his chair with his feet propped up as if he had not moved at all. This time, the guard did not so much as glance into the room. Had he done so, he might have noticed the sweat glistening on Kateb's brow.

As soon as Azzam's footsteps faded, Kateb unlocked his computer and deleted the duplicate keycard from the system. He breathed a sigh of relief. The leather satchel at his feet that usually carried his coffee thermos now held a titanium canister of the same size. The hard part was over. There were no metal detectors or X-ray machines to pass through on the way out of the facility. Kateb could walk out the front door as if it were the end of any other nightshift. After that, he had a little vacation planned—a very profitable one.

CHAPTER 6

Nick's phone chimed with a text at four thirty in the morning. He ignored the first one. At the second chime, Katy rolled over and elbowed him. "Make it stop," she complained. "Why can't you turn that thing off when we're in bed?"

He leaned across his pillow and kissed her on the cheek. "You know why. Suck it up."

Katy pushed him away with a palm to the forehead and rolled the other way. "You suck it up."

Nick laughed at his wife and sat up to check his screen. "It's the colonel. He wants me in his office, *now*." He turned the phone toward her. "See, he capitalized NOW. He's finally learned how to yell in text." Katy did not look. She had already gone back to sleep.

Forty-five minutes later, Nick pulled his midnight blue '67 Shelby through the gate at Andrews, flashing an ID card that identified him as an Air Force major. Five minutes after that, he parked in an unlit lot next to a large, mostly forgotten hangar facility on the southern end of the runway.

While he was pulling his duffel and sidearm out of the Mustang's trunk, a phantom black Audi R8 pulled into the next space over. A big operative, the size of the Rock and just as popular with the girls, pulled himself up from the bucket seat behind the wheel. "Does this early-morning get-together have anything to do with your adventure last night?" he asked as he shut the door. He locked the Audi with a quiet beep. "I heard you spent your afternoon wading through body parts on the Mall."

Drake Merigold had been Nick's teammate for more than a decade. Like Nick, he was a pilot and an Air Force major, though neither of them wore an official uniform. Both were dressed in simple khaki slacks, black golf shirts, and winter jackets.

Nick closed his trunk, his face showing mild surprise. "Did CJ call you?"

An impish grin spread across Drake's chiseled Greek features. "All the girls call me. You should know that by now."

Nick rolled his eyes and glanced around the lot, looking for a beat-up '71 Charger that wasn't there. "Where's the kid? He lives on base. He should be here by now."

"Millennials," said Drake, slinging his own duffel over his shoulder and starting toward the hangars. "They have to spend an extra hour in front of the mirror with hair gel to perfect that just-got-out-of-bed look."

The two threaded their way through the empty corridors of a low building attached to the hangars until they came to a black door with no knob or handle. White block lettering read:

R7 PERSONNEL ONLY

LETHAL FORCE IS AUTHORIZED

Nick swiped a key fob across a gray sensor, punched in a code, and then waited impatiently. There was a whirring sound behind the door, punctuated by irritating squeaks. He frowned. "I think it's getting slower."

"I'll have it checked," said Drake.

Finally the whirring and squeaking stopped, and the black door slid open, shuddering on its track. They stepped into a circular white chamber, watched the wall rotate 180 degrees, and then steadied themselves as the whole thing jerked into motion and began a long, slow descent. The whirring and squeaking was much louder now that they were inside.

Romeo Seven, the headquarters of the Triple Seven Chase squadron, was five stories beneath Andrews. The facility was constructed from a defunct presidential bunker and boasted a wealth of resources, including a well-stocked clinic, an engineering lab, and its own freshwater supply. The jewel of the bunker, though, was the two-story command center that Nick and Drake entered when they stepped off the aging elevator.

A wide platform spread out before them, lined with crescent-shaped workstations, all facing a forty-foot-wide floor-to-ceiling screen—a screen that Drake had used more than once for a late-night Call of Duty marathon. At the back of the platform, an iron staircase led up to the colonel's office. Three of the colonel's four walls were made of smartglass, so he could keep an eye on his minions.

Most of the workstations were empty, but the Triple Seven's diminutive chief intelligence analyst was clicking away at the one closest to the elevator, pausing occasionally to brush back a thin strand of deep brown hair. There were three pale blue mugs of coffee sitting on the edge of her desk—one black, the other two blond from an excess of cream and sugar. Nick handed one of the desserts to Drake and took the black coffee for himself. He raised it in toast. "Thanks, Molly."

The analyst looked up and gave him a fleeting smile. Then returned to her computers.

A year before, Molly had been the team's brown-eyed girl, always smiling, chatty, the brightest and most innocent among them. Then she had fallen in love. She never said a word about her infatuation, and a CIA traitor murdered the object of her passion before she got up the nerve. After that, she collapsed inward. The smile was gone.

Molly didn't talk much in person, but she did better over the comm links when the ops team was out in the field. Drake had postulated that the digital wall made her feel safe.

As Nick and Drake sipped their coffee, the elevator door squeaked open once more, and the newest and youngest member of the Triple Seven Chase stepped into the command center. Ethan Quinn was a special tactics para-rescueman who had joined the ops team to replace the team member lost in Iran. He was a little shorter than Nick, with wayward brown hair and green eyes that made you think he knew something he wasn't saying. Over the past year and a half, Nick had beaten some of the youth-ful cockiness out of him, but not all of it.

"This for me?" asked Quinn, reaching for the last mug of coffee.

With her eyes still on her monitors and one hand still typing on the keyboard, Molly pulled the coffee away and set it down on the other side of her desk.

"That means no," said Drake.

"Get in here, all of you." Colonel Richard T. Walker appeared at the door of his glass tower. While the ops team wore khakis and polos, the colonel wore his green Army uniform, with crisp edges ironed into the shirt-sleeves and pant legs. The unit's paper cover as a subsec-tion of the DIA's Directorate of Analysis required it. The colonel had to maintain appearances while working his magic amid the alphabet soup of D.C. organizations.

"What'd I do this time?" asked Drake.

Walker shook his gray crew-cut head. "Not you"—he pointed at Nick—"him." The colonel's scowl looked more foreboding than usual. Then Nick saw that he was not alone in the glass office. CJ was up there with him.

CHAPTER 7

s there anything you want to tell me, Major Baron?"
asked Walker. The colonel had returned to his desk chair
and sat leaning back with his arms folded. CJ was next
to the front wall, wearing a scowl as deep as the colonel's.
Their posture suggested an ambush. Nick kept quiet.

"Fine, have it your way." The colonel rocked forward
and slapped a large black button on the corner of his desk
and the lights dimmed. The smartglass walls turned the
color of pearl. The long wall that overlooked the command center became a digital workspace. At its center, a
picture of a burnt photograph appeared.

CJ raised a manicured hand toward the photo. "We
found this in the bomber's wallet. Does it look familiar?"

The photo was a close-up of a man's face, but it was
too warped and discolored to break out the features. Still,

Nick found the shape strangely familiar. A pit started to open in his gut. He shook his head in the negative.

"What about this one?" Another picture appeared. CJ's forensic team had run a scan of the burnt photo through a digital-enhancement program, reconstructing the face. The pit in Nick's gut widened to a chasm. The improved photo left no question. The face in the close-up was his own, confirming fears that had haunted him for the past eighteen hours. The ramifications were staggering—all those lives snuffed out or changed forever, somehow all because of him. He slowly sank into the leather chair in front of Walker's desk.

CJ stepped closer, towering over Nick in four-inch heels. She tilted her head slightly back and looked down her nose at him. "Would you like to explain to me how your picture got into the wallet of the D.C. suicide bomber?"

Nick remained silent, staring at the burnt photo of himself.

She returned to the wall and tapped a file at the edge of the digital space. Another photo opened up next to the other two. A young man stood behind a motel reception desk wearing a purple shirt with the word *Paradise* stitched over the breast pocket. "Jamal Shahat," said the FBI agent. "Have you ever heard of him?"

"No."

"Neither had we. He was a nothing, a nobody, at least as far as the U.S. government was concerned. He was an illegal, and yet he had been the assistant manager of the Paradise Motel in Seaford, Delaware, for over a year." CJ turned her scowl on the photo of the bomber. "This is the first time he's come up on the FBI's radar. He has no affiliation with any known cells."

"What about the motel owner?" asked Drake.

"Jordanian, with a valid green card. Says he was only trying to give a bright young man a chance. Our interrogators don't think he's guilty of anything beyond hiring an illegal."

Nick tore his eyes free of the photo and looked up at her. "So you've got nothing."

"I didn't say that. We have his apartment. Even better, we have his laptop, which he tossed into a Dumpster behind his building. That rookie you gave such a hard time yesterday ran down the garbage truck and saved it."

"I'll buy the kid a soda."

"Cute. The NSA decoded e-mails on the computer and traced them to a known source." CJ opened another file that covered the other three. In this picture, straight lines connected four names to a central square that read *Grendel*.

Ethan Quinn pushed off the back wall and scrutinized the chart. "So we're looking at a cell?"

"Not really. Grendel is not a cell or a network. It's an NSA code name for a set of IP addresses." CJ gestured to the four names. "These represent four plots that were uncovered over the last six months, all of them in Europe." She pointed to each name in sequence. "This one planned to bomb a train in Germany. This one, a Russian in Budapest, attempted to sell rocket-propelled grenades to a known al-Qaeda buyer. This one was a subway bomber in the UK, and this one an Algerian radical buying explosives in France." She turned and faced the group. "None of the four were working together, but the NSA pulled similar IP addresses from e-mails on each of their computers."

"If they have the IP addresses, then they have a physical location," said Drake, starting to boil. "The NSA could have rolled this Grendel up and stopped the Washington attack before it happened."

CJ held out her hands to calm him down. "Easy, tiger. The NSA has a location, a building in northern Budapest, but Grendel is not a ringleader or an umbrella organization. The IP addresses indicate Grendel is a hacker, providing a secure communications network for hire. Chances are, whoever sent the D.C. bomber had never used him before."

"Can we read Grendel's mail?" asked Nick.

"Not yet." CJ tapped the digital wall, and the Grendel chart shrank back into the tray, leaving the previous three pictures up on the screen. "The NSA hasn't cracked the outgoing or incoming paths to the IPs. If they could, they'd have a simultaneous wiretap on every terrorist that uses the network. They've had their long-haired geniuses working on it night and day for months."

Nick nodded. "That's why they left Grendel in the wind, but tapping the network isn't the goal anymore, is it?"

"No." Walker stood up from his chair. "The D.C. attack is a game changer. The president doesn't care about using Grendel as an intelligence source. He wants the mastermind behind the D.C. bombing, and that means capturing both Grendel and his hardware."

Nick cringed at the mention of the president. He hadn't met this one and he didn't want to, particularly under these circumstances. "Does the White House know about my picture?"

"As soon as I saw it, I classified it Special Access Required," said CJ. "That won't keep it out of political hands forever, but it will delay things until we can get a handle on the situation."

The colonel stepped out from behind his desk and stood next to CJ, silhouetted in front of Nick's picture. "We need to understand how you became a target. Is there anything else that connects you to this attack?"

Nick stared up at the two of them a moment longer. Then he pushed himself up from the leather chair and pulled his phone from his pocket. "Yes, sir. There is."

———

"A telephone chess game?" asked Walker when Nick had finished explaining himself. He followed his question with a snort.

CJ did not share the colonel's skepticism. Her eyes narrowed. "Have you accepted the game?"

Nick glanced down at his phone. "I haven't even opened the app, and I don't plan to."

"You don't have a choice," said the FBI agent. "We can use this. It's not the same as a phone trace, but it's not too far off either. We can tap into the app company's servers, find out where this guy is."

"We may not even have to burn Grendel," offered Quinn. "The NSA could keep working to crack the network."

The colonel shook his head. "No. I'll allow Baron to

keep this Emissary on the line, but we're still going after Grendel." He glanced up at the reconstruction of Nick's photograph. "Somehow, this mess belongs to the Triple Seven Chase, and we're going to pull out all the stops to clean it up."

Nick nodded. "What's the profile on Grendel?"

"One hacker, some serious hardware," said CJ. "Multiple targets at the hub are unlikely, unless the Grendel has personal security."

"How soon do we leave?"

"This afternoon."

"Today?" Nick's team was known for its rapid-response capability, but *rapid response* generally meant less than seventy-two hours, not twenty-four. "Why so soon?"

"There's one more piece of evidence I haven't shared," said CJ. "One of the victims briefly regained consciousness in the middle of the night, right before she passed. With her last words, she told her doctor that she heard the bomber say something in English."

"And that was?" prompted Quinn when the FBI agent paused too long.

"'I am the first sign.'"

They all gazed silently at the face of the suicide bomber for several seconds. Nick furrowed his brow. "The first of how many?"

CHAPTER 8

Istanbul, Turkey

Pavel Ercan whistled as he walked. He loved the acoustics of empty hallways. He enjoyed solitude. That's why he requested the late security shift at the university's new biochemical research facility. He led a team of three guards that each manned a floor. As the senior guard, he could have taken the desk at the entrance—where there was a television—but he preferred it here, on the third floor, in the quiet.

The *click* of a closing door echoed from the crossing hallway ahead. Usually by this time, all the staff and students had gone home. The floor should be empty. Pavel placed a hand on his nightstick, but before he reached the hallway, a short, white-haired man in a lab coat rounded the corner at an urgent pace. Pavel relaxed. He recognized Dr. Varga. The facility chairman always moved at such a pace, always had someplace to be.

Pavel waved smartly and smiled, but the professor ignored him and continued toward the bank of elevators at the center of the floor. The security guard did not feel particularly snubbed. Dr. Varga never acknowledged anyone beneath his station, unless it was to bark an order or chew them out. He watched the man jab at the down button until one of the elevators finally opened and he stepped inside. Then he inclined his head and spoke into the radio handset hanging over his shoulder. "Big man is coming your way, Janos," he warned, prompting the guard at the entrance to turn off the TV and pretend to watch the door until Varga exited the building.

"Yah, yah," the radio crackled back.

With the most exciting event of the evening behind him, Pavel retreated to a chair at the end of the hallway and sat down to enjoy his dinner. He removed a paper-wrapped chutney sandwich and thermos of coffee from his backpack, and was just about to bite into the sandwich when he heard an echoing crash from far below.

Pavel sighed. He set the sandwich down on top of his backpack and keyed his radio. "Janos, what have you done?"

Janos made no response.

"Adnan, go down to one and check on Janos. Find out what that *imbecile* has broken this time." Pavel emphasized the word *imbecile*, hoping that Janos could hear him.

"I always check on him. Why can't you check on him?"

Pavel glanced down at his chutney sandwich. It called to him. "Because I am in charge and you are closer. Now get moving."

Half a minute passed as Pavel took a sip of coffee and

then raised his sandwich for the second time. As his teeth sank into the soft white bread, the hallway went completely dark. "What now?" he mumbled through a mouth full of chutney. He swallowed and picked up the radio again. "Adnan, come in."

Adnan did not reply.

"Adnan? Janos?"

Pavel got up and started walking toward the elevators, muttering about the incompetence of his crew. He tried to raise his flashlight, but the lanyard tangled on his belt, forcing him to hold the sandwich in his mouth and look down to unhook it. Finally, he flipped on the bright beam and looked up again. His blood ran cold. The chutney sandwich fell to the floor with a light splat.

A menacing figure barred his path barely a meter away, cloaked in black with a wide hood that obscured his face. The security guard went for his nightstick, but he was too late. He barely saw the flash of the knife before it ripped across his throat. He grabbed at the wound with both hands and felt the sickening gush of his own warm blood pulsing through his fingers. He tried to speak, but he couldn't. He couldn't even scream.

———

The hooded figure stepped around the gurgling guard without waiting for him to fall. It was not until he turned down the next hallway that he heard the *crack* of the man's skull hitting the tile next to his ruined sandwich. At the far end of the hall, he found the facility's cold-storage locker. A red light glowed above the door, warning that structural power to the refrigeration units had been compromised, leaving them on the auxiliary batteries. The door was still locked, secured by a keycard reader and biometric pad that were also supported by backup batteries, but that was expected.

The intruder reached into the fold of his cloak and removed an access card that read VARGA, BIOCHEM. He swiped the card, causing the red LED on the biometric pad to turn orange and blink. Letting the card fall to the floor, he reached into his cloak again. This time he produced a white cloth, stained with blood, pinched between his fingers. As he raised it to the pad, the cloth unraveled over his hand to reveal a severed thumb. He pressed the thumb against the pad and the LED turned green. The lock clicked open.

Inside, the intruder opened a large canvas satchel and began sweeping chemicals off shelves. Most fell into the bag. Others fell to the floor. Glass vials filled with blue, amber, and clear liquids shattered at his feet. When the bag was half-full, he went to the rear of the locker and found a tall locked cabinet. He smashed the glass with his elbow. Again, the intruder indiscriminately swept vials and bottles into his satchel—this time continuing until it was full. Then he bent down to the bottom shelf and carefully lifted a pressurized titanium container. On all four sides of the box, bright yellow labels read BIOHAZARD: CONTROLLED SUBSTANCE.

CHAPTER 9

"et packed," said Nick, letting the door slam behind him as he rushed across the tile foyer of his home. Katy sat on the living room couch working on her latest hobby. Photos and colored paper lay all around her on the cushions, a large open binder on her lap. Their son sat on the carpet at her feet, giggling as he knocked down stacks of blocks.

Katy did not look up from her scrapbooking. "My day was fine, dear. How was yours?"

"My day's not over yet. I have to ship out tonight. Pack up. You're going to stay at your mother's while I'm gone."

That got Katy's attention. She put her scissors down. "What's going on?"

As a young officer, Nick had learned to discern when it was appropriate to follow orders without questioning. His subordinates also had that skill. He often wished his wife could learn it too. "Look, it's not complicated. I don't want you and Luke here alone. As soon as you drop Dad off at the airport tomorrow, I want you on the road to your mom's house. Don't even come home in between. Pack up the car before you leave with Dad. If he asks why you're going out of town, make up an excuse."

"Or you could tell him the truth," said Kurt Baron, emerging from the hallway to the guest room. "What's all this about?"

"It's nothing, Dad." Nick turned away from his father and shot Katy a look that said, "Do as I say."

Katy shot a glare right back at him, suddenly in one of her moods. "How is it nothing?" she argued, standing up and crossing her arms. "You're telling me to flee our home, but you won't say why."

Nick heard a sniffle at his feet. "Dada?" Luke stared up at him, on the edge of tears, his hand frozen above the tumbled blocks as if he had caused all the anger in the room by knocking them down. Nick willed his tense features to relax and gave his son a reassuring smile. Luke smiled back and returned to his game.

When Nick looked up again, his wife's expression had not softened. He slumped down into an oversized chair, defeated. "Our presence at the attack wasn't happenstance," he said, watching her hardened glare collapse into shock.

"You mean the bomber was trying to kill you?" asked Kurt.

"Maybe, or at least get my attention."

"That doesn't make any sense. Why would a suicide bomber target you? You're just an adviser."

Just. Nick hated it when his dad used that word. You're just a kid. You're just an outfielder. You're just a lieutenant. *Just* meant you didn't matter. He bit back what he wanted to say and offered his dad a very uncomfortable truth. "I don't know why."

"Then how can you be sure?" asked Katy.

"The FBI has evidence."

The older Baron stepped deeper into the room, a stern expression—his colonel face—bearing down on Nick. "What evidence?"

"*Classified* evidence, Dad." Nick sat forward in his chair and sighed. "The how and the why don't matter now. The fact remains that I've come up on some terrorist group's radar, and if they were able to find us on the Mall, then they probably know where we live. I have to leave the country tonight, and I'm not comfortable leaving Katy here alone." He matched his father's stare. "I told Katy to go to her mother's place. I'm trying to keep my family safe, and I would appreciate your support."

"You don't have it. You're not making sense."

Nick almost came out of the chair swinging at his father's defiance, but he caught himself when Luke stopped playing and looked up at him again. He took a deep breath and settled back down into his seat. He settled his voice as well. "Dad, I've already explained that the FBI is sure about this."

The elder Baron made a T with his hands, signaling

détente. "That's not what I meant. Listen, if they can figure out where you live, it won't be long before they can figure out where Katy's folks live. You can't protect her by sending her to West Virginia."

Nick leaned back against the cushion and looked up at his father. "You have a better idea?"

"As a matter of fact, I do." Kurt bent down and scooped up his grandson, to the delight of the child. "Katy and Luke can come with me to Israel."

"What?" Katy abruptly turned to face her former ally.

"I'm serious. My invitation to speak included travel and accommodations for two. That's standard practice. Guest speakers usually bring a spouse or an assistant." He sat down in the chair across from Nick and started bouncing Luke on his knee. The toddler laughed and squealed. "Two days in Frankfurt to speak at the campus there, two in Jerusalem, another day in Frankfurt on the way home. No terrorist would anticipate Katy and Luke hopping back and forth between Europe and the Holy Land. If you want to protect your family, keep them on the move." He smiled down at his grandson and lightened his voice. "It will be fun! There's going to be a total eclipse visible from Jerusalem. Not everybody gets to see one of those."

As much as he wanted to find a flaw in his dad's idea, Nick couldn't argue with the logic. When crossing borders, vacationers only had to manage their suitcases and their children. Terrorists, on the other hand, had to manage identities and weapons, and those things took time. Katy's surprise travel would keep her one step ahead.

Katy's hands were on her hips. "Excuse me. Does the little woman get a say?"

"Of course, my dear. How thoughtless of us." Kurt offered her a chivalrous bow, playing the white knight opposite Nick's tyrant king.

Katy responded to the knight with a sweet nod of thanks and then knelt next to the tyrant's throne, placing a hand on his arm. "I've always wanted to see Israel. And I think your son and I would be a lot safer traveling with your father than driving ourselves to Lewisburg." Her light grip on his forearm became a heavy squeeze, with a couple of fingernails added for emphasis. "Don't you?"

Without waiting for a response, Nick's dad set Luke down and stood up, clapping his hands together. "It's settled then. I'll call the travel company right now and make all the arrangements."

———

Had that been the end of it, Nick would have considered the status quo maintained—Dad wins and everyone else plays along. But that wasn't the end of it. Shortly before he left for the base, Nick informed Katy that he had to take away her phone to keep her from being tracked. He had delayed the conversation because he knew it would turn into a fight, and it did. Katy cried, which set Luke off, and then of course his dad had to butt in. This time Nick did not back down, and he ordered his dad to minimize communications too. He was certainly not to call or text Nick. The elder Baron fought back. He could call his own son whenever he wanted to. "Fine," said Nick, "but don't expect me to answer."

Nick made up with Katy, kissed her good-bye, kissed his little boy, but those were the last words he said to his father.

CHAPTER 10

Like the repurposed presidential bunker below, Romeo Seven's hangar facility was a relic of days gone by, a testament to the excess of the Cold War. The two massive adjoining structures had been erected in 1958 to house Ike's new Boeing 707 presidential fleet. There were only two aircraft, but like every Strategic Air Command endeavor, the grandeur of the new facility far exceeded its purpose. One hangar alone could have sheltered three 707s and included offices and shop space for an army of maintenance personnel.

As with the bunker, Walker had renovated the out-of-use hangars with black funds. On the outside, they looked the same as any of the unused hangars found on Air Force bases across the country. On the inside, they housed a state-of-the-art facility with propulsion, hydraulic, and avionics shops; a subterranean engineering lab; and a small fleet of aircraft, of which the flagship was a jumbo-jet-sized stealth striker called the M-2 Wraith.

As Nick entered the hangar an hour before the mission launch, two CIA pilots were preflighting the latest addition to Walker's air force—a sleek, gray and black Gulfstream C-37B. Normally Nick and Drake piloted the Triple Seven's aircraft, but the colonel had worked out a deal to have Agency pilots fly this militarized version of a G550 luxury business jet. Walker wanted his operators to use the Gulfstream as a mobile command center, and they couldn't do that if they spent all their time playing around in the cockpit.

A blonde in greasy blue coveralls hopped down off one of the Wraith's massive landing-gear assemblies and flagged Nick down with a dirty oil rag. "Aren't you taking my baby with you?"

Amanda Navistrova led the aircraft maintenance team. She was also one of the Wraith's principal designers, with multiple degrees from MIT. The coveralls, the unkempt ponytail, and the safety goggles strapped to her forehead did little to detract from her gorgeous features. In fact, Nick decided, few women could pull off that ensemble better.

"If you mean the Wraith," he said, closing the distance between them, "I've got to leave her in the barn. We're looking for subtle, and landing the world's largest stealth aircraft at Budapest International doesn't fit the bill. If you mean your other baby—"

"I don't." Amanda cut him off, casting an evil glare toward the entrance behind him.

Nick glanced over his shoulder and saw Drake stepping

into the facility. When he turned back, Amanda was walking away beneath the broad belly of the striker. She slapped the rag down on a worktable and disappeared into the maintenance section.

"What did you do this time?" asked Nick, meeting Drake at a table covered with black duffels and hard equipment cases next to the Gulfstream's cargo bay.

Drake unzipped one of the bags. "Nothing. I don't know what her problem is."

Amanda and Drake, known collectively as Mandrake by Walker's techs, had been the Triple Seven's token office romance for years. In Nick's opinion, they should have been the Triple Seven's token married couple, but Drake couldn't pull the trigger. Every time things got serious, he did something stupid to pick a fight, like flirting with their waitress at dinner. Nick didn't believe Drake's *nothing* for an instant. "You're an idiot."

Drake lifted a Heckler and Koch MP7A1 compact submachine gun from the duffel and checked the chamber. "I know."

Both fell silent and continued their equipment checks. While Drake moved on to a nine-millimeter Beretta Nano micro-compact, Nick popped open a wide, flat case, revealing six black boxes set in gray foam, each the size of a deck of cards. Each had a small screen and keyboard, and each had a tiny earpiece mounted on copper contacts in the upper left corner. These would serve as the team's field radios, controlled by an app on their smartphones, or by touch and voice commands should the phones become unavailable.

Nick activated all the screens to make sure the earpieces were charged and then shut them off again. When he closed the case, Ethan Quinn was standing in front of him, glancing back and forth between the two quiet operatives. "What'd I miss?" he asked.

The older operatives responded simultaneously.

"Nothing," said Drake.

"He's an idiot," said Nick.

Quinn clapped his hands and rubbed them together. "Situation normal then. I guess it's time to go catch ourselves a hacker."

CHAPTER 11

Budapest, Hungary

Nick parked his team's rented Suzuki Vitara against the chain-link fence of a snow-covered rail yard and glanced across the street at the target address, a six-story brick structure. "An apartment building," he said. "That confirms the NSA's assessment."

"Why couldn't it have been a mansion with armed sentries and killer guard dogs?" asked Drake, slowly shaking his head. "That would be so much easier."

Dr. Scott Stone, the Triple Seven's lead engineer and tech guru, leaned forward from the backseat and pushed a pair of wire-framed glasses up the bridge of his nose. "Exactly *what* makes hired guns and killer dogs easy?"

"Not easy. Easier," corrected Drake. He gestured at the building. "The IP addresses captured by the NSA all trace to this structure, but not to a specific apartment.

We have to find a way to narrow it down without terror-izing the locals or spooking the target."

Scott shot a glance at the icy slush that covered the street between the Vitara and the apartment building. He pulled his overcoat tighter around his small frame. "I have to go in with you."

"Out of the question," said Nick. "Your job is to sit in the car and play lookout until I send for you." He hadn't wanted to bring the engineer along at all. Scott had no field experience, but he convinced the colonel that he might have to hack Grendel's hardware on-site, something he claimed would prove impossible for the knuckle-dragging ops team, even with his guidance over SATCOM.

The engineer scrunched his gaunt face into a sneer. "So, what then? Are you planning to search the entire building? Blow in a few doors, rough up a few old ladies and hope that one of them is the hacker?" He shook his head. "Get me into the utility room, and I can tell you exactly which apartment Grendel is hiding in."

Nick and Scott stared at each other across the seat back for a few moments. Then Nick shut off the engine and cracked open his door. "Fine. Come on."

The three older operatives gathered at the back of the Vitara, dressed in dark overcoats and slacks to blend in with locals. Scott had added a Windsor flat cap to cover his thinning hair. At the same time, Quinn made his way toward a bus stop a half block west of the apartments. He wore grunge jeans and a long-sleeve T-shirt beneath a gray canvas jacket, better suited to the twentysomethings in the area.

"Nightmare Three, I'll call you if Grendel makes a break for it," said Nick, speaking through his SATCOM earpiece and using Quinn's mission callsign. "I'll give the best description I can. Taser is primary, drugs to knock him out. I want a live prisoner."

"Copy that, Nightmare One. Check your ten o'clock. I think a good prospect for entry is heading your way."

Nick glanced left and saw a grizzled old man in a hat with earflaps pass the bus stop and continue down the sidewalk toward the apartment building. He walked briskly, keeping his head down and his hands tucked deep into the pockets of his brown coat.

"That's our cue," said Drake. He pulled a large cardboard box marked AQUASTELLA WATER from the back of the Vitara, pretending to struggle with the weight of it. "Act like this is heavy," he said, passing the box to Scott.

"It *is* heavy," grunted the engineer as soon as Drake allowed the full weight to settle into his hands. "What's in here?"

"Your tools, genius," said Nick. He and Drake each pulled a similar box from the Vitara and then Nick closed the back end and led them across the street. He timed his approach to arrive at the apartment building's entrance just before the old man. He barred the local's way, pretending to struggle with his box and fumbling in his pocket for a nonexistent set of keys.

Within a few seconds, the old Hungarian lost patience. *"Elnézést,"* he said, gruffly excusing himself and squeezing around Nick. He used his own key to unlock the door and pushed through.

Nick caught the door and held it open with his foot. *"Köszönöm,"* he said, but the old man continued on without reply, trudging up a flight of stairs to the left of the door.

As soon as the local was out of sight, Nick led his team down to the basement level and into a short, dimly lit hallway. There were four wooden doors, each bearing a plastic sign. "Anybody know the Hungarian word for utilities?"

"This one." Drake tilted his head toward the door closest to him. "Has to be. I can hear the heating unit."

Nick shifted his box to one arm and checked the knob. It turned. The three of them moved quickly inside and set their boxes down. Drake closed and locked the door behind them.

"All right, Scott, you're in," said Nick, pulling a black duffel from one of the boxes. "Now tell me which apartment is our target." He tossed the heavy bag at the engineer, hitting him in the chest and nearly knocking him over.

Scott glared at him for a moment and then pushed his glasses back up on his nose and turned to scan the room. He zeroed in on a gray plastic box mounted on the wall next to a row of water heaters. "This area uses DSL. Their Internet will be running through the phone lines."

Inside the panel was a black hub with sixty phone lines running out of it. Each connection was labeled with an apartment number. "All we have to do," said Scott, pulling a wire-stripping tool out of his bag, "is find the line with the right IPs. We don't even have to disconnect them."

While Nick and Drake looked on, the engineer stripped

the line labeled 101. Then he traded the wire stripper for a black box with a small LCD screen and a set of alligator clips. He attached the clips to the exposed phone line. A series of numbers scrolled up the screen. Scott compared them to a document from the NSA and shook his head. "That's not the one."

Drake raised an eyebrow. "That's your method? This is going to take all night."

"Agreed," said Nick. "There has to be another—"

Before he finished the statement, his eyes fell on the rows of electricity meters mounted on the wall opposite the phone box. "Hey, Scott," he said slowly, walking over to the meters, "would you ever be caught dead in a dump like this?"

Scott was busy stripping the line for apartment 102. "I believe you've seen my condo in the Southwest Waterfront district. You already know the answer to that."

Drake started to catch on. "And you're a megalomaniac techno geek just like our terrorist hacker. No offense."

"Genius. The word your gorilla brain is looking for is *genius*." The engineer put down his strippers. "And just because you say 'no offense' after calling me a megalomaniac geek doesn't make it okay. What's your point?"

"This place is in one of the poorest sections of Budapest," said Nick. "You wouldn't live here, and neither does Grendel. He's just using the apartment to house a small stack of servers. No oven use. Minimal heating. I bet he's drawing way less power than the other residents."

Nick's finger moved along the panel as he scrutinized the readout of each meter. It came to rest three rows down from the top and seven units over. The dials were hardly moving. "This one. Three oh seven."

The door behind them rattled, and then rattled again. A tired voice grumbled in Hungarian just outside. Keys jangled.

Drake shot a withering look at the engineer and hissed, "What did you do?"

Scott stuffed his equipment into his bag. "Nothing! There's no way my reader alerted anyone."

A key slipped into the lock. Nick pushed the engineer behind the water heaters and rushed to one side of the door. Drake was already on the other side, bent down and digging through a black bag in one of the cardboard boxes. He raised up with a heavy flashlight and two pairs of dark glasses just as the knob turned.

The big operative lobbed one pair of glasses over the opening door and Nick grabbed them out of the air. The two of them backed into the shadows.

A balding man with a sagging middle and two days of dark gristle on his chin shuffled into the utility room, still grumbling. He started toward the row of water heaters where Scott was hiding, but he stopped when he saw the open phone panel.

"*Mi ez?*" he asked, walking over to the panel. He touched the first line with his forefinger, squinting at the section Scott had stripped bare.

While the intruder's back was turned, Nick nodded to Drake. Both men donned their dark glasses and then the big operative strode into the open behind the Hungarian. He whistled.

The heavyset man spun around, and Drake aimed the flashlight at his face and depressed its trigger, filling the room with strobing green and blue light. The Hungarian fell forward in a dead faint.

"A little help here," grunted Drake, catching the overweight super in his arms.

Nick rushed to help his teammate lower the man to the ground. Then he pulled a small cylindrical CO_2 injector from his pocket and gently dosed the super with a sedative. "That'll keep him down for a while. He removed his dark glasses and glanced around the room. "What happened to the geek?"

They found Scott lying flat on the floor behind the water heaters, passed out. Drake slapped him on the cheek a few times. "Wake up, Sleeping Beauty."

"Ohhh. Why did you do that to me?" the engineer moaned.

Drake lifted him to his feet and guided him out of his hiding place. "I used a MOID," he said, pronouncing the acronym as a word, "a multifrequency optical interference device. It knocks you out with sequenced pulses of light."

Scott doubled over and put his hands on his knees as soon as Drake let go of his arm. "Yes, I know what the MOID is, you idiot. Why did you use it on me?"

"He used it on the super." Nick nudged the unconscious Hungarian with the toe of his boot. "If you're going to hang with us in the field, you've got to pay attention."

"I didn't think the MOID would get you in your hiding spot," offered Drake. "Normally it only knocks people out who look directly at it. Even then it doesn't always work. Some just get nauseated."

As if on cue, Scott stumbled over to a wastebasket in the corner of the room and heaved up the contents of his stomach.

Drake stifled a laugh. "Apparently some people get both effects."

Nick was not amused. Before Scott was done retching, the team lead had him by the shoulder, dragging him back to the phone panel. "We're on a time limit now. I dosed our friend here with six hours of juice, give or take, but if someone comes looking for him, our clock will run out fast." He pulled the reader and the wire strippers out of the bag and shoved them into Scott's hands. Then he used the inside collar of the engineer's coat to wipe the bile from his chin. He slapped the man lightly on the cheek. "I need you back with me, Scott. Apartment three oh seven. Get on it."

Scott mechanically did as commanded, stripping the wire and setting the clips in place. Once the numbers started rolling up his LCD screen, he stared at them blankly.

Nick's patience grew thin. "Well, genius?"

The engineer blinked a few times and then finally came out of his daze. He nodded. "This is—" He choked on the words, fighting the bile still in his throat. "Ahem. This is the correct line. This is Grendel's apartment."

CHAPTER 12

The team propped the building super up on a chair and left with their black bags slung over their shoulders. They locked the door. With any luck, no one would disturb his slumber.

Despite the late hour, a woman in a flower-print head-scarf, stooped with age and leaning on a cane, came through the entrance just as the three of them came up the stairs. She eyed the bags suspiciously.

"*Jó estét*," said Nick, bidding her good evening. He did not speak Hungarian, but he had picked up a few phrases on previous operations and had boned up during the crossing. The woman just frowned at him and started up the stairs.

"These people keep odd hours," whispered Drake once she had passed the first landing.

They gave her three minutes to clear the stairwell and

then started up, pausing to listen at the third floor. A rhythmic thumping sounded from the hallway. Nick peeked around the corner and couldn't believe his bad luck. The old woman lived on this floor. Her cane thumped into the worn carpet with every shaky step. Nick stepped aside and nodded for Drake to lean out and take a look.

"You've got to be kidding me," said the big operative when he ducked back into the stairwell. His eyes widened. "You don't think she's—"

Nick shook his head. "No, although, at this point, I'm not averse to Tasing her."

After another few seconds, the thumping stopped and they heard the scrape of a key in a lock. They waited until they heard the door open and click closed and then Nick checked the hall one more time. "We're on."

They moved quickly, padding down the hall without a sound until Scott caught a toe on a lump in the carpet. His shoulder thudded against the old woman's wall. Nick shot him a glare.

The engineer winced. "Sorry."

The old woman did not reappear and they continued on. At the door marked 307, Nick pulled a small black leather wallet from his coat and flipped it open. A few years ago, it would have held the snakes, rakes, and hooks of his lockpick set, but picking locks was now a dying and largely unnecessary art. These days, the wallet held bump keys. Nick checked Grendel's dead bolt and doorknob and then selected a matching pair, handing one to Drake.

Both men drew pistol-style Tasers from their coat

pockets and inserted their keys into the door locks, Nick standing at the dead bolt, Drake crouched in front of the doorknob. After a final check that his teammate was ready, Nick whispered a count to three and they both gave their keys a sharp bump and a turn.

As the door swung open, Nick and Drake rushed in with their Tasers leveled, searching for targets. They saw no one. Scott opened his mouth to speak, but Nick shut him up with a sharp look. He pointed at Drake and with a wave of his hand, directed him toward the kitchen while he moved silently into a short hallway at the back.

The door on the left of the little hall was too narrow to be an entrance to a room. It had to be a closet. Nick checked the door to the right. The knob turned easily and he pressed into the room. Again, there was no one.

Drake appeared at his shoulder. "The kitchen and living area are clear."

"Same," said Nick, pocketing his Taser. "No one's here." He returned to the living area and shut and locked the apartment door.

"Do we even have the right apartment?"

"If I could have permission to speak now, I think I can answer that," said Scott.

Nick nodded. "Speak."

The engineer pointed over Nick's shoulder to a short, unobtrusive rack that stood against the front wall of the apartment. There were four shelves, each holding a whirring silver box, ten inches wide, flat and unadorned except for a single green LED blinking on one end. A bundle of cables ran from the rack to another silver box that sat on a small desk. That box was connected to a laptop with a simple USB cable. "This is the place," he said.

"That's it?" asked Drake. "That's our terrorist communications network."

"It is. At least, it's the heart of it."

Drake strode over to the rack. "Then let's pull the plug and get out of here." He bent down to pull the servers away from the wall. "You can hack into the servers at the hotel while we search for Grendel."

"Wait!" said Scott, rushing toward him with an outstretched hand.

Drake abruptly stepped back, surprised by the command carried in the engineer's voice. "What?"

"The servers will be booby-trapped."

"You mean a bomb?"

Scott frowned at him. "No, you Neanderthal, I mean a delete program. It's common practice in the hacker underground. Almost any computer can be hacked if you can get it to the right people, so you have to rig your servers to wipe clean if they're moved."

Nick eyed the laptop. "Can you hack the system here?"

"Yes, but it's likely that Grendel included additional security measures. If I work too quickly, I could miss a digital trip wire that has the same effect."

"Then get to work. The clock's ticking."

Scott picked up his black bag and tentatively approached the desk. A foot away from the chair, he froze.

"What is it?" asked Drake. "Is the desk booby-trapped too?"

"No. It's filthy. How can any hacker work in an environment like this?" Scott pulled a handkerchief from his pocket and dusted the laptop keys and the chair cushion. When he finished, he considered the handkerchief for a moment and then flung it at the wastebasket next to the desk. It flopped across the top, knocking a crumpled paper onto the floor where several others were already gathered.

Nick picked up the paper and unraveled it. The fading print listed the address of a nightclub and a hefty bar tab. He set it on the desk and picked up several more. All of them were receipts from the same club, all paid in cash. "We have a hangout," he said.

"And we have a picture," said Drake. He nodded at the laptop that Scott had brought to life. The screen saver showed a young man in his early twenties, reclining on a leather bench with three women in micro-miniskirts. His hand was raised to the camera in some gesture that Nick did not recognize and his tongue was hanging out. The women looked bored.

"It looks like our hacker has a taste for the nightlife," said Nick. "I'll take Quinn and stake out the bar." He turned to Drake. "Watch the door. Grendel might come here at any time. If he does, bag him and call me on SAT-COM. Whatever happens, be out of here in five hours."

CHAPTER 13

A well-executed snatch-and-grab required weeks of planning. A CAT, a covert abduction team, might burn a hundred or more man-hours documenting a subject's routine—learning his habits and clearing away the chaff of random daily occurrence to isolate predictable behaviors. Nick didn't have a team. He had Quinn, and he had the time span of a drive across Budapest to plan the abduction, using nothing but a smartphone and a bar receipt.

In ad hoc situations like this one, common sense dictated that the team at least take the subject at a point with no potential witnesses and with easy access for the abduction vehicle. The satellite imagery on Nick's smartphone showed that the Black Dog—Grendel's favorite nightclub—offered neither.

"Maybe we could wait for Grendel to come out and

then follow him," said Quinn, eyeing the steroid-pumped bouncer outside the bar as he and Nick approached on foot. The Black Dog was a basement bar, with its primary entrance in a stairwell on an otherwise dark and narrow cobblestone street. In addition to the bouncer, there were three large men hanging out at the edge of the alley, chatting up a couple of bleach blondes in tight jeans.

"We can't afford the time," replied Nick. "We don't even know if he's in there. You want to stand out here all night?"

"What if the bouncer pats us down?"

"He won't."

As Nick led his young teammate into the alley, the girls broke from their conversation to cast flirtatious taunts in their direction, alternating between stunted English and only slightly better German. A muted, pulsating beat emanated from the stairwell—club music stripped of everything but the bass by the heavy black door.

The bouncer pushed off from his post against the brick wall and barred their path, his hands gripping the lapels of his black leather jacket. His eyes shifted from Nick's blue irises up to his blond hair and back. "This is Hungarian bar. We don't take dollars or euros here."

"*Kak naschet rubley?*" asked Nick in cool Russian, roughly pressing a thousand-ruble bill against the brute's chest.

The bouncer smiled. He took the bill, the Russian equivalent of a U.S. fifty, and stepped aside. "*Naslazh-daytes', ser.*"

A blast of heat greeted Nick as he opened the door,

and a cacophony of digital tones joined the thumping bass. Dim red light glowed through a haze of cigarette smoke. He and Quinn cut through the sparse crowd of dancers, making for one of the shiny black couches that lined the walls. A few of the patrons looked their way, but no one challenged them. They had already passed the gatekeeper at the top of the stairs. That was enough.

"How did you know to bring rubles?" asked Quinn once they had settled onto a secluded stretch of over-stuffed vinyl.

"In this country, rubles almost always grease palms better than dollars," said Nick, slipping his hand into the inside pocket of his coat, but he immediately removed it again as a fair-skinned girl with raven hair approached the table. She was young, far too young to be dressed as she was, in a thigh-length minidress that might have been cut from the same cheap vinyl as the couch.

The girl bent down with a tray of drinks and said something in a sultry voice that did not fit her young features. Her eyes flitted over to Quinn.

Nick didn't pick up all the Hungarian, but he could gather the gist of what she said. The thought made him ill. He selected a pair of dark beers from the tray and replaced them with a wad of rubles, letting his hard expression tell the girl that he and his young friend were there for drinks and nothing more. She didn't press him, almost looked grateful. She straightened and turned back toward the bar, wobbling on her stiletto heels as she did.

Nick watched her go for a moment. He knew what she was, and he could easily reconstruct how she got there.

He wanted to drag her back to the airport and put her on the team's Gulfstream, send her home to D.C. where she could be a barista instead of a barmaid, but his team wasn't here for her.

Quinn also watched the girl walk away, likely with different thoughts. "Snap out of it, junior," said Nick. "Let's find our boy and bag him."

He reached into his coat again and withdrew his phone, a slim unit a little larger than an iPhone. The device consolidated both his civilian and company needs into one unit, with a firewall that separated the more interesting functions from the mundane. Walker had placed only two restrictions on apps for the personal side. No Facebook. No Twitter. No big loss.

Nick had Angry Birds, though. Everyone had Angry Birds.

The program he used now came from Scott rather than the App Store and resided on the classified side of the firewall. The engineer had pulled the screen saver from Grendel's laptop, trimmed it to just the face, and transferred it to Nick's phone. The app identified the subject's key features: skin tone, hairline, bone structure. Then an algorithm built a three-dimensional predictive model.

Nick held the phone flat between them so that Quinn could see, showing him the screen as if showing pictures to his friend, working it with his thumb. He wore a ring on his left hand—titanium, bulky. There were three square black stones across the top. The middle square housed the lens of a micro-camera that fed video to the phone. He scanned the room with subtle movements of his hand, combining them with the natural movements of his body.

Nick paused on each group of patrons while the software went to work. It placed a red X over the faces it rejected, working quickly on the girls, taking more time with the men, but not much. Most of them were too big, with flat foreheads and square jaws. Their faces screamed Bratva, Russian mafia, and their eyes were glancing his way. Nick looked up for a moment and noticed his young teammate staring stone-faced at the phone.

"Pick up your drink and smile a little," he said through his teeth. "Or you're going to get us killed."

"I quit drinking a while ago. You know that."

The kid had been a passenger in a drunk-driving accident during his special ops training. He was too blasted to save the life of the driver, his best friend, despite being a qualified medic. He hadn't tasted a drop since.

"That doesn't mean you can't hold a beer in your hands." Nick didn't drink either, but for completely different reasons. He let out a laugh, big enough to be seen by anyone watching and subtle enough to appear legitimate. "Quit acting like you're at work. This is a nightclub, not Kandahar."

Quinn picked up his beer and responded with a fake laugh of his own. "At least in Kandahar there was no pretending. Everyone was as miserable as we were. Where is this guy?"

Nick continued to pan the camera around the room. Brick pillars rose from the floor at wide intervals, topped with arched buttresses that supported the building above.

Each had a circular cushion of cheap vinyl surrounding its base, and most of those were occupied by two or three patrons. Nick's program rejected them all, until the camera finally fell on a young man sitting alone in a recess in the far wall. A pair of spent beer bottles and a full tumbler of liquor sat on the black lacquer table in front of him. The software chewed on him for a while, with tiny white circles dancing over his features, but it couldn't make up its mind. Then the subject leaned out into the red light to signal a waitress. Instantly, a green box surrounded his face. A number below it proclaimed him a ninety-two-percent match for Grendel.

"Time to go," said Nick.

There were no direct exits on Grendel's side of the club, but the waitresses occasionally moved in and out of a swinging door behind the bar. As Nick and Quinn crossed the floor, Nick wrapped an arm tightly around the kid's shoulders and shook him, leaning close to his ear as if sharing a drunken joke. "If Grendel bolts, stay between him and the entrance. I've got the door behind the bar." Then he pushed Quinn away again and reached into his pocket to palm a fresh CO_2 injector.

The skinny hacker didn't notice the two foreigners approaching. He was preoccupied with getting a passing waitress to keep him company, the same one who had brought Nick and Quinn their drinks. He called after her using the haranguing tone universal to twentysomething males with a little too much alcohol and way too much confidence.

The girl rattled off a curt response and punctuated it by spitting on the floor.

Grendel would have none of it. He shouted at her and slammed his fist on the lacquer table, knocking over one of the beer bottles. His rant caught the attention of the indoor bouncer, the same size as the man outside. The big Hungarian came out from behind the bar.

"Back off," said Nick, touching Quinn's arm. "This window is closing."

As they turned toward the bar, a drunk stumbled past, bumping hard into Quinn and loudly excusing himself. The stench of old booze assaulted Nick's nostrils. Grendel looked up from his confrontation and stared. His eyes locked on Quinn's midsection. The jostling from the drunk had knocked the kid's jacket open. The butt of his forty-five was exposed. They were blown.

CHAPTER 14

Grendel upended his table with both hands, launching the bottles and the full tumbler at the bouncer, who reeled back into Nick and Quinn. As Nick caught the big Hungarian, the hacker scrambled over the bar and vanished through the swinging door.

"Get to the street," grunted Nick, shoving the bouncer back to his feet. Quinn obediently headed for the entrance while Nick took off in pursuit, leaving the bouncer standing alone in utter confusion. He reached the bar in two strides and vaulted over. His low foot caught a whiskey bottle and sent it flying into the mirrored backdrop. Glass and booze showered down.

Nick shouldered his way through the swinging door into a red-carpeted hallway, bound on one side by a brick wall and on the other by a row of rooms. A stunned waitress came out of one and then screamed and retreated back inside, slamming the door. The rest were closed, but the door at the far end of the hallway stood open. Immediately behind it there was another that opened the opposite direction. That one hung loose on its hinges. The dead bolt had been knocked through, splintering the old wood frame.

The buildings here were pressed against each other, with varying heights but with shared walls. Pairs of doors like these connected their cellars. Nick touched his ear. "Nightmare Three, he's headed southeast through the sublevels. He'll have to surface when he reaches the end of the row. Get in front of him."

"Copy, One. I'm on it."

As soon as Nick opened the second door, a heavy shelving unit came crashing down from his right. He jumped back. A shadow flitted away across a dark storeroom.

"We just want to talk," Nick called after him, clambering over the half-fallen unit, but Grendel kept running, toppling more shelves before escaping through a heavy door. Dim blue light spilled in from the other side.

"He's coming to you, Nightmare Three. I think he's in an outside stairwell."

Nick made quick work of Grendel's obstacle course and hit the door's push bar hard. He expected to slam into the wall of a stairwell on the other side. Instead, he almost plunged headfirst off a narrow concrete platform.

"I don't see him," said Quinn.

"Scratch my last. We're in the subway. I'm turning southwest." A few dim fluorescents lighted the narrow platform. There were no travelers. Nick spotted the hacker at the far end and drew his Beretta. "Stay where you are!"

The clacking rush of an approaching train drifted into the platform—one of the express lines that served the main stations in the off hours. The hacker raised his hands and slowly turned, but his eyes shifted down to the tracks. He sidestepped closer to the edge.

Nick raised his gun and advanced. "That's a bad idea, kid."

As the rush grew louder, a growing light shined from the tunnel behind Grendel. The hacker lifted his eyes to meet Nick's. There was fear in them, but Nick could see something else. A taunt. A half second later, Grendel flashed a smile and jumped down to the tracks, fleeing toward the oncoming train.

A horn blared. Lights flickered and brakes locked with an earsplitting shriek. Nick leaned out over the tracks to see what had happened, but he had to jerk back again as the train blew by. Inertia carried it six car lengths into the station before the driver got it stopped.

"He jumped in front of a train," said Nick, hopping down to the tracks and racing toward the cab.

"He what?"

"He jumped down onto the tracks and ran into the tunnel in front of the Metro."

"I see the street entrance, One. I'm coming down."

At the front of the train, Nick holstered his weapon and bent down to examine the bumper. The bewildered driver shouted a stream of Hungarian through the Plexiglas above. Nick didn't look up. He ran his hand along the dirty aluminum and then held it up in the light of the cab's left headlamp, rubbing the grime between his thumb and fingertips. "Negative. Hold your position. There's no blood here."

He jogged down the other side, bending down every few paces to look beneath the cars for body parts. He saw none. Above him, the late-night passengers peered out their windows. A few shouted and pounded on the glass.

During the course of his career, Nick had witnessed two suicides at close range. He had stood face-to-face with a suicide bomber in Bagram, and he had watched a Pakistani ISI agent pitch himself off a cliff to avoid capture. Of the two, the bomber had smiled, but not like Grendel. The hacker's face did not show the same placid acceptance of death. Nick stood up and ran, turning sideways and pushing against the car as he squeezed past tunnel supports. "Is my locator breaking the surface, Three?"

"Affirmative."

"Follow my signal. Stay above ground."

Twenty feet down the track from the far side of the platform, he saw it—an alcove cut into the tunnel wall beneath a faded emergency-exit sign. "I'm turning east." He pushed through the exit into a long low passage. As soon as he was in, he heard the echo of a door clicking closed on the other end. "He's out! Find him!"

"Working on it. I had to divert around some buildings."

Nick raced down the passage, up a flight of stairs, and slammed through another heavy door into cold night air. It had started snowing again. Big, airy flakes fell lazily down through the yellow cones of light beneath the streetlamps. Quinn came running around the corner a half block away and pulled up short. The two stared blankly at one another. "Where is he?" shouted the young operative.

The row of buildings between them faced a small park. Nick spotted movement among the bare trees. "There!"

Both men broke into a run, and Quinn pulled ahead as they crossed into the park. The young operative had his forty-five out. With the long, fat suppressor fixed to its nose, the bulky XDm looked about as subtle as an RPG. Nick was thankful that the area was deserted.

Quinn stopped at an old-school carousel and rested his forearms on the rail, leveling his weapon. "He's making for the buildings across the street. Let me shoot him."

"Cleared hot. One to the calf. I don't want him bleeding out."

"Copy that."

Nick never broke stride as he raced past, just right of the line of fire. He had complete faith in the kid's aim.

At the same moment the muted *thud* of the shot reached Nick's ears, Grendel stumbled. He cried out and pitched headlong onto the snow-dusted grass, but he did not stay down for long. Nick had to give him points for tenacity. The hacker got up, pinballed off a tree, and limped on, leaving a crimson trail through the snow.

Nick was closing the distance now. "Give it up," he called, drawing his Beretta again.

The hacker only quickened his pathetic gait, letting out small cries of pain with every other step. He looked back over his shoulder. No taunting smile this time, only fear. He limped past the trees at the edge of the park and turned south onto the street, where a black sedan plowed right through him.

Grendel's body flipped over the hood like a rag doll, glanced off the windshield, and slammed down into the gutter at Nick's feet. His head hit the curb with a hollow *thock*. Blood and gray matter spattered across the snow. The driver's window was down and he locked eyes with Nick as he passed. The young face looked oddly familiar, and there was something else—a tattoo on the left forearm, a simple geometric shape set within a circle, a crescent moon with an eight-pointed star nestled in its bend.

Where had he seen that mark before? An image flashed in Nick's mind—the drunk at the Black Dog, the one who had stumbled into Quinn and outed them to Grendel. Then a second image overpowered the first—the same youthful face under a ball cap, asking if Nick needed help, a green medical kit slung under his arm.

Nick raised his weapon and fired, but the sedan was already at the next intersection. His rounds blew out the back windshield and sparked off the bumper as the killer fishtailed around the corner. Then he passed behind a building, out of range.

CHAPTER 15

Nick and Quinn sprinted up a wet cobblestone street, heading for the Vitara. "Lighthouse, I need a patch to NSA reconnaissance right now!"

"Coming up, Nightmare." The voice in Nick's ear belonged to Molly, manning the SATCOM station at Romeo Seven. A moment later, she connected him to an NSA space-based reconnaissance crew.

"This is Raven Zero One. Send your code and request."

"Raven, this is Nightmare One, authorization seven zero one, requesting a priority-four retask for your bird."

A short pause. "Nightmare, you are authenticated and authorized. Go with retask."

"Do you have my grids?"

"Affirmative."

In midstride, Nick glanced down at his watch and did some quick math. "I need a two-mile-radius scan. You

are looking for a sedan with a blown-out back window."
He didn't bother giving the color. At night, it wouldn't
matter. The crew would start the search with synthetic
aperture radar, taking rapid, highly detailed radar photos,
the best way to find a vehicle with a missing window. Then
they would switch to infrared to track it. Neither sensor
used true color. "Send me your feed. Lighthouse will pass
you my streaming address."

"Raven copies all. We'll have the bird on target in two
mikes."

————

Nick's foot was on the Vitara's gas pedal before his door
had even closed. He took a hard right at the end of the
street and then right again on the next one over, working
south toward the point where Grendel was run down.
"Anytime now, Raven."

"Copy, Nightmare One, our bird is overhead. Stand by."

Nick held out an open palm to Quinn and snapped his
fingers. "Eyes, please."

Quinn was ready for him. He placed a compact head-
mounted display in Nick's hand, a composite frame with
a tiny screen positioned at the edge of the right eye—the
military version of Google Glass. Nick put it on and
then slapped his smartphone into the kid's chest. "Sync
it up and give me Raven's feed. I want to see this guy as
soon as they lock him up."

Quinn busied himself with the phone and a few seconds later, a black-and-white video appeared at the corner
of Nick's right eye. A stream of photo-quality radar stills

flashed by like pages in a flip book. After drifting south-west over urban Budapest for nearly a minute, the satellite feed settled on a sedan heading west on a two-lane street. The radar return showed every surface of the car in varied shades of light gray, except for the back windshield. That part came through as an empty black hole.

"That's him, Raven."

"Copy Nightmare. Switching to infrared. The target vehicle is two miles southwest of your current position, heading west toward the river."

The video switched from radar stills to gray-scale infra-red and showed the sedan moving along a two-lane road at moderate speed. The killer paused at the next intersec-tion like any other law-abiding citizen.

Quinn watched the feed on Nick's phone. "He doesn't look like he's in a hurry."

"He already has a busted rear window. He doesn't want to draw any more attention to himself." Nick turned west down an unlit street and floored it, but a block later, a brick wall materialized out of the dark. He gritted his teeth and slammed on the brakes. A dead end.

He smacked the steering wheel with his palm. "Get me a street map," he said, shifting into reverse.

As Nick floored the Vitara backward down the alley, Quinn shrank the satellite video to one side of his heads-up display and added a street map. Nick's blue dot was trapped in a web of city streets. The target's red dot had just reached the wide road next to the Danube. It turned south and accelerated. The killer's lead was growing.

Nick hit the brakes and spun the Vitara 180 degrees

on the slick road, coming to a stop at the intersection he had just left. He let it idle.

"Boss?"

"Give me a sec."

Quinn stared at the feed. "He's getting away."

"I know. Shut up."

Nick studied the map. None of the main roads in Budapest were straight. All of them led in big circles except for the winding river road and a four-lane highway that cut diagonally through the web, heading southeast to the airport. A half mile ahead of the red dot, a side street connected the river road to that highway.

Nick shoved the Vitara into gear. He turned left, backtracking for two blocks before hopping a curb and cutting across a grassy park to get to a two-lane road heading northeast.

"You're going completely the wrong way," said Quinn, gripping the dash as they bounced onto the road. "The target is headed south. He's headed out of town."

"He's going to turn east."

"How could you possibly know th—"

"Nightmare, your target is turning east," said Raven. "He's leaving the river."

Nick took his eyes off the road long enough to purse his lips at Quinn. "Copy that, Raven. Moving to intercept."

After continuing two blocks in the wrong direction, Nick turned south onto a four-lane road that made a wide circle around the city. The dots on the map were finally converging again, both heading for the highway to the airport—the blue from the northeast, the red from the west.

Nick reached the highway first, two miles north of the street the killer was on. The engine screamed as he pushed the little SUV's tachometer to the limit.

Seconds later, the target reached the highway, still a mile and a half ahead. The red dot turned southeast and accelerated beyond the speed limit.

"I think he's made us," said Quinn.

"Impossible. We're too far back."

"Target is stopping," said the satellite controller. "He's pulling over, still well short of the airport."

Just as Raven described, the sedan slowed to a stop on the side of the highway. The killer jumped over the barrier and climbed a set of stairs to a footbridge next to the road. "Zoom out one, Raven," ordered Nick, and the image blinked to a wider view. The footbridge led across the road and over a small field to a Metro station. Nick's target was about to disappear. "Raven, go optical, now! Get me some details before we lose him."

The crisp gray-scale image turned to dull black, broken only by a few orange lights on the street and on the train platform. The target ran beneath a dim lamp on the footbridge. He was barely a shadow.

The image flashed back to gray scale. "Negative, Nightmare. There's not enough light. Sticking with infrared. Suspect is wearing a hoodie, dark in color. That's all we got."

The sedan came up fast, abandoned on the side of the

road. Nick skidded to a stop behind it and threw open his door.

"Boss—" said Quinn, but Nick was already out of the car.

He ran across the short grass field underneath the footbridge and half climbed, half vaulted over the chain-link fence at the edge of the tracks. By the time he reached the platform, the train doors were closing. There were a number of passengers. Sunrise was approaching and the early commute had begun. As the train pulled out, Nick counted at least six dark hoodie sweatshirts among the passengers near the windows. He let out an angry shout and punched the schedule display. The Plexiglas cover cracked. The few remaining passengers on the platform stared and backed away.

Quinn appeared at Nick's shoulder. "He's gone, boss. We lost him."

CHAPTER 16

He was there, at ground zero."

Drake looked incredulous. "You sure about that?"

"Absolutely. I spoke to him. It was the same guy." Nick stared out his cabin window. The sun was just breaking over the eastern horizon, spreading its light across a solid cloud deck far below the aircraft. The two older team members sat facing each other in club seats with a faux wooden table between them. Quinn was across the aisle, sound asleep. Their flight to Turkey would last another hour.

Nick and Quinn had returned to the killer's car to find it completely clean—no papers, no prints, even the VIN had been scratched off. The license plates were stolen. Drake and Scott had fared little better at the apartment. Scott cracked the hacker's laptop and disabled the booby traps on the servers, but the servers did not reveal the

Emissary's identity. All he found were some scraps of code that looked like a virus and a second e-mail that went out on the day of the D.C. bombing. That e-mail had prompted a robbery at Istanbul University, one that had already made the news. They had no other leads.

After a long silence, Nick pressed a switch on his armrest to darken all the cabin windows. Then he glanced across the table at Drake. "I know you did something to make Amanda mad. What was it?"

Drake had started playing with his phone. He kept his eyes on the screen. "Seriously?"

"Seriously."

"Terri Belfacci invited me to coffee. I went."

Nick nodded. That would do it. Terri was their primary contact at the CIA—striking, flamboyant, and quite open about her designs on Drake. She referred to Amanda as "the grease monkey," even when Amanda was in the room.

"You're an idiot."

Drake dropped his hands to his lap and looked up. "I know."

Before Nick could follow up with all the reasons why Drake was an idiot, the big operative changed the subject back to the Emissary. "So, has our new friend made any more chess moves?"

"He made another one while we were on our way to pick you up last night. So far, he's given me two pawns, sending them up the edges of the board. I'm no chess master, but that's a very unconventional opening."

Drake shrugged. "So he's just using the app as a conduit to get your attention. He doesn't know a pawn from a pineapple."

"Maybe." Nick let his head settle back onto the leather cushion. "Or maybe he's a grand master and he's setting me up to take a beating."

The door separating the main cabin from the aircraft's aft comm station opened and Scott peeked out. He nodded to Nick. "The colonel's on the line. He wants to speak to you."

———

Colonel Walker's face was on the workstation's live video feed, his eyes roving the peripheries of the monitor as if he were trapped in the box. The old man spared no expense when it came to the Triple Seven Chase's technology, but he never fully adapted to any of it. He looked out of place using anything that wasn't built before or during the Cold War.

"Go ahead, sir," said Nick, dropping into a desk chair that was bolted to the aircraft floor.

Walker's scowl abruptly centered on the screen. "Baron?"

Nick rolled his eyes. "Yes. It's me, sir. What did you want to tell me?"

"CJ got herself a warrant to tap into the chess application's servers."

"And?"

"And they pulled the IP addresses for the Emissary's moves. He made one a couple of hours ago—"

"From a train in Budapest," said Nick, finishing the colonel's statement.

Walker squinted at him. "No. He made that move from the same place as all the others, from a wireless hot spot at a coffee shop on C Street, two blocks west of the D.C. bombing site."

Nick's eyes widened a touch. "That's impossible. I saw the driver who ran down Grendel. The same guy was at ground zero right after the bombing, posing as a responder. He has to be the Emissary."

"Not necessarily. Someone was at that coffee shop, and that someone is sending out the chess moves. He may be running the operative you saw in D.C. and Budapest, or he may be working for him." Walker took a swig from a foam cup of coffee, savoring the bitter liquid for a moment before continuing. "We need more data. Keep playing the game. Keep the Emissary on the hook. CJ is setting up a surveillance van to see if her team can't pinpoint which of the café's patrons is sending the moves. You have anything else?"

"Only the tattoo on the driver's arm," said Nick, sitting back in his chair. "I sent a drawing to Molly."

"Dead end. I saw your drawing. It looked common enough. I expected Molly to get a dozen matches, if not a hundred." Walker shook his head. "She got nothing. There's not a single person in the joint databases—good guy, bad guy, or otherwise—that bears that mark."

He polished off his coffee and then frowned at the empty cup. "So far, this investigation has netted us little more than a dead hacker and some useless computer files.

We're no closer to figuring out who these people are than we were yesterday morning."

Nick's eyes drifted to the clock at the bottom of his screen. "And no closer to stopping their next attack."

———

Luke Baron had never flown before. His little ears had never experienced the alarming compression that occurs when an airliner's cabin pressure descends from eight thousand feet to five hundred in the space of twenty minutes. In Katy's admittedly biased estimation, her toddler had endured the bumps and boredom of the grueling eight-hour flight with admirable calm, but the descent into Frankfurt was too much. Luke started to cry. Katy could feel the weighty glances of the passengers around her, all of whom surely regarded her as the worst mother on the face of the earth.

Nick's dad offered to take his grandson, but Katy shook her head and hugged Luke to her chest. She needed to hold him close right now. She was on the verge of tears herself.

Katy was used to Nick's travels. She was used to worrying when he disappeared for days or even weeks without contact, but she never left home during his trips. Somehow that made this one different. The house in Chapel Point—their home, their life together—sat empty and frozen in time while the two of them ventured off in different directions.

Between baggage claim and customs, it took Kurt and Katy a miserable hour and a half to get from the gate to the curb. Luke squirmed in his stroller the whole time, hungry and tired. Katy knew exactly how he felt. As they waited for the hotel van, she breathed in the crisp air and tried to put a better face on the situation. She was in Europe after all. That was fun. And in two days she would be in the Holy Land. Hadn't she always wanted to see it? She glanced around at the other passengers. None of them looked happy either. Most hunched down into their coats and stared anxiously down the pickup lane.

As her eyes roved the faces, Katy caught one individual looking her way, a short stocky man with a dark complexion and graying black stubble covering the lower half of his face. When she saw him, he cast his eyes down at the curb.

Katy quickly realized that she was now the one staring. She turned and joined the rest in watching for the next van, trying to let the moment pass, but the back of her head burned. Was that man watching her? She had told her husband that he was paranoid, overreacting to this whole thing, but now she wondered. Had she become a target?

After thirty seconds of pretending to look for the van, Katy couldn't take it anymore. She knelt down on the pretext of tucking Luke's blanket around him, and stole a glance behind her.

The short man had disappeared.

CHAPTER 17

Istanbul, Turkey

The spray of blood from the guard's throat sent a chill through Nick's body. Six hours after leaving Budapest, the three Triple Seven field operatives stood in the main security office of Istanbul University's biochemical research facility, watching videos of the robbery over the shoulder of the university's head of security. As far as the Turks were concerned, they were Interpol agents, thanks to a set of identities created by the techs at Romeo Seven. They watched the playback until the mysterious thief in the flowing hooded cloak disappeared from the frame.

"Holy cow," said Drake. "You guys were hit by Darth Maul."

Nick smacked his teammate's arm with the back of his hand. The security officer looked up from his bank of monitors and glared at him.

"What? Too soon?"

The next video showed the same figure in a cold-storage locker, sweeping vials of chemicals into a bag. Nick straightened up and let out a short, frustrated breath. "There's not much of use here. He keeps his face well hidden, and despite the drama and the brutality, the whole thing looks like a run-of-the-mill robbery."

The security man nodded, this time keeping his glare fixed on the cloaked figure on the screen in front of him. "It was. The thief took the lives of three guards and a highly respected department head, but to him, the murders were well worth it. Those chemicals will fetch a high price on the black market—tens of thousands of euros, maybe a hundred thousand."

Nick watched as the cloaked figure lifted a box through the broken door of a glass cabinet, careful to avoid the remaining shards. Surprisingly, he wasn't wearing gloves. "Did he leave fingerprints?"

"Yes, plenty. But they did us no good. We could not find a match in any database." The security officer raised an eyebrow. "Even Interpol's."

"We need to know exactly what he took."

"For that, you must talk to Dr. Osman, the new chairman of the facility."

———

Dr. Osman dismissed the security officer as soon as he introduced his guests. "My heart is heavy with this tragedy," he said, standing and shaking Nick's hand over his desk, "and I am reticent to go over it all again." He took his seat again. "I told the police everything I know. Can't you get what you need from their records?"

"I'm sorry," said Nick, "but we have our own interview procedures. It may be painful, but if you want your colleague's murderer to come to justice, the best thing that you can do is help us."

The doctor stared at Nick for a moment and then spread his hands. "Of course. What do you want to know?"

"A good start will be a list of the stolen chemicals."

Osman scooted forward to his computer. "I'm not sure how much it will help. There seemed to be no method to it. Some of the most valuable chemicals fell to the floor. Others worth only a few euros went into the bag."

The printer at the edge of the doctor's desk whirred to life. Nick took the first page it spat out. He scanned down the list. None of the compounds stood out to him. "I'm curious," he said, still scanning the page. "Your head of security told me the thief could make a hundred thousand euros on the black market, but you just said he left the valuable chemicals behind."

Osman shook his head. "I told you he left *some* of the valuable chemicals behind. Our security chief is correct. The thief got lucky." He stood and pulled the rest of the pages off the printer, thumbing through them. When he found the page he was looking for, he shifted it to the top, tapped the stack on his desk to straighten it, and handed the whole pile to Nick. "There," he said, pointing to an item halfway down the top page. "That was the most valuable item in the room, by far."

Nick read the entry out loud. "Lithium-six: three kilos."

Osman nodded. "Worth a hundred thousand euros, maybe more."

"Why so much?"

"Lithium-six is rare and it is highly controlled. Supply and demand. Basic economics." The doctor sat down again and gestured at the door. "Now, if you'll excuse me, I must attend to the unhappy task of taking over my late superior's position."

Nick stayed where he was. "Just one more question before we go. Let's say for the sake of argument that your thief had a use for the lithium-six other than selling it. What might that be?"

"I can't imagine." Osman returned his attention to his computer. "We use it here to track the transportation of submicroscopic agents between host cells."

Nick cast a glance at his teammates. Drake shrugged. Quinn shook his head.

"Could you put that in layman's terms, Doctor?"

Osman let out a sigh and looked up at his unwanted guests. "Viruses, gentlemen. Lithium-six is used in tracking and engineering viruses."

———

"The Emissary is building a bioweapon," said Nick. He held his phone to his ear as the team descended the marble stairs that led to the lobby of the research facility.

"You have evidence?" asked Walker.

"I have a pretty solid hunch. The terrorists stole a box

of controlled material from Istanbul University, material used to modify viruses."

"I can't have the CDC act on your hunch alone, Baron. Maybe the Emissary is making a bioweapon, or maybe he's planning to sell the material for cash to support another suicide bombing. Get me hard evidence. And if there is a virus, find out what it is and where it's going. Actionable intelligence, Major. You know the drill."

As Nick pushed through the building's glass double doors, a glint of light caught his eye. Something atop the old tower gate that dominated the university park had flashed in the winter sun. He recognized the distinctive play of light.

"Down!"

He shoved Drake and Quinn to the pavement behind the rental car as the door they had just come through shattered behind them. Glass rained down on the sidewalk. A thunderous report ripped across the campus, followed by another.

The shooter gave them no rest. High-velocity rounds pounded the small SUV. Terrified students screamed and ran for cover. Suddenly Quinn let out a pained cry. Nick and Drake were protected behind the engine block, but the younger operative had taken cover behind the rear tire. It was not big enough. One of the rounds had passed through the rental's thin frame and penetrated Quinn's body armor. He sat back onto the pavement with his hands over his belly. When he pulled them away, they were covered in blood.

While Drake dragged their teammate to the relative

safety of the vehicle's front end, Nick searched for his phone. He found it within reach at the edge of the sidewalk, beneath a pile of glass. He could hear Walker shouting on the other end.

Nick interrupted the colonel. "Get me a medevac chopper! Quinn's been hit!"

Beside him, Drake ripped off his outer shirt and pressed it to their young teammate's abdomen.

"How bad?" asked Walker.

Nick watched as Quinn's blood quickly soaked through the makeshift bandage. The kid's eyes lost their focus.

"We need that chopper now, sir. He's bleeding out."

CHAPTER 18

Ten rounds, almost universal to clip-fed sniper rifles. Nick waited for the inevitable pause as the shooter reloaded. As soon as the impacts stopped, he crawled forward, opened the rear passenger door of the rental and pulled a black duffel from the backseat. The first round of the sniper's second clip passed through the driver's door right above his shoulder as he dragged the bag back to their cover position behind the engine block.

"Come up on comms. Stay with Quinn," he ordered Drake, handing him one of the team's H&K MP7A1s and a SATCOM earpiece. Then he put his own earpiece in and withdrew his Beretta Nano from the bag. "Cover me."

After the second set of ten rounds, Drake popped over the hood and fired a volley at the shooter. Nick sprinted into the open. His objective was a good 150 meters away at the other end of a green park, a four-story tower gate bracketed by a pair of three-story turrets. He made it across the street and twenty meters into the sparse trees before the bullets started flying again. Heavy rounds splintered the trunk of an ancient cypress as he passed. "Any questions about what 'cover me' means?" he panted.

"Working on it," replied Drake through the comm link. "I'm dealing with a wounded man here."

As Drake spoke, Nick heard the *rat-a-tat* of his team-mate's MP7 over the comm link, followed an instant later by a matching report, echoing across the park. Drake kept the sniper's head down until Nick reached the base of the structure. Then his clip ran out and the shooter opened up again. A slow steady rhythm of earsplitting cracks sounded from the top of the tower.

A crowd of terrified pedestrians huddled beneath the main arch of the tower gate. A young man pointed at the gun in Nick's hand and shouted to the others. Nick ignored him. To the left of the crowd he spied an ancient wooden door, slightly ajar, and pushed through into a stone stairwell. The gunfire above stopped. The shooter was reloading again. Nick raced up the steps.

At the top of the stairs, he kicked open the door and leveled his Beretta. No one. The ledge that faced the research facility was directly ahead, but the sniper had abandoned his perch. Then Nick heard the crunch of a footstep to his right. The shooter struck before he could bring his gun around, knocking him off his feet and knocking the Beretta from his hand.

Nick hit the gravel rooftop hard, but he rolled backward over his shoulder and came up facing his attacker.

The man wore the same black cloak as the killer in the security video. The face under the wide hood looked Turkish, with a thin black mustache and beard, not much more than stubble. His hands were open, ready to fight, and his right palm bore a black marking similar to the tattoo on the driver in Budapest, a geometric shape within a circle.

In the distance, Nick could hear the rescue helicopter approaching. He circled the shooter, muttering a command to Drake. "Nightmare Two, I'm keeping our sniper busy. Move now. Get the kid to the roof and get him on that chopper."

"What about you?"

"I'll be fine."

The shooter lunged. Nick caught him by the lapels of his cloak and fell backward, twisting mid-fall, slamming him to the ground. Usually that maneuver knocked the wind from an opponent, but the impact did not faze this enemy at all. With terrifying strength, the shooter rolled Nick onto his back and came up on top. The two of them bumped against the low lip of the tower roof, and Nick felt the eerie threat of four stories of empty space.

Nick threw a left-and-right combination, connecting with the left before the shooter reared up, out of range. As if by magic, a knife appeared in his hand, an ornate curved hilt with two black blades on either end, forming a crescent. He grinned and slashed down at Nick's throat.

Nick caught the wide sleeve of the cloak and redirected the shooter's momentum rather than blocking it, pulling his arm across his body. The first blade missed his neck by an inch. The tip of the second blade missed it by a millimeter. After the knife cleared his throat, he kept pulling in an arc, stretching his arm back above his head to pull the shooter forward and off balance. At the same time he bumped upward with his hips and twisted right. The lip of the roof acted as a stop, blocking his opponent's knee. The shooter's eyes widened and he toppled over the edge.

After taking a moment to catch his breath, Nick stood and peered over the side, expecting to see the sniper's broken body lying on the pavement below and a crowd of students gathering around it. There was no one, no onlookers, no shooter, not even a scrap of cloak or a spot of blood.

Across the campus, the rescue chopper lifted off from the research center and nosed forward to rush Quinn to the hospital. Nick's phone chimed, a message from his chess app. The ivory text read, *The Emissary has taken your knight. Your move.*

CHAPTER 19

A search of the roof revealed no weapon and no shell casings. The sniper had to have ditched his rifle before Nick made it up the stairs. Then a flash of gold caught his eye. The shooter's strange knife lay on the lip of the roof.

Nick retrieved it and turned it over in his hand. Its workmanship was beautiful. Gold and silver arabesque inlays formed an intricate pattern of vines with heart-shaped leaves, weaving in and out of eight-pointed stars—all set into a dark alloy that he could not identify. The shooter must have dropped the knife when he went over the edge, though he managed to retract the blades. Nick could not figure out how to get them out again.

The woven designs on one side of the hilt surrounded a small silver inlay circle, enclosing two crescent moons set back-to-back, the same symbol tattooed on the sniper's right palm. Lacing through the vines on the other side of the hilt was a phrase in flowing gold calligraphy. Nick understood the Arabic words, but he was not certain of their meaning.

"Nightmare One, did you get him?" asked Drake over the comm link.

"Negative. What about Three?"

"He looked bad when I put him on the chopper, no color at all. Lighthouse scrambled a C-17 out of Incirlik with a surgical team. The colonel doesn't trust Turkish hospitals."

The crowd filtered out from below the tower. Some of the young men stared up at the Western intruder. Nick could see blame in their eyes. "We need to get out of here. Get the gear from the car and see if Romeo Seven can arrange some transpo."

"Back to the hotel?"

"Yeah. And then the market." Nick glanced down at the ornate knife in his hand. "I need to talk to an old friend."

Two hours later, Nick and Drake parked a new rental in a metered spot along the outer wall of Istanbul's Old City. That morning they had been Interpol agents, now they were tourists. Nick wore jeans and a Columbia jacket. Drake wore khakis with a *Walking Dead* T-shirt under a windbreaker.

While they waited in the car for their appointment, Nick's phone buzzed. He pressed it to his ear. "What've you got, CJ?"

"More than I want and not enough," replied the FBI agent.

"What does that mean?"

"It means that while you're running around, terrorizing Turkish college kids, I'm getting nowhere. I keep coming up with dead ends."

"Don't kid, CJ," said Nick. "The Emissary sent out another move. You were watching the coffee shop. You should have bagged him by now."

"It's not that easy. If we roll in before pinpointing the exact customer, we'll violate the civil rights of every legitimate caffeine addict in the joint. We can't do that. Not in this girl's America."

"Have you made a list of regulars who were around when the moves were made?"

"Of course, but I need more data so I can rule more of them out. I need you to keep playing."

"Roger that." Nick heard voices and laughter. Drake was watching a YouTube video on his phone. He slapped the big operative's arm with the back of his hand and gestured for him to keep an eye on the street. Drake frowned at him and rolled a finger in the air, signaling him to move the conversation along. Had he been born to another generation, Nick was certain his teammate would have been one of those ADD kids. He returned his attention to CJ. "I have something new for you to chew on."

"I'm all ears."

"Scott has been digging deeper into the scraps of code we found on Grendel's servers. They are definitely part of a virus."

"You have specifics?"

"Some." He explained that the fragments resembled Stuxnet, the virus the NSA sent into Iran to wreak havoc on their nuclear centrifuges in 2010. Stuxnet was a very specific and very powerful program. It had no effect on the computers it passed through, but when it reached its target, it became the first virus to enter through Windows and cross-talk to an industrial control system. On the upside, Stuxnet spun the Iranian centrifuges out of control, doing as much damage as a gaggle of bunker busters. On the downside, it left copies of itself on millions of computers, becoming a blueprint for hackers worldwide.

"It was only a matter of time until one of these bozos found a way to adapt it," said CJ. "What does Grendel's version do?"

"We don't know, but Scott is convinced that the virus and the messages to the suicide bomber are linked because they were kept on the same section of the server. I'll have him send you a summary. For now, that's all I've got."

"You haven't asked about the 'more than I want.'"

Nick rolled his eyes. CJ could never just spit things out. She had to play games, a sign of the control freak inside. "Okay, I'll bite. What did you mean by 'more than I want'?"

"I'm so glad you asked. I've had more attention than I want from a certain Mr. Cartwright, the senator from Virginia—a lot more. It seems one of his staffers was injured in the bombing on the Mall, and a first responder refused to treat him. Ring any bells?"

"Not yet."

"Tall guy. Lawyer. Claims that the first responder not

only refused to treat his eye, he also punched him in the chest."

Nick cringed. "Oh, yeah. That was me."

There was a pause. In his mind's eye, Nick could see CJ's head cocking to one side, her free hand going to her hip. "Are you insane?"

"The guy had it coming. I had to get to people with more serious injuries, and he wouldn't leave me alone. He got physical. I returned the favor."

"I shouldn't have asked."

"Keep the senator at bay, CJ. We don't need interference from power-hungry politicians."

"What's it worth to you?"

Nick closed his eyes. "Dinner?"

"He's a U.S. senator."

"Fine. A nice dinner. An expensive one. Whatever you want."

"Tell you what, I'll plead ignorance as long as I can, but if he keeps digging, he's going to turn something up. He has the ear of the president. These days there's no defense against that."

Drake tapped Nick's shoulder and pointed to his watch.

Nick acknowledged the signal with a nod. "I've gotta go."

"Sure you do," said CJ. Then her voice became distant, like she was holding the phone in front of her face. "Dinner, Nick Baron. A very *expensive* dinner."

The line went dead.

CHAPTER 20

The Grand Bazaar was a sprawling labyrinth of roofed-in streets, all hopelessly narrow, all packed with rugs and hookahs and knickknacks, and all echoing with the shouts of merchants and the buzz of more than three hundred thousand daily visitors. It was a claustrophobic man's nightmare and a covert operative's dream.

Drake sniffed the air and grinned. "I love this place. Why have you never brought me here before?"

"I've never had a reason, dear."

Nick had not been to the Grand Bazaar in years, but he found his way through the maze with little trouble, mostly by following his nose. Hadad liked to meet at a favorite tea shop, and all of the tea, coffee, and spice shops in the bazaar were concentrated into one long row—the same row that had housed them for more than half a millennium.

In this section of the bazaar, *shop* was a loose term. *Bay* would be better. The cafés amounted to little more than shallow caves lining the covered street. The kitchens took up most of the space, while the patron seating—painted iron chairs and little round tables—spilled out into the narrow street. Nick and Drake each ordered a mint tea from Hadad's chosen shop and took a seat at the edge of the bay.

"He should be here," said Drake, checking his watch.

Nick raised a tiny glass to his lips. "This is Turkey," he said before taking a sip. "Any appointment time comes with an implied 'ish' at the end. Besides, he's already here. He has protection posted." With a subtle movement of his elbow, Nick indicated a waiter that haunted the opposite corner of the bay. His grim expression contrasted sharply with his bright red jacket and fez.

Drake brushed a hand through the hair on the back of his head, a pretext to get a look at the sentry. "That guy could play for the Patriots," he said when he turned back.

"He's scoping us out. Hadad will show up in his own time." Nick took another sip of tea and then drew the shooter's knife from the pocket of his coat. He held it with both hands, running his thumb across the gold calligraphy. *"Ana al-muftaah,"* he read out loud.

"Say again."

"It's Arabic. It means, 'I am the key.'"

He handed the knife to Drake, who held one end up to his eye, trying to look down inside. "How do you open it?"

"I don't know, but I assume each blade comes out like a spring stiletto, so I wouldn't do that if I were you."

"That's good advice." Thin and cracked with age, the

voice came from close by Nick's left shoulder. He had not heard the old man's approach, despite the fact that he walked with a cane. Nick smiled, but he did not turn. "It has been too long, my friend. God's peace be upon you."

"And upon you, Nicholas, though it never seems to stick." Hadad placed a withered hand on Nick's shoulder and lowered himself into the chair between the two operatives. He was small, shrunken by his many years, which Nick figured to be at least ninety. He rested a cane with a gilded head between his knees and then, without asking, he reached out and took the knife from Drake. "What an exquisite piece," he said, wrapping his gnarled fingers around the hilt. The two blades shot out from the sides with a metallic *ring*. "And it is functional. Remarkable. I presume you are looking for a trade? I've been working on a new shoulder-launched missile that you might like."

"Easy, Hadad. We just need information. We need to know where the knife came from."

The blades retracted as quickly as they had shot out. "I see." Hadad gently laid the knife on the table and smacked his lips, pushing a tobacco-stained tongue off the roof of his mouth. "I am thirsty, Nicholas. And too much talk dries out an old throat. Perhaps some tea might strengthen my voice." He raised a hand, and the grim waiter in the red jacket and fez came over with a glass of tea and plate of sweet halva wafers on a tray.

Nick knew the drill. He slipped the waiter a small stack of bills, much more than tea and wafers were worth. The waiter left the refreshments and returned to his post.

Hadad sipped his tea in silence for a while, watching

the tourists passing by. Finally, he set down his glass and picked up the knife again. He pressed his thumb against the back of his cane and the tip of the gold head swung open, revealing a set of bifocals. These he put on before examining the hilt, slowly rotating it with his fingers.

"How did you get it to open?" asked Drake, losing patience with the old man's silence.

Hadad grinned at the big operative, exposing an uneven row of yellowed teeth. "It is an ancient design using cogs and springs. You could call it clockwork. The switch is hidden. Look here." He flipped the hilt to the side with the silver circle and crescent moons and pressed the symbol inward with his thumb. The blades shot out. As soon as he released it, they retracted again.

"That explains why they retracted when the shooter dropped it," said Nick, but Hadad did not seem to hear him. The old man had fixated on the symbol. He adjusted his bifocals and brought the weapon to within an inch of his nose. "Did you say that you fought a man who wielded this knife?"

Nick nodded. "He had the same symbol tattooed on the palm of his hand, the circle with the crescent moons."

Hadad removed his glasses and looked up, dropping the quaint, dotard expression he had maintained since he arrived. He was suddenly alert, and very grave. "The man with the tattoo. Did you kill him?"

"I threw him off a roof."

"But did you *kill* him?"

Nick found the urgency in the old man's voice perplexing. "No. He disappeared."

Hadad pushed the hilt into Nick's hand and leaned on his cane to stand. "I have told you all that I can. Thank you for the tea."

Nick took hold of his arm to keep him at the table. "You saw something on that hilt. What was it?"

"It was nothing. Let me go." Hadad pulled against Nick's grasp. The Turkish linebacker started toward them. Out of the corner of his eye, Nick saw Drake reaching for his Beretta. This meet was going sideways, fast, but he needed answers. "Please, Hadad. For an old friend."

Hadad hesitated for a moment longer and then settled back down in his chair. He motioned for his protector to back off. Drake withdrew his hand from his jacket.

"Only for you, Nicholas," said Hadad as he set his cane between his knees again. He lowered his voice so that Nick could barely hear him over the echo of the crowd. "At first, I thought you had brought me an artifact. The design is centuries old. So are the symbol and the motto on the hilt. They all belong to an ancient order."

"Which ancient order?" asked Nick.

Hadad glanced up and down the street as if his answer might bring enemies flying from the shadows. "The Hashashin," he whispered.

"The society of killers from the Middle Ages?" asked Drake, sitting back and folding his arms.

The old man winced and motioned for him to keep his voice down. "Not killers. Assassins."

"The Hashashin died out eight hundred years ago," said Nick. "What are you so afraid of?"

"This weapon is newly fashioned."

"So? It's a fake, then."

"You don't understand. This is not one of the trinkets we sell to the tourists. Its construction requires methods and materials forgotten to history." Hadad handed Nick his bifocals. "I have only known one smith who still retains these skills. His family was rumored to have served the Hashashin as armorers." He slowly tapped the hilt at the bottom of the silver circle. "That man's name was Ayan Ashaq."

Nick held one lens of the bifocals like a magnifying glass over the spot that Hadad indicated. There he saw a blacksmith's touchmark etched into the hilt in Latin letters—the initials *AA*.

Hadad retrieved his bifocals and returned them to their place in the head of his cane. "Ayan's family once had a smithy in the Ankara Citadel. I trust you have the resources to find it, if it is still there, but I must caution you. The Hashashin are not as dead as the world believes. The man you fought today is proof of it. The wisest course is to leave them be."

Drake snorted. "We can handle them."

Hadad shrugged his narrow shoulders. "Perhaps."

Nick stared down at the knife, the beautiful inlays, the strange, dark alloy behind them. "Hadad, if the Hashashin have been in hiding for eight hundred years, why would they surface now?"

"Only one reason." The old man stood, sweeping a couple of halva wafers from the plate as he stepped around the table. "Armageddon is approaching." Then he melted away into the passing crowd.

CHAPTER 21

Cairo, Egypt

The Emissary smoothed out his white hooded robe and shifted his hands behind his back, clasping the lifeless prosthetic fingers as if they were real. In this pose he gazed across the Nile from the window of a forgotten watchtower, considering the thousand minarets of Cairo. He admired their workmanship. Each one was beautiful, unique. And like the mosques below them, each would soon become entirely meaningless.

The time of the true *Qiyamah* rapidly approached. The time long predicted by Ismaili scholars when mankind would join together in enlightenment, and these places of both worship and segregation would become merely architectural curiosities. But the advent of the *Qiyamah* required a purge. Looking out from the watchtower, the Emissary could see the path to Armageddon in a whirling, winding pattern of outcomes as complex as the motifs that adorned those many minarets. That was his gift—to see events unfold before their time, to shape them as he saw fit, to use them to draw an opponent to destruction.

Armageddon would bring both global peace and personal justice. The man who had stripped the Emissary of the one thing he cared for would now be stripped of everything he loved, piece by piece, outcome after outcome. The dominoes would fall one by one, bringing Nick Baron's world crashing down around him, until he was left in the same state he had left the Emissary—utterly alone.

Then the two of them would die together.

The Emissary withdrew from his vision and turned expectantly to face the open archway to the tower's spiral staircase. A half second later, a young Syrian appeared. Kateb, the assistant security clerk from the Latakia weapons storage facility, entered the room carrying a brown leather satchel.

"*Ya Sheikh,*" said Kateb, offering a short bow. "I have brought the item you . . ." The clerk's voice faded. His eyes fixed on an old wooden desk in the corner of the room where a white-haired Pakistani busily soldered electronics together. A shiny metal box on the edge of the desk was marked with a yellow-and-black radiation-hazard label.

The Emissary smiled reassuringly. "Do not worry, young man. The material is quite safe in its present form." He gestured toward the man at the desk. "Dr. Wahish has assured me so."

Before Kateb could respond, another man entered the

room, this one carrying a green canvas backpack. He stepped around the security clerk and silently approached the Emissary. The newcomer wore the practical attire of a desert traveler—a brown vest and a tan shirt over loose-fitting olive pants, a black and tan *shemagh* scarf around his neck. There was a curved knife in a simple leather sheath tucked into the sash around his middle. When the Emissary nodded, he set the backpack down and with-drew a metal box marked LITHIUM-6.

"Excellent, Amran." The Emissary took the box and motioned his lieutenant aside. "Dr. Wahish?"

Without a word, the Pakistani doctor rose from the desk and unfurled a six-foot roll of plastic sheeting onto the floor. He set the box of lithium-6 on the sheet and opened it. Inside, there were a number of soft silver chunks of metal, suspended in mineral oil. The doctor used a pair of tongs to transfer two small chunks into a metal cylinder the size of a 35-millimeter-film canister, spilling only a few drops of oil on the plastic. Then he closed both containers. He put the box on his desk, a good distance from the box with the radiation-hazard label, and then handed the small cylinder to the Emissary and returned to his work.

Kateb watched all of this with mild interest, patiently waiting his turn. When all was complete, the Emissary signaled for him to come forward. He approached, uncon-cerned that he was now standing on the plastic sheet. *"Ya Sheikh,"* said the clerk, bowing as if starting a rehearsed scene over again, "I have brought the item you requested."

When the Emissary said nothing, Kateb hesitated, unsure of himself, and then handed over the satchel.

The Emissary opened the flap and checked the thermos-sized cylinder inside. Satisfied, he slipped his small canister of lithium-6 into the bag with it and lifted the strap over his head, letting it settle at his side. He smiled at Kateb and gave an almost imperceptible nod.

In the awkward silence, Kateb shifted his weight from one heel to the other. "*Ya Sheikh*, about my payment." The clerk did not see the Emissary's lieutenant slip around behind him, or hear him draw the knife from its sheath.

CHAPTER 22

D r. Patricia Heldner sat at her computer, reading data bursts from the airborne team watching over Quinn during his transport back to the states. She started typing a response to one of them when she heard a gentle rap on her office doorframe.

"Yes, Dick?" she said, still typing. She did not have to look up. She recognized the knock. It was the knock of a man who entered every office in this bunker with a loud, boorish comment or the pound of his fist against the frame—every office but hers. Pat and Walker knew each other too well for him to wear that facade around her. Now in her late forties, Heldner had played doctor and team mom for Dick's operations long before the Triple Seven came into being. She knew all his secrets, and he knew hers—like the fact that not all of her shoulder-length red hair was still naturally that color.

"How's our boy, Pat?" asked Walker, coming around her desk so that he could see her monitors.

Heldner pressed enter to send her message and then sat up in her rolling chair, straightening her white lab coat. "We're still touch and go. Quinn is on the C-17, headed for Landstuhl, and unless the flight surgeon does something stupid, he's going to live. Whether or not he'll ever see field ops again remains to be seen. He won't be shooting so much as a cap gun for months, I can tell you that." She glowered up at Walker. "When Nick checks in, I want to talk to him."

"You want to yell at him. There's a difference."

"He's the team lead. It's his job to protect them."

"And he does, as best he can. You know that. You've seen how far he'll go to protect his own."

"From the dangers that *he* puts in their path. Just like you, I suppose." The doctor wasn't really looking for a fight, but she wasn't averse to one either, not while one of her boys lay bloodied and unconscious on a gurney, thirty thousand feet over the Balkans. "Don't think that I don't see the pride in your eyes every time Nick takes his team into the field. You think he's a younger version of you." She narrowed her eyes. "You're being unkind."

"To Baron or to myself?"

"Let me talk to him, Dick," Heldner pushed. "I need him to tell me what Quinn had for breakfast before he was shot."

Walker smiled. "No, you don't." He started for the door. "I don't need you giving Baron a guilt trip right now. I need his mind free so he can figure out our latest puzzle."

CHAPTER 23

yan Ashaq was dead. Amid all his mysterious gloom and doom, Hadad had failed to mention that little tidbit. Although the revelation was nothing earth-shattering, not when taken with the rest of the data Molly had mined out of the Turkish system.

Living to the ripe old age of ninety-seven, Ayan Ashaq had led a quiet, assassination-free life, never traveling far from Ankara. He had died just as quietly not two years before, and he had no male heirs, though his sixty-four-year-old niece, Safa, had retained ownership of the family's ancestral shop in the Ankara Citadel. City records currently listed the shop as closed.

Only one item in all of Molly's results hinted at anything out of place—a close-up photograph of Ashaq dated 1952. The man in the picture, the man who died a senior citizen almost two years ago and bore no male heirs, looked identical to the man Nick had fought on the tower rooftop.

Under a moonless sky, Nick and Drake raced along the high red-stone wall of Ankara's Byzantine Citadel. They wore MultiCam fatigues and steadied equipment satchels and suppressed MP7s slung at their sides as they ran. On their left, a jagged, near vertical slope fell away from the thirty-foot ramparts to the rocks below. On their right, inside the wall, stood a hilltop settlement that traced its origins back to the early Hittites, four thousand years ago. Narrow cobblestone streets wound between two- and three-story houses constructed of dark timber and whitewashed mud brick. The oldest structures were built into the wall itself, constructed of the same ancient red stones. Ashaq's place was one of these.

"Hurry up, you two," said Scott, his voice tinged with annoyance. The engineer waited in a Renault Clio near the bottom of the hill, monitoring their progress on his laptop. "And someone tell me why I'm sitting in a parking lot and not sitting comfortably at my desk in the hotel room."

"You're here in case we need the car on short notice," said Nick. He kept his voice at a whisper, easily heard by the other two in their SATCOM earpieces.

"With Nightmare Three out of commission, you have to fill two jobs," added Drake. "You get to be wheelman *and* tech geek. No offense."

Scott sighed into the comm link. "I hate you."

The shop's tile roof was twenty feet below the top of the wall. Nick looped a camouflage rope around one of several thick spikes meant to keep birds from roosting on the ramparts and secured it with a heavy polymer clip. He gave it a tug to make sure it would hold and then slid down, managing his speed with the grip through the leather pads on his Nomex gloves.

Drake followed him down, and the two of them crept to the front of the roof where Nick installed an early-warning device on a timber that jutted out from the peak. The booger cam—Drake's name for it—was a micro-camera set in a marble of green sticky material. The gum adhered to almost any surface and would hold any angle.

"So what do an undead sniper and a mythical society of assassins have to do with our D.C. bomber?" asked Drake, watching the street while Nick worked.

Nick waved a hand in front of the camera and checked the corresponding feed on his smartphone. "Ashaq is not undead. This group must keep their male children hidden, raise them outside the system. It's the only explanation."

Drake raised an eyebrow. "Says you. Either way, how does he relate to the suicide bomber?"

"I don't know." Nick pushed back from the edge. "Let's find out."

The structure next door shared a wall with Ashaq's shop, but its roof was four feet lower. Scott's satellite imagery had caught the glint of a window there. Nick and Drake carefully lowered themselves down to the next roof and found a single pane in a two-foot-by-three-foot frame. "It's big enough," said Nick. "This is where we go in."

While Drake affixed a suction cup to the mottled glass, Nick pressed what looked like a small cordless drill into the crux of the frame and dragged it along the window's edge. The device generated a high-power laser, outside the visible spectrum; Nick had no indication it was working except for the red LED on the handle and the whisper of micro-fractures forming in the glass.

After Nick completed the circuit, Drake held the suction cup fast and gave the window a light bump with his fist. The whole piece came free. He handed it to Nick with a grin. "Don't drop this."

One after the other, they slipped into the top floor of the structure and activated the red tac lights on their MP7s, illuminating a smithy from another age. An old wooden table beneath the window was cluttered with iron tools and sticks of soft metal. Next to it was a pedal-powered grinder, and in the back corner, a blackened brickwork stove with a chimney running up through the roof.

"I know what I want for Christmas now," said Drake. He had moved to the front of the room, and stood over a long bench where several ornate knives lay on a black velvet cloth, their silver and gold inlays shimmering red under his light.

"Don't touch," said Nick. "We're not here to shop."

"Yeah, but maybe they have a Web store."

Nick wasn't exactly sure what they were looking for—records, a recent photo, anything that might help them find the shooter. After the events of the morning, he had a deep desire to spend some quality time with the guy. The two of them panned their lights across every inch of the stone walls and floor, but there were no pictures, no safe, not even a file cabinet.

"I guess we go down," said Drake, nodding toward a narrow flight of stairs.

They doused their lights and moved cautiously down the steps—Nick first, Drake above him, his weapon leveled over his teammate's shoulder. Nick saw no movement in the dark and flipped his light on again to get a better look. A wide, old-fashioned desk against the opposite wall looked promising. So did a tall gun rack at the back of the room, though its dozen rifle slots were all empty.

"This is more like it," whispered Drake, joining him at the bottom of the steps, but his optimism turned out to be premature.

While Drake examined a set of black-powder-coated shelves next to the gun rack, Nick searched the desk. Every drawer was empty. A corkboard mounted above it had only a few torn scraps pinned beneath its thumbtacks, as if someone had hurriedly stripped it bare.

"Nothing over here," said Drake. "The dust pattern tells me these shelves were full recently, but they're empty now. Same with the gun rack."

"We're too late," grumbled Nick. "Whoever was using this shop has bugged out." He shoved the last drawer into place, jolting the desk. There was a light *flap* of paper falling to the floor.

"Find something?" asked Drake.

"Maybe." Nick bent down and searched the floor, rising a few seconds later with an eight-by-ten photo with one corner torn off, probably a former tenant of the corkboard that got trapped behind the desk when the room was hastily cleared. It depicted an Indian man with thinning gray hair exiting a building. The lettering on the glass doors behind him read IBE LABS.

Nick switched his tac light to white and took a snapshot with his phone. Then he texted the picture to CJ, with the message *WHO AND WHERE?*

As he pressed send, an alarm sounded in his earpiece. Video from the booger cam replaced the text window on his screen. A figure approached the shop door. Nick couldn't tell if it was their shooter, but it certainly wasn't the elderly woman who was supposed to own the shop. He signaled Drake and they took up positions on either side of the door.

"What's happening?" asked Scott, sensing the urgent silence on the comm link.

Before Nick could tell the engineer to shut up, the door swung open. Incandescent bulbs flashed on overhead, filling the room with yellow light. Nick leveled his MP7 at the man's head. "Close the door. Slowly."

The intruder obeyed. He was the same man Nick had faced on the roof of the university tower, the man who bore such an uncanny resemblance to the old picture of Ayan Ashaq. This time the killer wore black slacks and a green button-down, looking much less like the grim reaper than before. He stepped away from the door. "Don't move," ordered Drake from behind him. "Show us your hands."

The sniper understood English, or at least he understood the order from the tone of Drake's voice. He slowly raised both hands. His left was empty. His right, still balled around his keys.

"Who are you?" demanded Nick. "Who do you work for?"

The shooter remained silent and took another step into the room, moving closer to the desk. Nick couldn't read his intentions. That desk was empty, unless there was a hidden weapon he hadn't found. He sure wasn't going to let the shooter get any closer so he could find out. "Do it," he said to Drake.

Drake had the shooter covered with a stun gun instead of his MP7. He fired it into the man's back from short range and the sniper's face contracted for an instant. Then it relaxed. He took another step toward the desk. Drake pulled the trigger again, pumping another charge into the man's back, but it had no effect at all. The shooter gave Nick a defiant grin and opened his right hand, dropping its contents. Nick could plainly see the black Hashashin symbol on the sniper's palm. He could also see a tin ring with a short pin hanging from the sniper's middle finger. Those were no ordinary keys.

"Grenade!" Nick shouted, backing away and diving to the floor.

A flash filled the room, along with a deafening *boom*, followed by a cloud of foul smoke.

Stupid. A flash bang. Nick heard Drake coughing in the haze. "You okay?"

"I'm good," said Drake through his cough. "I had the door. He didn't go that way. Didn't take the stairs either. You got a tally?"

"Negative."

As the smoke started to clear, Drake materialized near

the stairs, but Nick saw no sign of the shooter. He kicked the old desk. "There's no way! Not again!" Then he noticed the Persian rug at his feet. It was actually two pieces, fit together at the middle to form one continuous pattern. He hadn't seen it before, but now the seam was disturbed, one piece slightly above the other. He crouched down and threw both sides back, revealing a wooden hatch in the stone floor underneath. "Here! Come on!"

Nick yanked open the hatch and pointed his MP7 down the hole, ready to shoot first this time, but all he saw was a ladder leading down into darkness.

CHAPTER 24

Nick dropped down off the ladder into a narrow tunnel hewn from the bloodred rock of the citadel hill. Stone block pillars held the weight of the ceiling, spaced two meters apart along the walls and extending as far as his white tac light could reach in either direction.

"Which way?" asked Drake, dropping off the ladder.

Nick shook his head. "Didn't see him."

"What's going on, One?" Static shrouded Scott's voice, interference from the tons of earth and stone above them.

Nick covered one ear so that he could hear the engineer better. "The target from the university showed up. He dropped a mini flash bang and disappeared into a tunnel under the shop. Find out what this place is."

There was a long pause. "I called up the archaeological records of Ankara. You must be in a cellar of some kind. There are no tunnels beneath the citadel."

Nick squinted at the gloom beyond his light. "I beg to differ."

"We've got to move if we want to catch him," prompted Drake, switching his tac light to white as well. "Do we split up?"

"Negative. We take this guy together." Nick stuck his index finger in his mouth and then held it out into the center of the tunnel for a few seconds. "This way," he said, nodding to his front. "There's a breeze." He wiped his finger on his pants, raised his weapon to his shoulder, and started forward.

Drake followed behind. "I can't believe you just did that. Who are you, Daniel Boone?"

"You have a better idea?"

"No."

"Then shut up."

After a few paces, Nick's beam illuminated a wall at the end of the arches.

Drake let out a short sigh. "Dead end. You picked the wrong direction, Mr. Boone."

Nick nodded and began to turn, but then he felt a breath of air tickle the sweat on his neck. He quickly shut off his light, motioning for Drake to do the same.

"That's not a dead end," he whispered, leading his teammate forward in the dark, feeling his way along the tunnel wall. "It's a ninety-degree turn."

Without the lights, the crushing weight of the darkness pressed in, and Nick had the unsettling feeling that something waited for them on the blind side of that corner, something accustomed to the dark, something that thrived on it.

The air had grown colder. The dank smell it carried had grown stronger. He paused and knelt when they reached the end of the wall, reaching back to tap Drake's boot in slow cadence: *Three, two, one . . .*

Nick took the corner low while Drake went high. Both tac lights came on as they twisted and flung their backs against the tunnel's far wall.

A cloaked, hooded figure hovered above them, suspended in midair. Drake fired, spitting two rounds through his MP7's suppressor. Dust exploded from the apparition's chest. A grotesque head rocked forward into Nick's light.

"Hold your fire," whispered Nick. "It's a body."

Drake's eyes were pinned to the ghastly thing, hanging from a recess in the tunnel wall. "It's not a body. It's a mummy," he whispered back. "I hate mummies. They're just zombies with better embalming."

Nick panned his light down the passage. More bodies hung along the wall in arched alcoves, four feet off the floor. All of them wore tattered black robes, all were mummified so that their skin had turned gray and shrunk tight against their bones. Their eyes and mouths were sewn shut. He smiled at his teammate. "At least we know they can't bite you."

The passage remained narrow for a short stretch before it opened into a wide chamber. The ceiling rose to a height of at least five meters, supported by columns cut directly from the cave rock. The dead filled the walls, hanging in rows of recessed niches with their heads bowed and their arms crossed. More bodies lay on stone slabs beneath them. Some were empty, perhaps waiting for a future occupant. Directly ahead, at the far end of the chamber, was a large arched portal, leading into a black void. There were no other exits.

They crept forward with Drake in the lead, staying in the narrow aisle between the left wall and the slabs at its base. "A few of these mummies are fresher than others," the big operative whispered, shining his light on the bodies on the slabs. "I think the Hashashin are still embalming their members."

His words were followed by a faint *click* that sounded from the darkness to their right. Both men instinctively dropped to the floor, and an instant later, bullets riddled the bodies behind them. Dust and decayed flesh filled the air. Nick's light cracked off the corner of a stone slab as he dropped and it flickered out. Drake's flashed around the room as he scrambled for cover, playing havoc with the shadows of the dead. For a few seconds there was movement everywhere. Then the chamber went silent again. Nick lay prone behind an empty slab. Drake was on his back behind one that was occupied.

Nick glanced up at his partner. "Did you see him?"

"Negative. I've got nothing." Drake adjusted his position, bumping the mummy. Its hand slipped down and rested on his forearm. He grimaced and tossed the rigid arm back across the corpse's chest.

Nick inched forward so that he could get his barrel around the edge of his slab. Then he waved to Drake, touched his broken light, and pointed outward toward the void at the center of the room.

Drake nodded. He kept low, but he swung his weapon over the mummy, laying it across the corpse to shine his tac light out into the chamber. A cloaked shadow fled from the beam. Nick fired at it through the space between the slabs, emptying his clip.

If the Hashashin was hit, he gave no indication—no scream, not even a grunt. Instead, he responded with another hail of bullets, forcing both operatives to pull back. The mummy's hand fell down and rested on Drake's arm a second time.

Nick pocketed his empty clip and replaced it with a new one. "I don't like this at all."

"Tell me about it." Drake tossed the mummy's arm up to its chest again. "I can't stay here. This guy won't keep his hands to himself."

Another torrent of automatic fire dug into the slabs and bodies, kicking up dust all around them. Nick judged the angle of the incoming rounds by the line between the slab hits and the wall hits. The shooter had moved ahead of them.

"He's trying to flank us at the far end," he said, firing a blind burst to keep the Hashashin from breaking their line of cover. As he did, more shots came from behind them, near the entrance. Nick rolled over, firing another blind burst to the rear. "Scratch that. There are two of them, and they're trying to flank us on both sides."

As he spoke, his tac light suddenly flickered on, still pointed behind them. A black figure ducked out of the cone of light. Nick shifted to follow, but all he saw were dozens of black-robed figures. He couldn't tell which were dead and which were alive, and he didn't have the bullets to find out.

Then a solution dawned on him.

"Shine your light at the portal ahead of us. I'll watch our six. If anything enters your beam, shoot it. As long as we keep them away from the ends of these slabs, they can't flank us. Move!"

Both men started crawling, Drake on his belly with his light pointed at the portal, Nick face up, scooting backward on his shoulders so he could keep his light and his weapon trained on the kill zone behind. Spurts of automatic fire tracked along with them, but the slabs deflected the rounds. The killers couldn't get an angle on them. The plan was working.

Until Nick's damaged light flickered out again.

A curtain of darkness closed over his kill zone.

"Go now!"

Drake doused his light and made a break for the large portal. Nick fired two more bursts into the black behind them and then rolled over and followed. Debris kicked up at his feet. Then a long suppressor appeared out of the dark to his immediate right. He let go of his MP7 and pushed the hot cylinder up and away, wincing as a burst of fire shot past his ear. Still fighting for control of the attacker's weapon with his right hand, he grabbed the MP7 with his left and shoved the suppressor up into the man's ribs. He pulled the trigger. The MP7 gave an empty *click*.

The assailant laughed and shouted in a language Nick did not recognize. Immediately, another volley ricocheted off the archway ahead. The Hashashin was trying to guide his partner's shots using the sound of his own voice.

"Quiet, you." Nick punched the killer repeatedly in the mouth before committing both hands to wresting his gun away. He shot his right hand under the assailant's biceps and then weaved it back up to grab the barrel, making a modified figure four. Then he cranked the trapped arm backward and down, all the way to the floor. He heard the muted pop of a shoulder coming out of the socket. Even then, the Hashashin did not scream, but the machine gun came free.

Nick turned and flipped the weapon around, firing it into the dark with one hand while dragging his attacker backward through the portal by the collar of his robe. His captive fought against him, trying to gain a footing, but Nick put a stream of rounds into his legs to settle him down, finally getting a human response. The Hashashin let out a furious howl.

Two steps past the arch, Nick heard Drake's voice in his ear. "Through here." Invisible hands took hold of Nick and his captive and dragged them into a side room. A heavy door slammed shut. A bar slid into place. Drake's tac light came on. "You hit?"

"No. You?"

"Not that I can tell. Who's your friend?" The big operative had propped the Hashashin against the wall next to the door. He shined his light in the man's face. He was their original target, the risen Ayan Ashaq. His legs were bleeding profusely and his face was battered.

Blood dripped down his chin from both sides of his mouth.

Drake grimaced. "Nice work, boss."

"Who sent you to kill us?" demanded Nick.

"I am the servant of the Emissary," said the Hashashin in perfect English. "But you already know that." The words brought on a fit of coughing and his robe fell open, exposing the green button-down shirt. A red stain grew at the center of his chest. Nick didn't have much time.

"We know you're planning a bio attack. What's the target?"

The Hashashin gave him a grisly smile, showing two rows of bloody teeth. "You don't know anything. You cannot . . . stop . . . the signs . . ." His voice trailed off and his head fell to the side.

"Nick, don't," warned Drake.

But Nick had already dropped into a crouch next to his captive. He shook the limp body like a rag doll. "I'm not through with you! What is the target?"

Suddenly the Hashashin came to life, lifting his torso off the wall. His eyes opened wide and bloodshot and he screamed with rage. He swung his left fist sideways at Nick's head. Within a quarter of a second, Drake put two bullets through the assassin's forehead. The man fell back against the wall again and his hand dropped onto his thigh. It fell open, and a long metal spike rolled to the floor.

"Back away from him, Nick," ordered Drake, his weapon still trained on the Hashashin.

Nick stayed where he was and patted the man's cloak,

looking for pockets. "Relax. I think he's really dead this time."

"You clearly don't watch enough late-night movies."

"No wallet. No ID." Nick stood up. So much for getting some answers. He glanced warily at the door. "I wonder what happened to his friend."

"My guess is he's watching the door, waiting for reinforcements," said Drake, searching the small chamber with his tac light. "He'll try to pick us off the minute we step into the tunnel. When more arrive, they'll breach the room."

Nick stared down at the dead Hashashin. "I was praying that arch would lead us to an exit as I dragged him through. I should have prayed harder."

After a heartbeat of silence, Drake nudged him and smiled, nodding toward the far corner of the room. He trained his light on a set of footholds cut into the rock wall, leading up to a stone hatch in the ceiling. "I think you did just fine."

CHAPTER 25

While Drake climbed the footholds to test the stone hatch, Nick's eyes drifted around the dark chamber. The walls were flat and bare. There was no furniture except for a wide circular pedestal that rose from the floor, perhaps serving as a table. He moved closer and knelt next to it, running his fingers along the side. He felt the indentations of script spiraling down from top to bottom.

"What've you got?" asked Drake, pressing his shoulders up against the heavy stone.

"I don't know. Verses of some kind."

Drake let out a long grunt. The hatch moved, but not far. He relaxed and it settled back into place. "Verses from the Quran?"

Nick used the glow of his smartphone screen to examine his find. "I don't think so. Usually Quranic verses are written in Arabic. This appears to be Farsi."

"You mean Iranian."

"I mean Persian, and that's not a language in my skill set." He walked around the table, taking pictures. "We'll have to get these translated."

When he finished with the verses, Nick moved his light to the top of the pedestal. There were more carvings—a series of five symbols, four at the points of the compass and a larger one at the center, worn smooth and partially erased by time. Each was a simple shape or combination of shapes within a circle. Two of them matched the tattoos Nick had seen on his Hashashin targets.

He recognized the nearest of the four minor symbols as the double crescent moon worn by the incarnation of Ayan Ashaq, now lying dead a few feet away. The next around the circle was a combination of two triangles with their points overlapping, and the next a sort of sawtooth with a narrow base. The fourth symbol was nothing more than a horizontal crescent moon, its points directed downward.

Nick also recognized the fifth symbol, the larger one at the center of the table. Despite the wear of the stone, he could see the remnant of a crescent moon and an eight-pointed star, just like the tattoo on the man from Budapest and the D.C. bombing. Its honored position on this pedestal solidified what Nick already suspected. The man bearing that mark was in charge. He had to be the Emissary.

"Hey, professor," said Drake, growing impatient in his

awkward perch. "We can move this hatch if we both push together. You coming or what?"

———————

No one spoke when the team finally reached its three-room hotel suite in downtown Ankara. Against the objections of his teammates, Nick had kept them out an additional hour after they escaped from the catacombs, driving a preplanned surveillance-detection route to make sure they weren't followed.

Nick went straight to his room and shut the door, dropping his gear on the floor and collapsing onto his bed without bothering to undress.

He slept fitfully, his dreams full of half-decayed corpses in black robes, reaching for him out of a murky black ether. When he woke in the dim hour before sunrise, he couldn't move, trapped in that place where the mind is awake but the body is not. The feeling of an evil presence weighed heavily on his senses. The curtain fluttered. The silhouette of a hooded man materialized in the corner next to the window, its edges bleeding into the shadows around it.

Though he tried to call out, Nick could not speak. He could not utter a sound. His MP7 lay on the floor, not three feet from his left hand, but he could not move to grab it.

The shadow glided to the foot of the bed, reaching into its cloak with a skeletal black hand.

Nick fought against his paralysis until all at once his voice and body broke free. He cried out with something between a growl and a scream and rolled over to grab his weapon.

When he rolled back to fire, he saw nothing but an empty wall.

Drake burst through the bedroom door with his Beretta in hand, but he stopped short, his eyes flitting from the weapon in Nick's hands to the blank wall under his crosshairs. He blinked. "You . . . um . . . have a call on Scott's video setup. It's CJ." The big operative watched Nick until he lowered the MP7. Then he slid his Beretta into his waistband and walked out of the room.

Both Scott and Drake eyed Nick with curiosity as he crossed the suite to their temporary computer station. Nick said nothing. He did not want to discuss it.

He sat down in front of a live telecom image of CJ on the center of three laptops. "You have something for me?"

"You look like death warmed over," said the FBI agent, scrunching up her face.

"It's the SATCOM link. It adds ten years. Come on. Don't keep me in suspense."

The FBI agent squinted at Nick for a second longer, but then she clicked her mouse and a photograph replaced her face on the screen. "We had to outsource to some folks at the National Archives," she said, "but we finally restored that photograph from the bombing."

Nick took in a breath. Except for some small discoloration and fading, he could swear he was looking at an unburned photo. He would never have thought that kind of restoration possible, not after seeing the damage done to the original.

The picture was clearly a surveillance photo, from the chest up, taken with a telephoto lens. The younger version of Nick was looking off camera. He tried to place the drab urban scene in the background, but the flat mud structures looked like any number of villages in the Middle East.

"Ring any bells?" asked CJ.

Nick shrank the picture with his mouse and moved it into the corner of the screen. "Give me a little time. It will come to me."

"Time is something we don't have. The president is certain that another attack is imminent, and I have nothing to give him. Please tell me you haven't been gallivanting around Eastern Europe for two days only to come up empty-handed."

"I wouldn't call it empty-handed." Nick told her about their fight in the catacombs. "We found script that may be useful," he said, plugging his phone into the laptop, "along with some symbols that match our mystery tattoos. I'm sending you the pictures."

CJ wasn't impressed. "Cave drawings and mummies, huh?" She shook her head. "You're slipping, Nick Baron. And another thing—your buddy Senator Cartwright is getting more persistent. I've got one of his staffers banging on my door every couple of hours. It's like they're taking shifts. I've blocked them with special access orders, but that won't last. He's on the Intelligence Oversight Committee."

"My team isn't under that committee," said Nick.

"Well, mine is," she countered. "And I told you about Cartwright's White House connection. In another forty-eight hours, he'll have all the clearances he needs."

Nick didn't want to hear about the idiot politicians. He pushed her back on track. "I sent you a text from the room where we entered the tunnels. Did you get it?"

She cocked her head. "Random picture with a 'who and where' attached? Yeah, I got it. How should I know who that is?"

"I'm tired, CJ."

"Fine. Be that way. His name is Dr. Nashak Maharani. It took our software under an hour to come up with a match. We also know the where. International Biological Engineering. The good doctor is a molecular biologist." She paused and leaned closer to the screen. "Nick, he's noted for his achievements in genetically modified viruses."

Drake appeared at Nick's shoulder. "Bingo, we have a winner. That confirms we're facing a bio-attack."

A torso in a black suit, made headless by the limits of the webcam, approached CJ's desk. The suit handed her a note and she looked up and said a few words that the microphone didn't pick up. Then he moved offscreen again. CJ turned back to the monitor. "We got a video hit on your tattoo from Budapest."

"Where?" asked Nick and Drake in stereo.

"An airport cam at Heathrow, ten hours ago. Just a glimpse of the mark itself, though, no face. Two significant flights came in around that time, one from Cairo, one from Jordan. My guys pulled the customs feeds, but no dice."

"Ten hours," muttered Nick.

"Suck it up, princess," retorted CJ. "Legitimate gov-

ernment agencies like mine have to follow rules, file paperwork. Ten hours is some kind of record. You should be
singing my praises."

"So do we go after Maharani or Tattoo Guy?" asked
Drake.

"Both. The bioresearch firm that Maharani works for
is also in London. I'm guessing that's no coincidence."

Nick looked back at Scott. "Call our pilot. Have him
warm up the jet. Start packing the gear."

"Hey! I'm not finished." CJ tapped her screen to
reclaim his attention. "Maharani's a start, but I need
more. The picture showing up at the bombing tells me
our quarry is someone from your past. You've seen his
face twice so far. You have to dig down and try to remember him. You have to tell me who we're up against."

Nick glanced down at the picture in the corner of the
screen. In the photo, he was younger, several years at least.
He shook his head. "The man I saw was young, early
twenties. If I was chasing him when this picture was
taken, then I was chasing a teenager—"

He stopped. That was it. Suddenly he saw the face of
the Budapest killer—the face of the mystery man at the
D.C. bombing—in a new light. He knew the identity of
the Emissary.

PART TWO

GAMBIT

CHAPTER 26

Yemen
35 kilometers northwest of `Amran
September 2005

Hatchet, this is Zombie One. Confirm you saw the target enter the building?" asked Nick, pressing a button on the fat comm unit hanging from his ear. He turned to Drake, who was lying prone right next to him. "I'm not letting you pick our callsigns anymore."

They were crammed into a crevice in the side of a sandy hill, watching a mud house in a tiny desert village. Kattan had crossed from Iraq into Saudi Arabia, and then through the desert mountains into western Yemen. They had been on his trail for months. It was hot, it was stuffy, and they were surrounded by some of the biggest flies Nick had ever seen. He wondered if he smelled as offensive to Drake as Drake smelled to him.

"Zombie, affirmative," said the pilot of the drone circling above, high and out of sight. The CIA Predator-B was a limited production model of the Air Force MQ-9 Reaper, able to carry eight times the munitions of the original Predator. "Your target is inside. There are two sentries. One on the east side of the structure, the other on the west."

Colonel Walker's voice interrupted through Nick's satellite comm link, much more clear and crisp than the voice of the pilot relayed through the Predator-B's five-watt radio. "Zombie, this is Lighthouse. The risk of collateral damage has been assessed low. A strike on the building is approved. Do not wait for the target to leave. I repeat: do not wait for the target to leave. This is our best chance to take him down."

Everything had come together for this strike. The CIA asset had confirmed Kattan's presence, and it was carrying the best surgical strike weapon that current technology could provide—a dual GPS/laser-guided bomb called a GBU-54. The new bomb wasn't even fielded with regular units yet. At five hundred pounds, it was big enough to do the jobs that a Hellfire missile couldn't, and small enough to minimize collateral damage in a village like this one.

The numbers, the intelligence, the timing, all the data told Nick that striking now was the right move.

He checked the hardened laptop that Drake held open beside him. The high-definition video feed from the Predator-B showed the house and the two sentries in perfect clarity. "Hatchet, Zombie, I will be your tactical controller for this strike," said Nick. "Keep your laser cold. I'll take care of terminal guidance. Your aim point is the center of the house. I want *one* GBU-54 and *one only*. Call in with direction."

"Hatchet copies one bomb and one only. Laser cold." There was a long pause while the drone pilot lined his aircraft up for the attack run and then, "Hatchet is in from the north."

Nick checked the video one more time. Then he squinted through the scope of his laser designator, adjusted his crosshairs, and flipped on the beam. "Hatchet, you are cleared hot," he said into the radio.

The moment Nick spoke those words, the door on the south side of the structure opened and a boy walked toward a nearby water pump. It took Nick a long moment to process the unexpected sight. Instinctively, he backed away from the scope. The wider view with his naked eye confirmed the newcomer was way too short to be one of the sentries.

"Abort, abort, abort!"

"Too late, Zombie. The weapon is away, tracking your laser. Time of flight now twenty seconds."

Unaware of the danger, the boy went about his business. He hung a pail on the end of the pump and started working the handle.

Nick lost sight of the kid as he returned to his scope and started dragging his crosshairs into the desert. He moved the weapon's laser aim point toward his own position. It was the only direction he could shift the bomb without endangering another house in the village.

"Ten seconds."

"Take cover!" Nick reached blindly behind him, motioning for his teammate to move deeper into the crevice. "I'm bringing the bomb closer to our hill."

"You're what?"

"Five seconds." The Reaper pilot's voice remained even, almost robotic.

"Just get back!"

Nick knew that shifting a GBU was a long shot. The bomb's flight controls could not handle large changes with the laser spot. If he did not move the aim point far enough away, the house and the kid would still be inside the blast radius. If he moved it too far, too quickly, the bomb's logic would reject the laser signal and revert to GPS.

"Three, two, one . . . "

The impact shook the earth, threatening to bring the whole hill down on top of them. Debris ranging from small pebbles to softball-sized rocks pummeled Nick's back and shoulders and glanced off his Kevlar helmet. He kept his head low, waiting for the quaking to settle.

When Nick finally lifted his eyes, all he saw was a uniform curtain of light brown dust. He allowed himself a dirt-caked smile, certain he had successfully dragged the bomb closer to his own hideout.

Then Hatchet shattered the illusion.

"Splash. Direct hit on target building. Stand by for damage assessment."

With a gust of wind, the curtain of dust swirled apart, confirming Hatchet's report. The five-hundred-pound weapon had rejected the laser spot and reverted to the original coordinates, obliterating the mud structure.

Nick dropped into his scope and shifted it back to the water pump. At first, he could not see anything—the haze played havoc with his focus. Frantically, he rubbed his eye with a gloved knuckle and looked again.

On that second look, he found him: the young boy, lying still and bloodied in the dust.

CHAPTER 27

15,000 feet over France

Hey, are you awake?" asked Drake, reaching across the Gulfstream's aisle to poke Nick's arm.

Nick sat up slowly, rubbing his eyes. "I'm awake. I was just replaying the Kattan strike in my head."

"We acted on our intelligence," said Drake. "And we had no choice. That guy engineered attacks in Iraq that killed thirty-four U.S. soldiers and more than a hundred Iraqis. He was going to do it again."

"His son was twelve years old. He was an American citizen." Early in the Kattan chase, they had learned about his affair with a woman in New York. They knew about the boy, Masih, but they had no record of him ever going to Yemen.

Drake waved his hands. "Kattan is the one who brought the kid out there. That's on him. We didn't know."

"But we knew afterward. We should have tried to

recover the boy's body. We owed him that much." Nick laid his head back again and stared up at the cabin ceiling.

The CIA had operated its remotely piloted aircraft in Yemen with the consent of the Yemeni government, but there were compromises in the deal. One of those was the sanctity of Muslim bodies after a strike. The CIA could not touch them. The remains had to be left for the Yemeni authorities to collect for proper burial. All the Agency could do was monitor the removal and hope they got enough video to confirm that a target was dead. Once the bodies were out of sight, the word of the local coroner would be highly suspect.

But Nick and Drake were not bound by any international agreement. They were not CIA, and the Yemeni government had no knowledge of their presence. They could have reached the target area before the local authorities arrived. They could have confirmed the death of the child. Instead, still numb from the strike, Nick and Drake had packed up and left.

"I didn't want to see that boy up close," said Nick. "I didn't want that image locked in my head for the rest of my life."

"I know," said Drake. "I didn't either."

"But if we had, if we had gone down there and checked the bodies"—Nick rolled his head left to look his teammate in the eye—"we would have realized the kid was still alive."

The team left the Gulfstream in a hangar at London City Airport and set up shop in a two-bedroom apartment at Cygnet House, in Greenwich.

"Why do I always get the couch?" complained Scott, setting up a spiny SATCOM antenna on the balcony. Despite the cold, he wore only a lime-green T-shirt with his jeans. Block lettering on the front said: I'M SMARTER THAN YOUR BOYFRIEND.

Nick was running the antenna's cable along the baseboards behind the couch in question. "Because *your* room has to be the command center, and the command center has to be in the living room. Do you want me to put Drake in charge of your equipment?"

Scott winced. "Absolutely not."

"Then quit complaining." Nick secured the cable to the back of one of Scott's three laptops with a multi-tool and then stood up, slipping the tool into the leg pocket of his cargo pants. He brushed the dust off the long sleeves of his black thermal and turned to face the engineer. "What are we doing about Masih Kattan?"

The engineer cast one more wary look at the frayed couch cushions and then waved Nick back from the computers, out of his way. "While you two were lounging on the plane, I was back in the workstation getting us a head start." He sat down and tapped at a wireless keyboard, bringing all three laptops to life. Two of the screens showed freeze-frames of their Budapest target, one captured from Raven's satellite footage and the other from the camera at Heathrow airport. The third screen showed a facial sketch that Scott had built from Nick's description. "I took what surveillance images we had and fed them into the same program that helped you identify Grendel. Neither caught the subject's face. For that, I had to depend on our sketch. So the digital profile is much less complete."

"Nice pick on the digs, boss," interrupted Drake, emerging from his bedroom. He wore a loud, orange and yellow Hawaiian shirt, the one he called his relaxation shirt. He grinned at Scott. "Who knew you could find a California king in jolly old England. That baby is already calling my name."

Nick ignored him and pressed the engineer. "So you're saying our chances of finding Kattan are slim."

Scott shrugged. "If I set the program to scan the feeds from London's traffic and rail-station cams, we might get lucky. The tattoo will be the clincher. The software is set to view anyone with the same mark as a dead match. London has a lot of cameras. Kattan can't hide forever."

"No, but we don't have forever to find him. We need to locate this Dr. Maharani and find out what he knows." Nick grabbed his satchel from the couch and turned toward his room. As he did, the photo he had found at the knife shop fell onto the cushion. He picked it up, and for the first time he noticed a handwritten equation on the back.

$$632,000 \times 0.05 = 31,600$$
$$\underline{-31,600}$$
$$600,400$$

The final number was circled.

"Hey, I know what that equation means," said Drake, looking over Nick's shoulder. He pointed to the first number. "This is a population figure before an outbreak. The subtracted amount represents potential survivors. Five percent is the standard estimation of people who will be immune to a virus."

"How could you possibly know that?" argued Scott.

"Zombie apocalypse," countered Drake, folding his arms. "Every prepper takes it for granted that he's part of the five percent. It's the only hope we have."

"Finally we get something useful out of your ridiculous hobby."

"It is not a hobby, it is *survival*."

Nick snapped his fingers at his teammates. "Focus, please." He held the picture in front of Drake's nose. "What does the last number mean, the one that's circled?"

Drake shrugged. "That's the fatality estimate, the number of people the virus will kill."

Nick pushed past him and slapped the photo down next to Scott's computers. "I've been carrying around the answer to one of our biggest questions for hours, and I had no idea. Scott, how many cities have a population of 632,000?"

The engineer clicked at his keyboard and quickly came up with a result. "A few," he said, rolling out of the way so that Nick and Drake could see the screen.

Only one result from the short list of cities stood out to Nick. Only one made any sense. "These numbers tell us the target for the bio-attack," he said, picking up the photograph again. "They tell us it's Washington, D.C."

CHAPTER 28

Drake regarded his phony Interpol ID with a sour look, rubbing his thumb across the brass shield. Crammed into the right seat of the rented Peugeot hatchback, the big operative could easily have passed for Gulliver in Lilliput. Like Nick, he had exchanged his grunge clothes for business attire appropriate to the Interpol persona, and the overcoat he wore only amplified his disproportionate appearance in the small car. "Why Drake Martignetti?"

"It's Italian. It suits you."

"I'm Greek."

"Who can tell? You Mediterranean types all look the same."

Nick adjusted the dials of a microwave camera sitting on the dash, tuning an image of Maharani's three-story Kensington row house that a USB cable fed to a tablet computer on his lap. The video feed looked something like an ultrasound, assuming the doctor conducting the ultrasound was drunk. Intel techs often likened interpreting microwave video to interpreting chicken entrails.

"I don't like this," said Drake.

"It's too late to get a new cover name."

"Not the name, the plan. We need to take a step back and stake this guy out for a couple of days. If the doctor's working for Kattan, we might be walking into another firefight."

"We don't have a couple of days. And there's no ambush here." Nick lifted the tablet so that Drake could see. He pointed to a green, vaguely human-shaped blob, undulating across the first floor. "I see one guy, probably Maharani. You have to trust the equipment."

"Right. Because microwave is so dependable." Drake flipped the Interpol ID wallet closed with a *slap*. "I don't look Italian at all."

Nick rang the bell next to Maharani's carved oak door and waited. When no one answered, he rang again. After a few seconds, he glanced up at Drake and jerked his chin toward the near end of the joined houses. "Head around back."

After selecting a bump key, it took Nick less than four seconds to unlock both the dead bolt and the knob and silently push through. He stepped into a hall with dark wood flooring that ran all the way to the back of the house. Up and to the left, an open doorway led to a carpeted living area, and farther down another led to a kitchen. To his immediate right, a stairway led up to the bedroom floors above. He closed the door behind him, pocketed the bump key, and drew his Taser.

The microwave camera had last shown the flat's one occupant on the first floor, in a room on the right side. By now, he could be anywhere. Nick checked the living area first. He saw no one, just some ugly green furniture and a couple of ebony curios full of knickknacks. As he returned to the hallway, Drake appeared at the other end. Nick pointed at his own eyes and shook his head and then pointed at Drake. His teammate shook his head as well. Drake had not seen anyone either. Then Nick heard a *bump* from the wall to his right.

Drake heard it too. The two operatives converged on a closed door beneath the stairwell. Nick held a finger up for his teammate to wait, raised his Taser, and then nodded.

As soon as Drake turned the knob, the door swung open. A broom handle came crashing down and smacked him in the forehead. Nick would have laughed if the handle hadn't reared back again for another blow.

Drake grabbed the stick and yanked hard, and a young Indian woman stumbled out into the hall, still maintaining a death grip on the other end of the broom. She struggled hopelessly against Drake for a couple of seconds and then abandoned her weapon and ran, hitting Nick in the ribs with a sharp little shoulder as she shot between them. She disappeared into the kitchen.

"Why didn't you Tase her?" asked Drake, rubbing the welt on his head.

"Why didn't you?"

Nick tilted his head toward the kitchen. "She's going for a knife. We should probably go get her."

"After you, then."

The girl took a swipe at Nick with a chopping knife as soon as he passed through the doorway. He lurched back and then maneuvered deeper into the room so that Drake could follow and hem her in. He assessed the subject. Other than the knife, she hardly looked threatening—five foot three in her heels and a buck ten, if that. She wore formfitting gray slacks and a forest-green blouse, not the typical attire of a burglar or a terrorist. He kept his Taser pointed at her shins. "We're Interpol, ma'am. Drop the knife."

"Please, ma'am," Drake chimed in, circling right. "Drop it."

Before Drake finished the command, it was Nick's turn again. "Drop the knife. We don't want to Tase you."

The technique was called barrage. A single, rapidly repeated command issued from multiple angles. Sensory overload blocked a subject's ability to make complex decisions, leaving them with only three basic options—fight, flight, or compliance. All but the most hardened criminals chose compliance.

After the second round of commands, the woman dropped the knife onto the counter with a heavy *clank* and raised her hands. Tears formed at the edges of her almond eyes. "Who are you? What have you done with my father?"

Nick held out a badge that declared him to be Nicholas Stafford of American Interpol, the same badge he had used in Istanbul. While the girl's eyes were focused on the wallet, Drake stepped in and pulled the knife away. "We haven't done anything with your father," said Nick. "We just want to ask him a few questions."

It took several minutes to calm her down, and Nick was forced to produce a British search warrant that Scott had created, signed by a local magistrate who did not exist. When she was finally convinced that the two Americans were not there to kidnap her, the young woman introduced herself as Chaya Maharani, the biologist's daughter. She led them into the living area and invited them to sit down in a pair of worn mint-green chairs. Chaya remained standing, pacing in front of the matching sofa, her reflection ghosting back and forth across a polished ebony coffee table.

"I have not heard from my father in two days," she explained. "His company claims that he came to the office yesterday afternoon and took a leave of absence." Fresh tears rolled down her cheeks. "Mother is gone. I am his only family. If he went on a vacation, I would know it."

"Did you go to the police?" asked Drake.

"They said he hasn't been missing long enough. Please, if you know something about his disappearance, you must tell me."

Nick did not have time to play things close to the vest. He put his cards on the table. "Miss Maharani, we believe that your father is involved in an attempt to create a biological weapon."

"Impossible." She sniffed and wiped her eyes and then her hands went to her hips. "My father's viral research is designed to improve life, not take it."

"What if he's being coerced?" asked Drake. "Is there

anything a terrorist group could use against him? Maybe an affair?"

Nick cast a sharp glance at his teammate.

Chaya scowled at him too. "I just told you that my mother is gone. If my father were seeing anyone—which he is not—it would hardly qualify as an affair."

Nick was losing her. He softened his tone, switching roles from interrogator to helpful outsider. "What about his finances? Does he have any large debts that might make him vulnerable?"

Chaya collapsed onto the sofa. "Everyone has mountains of debt these days. And what would I know about his finances? In my culture, a child does not question her parents about such things."

Nick smiled, hiding his frustration behind empathetic words. "My family is from the midwestern U.S.," he said. "We have the very same tradition." He stopped asking questions. This whole exercise was pointless. Molly had already delved into the biologist's past. His known financial dealings were clean, and just as Chaya had said, his work was aimed at attacking disease and genetic disorders, not symbols of democracy.

Nick stood and offered a hand across the black coffee table. "Thank you for your cooperation, Miss Maharani. We need to go."

The girl walked them to the door and saw them out without any pleasantries. They made it all the way back to the Peugeot before she suddenly called out from the doorway. "Mr. Stafford," she called, using the name from Nick's Interpol badge.

He turned to see her standing on her father's steps, holding his warrant out at arm's length. Nick patted his coat. Had he really left the bogus legal document in her hands? He put on his best government employee smile and hurried back across the street to keep her from raising her voice and involving the whole neighborhood. "Yes, ma'am?"

Chaya closed the door and walked down the steps. She had donned a tapered blue peacoat, like she was going somewhere. "You can drop the 'ma'ams,' Mr. Stafford. I'm not one of those Brits who equates all Americans with cowboys. I'm also not one who blindly accepts a warrant. When you looked into my father, you must have read something about me. Did you happen to notice what I do for a living?"

Nick winced. Yes, he had. "Chaya Maharani," he recited, "assistant solicitor for the firm of Taylor and Brown, London office."

"What does that mean?" whispered Drake, catching up to him.

"It means she's a lawyer," Nick whispered back.

"Oh. Not good."

Chaya offered him a congenial smile. She seemed to have gathered her composure rather quickly since the impromptu interrogation. "Mr. Stafford—may I call you Nicholas?"

"Nick's fine."

"Nick it is, then. As you might guess, I'm quite familiar with the magistrates in Central London." The girl held up the warrant pinched between a thumb and forefinger and jiggled the paper. "I find it odd that I've never heard of this one."

Nick reached up to retrieve the warrant, but Chaya jerked it away.

"What are you implying?"

"I'm not implying anything . . . yet. I would like to propose a partnership. My father is missing, and you are the only ones who seem to know anything about it. Why don't you let me tag along on your investigation?"

"Out of the question."

"Then Interpol won't mind if I give this document to one or two *nonfictional* magistrates that I know." She gave her hair a melodramatic toss and batted her eyes. "You've no idea how eager to please these judges can be around cute little solicitors like me."

"Oh, I think I do." Nick's hand went for his Taser of its own accord.

Drake caught his wrist. "She can help. Who knows Maharani better than his own daughter?"

Chaya flashed a sugar-sweet smile, showing perfectly straight white teeth, and then stepped around Nick and hooked Drake's arm. She tucked the warrant into the pocket of her peacoat. "I guess it's settled then."

CHAPTER 29

Frankfurt, Germany

H ad Katy known the power of Kurt Baron's lectures, she would have asked Nick's dad to move in with them a long time ago. Luke was sound asleep. Katy was on the verge herself.

The dark lecture hall offered a welcome break from racing around Frankfurt. Kurt, aka Clark W. Griswold, had been running them ragged since they arrived. They saw the cathedrals, the botanical gardens, the Frankfurt Zoo. Most of it was a blur, but she did find the enclosure full of guinea pigs at the zoo oddly amusing. Maybe they weren't considered disposable pets in Germany.

To stay awake, Katy took her eyes off the giant timeline of Jericho artifacts on the screen and let them drift around the room. About half the students were paying attention. The other half were either playing with their phones or passed out like Luke. None of them took any notice of her.

Good.

Throughout their tourist activities, Katy had noticed people watching her—the tall guy at the zoo, the car that followed them all the way to Mainz, the blonde woman who stayed with them from the train to the botanical gardens and then reappeared when they came out. And there were others. Maybe some of it was her imagination. Maybe all of it. Kurt had said as much, but he didn't know the history. He didn't understand what Nick did for a living. He didn't know what Katy had been through already.

She was jet-lagged. She missed her husband. She told herself these things were making her paranoid. She needed to let go and start enjoying herself.

Katy squeezed her sleeping son, took a deep cleansing breath, and focused on her father-in-law's lecture, but Kurt was droning on about a broken oil lamp preserved in the shelter of the Jericho wall. She sank a little in her seat. Maybe she could start enjoying herself later.

————

When the lights came up, a short, stocky individual stretched in his seat and picked up his pile of books. He started up the stairs with the rest of the students rather than hanging around to wait for Dr. Baron to pack up. That would be far too obvious. Besides, he knew where the professor and his daughter-in-law would exit, from the green room backstage. He could pick them up in the hall.

The woman came down the stairs on the other aisle as he went up. She did not see him this time, but this time he was more cautious. He wore a yarmulke. It was amazing how a little cultural item could become camouflage. He had also shaved, removing the beard of stubble, and he carried a thick pile of books under his arm, naturally raising his shoulder and ruffling his jacket to disrupt his form and cover his face.

He examined the woman with his peripheral vision only. She looked wary, alert. Baron had trained her well.

Out in the upper hall, he found a dark alcove and dialed his phone. The man who answered spoke German— a courtesy to him and a way to minimize the risk of inadvertent exposure.

"How was the lecture?"

"Enthralling."

"Any further problems?"

The short man glanced over at the lecture-hall doors, watching the last of the students filtering out. In a minute or so he would need to reposition to keep tabs on his quarry. "No, we've adjusted."

"I told you not to underestimate her."

"Yes. You did. I assume you want me to remain hidden?"

"For now, but be ready to move in if I need you."

The man reached into his coat and felt the butt of the Glock 42 holstered in his waistband. "Always."

CHAPTER 30

London, United Kingdom

Although common sense seemed to have taken a backseat, Nick had enough of it left to keep Chaya with him when he and Drake split up. Between his teammate and the girl, it was hard to tell who was the wolf and who was the prey. Either way, Nick knew leaving them alone together was a bad idea. Amanda could thank him later.

To keep Drake out of trouble, Nick sent him up to Cambridge in the Peugeot to chase down a hunch. Meanwhile, he took the unscrupulous lawyer to her father's office to see what they could dig up. Without a car, that meant twenty-five awkward minutes on the Tube's Central Line—great place to sit and be a target, in multiple senses of the word.

"I take it you're single too?" asked Chaya, breaking the silence as they left Kensington Station on their way to Holborn.

"No."

The monosyllabic answer shut her down, but not for long. Passing through Oxford Circus, she gathered her courage again. "Sooo, you leave the wedding ring at home then?" She glanced pointedly down at his bare hand.

Nick took in a long breath. He didn't like her tone, and she was way off. He missed his wife and son, and he worried about them—constantly. Katy and Luke made up the part of his life that he could never fully compartmentalize. Everything else—the mortgage, plans for the future, even his other family members—he could pack in mental boxes to save for when he came home. Most of his day-to-day life did not exist when he was out on a mission, but Katy and Luke could not be tucked away so easily. He had learned that the hard way more than a year ago, while hanging by his wrists in a Chinese interrogation room.

Nick put his hand in his coat pocket, out of sight. "It's not like that. It's . . . policy. When things get heated in the field, jewelry causes issues. Rings can get hung on clothes or weapons."

Chaya looked up at him with those big almond eyes. "Do things often get *heated* in the field?"

"No."

Like a gift from heaven, the word *Holborn* emerged from the left side of the car's LED display and moved to the center. The train slowed to a stop. Nick got up and headed for the doors.

———

The sloped glass facade of International Biological Engineering stood as a modernistic affront to the stark gray

Edwardian style of the rest of Kingsway and the Strand. The echoing lobby with its concrete walls and aircraft-aluminum trim continued the theme. Everything screamed high-tech. Nick's badge got them past the security desk and up the elevator to the third-floor research section. There, a curving hallway walled with faceted aluminum panels led them to a faux redhead, bunkered behind a concrete reception desk.

"How can I help you?" she asked in Estuary English, covering the receiver of her cell phone as Nick and Chaya approached. Then she recognized Chaya and the plastic customer-service smile fell away. "I'll call you back, love," she said into the phone. She put it down and folded her hands on the desk, staring Chaya in the eye. "Dr. Maharani is on leave, same as I told you this morning. He lef' strict instructions tha' he was not to be disturbed."

Chaya grabbed the ID wallet from Nick's hand and thrust it in the receptionist's face. "And I told you I'd be back. This man is from Interpol. You *have* to tell him where my father is."

Nick gently but firmly pulled Chaya's hand back and reclaimed the badge, using the pressure from his fingertips to tell her, *You're not helping.* Confrontation rarely worked with witnesses. As Walker once told him, no matter how loud you shout, you can't argue a fish into your boat.

Nick quickly shifted the mood, baiting his hook. "What Miss Maharani is trying to say is that her father may have vital information relating to a counterterrorism investigation."

The receptionist's eyes widened. *"Counterterrorism?"*

"Yes, counterterrorism." Nick slowly turned the reel, bringing the bait to life. "Of course, I must inform you that anything we discuss from this point forward is strictly classified. You cannot share our conversation with anyone."

The receptionist glanced down the hallways on either side of her pill box and then leaned forward on her elbows, brushing back the ragged strands of mauve that fell about her face. "You can count on me, love. How can I help you?" This time the question sounded much more sincere. The fish was on the line.

Unfortunately, the fish knew very little. She explained that Maharani's leave of absence was nothing unusual. Bioengineering was a high-stakes, high-pressure field, and minds like his needed the occasional respite. IBE had a generous leave policy, and all of its researchers took full advantage, Chaya's father included. The receptionist handed Nick the researcher's leave request. "He only lef' me his home address," she said. "No resort or vacation house."

"Then shouldn't you be concerned that he isn't *at* his home address?" asked Chaya.

The receptionist pursed her lips. "They *all* put down their home addresses. I've got a department full of regular absentminded professors who can make a rat grow purple hair but can't remember the name of the resort they're headed to."

Nick examined the form. There was a list of equipment at the bottom. It appeared the doctor had signed out assorted beakers and containers, a pair of laptop computers, and some culturing solution. "What's all this?" he asked, pointing out the list to the redhead. "Did Dr. Maharani indicate that this was a working vacation?"

The girl bobbled her head, making the mop of red flop back and forth inconclusively. "Not really. The professors of'n take a few supplies along, 'case they get ideas halfway through their holiday." She raised her penciled eyebrows and took on an expression she must have thought looked quite intelligent. "A true genius does not choose his moments of inspiration."

Nick scanned the list of supplies again. "There's a lot of glass here. More than an older gentleman like the doctor can carry."

"Oh, he had help, love." The receptionist's eyes drifted and she smiled to herself. "Tall, dark, and handsome help—with a bit of a prison vibe, but the kind a girl likes, if you know wha' I mean." She winked and poked Nick in the arm with a press-on nail.

"No, ma'am. I don't know what you mean."

"He had a *tattoo*, love. Right here." She pointed to her pasty white forearm. "But not a cheesy set of flames like the boys at the pub have." She looked around again and lowered her voice. "It was a proper marking. You could tell it meant some'n serious."

Nick flipped over the paper between them and drew the circle with the crescent and star. As soon as he finished, the receptionist jabbed her finger at the paper. "That's it, love. That's the one."

"Are you certain?"

"Do I look like I'm blind? *'Course* I'm certain."

Nick glanced up at the security camera behind the desk. This might be the break he needed. He tucked his badge into his coat. "Thank you, ma'am. You've been most helpful."

"Have I?" asked the receptionist, her cheeks beginning to flush.

"Yes, but remember, our conversation here was strictly classified."

She waved her hand in a slow arc, fluttering her fingers. "You were never here, love."

———

On the elevator back down to the lobby, Chaya tugged at Nick's elbow. "How could you know to draw that tattoo unless you already knew who took my father?"

Nick watched the red numbers tick by above the elevator door. "I didn't know, I suspected. We've been tracking a terrorist group with similar tattoos since the bombing in Washington, D.C." There was a loud *ding* and the doors slid open. He stepped out into the lobby at a quick pace.

Chaya was right on his heels. "And when were you planning to tell *me* that the people who bombed your capital had my father?"

"I'm telling you now." Nick reached the security desk and loudly slapped the polished concrete surface, startling the college dropout behind it nearly out of his chair. He flashed his badge. "I need to see yesterday's video files."

CHAPTER 31

n one hundred meters, turn left on Lensfield Road."

"This one?" asked Drake, putting on his blinker.

"No. Keep going. That one was thirty meters. I said one hundred meters to Lensfield."

"There are no street signs. How do these people find anything?"

"You're there. Turn now!"

Drake missed the turn.

Scott exhaled loudly into the comm link. "Stand by. I'm recalculating."

"Something wrong?"

"Oh, I don't know. Maybe I'm upset because you've taken one of the most brilliant technical minds of our time and reduced him to a TomTom. Make the next available U-turn."

Drake followed Scott's directions deeper into the

Cambridge University campus, crossing from modern to old to Old World. He stared up at the brownstone faces of the long renaissance buildings as if he might enter the maze within and never find his way out again. He hated the endless dusty halls of academia, and Nick knew it. Yet Nick had sent him up here anyway.

"CJ's databases won't have anything on a terrorist group that's been dormant for eight hundred years," Nick had explained as he peeled Drake away from Chaya and stuffed him into the Peugeot. "I need you to go up to Cambridge and consult Rami."

"What kind of database is Rami?"

"Rami isn't a database. He's a professor—my professor. Dr. Rami Fuad taught Middle Eastern studies at the Air Force Academy. A few years after I graduated, he abandoned that program as a lost cause and moved to Pembroke College, at Cambridge."

The interior of the college was as nightmarish as Drake had feared. Long, echoing halls, stairwells that only led down when he needed to go up, room numbers with no decipherable pattern to their order. He made several wrong turns and backtracks before he finally stumbled upon a half-open door with a frosted glass pane that read: DR. RAMI FUAD, MIDDLE EAST HISTORY, EGYPTOLOGY.

Drake rapped lightly on the glass and then pushed the door open and peered inside. He heard voices, but he saw no sign of the professor, only a narrow L-shaped room that might have once been Shakespeare's broom closet. The leg of the room ahead of him was lined with books, most on shelves, some in precarious stacks on the floor.

What he could see of the back wall sloped downward with the roof, except for a recessed window where sunlight held the dust of centuries past suspended in a thin beam.

A flustered student marched around the corner, clutching a heavy stack of loose pages and sending the dust flying in wild swirls. As the young man brushed past Drake and fled into the hall, a Middle Eastern voice called out from the inner sanctum in impeccably articulated English. "Next! And be quick about it. I have an important meeting."

With trepidation that his subconscious dragged up from his Notre Dame years, Drake crept around the corner. There, he found an aging Egyptian with neatly trimmed gray hair seated behind a desk cluttered with papers and more stacks of books. If there was a computer, Drake could not see it. The professor's eyes, partially hidden behind square-rimmed glasses, remained buried in a thick volume. "What do you need?"

"Dr. Fuad . . . um . . . ahem." Drake tried to banish the twenty-year-old student from his voice. "My name is Drake Merigold. Nick Baron sent me."

Rami abruptly looked up. His stern expression melted into a warm smile. "Ah, Mr. Merigold. I apologize. *You* are the important meeting." He stood and took Drake's offered hand, pumping it up and down. "Welcome to my castle."

Drake had to bend forward to accommodate the handshake. The professor's head barely came up to his chest. The rapid change in the Egyptian's demeanor left him off balance. "Um . . . was I interrupting something?"

"Hmm? Oh, you mean the student." Rami flicked a thick hand at the door as if he were shooing away a mosquito. "I just gave Mr. Wentworth my review of his dissertation. He still has a lot of work to do." He gestured to a wooden chair in front of his desk. "Please, sit down and tell me your tale. Nicholas did not give me much information over the phone."

Drake unlocked the screen of a tablet computer and passed the device over the stacks of books into Rami's hands. "Nick took these photos in what we believe to be a Hashashin catacombs," he said as he settled into the chair, "under the Ankara Citadel."

"There is nothing under the Ankara Citadel," argued Rami, taking the tablet. "Over the years, the Turkish National Museum has pelted that hill with enough sonar to raise a Russian submarine. They find it is solid rock every time."

"We beg to differ. In light of our recent intelligence, I'd say the museum was bought off." Drake shook his head. "But that's beside the point. Professor, those symbols may be the key to stopping a terrorist group planning to release a bioweapon. Can you identify them?"

Rami squinted at the screen in his hands, flipping back and forth through the photos. "You are certain these were taken beneath the citadel?"

"Absolutely certain."

"If that is true, then you've made a discovery of historic proportions. I must go and see it for myself."

Drake grimaced. "Not advisable. Not all the Hashashin

in that tunnel are dead." He forced a smile. "The symbols? Please, professor."

"Right. Of course." Rami glanced through photos one more time and then handed the tablet back across his books with a definitive nod. "Yes. You can tell Nicholas that these are, in my opinion, Hashashin."

"Is that all you can tell me about them?"

"Oh, no." The professor stood and pressed himself against the sloped ceiling to get out from behind his desk. He gave Drake an excited grin. "There is more, my boy. Much, much more."

CHAPTER 32

Rami walked the perimeter of his office, bobbing up and down at random, pulling books from shelves above his head and lifting them from the stacks on the floor. None of them seemed to satisfy him, and he kept putting them back, rarely in the place where he had found them.

"Doc, we're in a bit of a hurry, here," urged Drake.

"Shh." Rami held out a quieting hand and continued scanning his shelves. "You cannot rush knowledge."

Drake shook his head and left the professor to his searching, wandering impatiently around the small office. Amid the clutter and books, he saw the artifacts and memorabilia one would expect in the den of a professor of antiquities—fragments of pottery, blocks of hieroglyphics and cuneiform script. Then he came across an old Bible with dog-eared pages, lying open on a stand. He leaned closer to the Bible. It was open to the tenth chapter of

Romans. Faded orange highlighting covered the thirteenth verse. *For whoever calls upon the name of the Lord shall be saved.*

"Not all Middle Eastern people are Muslims, Mr. Merigold," said Rami, suddenly standing right next to him. "That is especially true in Egypt."

"You're a Copt. Nick didn't tell me."

"As well he shouldn't. It is not for him to tell." The professor held up a book bound in blue leather with both hands, one index finger holding a place in the text. "Come, I have found the information we need."

Drake eyed the weighty volume. "Doc, I don't have time for a history lesson."

"Trust me, you'll want to make time for this one." As if to emphasize the point, the professor made Drake wait while he squeezed back behind his desk and cleared the space between them.

"These are the writings of Hulegu Khan, the grandson of Genghis Khan," he said finally. "Hulegu sacked the Hashashin stronghold of Alamut in Persia and spent many hours in their library. In this book, he recounts the story of a splinter group that left Alamut a century before he arrived in the region. Scholars have always dismissed it as pure fiction."

"Why should they dismiss it?" asked Drake.

"Because there was no archaeological evidence to support it." Rami's thin lips spread into a conspiratorial smile. "At least, not until you stepped into my office with those pictures." He laid the book on the desk and opened it to the place he held with his finger. At the center of the page,

beneath flowing silver script, was a hand-drawn illustration
of the same five symbols that Nick had photographed in the
tunnel.

The professor's eyes shone behind his square lenses.
"What do you know about the Hashashin?"

"They were assassins," said Drake. "Everyone knows
that. But Nick said they were pragmatic killers, not apocalyptic zealots like the terrorists we're chasing."

Rami gave a dubious nod. "Nicholas was half-right.
The Hashashin leader, Hassan, used his assassins to con-
solidate power for his Ismaili cousins. He killed far more
Muslims than Crusaders and was, indeed, a pragmatist.
But"—the professor raised a finger—"his foot soldiers
were the *quintessential* apocalyptic zealots."

Rami swept backward through the text until he came
to a tinted illustration of a lush garden, lit by a radiant
sun. Four bearded men in long robes stood in a half circle, happily conversing.

"Where are the seventy virgins?" asked Drake.

"I am sure that many retired suicide bombers have
asked the same question," said Rami, sitting back in his
chair. He gave a dismissive wave of his hand. "The heav-

enly harem is a more recent invention. Hassan did not promise his followers postmortem sex. He promised them an earthly paradise instead."

"An *earthly* paradise?" repeated Drake, furrowing his brow.

Rami nodded. "Hassan promised his soldiers an eternal age called the *Qiyamah*, a final peace brought on by the return of the twelfth imam, the Mahdi. He convinced them that he was the Qaim, the ambassador who could speak to the Mahdi across the veil between worlds, and that all these assassinations were preparing the earth for the Mahdi's return." The professor shrugged. "The great Hassan was nothing more than a charlatan, and every charlatan has his comeuppance. That is where Hulegu's splinter group comes in."

He sat forward and flipped through the pages again, coming to rest on a picture of two cloaked men in peaked helmets. They carried curved scimitars and glared at each other with their pointed beards nearly touching. "Hulegu tells us that in the year 1120, Hassan reached the precarious pinnacle of his career. His society of assassins had hundreds of murders to its credit—"

"But still no Mahdi," interrupted Drake.

Rami smiled. "High marks for you, Mr. Merigold." He placed his elbows on the desk on either side of the text and steepled his fingers. "Hassan's only option was to fabricate a Mahdi. He paraded a child around his mountain stronghold as the incarnation of the twelfth imam and then hid him away and declared the *Qiyamah* had begun." The Egyptian grinned like a car salesman and spread his arms wide.

"Welcome to paradise! Now get back to work. Of course, Hassan remained the Qaim, the assassinations continued, and no one ever saw the child again."

"Great story," said Drake, growing impatient again, "but what does that have to do with our Hashashin terrorists?"

Rami brought his hands together with a startling clap. "I'm so glad you asked!" He laid a finger on one of the bearded men in the illustration. "This is General Insar, a foot soldier who survived too many suicide missions. He didn't buy Hassan's lies and started squawking about it among the faithful. When Hassan tried to arrange his death, Insar challenged him and killed him and then fled with his followers to another mountain fortress."

"The Ankara Citadel," said Drake.

Rami abruptly looked up from the book. "High marks again, Mr. Merigold! You're much smarter than Nicholas gives you credit for."

Drake opened his mouth to respond, but the professor kept going before any words came to him.

"Insar formed an unsteady alliance with one of the late Hassan's rivals, the Sultan of Rum—sort of an enemy-of-my-enemy arrangement. His splinter group of Hashashin, the Insari, lived and thrived at Ankara for a hundred years, making their living openly as assassins and blacksmiths and waiting for the return of the real Mahdi."

"Who, once again, never came."

The professor raised a pair of bushy eyebrows. "They never got the chance to find out. The whole group was wiped out in 1242. The new sultan saw them as a threat

and sent a huge army to Ankara in a preemptive strike."
He closed the book and sat back again, removing his
glasses. "According to Hulegu, the sultan's army finished
off the Insari Hashashin, but at great cost. Five thousand
men marched on Ankara. Only two hundred returned."

Drake narrowed his eyes. "If the sultan wiped out the
Hashashin in the thirteenth century," he asked, "then
who did we fight in those catacombs last night?"

Rami shrugged. "Why should we trust the word of the
sultan's men? Perhaps a remnant of the Hashashin survived at Ankara, living in secret all this time as assassins
for hire. There are rumors of it all throughout history.
Can every one of them be false?"

"That would mean the Insari Hashashin are remarkably
adept at keeping to the shadows, even in the modern world.
They've purposefully stepped out into the light. Why now,
after eight centuries? What changed?"

The professor pressed one stem of his glasses to his
chin, his face clouded in thought. After several seconds,
his eyes focused again, and he shook the glasses at Drake.
"They must have found another Qaim, another Hassan
more convincing than the original."

The word *Qaim* stuck in Drake's brain. "You men-
tioned Hassan pretending to be the Qaim before. What
did you say it meant?"

"Al-Qaim," said the professor, slipping his glasses back
on. "In English, 'the ambassador.'" He seated his frames
and looked across the desk at Drake. "Or perhaps more
accurately, 'the emissary.'"

CHAPTER 33

British food had always mystified Nick. How could the nation credited with the invention of the sandwich be utterly incapable of producing a basic ham and cheese? He dumped the caramelized onions off a dubious adaptation of a chicken club and then considered dipping the sandwich in his Americano. That might at least soften the hard roll, which promised to go down like broken glass.

Across the table, Chaya drummed the Formica with manicured nails and stared out the café window at the Strand. "You said the IBE security video was a major breakthrough."

"It was."

"Then what are you doing?"

Nick slowly chewed a bite of sandwich, grinding the stiff crust between his teeth until it was safe to swallow. "I'm eating."

Chaya muttered something in Hindi and pounded the table with her fist, sending a spatter of Nick's coffee onto the sleeve of his overcoat. He leisurely dabbed it away with a napkin.

Behind the stolid expression, Nick was just as impatient as she was. The security video from IBE showed Kattan's face from multiple angles, their biggest lead yet. Now they had a complete digital profile along with fixed points in time and space to feed into London's public-camera system, the largest Big Brother network in the world. Finding Kattan was only a matter of time, but Nick couldn't go back to the hotel to prepare to go after him—not yet, not with the lawyer in tow.

As he struggled to masticate his third bite of sandwich, Nick's comm unit finally crackled to life. "Are you there, One?"

Nick raised the phone to his ear to conceal that he was talking through the earpiece. "I'm here," he said to Scott. "Did you get it?"

"I hope you know how many international laws I had to break."

"Which makes this no different than any other day. Where to?"

"Take the Piccadilly Line from Holborn. Head for Piccadilly Circus."

"On my way."

Nick slapped a lid on his coffee and started for the door, leaving the sandwich languishing in its wrapping. Chaya scrambled out from behind the table to follow. "Your friend has something?"

"I have to get to Piccadilly Circus."

As soon as Nick hit the sidewalk, he extended his stride, forcing the short lawyer into a stilted jog. The Strand and Kingsway were crowded with lunchtime foot traffic, and he weaved his way through the oncoming droves, picking the path of most resistance. He could hear the uneven click of Chaya's power heels behind him, her panting apologies as she bumped into the people he side-stepped. Nick found it difficult not to smile.

When they came within sight of Holborn station, he felt the lawyer's fingers graze his back, grasping for him. "You're taking the Tube?" she asked, out of breath. "It will be packed at this hour. We should walk it."

"No time. The Tube is still faster. Besides"—he stepped onto the steep escalator descending into the station—"I'm a government employee, remember? I have to support the public-transit system."

Chaya clutched the arm rail on the step above him, gasping for breath. "You're not an employee of *our* government."

A cloud of static grew on Nick's comm link as the escalator took them deeper underground. "I'm going to piggyback on the Tube's cell-phone repeaters to keep the link open," said Scott through the interference. "Once you're on the train, give me an execute signal. After that you'll have only a ninety-second window, encompassing both stages. Will that be enough?"

"Should be."

Chaya looked up from straightening her rumpled coat. "What?" she asked.

"Nothing."

Chaya's concerns about the noontime traffic proved to be well-founded. The platform was packed. Nick jostled his way to the map on the back wall. "Which train?"

"All of them, you stupid Yank," said Chaya, scrunching her nose. "All the trains that pass this platform go to Piccadilly Circus."

"The next one," answered Scott through the earpiece. "It arrives in forty-seven seconds. Get on it, even if you have to crowd out other passengers. The rush at the up-channel station is beginning to slow. The following train will have too much open space."

Exactly forty-seven seconds later, the next train pulled into the station. The doors opened and a bright feminine voice warned, "Mind the gap." No one did. The masses crammed themselves into the already loaded cars. Nick herded Chaya ahead of him, shouldering a lanky teenager with green hair and studs in his eyebrows out of the way. As the cheerful voice advised them to mind the doors, he took a sip of his coffee and winked at the angry teen still standing on the platform. The kid slapped the door.

A moment later, the train lurched into motion and the crowd swayed as one body. Chaya gripped a vertical bar with white knuckles. The passengers around her engulfed her tiny form. She leaned a shoulder into Nick to gain a little space from a gristly, hairy individual. The man seemed all too content to have his oversized gut pressed against a pretty girl. As the train reached full speed, Nick took a final sip of coffee. It was much too sweet for his taste, and it had grown tepid. Perfect. He held the cup low and removed the lid. "Go," he said through his teeth.

"Executing," said Scott. "Three, two, one . . ."

The brakes locked, sending a terrific squeal ripping through the train. The passengers fell into one another. The lights flickered. With a little extra guidance, Nick's coffee flew from his open cup. A flying wall of brown liquid hit Chaya in the back of the head.

Her hands flew up in shock and surprise. "Ugh!"

"I am so sorry. What a klutz." Nick wiped her back with the sleeve of his coat, and her heavyset admirer joined in from the other side, a model of English chivalry. She batted them both away.

Scott's voice sounded in Nick's ear again. "Stage two in three, two, one . . ."

Every light in the car brightened and then popped. Sparks showered down. The passengers screamed.

Moments later, Chaya was still trying to get the coffee out of her hair, her fingers dripping. The dark and the screaming passengers did not concern her nearly as much as the horrible, sticky liquid.

The train operator made a desperate announcement over the PA system. "Remain calm, everyone. Please remain calm. We've only had a little power surge. Do not attempt to open the doors. The train will begin moving again shortly."

He was right. The train jerked into motion again, but the lights never came back, blown out by the surge. The big man next to Chaya patted her sleeve, leaving his hand there a little too long. "Don't worry none, darlin'. You're safe with me."

Right.

Chaya felt behind her back for Nick, but her hand went straight to the door. He was gone.

————————

Nick emerged from a utility stairwell into daylight on Russell Square. He felt a pang of guilt at leaving Chaya alone in the dark with her chivalrous friend, but only a small pang.

After all, she was blackmailing him—*was* being the operative word. He glanced down at the paper in his hand to make certain he had lifted the right one from her peacoat. Then he crumpled it up and tossed it into a recycle bin. So much for the fake warrant and Chaya's adoring magistrates.

CHAPTER 34

A nyone follow you?" asked Scott, checking up and down the hallway as Nick pushed past him into the apartment.

"You mean the girl?"

"I mean the police, the bobbies, Scotland Yard." Scott checked the hall one more time before he closed the door. "What we just did was highly public and highly illegal. It could be classified as terrorism."

"You've done a lot worse."

"Yes, but from the safety of a bunker on the most well-defended military base in America. Out here I feel exposed."

Geeks. "Welcome to field ops. Have you spoken to the colonel?"

Scott nodded.

"Katy?"

"She's fine. Walker's man in Germany has her well protected, and he hasn't seen any threats. He said she almost made him in the first hour."

"That's my girl." Nick strolled over to Scott's computer station and jiggled the wireless mouse. "Find Kattan yet?"

"I've made some progress," said the engineer, rushing after him and slapping his hand aside. "A timeline is taking shape."

Nick knew better than to joust with Scott for control of the workstation. Instead, he retreated to the couch and collapsed onto the cushions. He leaned his head back. "Keep talking."

"After I rebuilt the subject's digital profile with the videos from IBE, I ran a search against Heathrow's customs files." As Scott spoke, he bustled back and forth to either end of the couch, adjusting a pair of cigar-sized cylinders fixed to the top of telescoping stands. "My software achieved a ninety-percent match on a passport that came through yesterday from Cairo."

Nick's head remained a dead weight on the couch cushion. "Giving us an alias that he'll never use again."

"Yes, but it also gave us a solid starting point for our London timeline." Scott made a final adjustment to one of the cylinders and then sat down at his workstation. "Look."

Nick raised his head and saw that the living room wall had become a three-dimensional map of London, projected by the apparatus Scott had set up. Weaving through the digital buildings, a red line connected several dots, each with an associated time.

Scott clicked his mouse and the first dot expanded

from Heathrow, growing into a passport photo that seemed to stand out from the wall. The name underneath read Mohammed Jibreel, but Nick recognized the young Masih Kattan from his fleeting appearances in D.C. and Budapest. He must have suffered many reconstructive surgeries in the years following the strike, but he still bore a resemblance to his father, mostly around the eyes.

"This is a customs hit," said Scott. "The new digital profile gave me several more shots from Heathrow, but eventually Kattan disappeared into the Tube." The first picture shrank back into its dot and a new one sprang out of the next, showing Kattan getting into a van. "Our first piece of new data occurs here. Unfortunately, Molly and I can't determine where he got the van. Maybe he rented it—maybe it was left for him. I haven't recovered any shots of the plates. However, we're sure he drove it directly to IBE." Two video stills appeared. One showed Kattan entering IBE's lobby and the other, several minutes later, showed him leaving with Maharani. Both men carried boxes of equipment. No gun was visible.

"Maharani is a willing hostage," said Nick, rising from the couch and stepping closer to examine the second still. With the three-dimensional projection, he felt like he could reach out and grab the biochemist—yank him away from the terrorist. If only it were that easy. "There has to be some form of coercion, here, besides brute force. What do the Hashashin have on this guy?"

"Unknown." The stills shrank back into the map, and the last dot opened out of central London, this one a repeating video of Kattan and Maharani carrying their boxes across a small plaza. "This is where we lose him," said Scott, frowning as the two men disappeared into an office building. "There were no more hits yesterday."

"And this morning?"

"I'm still running searches on the last twelve hours." The chair squeaked morbidly as Scott slowly swiveled around to face the couch. His expression was deadpan. "Nothing so far."

Nick's phone buzzed. CJ. He put it to his ear and said, "Gimme a sec," and then covered the receiver and nodded to Scott. "Keep at it. I've got to take this."

Outside Nick leaned against the balcony rail, gazing across the rolling snowy hills of Greenwich Park to the domed observatory that sat on the Prime Meridian. "Go ahead, CJ," he said into the phone.

"My team made progress with those pictures you sent."

"The symbols?"

"Negative. Those are still a mystery, but we found a guy at Georgetown who could translate the calligraphy."

"Farsi, right?" Nick watched a group of children sledding on the observatory mount. His eyes followed a boy on a blue saucer, spinning in a slow circle as he sailed down the hill.

"Sort of. Our guy said the language was muddled by Turkic influence, but he's confident he got the general idea. I'm sending it to you now."

Nick put CJ on speaker and opened the file she sent him, turning away from the playing children to lean his back against the rail. There were four stanzas of text on his screen.

THE MESSENGER OF HIS MESSENGER SHALL DECLARE HIS COMING ON THE PLAINS OF THE GREAT EMPIRE,

AND THE MARKETPLACE WILL ERUPT IN TURMOIL SO THAT A LOAF OF BREAD SHALL COST MORE THAN A DAY'S WAGES,

AND PESTILENCE WILL SPREAD AMONG THE UNBELIEVERS, A DISEASE THE LIKES OF WHICH NO MAN HAS EVER SEEN.

THEN THE SUN WILL BE BLOTTED OUT AND MY SERVANT WILL OPEN THE GATE. A GREAT SMOKE WILL RISE UP FROM THE CENTER OF THE WORLD. THE SKY WILL BURN LIKE MOLTEN BRASS, AND FROM THE HIGH PLACE THERE WILL SOUND A DEAFENING NOISE, AS TRUMPETS, ANNOUNCING THE ENTRANCE OF THE MAHDI.

"Reads like the Quran, doesn't it?" asked CJ.

Nick took the phone off speaker and brought it back to his ear. "It's probably a hadith, a saying attributed to Muhammad. A lot of them mirror passages of the Quran."

"Whatever it is, it ain't good."

At that moment, one of Scott's laptops made a twittering sound, mimicking R2D2. "What was that?" Nick called into the apartment.

Instead of an answer, he heard a click, and then another, and then a furious stream of them. He poked his head into the room and saw Scott's fingers blazing over the keyboard. "Thanks, CJ," he said, ending the call before she could respond. Then he stepped into the living room and closed the door behind him. "You get something we can use?"

Scott changed the display projected on the wall. A new video showed Kattan walking across a plaza. When the killer reached the border of the camera's view, the display flashed and another camera picked him up. This one showed Kattan approaching the same office building as before.

Nick watched the assassin casually stroll beneath a concrete awning and disappear. "How long ago did the cameras record that?"

Scott stared up at the display, his hands still hovering over his keyboard. "The software didn't pull that video from the recordings. We're watching the live feed."

CHAPTER 35

The very sight of the dome of St. Paul's Cathedral enraged Kattan, the thought of the daily throngs crowding beneath its extravagant portico, gazing mindlessly at the stone idols of the crusaders. The cathedral was not a house of worship. It was a tourist attraction for bloodthirsty Christians.

The assassin lingered in the shadow of a concrete awning a moment longer and then turned and pushed his way through a set of glass double doors. As he descended a flight of carpeted stairs to his temporary headquarters, his anger gave way to rapturous anticipation. Soon the masses would see the cathedral and all others like it for what they were: empty monuments to a false religion.

Soon. Very soon.

At the basement level, Kattan unlocked a heavy wooden door and entered the lab he had constructed for

Dr. Maharani. A long table on one side of the room held a variety of electronic instruments, controlled by a pair of laptop computers. Most of the instruments were contained inside a large clean box, along with glass dishes and beakers and the canisters Kattan had brought from Egypt. The biochemist was on the floor a few feet away, completing his afternoon prayers.

"One day soon the *Qiyamah* will begin, and those rituals will be abolished," said Kattan as the doctor rose to his feet.

Maharani averted his eyes from his captor. His hands shook as he lifted a lab coat from a cot in the corner and slipped it on. "And this," he said, as he stepped up to the worktable, "this thing you have asked me to create will hasten that day's arrival?"

"It is a necessary step, yes. It is a sign that must precede the age of peace."

Maharani pushed his hands into the rubber gloves inside the clean box and carefully grasped the cylinder. "Are there other signs to perform? Is that the reason you are dressed as an electrician today?"

Kattan looked down at his blue jumpsuit and then back at the doctor. He frowned. Maharani's eyes were clearly not as averted as he pretended; and he was never this talkative before, never this inquisitive. Then the reason dawned on him. The scientist was stalling.

The amiable tone vanished from Kattan's voice. "Do not forget that I am on a schedule. How much longer?"

"I need six more hours."

"You have three."

For the first time, Maharani looked directly at Kattan. "You do not understand. There are biological processes at work here. They cannot be rushed."

Kattan was shocked by the doctor's stern expression. It seemed Maharani needed a reminder. "Do you know what your daughter is doing right now?"

The stern expression fell away in an instant. "Please. I am doing everything you ask."

"I am told by my people that she is on a train. What do you think would happen if there were an explosion in that tunnel?"

"But the timeline is beyond my control."

"How terrifying it will be for little Chaya. A flash of fire, incredible pain, then darkness. To which do you suppose she will succumb first? The slow drain of her lifeblood or the crushing press of a thousand tons of concrete?"

Maharani quickly returned to his work, removing a sample from the canister inside the clean box. "I will get it done. See? I am working. You do not have to do this."

"Three hours, Doctor."

"Yes. Three hours. You will have your weapon."

———

Nick left his car in a garage and hurried up Godliman Street toward the courtyard of St. Paul's and the southern access to Paternoster Square—the home of the London Stock Exchange and the location where the camera had caught Kattan a half hour before. In his slacks and overcoat, he mirrored the smattering of London businessmen around him, all rushing back to the office after their long lunches. Most of them carried some sort of portfolio, either a briefcase or a satchel. No one seemed to notice that Nick had two—one for him and one for Drake.

The big operative was racing back from Cambridge to meet him. Thankfully, Drake could push the limits of the Peugeot without much fear of police interference. The Brits relied on speed cameras. Walker could compensate the rental company for the photo tickets later.

As he drove, Drake back-briefed Nick on his conversation with Rami. "Long story short," he said over the comm link, "Kattan set himself up as the mouthpiece of the Hashashin messiah. They call him the Qaim, the Emissary."

Nick slowed his pace at hearing Kattan's screen name in the new context. "That doesn't make sense. I see the benefit of controlling the Hashashin, but Kattan should be trying to hide the connection from us, not flaunting it through the chess app."

A passing Brit glanced Nick's way and gave him a curious look, trying to assess whether the man talking to himself was mentally challenged or simply drunk. Nick put his phone to his ear to make the SATCOM conversation look normal.

"It's a mind game," said Drake, oblivious to the interruption. "Kattan is overconfident, like his father always was. He's giving you puzzles to break up your focus. Don't get sucked in."

CHAPTER 36

The building in the video, the building where Kattan disappeared, was twelve stories of glass and concrete owned by the financial conglomerate Fishman Zeller—two towers of offices, separated by a narrow glass atrium, standing at the western end of Paternoster Square. Fishman Zeller occupied all of the southern tower, but the company rented out the offices of the northern tower to smaller investment companies. Molly had done a little digging and discovered that one of those companies had a paper-thin corporate veil.

According to the Fishman Zeller records, Kingdom Ventures Incorporated was a ten-year-old Dubai investment company that opened its London offices less than a month before, leasing the entire sublevel of the northern tower— two thousand square feet of office space. Molly cross-checked KVI's tax filings with the City of London and uncovered two classic signs of a front company with a fictional corporate history—minimal transaction volume and earnings that matched to a percentage point year over year. No investment company was that consistent.

Scott had done some digging as well. "I own their cameras, their elevators, whatever you want," he told Nick over the comm link. "The firewalls to the tower security system were tragically easy to hack."

Nick nodded as if Scott could see him, his phone still at his ear to mask the SATCOM conversation. From the partial concealment of a Renaissance arch on the southwest corner of the square, he surveiled the entrance between the Fishman Zeller towers. Foot traffic was light, only a few people going in or out. None of them looked like Kattan or Maharani. "Any escape routes besides the obvious?"

"Do you see the big column?"

A gaudy Corinthian column rose out of the northwest section of the square between the towers and the London Stock Exchange. With the gold-plated flaming urn at its top, it reached a height of seventy-five feet or more, and with a base at least twenty-five feet in diameter and twenty feet tall, it blocked Nick's view of the western quarter of the exchange. "How could I miss it? Another monument to the empire."

"Except it isn't a monument at all," said Scott. "You're looking at the world's most overdressed exhaust vent. The London Stock Exchange has a basement level that extends out beneath the square, housing a massive server room—literally thousands of networked drives. It takes some heavy-duty air-conditioning to keep all those electronics cool, and that column is really a giant stack that vents the exhaust."

"And I care about the vent because . . ."

"Not so much the vent as the server room underneath it. There's a thirty-meter utility tunnel connecting it to Fishman Zeller. The access panel is in the front hallway of KVI."

"Kattan might run that way."

"He might try. The good news is, the tunnel is a dead end. The exchange side is secured by a steel door, four inches thick. If Kattan tries to sneak out through the crawl space, he'll be trapped."

"Copy that." Nick stared at the entrance for a few seconds. He still couldn't shake the feeling that this was coming together too easily. "Be ready to shut down the elevators and the elevator alarms on my call. And when you have that set up, go back and look at all the footage we have of Kattan. Find me something we haven't noticed before."

"I've already been over that footage several times."

"And I'm telling you to go over it again, every frame." Nick's eyes tracked another businessman leaving the Fishman Zeller towers. Like all the others he'd seen so far, this one was young, Caucasian, and not Kattan. From what he could tell, the target had not left the building, but Kattan wouldn't stay in there forever, waiting to be caught. They needed to move. "Nightmare Two, give me an ETA."

"Thirty seconds ago." The voice was right behind him,

not on the comm link. Drake walked beneath the arch from the cathedral side and joined Nick in the shadows against its eastern wall. "Where's the lawyer?"

Now that he had someone visible to talk to, Nick returned his phone to his pocket, but he kept his eyes on the tower entrance. "By that, you mean where's the hot chick?"

"You know me so well."

"I put her on a train to get her out of the way and keep her away from you. One day you and Amanda will both thank me."

"She went willingly?"

"Not really." Nick slipped the strap of one of his satchels over his head and handed it to Drake. "I brought you something."

"A European carryall? You shouldn't have."

"With an old friend inside."

Drake hefted the satchel, feeling the weight of the MP7. He grinned. "A good friend." Then he reached into his pocket. "I brought something for you, too, a gift from your old professor." He handed Nick a small green statuette, jade by the look and feel of it. The figure was a complex geometric shape—two faceted cones that blended together and then tapered down to a narrow base. "Look familiar?"

When Nick shook his head, Drake took the figure and laid it flat in his teammate's hand. "How about now?"

Suddenly Nick made the connection. Viewed in two dimensions, the figure matched one of the Hashashin symbols, the sawtooth with the narrow base.

"What is this thing?"

"A Persian chess piece."

Drake related the final bit of history that Rami had shared with him. The early Muslim leaders had outlawed traditional chess sets, fearing the lifelike figurines would be worshipped as pagan idols. Cunning adherents to the game revived it by simplifying the pieces. The elephant— the precursor to the bishop—became a double crescent moon, representing the tusks. The two spires of the piece in Nick's hand represented the two heads of chariot horses. Later, the Europeans would interpret them as castle battlements—the rook. Each of the Insari Hashashin symbols represented a chess piece. General Insar had been obsessed with the game.

Drake pulled out his phone and flipped through the symbols, explaining each one. "The overlapping triangles are the knight," he said, "and the horizontal crescent moon is the queen." He flipped to the last picture, the crescent moon over the eight-pointed star. "This is Kattan's symbol. Guess which piece it represents."

"The king," said Nick, pushing away from the arch and starting across the square. "I guess it's time to take him down and end the game."

The two operatives were halfway to the tower entrance when Scott spoke up over the SATCOM. "It's the boxes!" he exclaimed. His voice was both excited and nervous.

"We're a little busy here," said Nick, reaching a hand into his satchel to find the grip of his MP7. "Get ready to shut down the elevators. We'll take the stairs down to KVI and hem them in."

The engineer ignored the command. "You don't understand. You were right. We missed something in the footage. The boxes, they're empty."

Nick released his weapon and touched Drake's arm to slow their pace. "You're not making any sense, Four."

Scott gave a frustrated huff. "When Kattan and Maharani left IBE, pieces of lab equipment were sticking out of their boxes. The tops were only half-closed. When they carried them into Fishman Zeller, the tops were flat. I'm telling you, the boxes were empty."

Nick came to a complete stop and looked up at his teammate. "Why would they pretend to bring the lab equipment to KVI?"

Before Drake could respond they heard a muted boom like far-off thunder. The ground beneath their feet rumbled.

"The seismic alarms in the towers just tripped," said Scott. "The elevators are locking down on their own."

Another explosion sounded, and then another and another in rhythmic cadence. The Fishman Zeller towers visibly shook. The pedestrians in the square stumbled back and stared as glass fell from the atrium windows.

"Come on!" shouted Nick, and the two operatives ran toward the buildings.

CHAPTER 37

Nick and Drake pushed their way through the flood of suits pouring from the lobby. Periodic explosions still sounded from the sublevel—one every couple of seconds like artificial aftershocks. Smoke and dust billowed up through vents in the floor, and glass rained down from the bridges that crisscrossed the atrium above.

Nick spied an elderly man lying on the gray marble floor, bleeding from a deep gash in his thigh. He sent Drake to help and kept searching for wounded. Deeper in, a young woman in a white blouse and black business skirt stood frozen in fear, her knees pressed together and her hands spread out, trying to maintain her balance on the quaking floor. For a split second, she locked eyes with Nick. Then a final blast, an explosion that dwarfed all the rest, ripped through the floor, heaving granite tiles upward on a wave of concrete that launched the woman into the air. She came crashing down on Nick's side of the fissure and screamed in pain. As the echo of the blast settled, there was a rending and cracking of stone. The gap behind the girl began to widen.

Nick ran toward her and dove flat out onto the broken floor, catching her hand before the cave-in swallowed her whole. Wasting no time, he pulled her up and hoisted her over his shoulder and then sprinted for the exit with the floor collapsing at his heels.

As he emerged from the thick cloud of dust into the haze on the plaza, Nick heard a strange command.

"Set her down, mate. Nice and easy."

He slowed to a jog and then a walk, still a little disoriented. A dark-haired individual materialized to his right, tracking him with the short barrel of a Glock compact. He wore a suit and overcoat much like Nick's and held up a badge with an eight-pointed star and a crown. The badge made him Metro Police. The Glock made him Special Branch, a superbobby. Regular bobbies carried Tasers.

Nick kept walking. The woman had lost her shoes in the explosion, and he did not want to set her down on the broken glass that littered the square in front of the building.

"I said set her down, mate."

Convinced by the constable's behavior that Nick meant her harm, the woman started to thrash, kicking her feet and pounding his back with her fists. Nick bore the abuse and the threat from the Glock until he reached clear ground next to the gaudy fake monument. As soon as he set her down, she turned and limped away into the growing crowd.

"You're welcome," Nick said flatly. Then he turned to survey what was left of the building. The dust cloud still hovered, obscuring the first floor. Every window on the second floor had shattered, along with several more on the floors above. A few more accountants and stockbrokers stumbled out over the piles of glass, beating the dust from their expensive suits and squinting at the sunlight.

"Oi! Mate! Hands where I can see 'em."

Oh, right. The superbobby. Nick turned to face his accuser, not certain how rescuing a woman from a disaster area warranted the threat of deadly force. Then he became aware that Drake was right next to him.

"What's his problem?" he muttered to his teammate, raising his hands.

"Your answer is at nine o'clock," Drake replied, raising his own hands, "coming in hot."

Nick looked left in time to get slapped in the face by Chaya Maharani. Tears streamed down the lawyer's cheeks. "What have you done?"

"Oi! Doesn't anyone care about the man with the gun?" asked the constable, clipping his badge to his belt.

Nick and Drake glanced at each other and then back at the Brit. "No," they replied in unison.

"I told you," said Chaya, turning her anger on the policeman. "They're Interpol. They're chasing the terrorists who kidnapped my father."

A pair of uniformed bobbies in yellow reflective jackets closed in with their batons drawn and motioned Chaya back. They patted the two Americans down and removed the Beretta Nanos from the holsters under each man's shoulder. One of them found Nick's ID wallet and tossed it to the plainclothesman.

The superbobby flipped it open and frowned at the badge. "Right. Interpol. The thing is, if Interpol was chasing terrorists in London, they would have coordinated with Counter Terrorism Command at Scotland Yard. And if they had coordinated with CTC, then I would know all about it."

"You're SO15," said Nick.

"That's right. And if you're Interpol, then Bob here is the Prince of Wales."

Drake gave a little curtsy to the uniformed constable next to him. "Your Majesty."

Nick's phone chimed. He looked his captor in the eye. "I'm going to get that."

The plainclothesman raised his gun in protest, but Nick retrieved his phone anyway. On the screen, he saw another message in the ivory letters of his chess app. *The Emissary has put you in check.*

Even as he lowered the phone, the general murmur of the crowd on the square shifted. Heads turned from the shattered towers to the London Stock Exchange next door. Nick glanced over his shoulder and through the tall windows he could see all the numbers on the giant ticker display turning red. Every stock plummeted. One of the verses CJ had sent him jumped to the front of his mind. *And the marketplace will erupt in turmoil.* "Something bad is about to happen."

"Something bad indeed," said the plainclothesman, tucking his Glock into its holster and closing the distance to the Americans. "You two are under arrest."

One of the bobbies reached for Nick's wrist. He jerked it away.

"Easy, mate." The bobby reached for him again, slower this time.

Nick's eyes remained fixed on the ticker. The stocks kept falling. Cell phones were ringing all over the square. People were shouting inside the exchange. Suddenly all the numbers disappeared. Red dots flew in from all sides of the ticker and formed a slowly flashing message: NOW BEAR WITNESS TO THE SECOND SIGN.

Then the message stopped flashing and faded, replaced by a countdown from ten. Several people in the crowd counted with it. "Nine!"

"Fishman Zeller wasn't the target," said Nick as the bobby drew his hands together in front of him and locked them in steel cuffs. "It was the London Stock Exchange. And if they have control of the tickers, they must control . . ." His voice faded and his eyes drifted up to the top of the fake Corinthian column. A wisp of smoke rose skyward from the gilded rim. "The server room."

"Six!" Most of the crowd was now treating the countdown like an early New Year's. The explosions were all but forgotten. Pockets of laughter erupted all over the square.

Idiots.

"Get back!" shouted Nick. He slammed his shoulder into the plainclothesman's chest, lifting the Glock from its holster with his cuffed hands and firing it into the air. Then he leveled the weapon and turned in a circle. "Get away from the column! Get back! Get back!"

The tactic worked. Those nearest to the column stopped counting and backed away. One of the bobbies pulled Chaya into the crowd, trying to protect her from the crazed American.

As he heard the crowd count, "Three!" Nick dropped the gun and rushed the constable, Drake at his side. The two of them lifted the SO15 man by the armpits and dragged him toward the middle of the square.

"Two!"

"One!"

A wild cheer went up, and a fraction of a second later it was silenced by the biggest explosion yet.

Nick and Drake fell to the ground on top of the constable as a cloud of dust and smoke rolled over them. Twisting onto his side, Nick could see the seventy-five-foot column settle back down into the square and tip over. The concrete mask fell away and the huge rusted standpipe beneath it let out an angry groan and slammed into the face of the exchange.

Nick struggled to his feet and started toward the wreckage, but a heavy hand grabbed him by the shoulder and swung him around. "Where do you think you're going?" asked the man from SO15.

"Uncuff me! People are in there. I can help."

The constable took Nick by the front of his shirt with one hand and flicked open a telescoping baton with the other, hauling it back. "I don't think so, mate."

CHAPTER 38

Nick woke up facedown on a polished concrete floor, staring at the distorted reflection of four cinderblock walls and a cold fluorescent light. His vision was fuzzy and he had a splitting headache, made worse by Scott's voice in his ear, repeatedly insisting that he respond.

"I'm awake," he mumbled, just to get the engineer to shut up. His coat, shirt, and bulletproof vest were gone, leaving him nothing above the belt but his black Lycra undershirt. His hands, originally bound in front with steel cuffs, had been released and resecured at his back with flex-cuffs, cinched so tight his fingers were numb. He supposed stealing the constable's gun and threatening civilians with it had something to do with that.

The position of Nick's hands and shoulders made getting up an awkward process. He pulled his knees to his chest and then rolled up onto them. From there, he took his time standing up. Waves of nausea threatened to knock him back down. He found it hard to focus his mind.

"Where am I?"

"Scotland Yard," the engineer replied, his voice tight, his words quick. "The headquarters building on Victoria Street. I'm glad you're awake. What's the plan?"

The cell was small, maybe six by ten. Nick saw a camera staring down from the corner above the door, but he didn't see an audio receiver of any kind. Someone was watching, but they weren't listening. He staggered over to the opposite corner and leaned his shoulder against the wall, turning his face away from the camera. "Is Nightmare Two up on comms?"

Drake chimed in, as chipper as always. "I've had the rubber ducky song stuck in my head since the column fell. Do you think that's a side effect of a concussion?"

Scott sighed. "Yes. He's up."

"I'm serious. Why am I remembering songs from Sesame Street? I don't even have kids."

"How long, Nightmare Four?" asked Nick, ignoring Drake's antics.

"It's been sixty-one minutes since I last heard your voice. The colonel has been pinging me every five to find out if you're dead or alive. You have no idea the kind of stress you're putting me through."

"My sympathies. What about the virus at Paternoster Square?"

"Only the cyber kind."

"Are you sure?" argued Drake. "We don't know that

the explosions weren't the delivery method. This is how zombie apocalypses get started. You don't know you're infected until it's too late. One minute you're remembering Bert and Ernie. The next you're an undead freak. Maybe that's what's going through every zombie's head. On the outside they're all gore and brain-munching rage but on the inside it's 'Rubber ducky you're the one—'"

"Do you see what I've had to put up with?" interrupted Scott.

"You're fine, Two. The target is D.C., remember? Besides, the bioweapon isn't the second sign. It's the third." Nick closed his eyes and visualized the translated verses from the catacombs. "The Hashashin listed four signs before the return of the Mahdi. The messenger on the plain of the great empire was the suicide bomber on the D.C. Mall. The marketplace in turmoil is this cyber-attack. It was the third verse that talked about pestilence and disease. That has to be the bioweapon, and that's what's coming next. They're getting progressively worse."

"There were four signs," said Drake. "So there's one more after the bio-attack. What's worse than that?"

"Only one thing." Drake's point worried Nick. They had no leads beyond the third sign. "Four, have CJ go back over the evidence and look for links to the fourth sign, the sky of molten brass and the black smoke."

"Will do."

As the fogginess wore off, Nick became aware of a distinctive pain in his left arm. "Sixty-one minutes. That's way too long to be knocked out from a simple blow to the head."

Drake confirmed his suspicions. "You were drugged. That plainclothes bobby hijacked an EMT on our way to the paddy wagon. He had the kid inject a sedative into your arm, citing some regulation about 'excited delirium.'"

"I'm going to kill him."

"We have to get out of here first."

"Right. Four, where is Romeo Seven on securing our release?"

"About that," said Scott, dragging out the words. "Getting you out is proving more difficult than we thought."

CHAPTER 39

Washington, D.C.
Capitol Hill

No one *summoned* Colonel Richard T. Walker. Usually he informed the Joint Chiefs of an impending threat and went straight to the Pentagon. Occasionally the chairman or the White House notified him of a potential situation and scheduled a meeting. But no one had ever summoned Walker. Not until today.

The colonel sat fuming on a leather chair in a dim anteroom paneled with dark oak, waiting to see Senator Cartwright like a Virginia cadet waiting to see the commandant. He sat with his back rigid, refusing to relax because the chair's tightly stuffed cushion made an unfortunate sound every time he shifted his weight. He would not give the senator the satisfaction of making him look awkward.

Walker did not have time for this idiocy. A biological weapon was adrift in the terrorist nethersphere, and the team he sent to find it had been locked up by some two-bit Cockney cop. Now his team's Interpol covers had suddenly evaporated from the system. He should be running down the glitch and securing their release instead of running up to the Hill like an errand boy. The senator's office had not even given him the courtesy of a reason, but he had a pretty good idea.

The first explosions of the London attack had occurred at 0910 hours Eastern Standard Time. Thanks to Dr. Scott Stone's frantic SATCOM report, Walker knew about it within thirty seconds. The network news stations knew almost as quickly.

Molly's team of intelligence techs could barely keep up with the incoming reports as an unprecedented video timeline developed. Smartphones and tablets captured the events from the first quakes within Fishman Zeller to the moment the great column heaved up out of the square and crashed down onto the London Stock Exchange. Sky News released a dramatic tablet video in which the impromptu cameraman was thrown from one of the atrium bridges by the quaking. The tablet captured the young accountant's terrified face as he tumbled four stories to the granite floor, surrounded in the eerie freefall by shards of broken glass. A less-disturbing video showed an unknown hero carrying a woman out of the building through a billowing dust cloud. It was a miracle that his face remained hidden.

The TV hanging in one corner of the anteroom showed a live feed of emergency crews pulling bodies out of the rubble while a talking head babbled on in morbid appreciation of this new terrorist art—blending the physical destruction with the virtual.

The talking head explained that the virus, now called the Second Sign Virus by network consensus, targeted key commodities and banks on the London Stock Exchange. It worked subtly, artificially nudging some prices down and others up until it triggered a wave of automatic trades. That wave triggered another, more serious wave, and then another, and the digital snowball picked up speed.

Millions of transactions took place in the first minute alone, driving bank stocks and gold into the ground and oil through the roof. Then the snowball leaped across the Atlantic and hit New York as well. The Americans shut their markets down, but the damage was done. Within a few minutes, the Second Sign Virus had caused the single greatest destruction of wealth the world had ever seen. The talking head predicted falling markets across the globe for weeks to come, with losses reaching into the trillions. A well-timed ticker floating across the screen noted that three suicides had already been reported.

As the video switched to a leggy brunette asking the expert a question he had already answered, the senator's door opened. A stocky gentleman with thick white hair and a disingenuous smile emerged. "Ah, Colonel Walker," he said in an overstated Virginia accent, "I'm so glad you made it."

Walker stood without so much as a squeak from the

chair and took the senator's offered hand. "I was not under the impression that I had a choice."

"Very direct, sir." The senator motioned Walker into his office. "*Very* direct. I was told to expect that."

Moving from the dark oak paneling of the anteroom to the sunlit ivory walls and blond furniture of the senator's office gave Walker the impression of emerging from a dank cave into fresh air. He knew this was intentional. He had once played similar games with his own office at the Pentagon. The senator offered him a seat—a twin of the overstuffed chair outside except for the lighter color of the leather. Walker opted to stand.

Cartwright shrugged and sat down on the edge of his desk. "I often find that I am disadvantaged when it comes to first impressions," he said, opening his hands. "My life is an open book, always on public display. You must feel that you already know all about me."

"Only what I see on the news," Walker lied. In truth, Molly's team had started digging into Cartwright's background the minute the politician had started harassing CJ. Their report was worrisome to say the least.

The liberal senator from Virginia had served his state in that capacity since 2002, but he had not made his mark on the national stage until recently, elbowing his way into the limelight of the second campaign by becoming the president's most vocal supporter. Cartwright likely expected to be rewarded with a cabinet position for his loyalty. All he got was a seat on the Intelligence Oversight Committee and an occasional invitation to dine at the White House. The senator was not a major political player.

He was a minor player with a lot of ambition, and that kind was often the most dangerous.

"Why am I here?" asked Walker, checking his watch. "With all due respect, sir, I have a lot on my plate and the drive back to my office isn't exactly short."

"So I noticed. You took quite a while to get here. I was under the impression that you worked at the DIA's Directorate of Analysis. Heading up Section Seven, was it?"

"Romeo Seven."

"Right. But the DIA offices at Bowling are just a hop, skip, and a jump across the river—just a hop and a skip, really. Surely traffic wasn't that bad at this hour of the day."

"Romeo Seven is an off-site section. Our offices are in a different location."

The senator raised a set of bushy eyebrows. "And that would be . . ."

Walker's features remained a flat scowl.

Cartwright lightly punched the air with his fist and grinned. "G-14 classified. I get it." He stood up and walked behind his desk, backlit by a broad window with the U.S. and Virginia flags on either side. He placed his hand on the high back of his chair. "Colonel, you *do* know that I have a top-secret clearance with multiple caveats, don't you?"

"Yes, sir, and Romeo Seven is not one of them." The colonel checked his watch again. The more time he wasted here, the longer Baron and Merigold would sit idle in a British jail. "Again, why did you call me here?"

Cartwright nodded. "Very direct." He picked up a small remote and pointed it at the flat-screen TV that hung over his faux mantel. The muted feed from CNN blinked and became a paused video. Walker recognized the image of Baron with the woman slung over his shoulder. "Do you know this man?" asked Cartwright.

Walker cast a sidelong glance at the senator. Through all the subtle changes in Cartwright's expression, that phony smile never faded from his lips. He could not read the mind behind it. "Hard to say."

"Too true, what with his face hidden behind that young lady's rump and all. Let's see if I can fix that for you." Cartwright clicked his remote and the video began to play—the same video Walker's techs had recorded from the news stream. He wasn't worried. The bystander would stop filming before Baron's face came into view.

But the bystander did not stop filming. The video kept playing beyond where it had before. A man in an overcoat held up a badge and pointed a gun. The scene jostled around as the cameraman fiddled with the zoom to get the gunman's face. Then it shifted back to Baron, who had just set the woman down. Merigold was next to him. Both of them raised their hands.

Cartwright paused the video. "This is a *much* better picture. How about now, Colonel? Do you know this man—the blond guy with the angry scowl?"

"Never seen him before."

"Well, that is disappointing." Cartwright came around his desk and stood between Walker and the screen. "I suppose you already know that I have a vested interest in these attacks."

"Why would I know that?"

"Oh, right." The senator touched the side of his nose. "G-14 classified. Okay, I'll play along." He walked over to the screen and scrutinized the men in the video, keeping his back to Walker. "One of my staffers was injured in the first attack, you know. He lost an eye."

"I'm sorry to hear that."

"Me too. Anyway, the injured party swears up and down that a blond man was on the scene right after that suicide bomber blew up on the Mall. That same blond fella refused to help him with his eye and even punched him." Cartwright tapped the image of Baron. "Isn't it funny that another blond fella, who matches the description of the first blond fella, appears here, smack in the middle of the second attack?"

Walker nodded. "That does seem suspicious."

Cartwright turned from the TV and shook the remote at Walker. "You're telling me, but it gets even more interesting."

He pointed the remote over his shoulder and pressed play. On the screen, the constable flipped open Baron's ID wallet. The bystander got a nice shot of the badge before a policeman waved his hands in front of the camera and the screen went black.

"Are you sure you don't recognize that man?" asked Cartwright. "Last chance."

"Positive."

The senator nodded. "I know you have a lot of friends, Colonel. It seems that half this town owes you a favor, even though no one knows quite what section Romeo Seven does for the Defense Intelligence Agency's Directorate of Analysis."

Walker raised one eyebrow. "We analyze stuff. Mostly intelligence."

"That's clever." Cartwright carefully set the remote down, squaring it with the side of his desk as he spoke. "I have friends too—like the one at CNN who kept that blond fella's face off the television. You're welcome. Another friend told me that the Brits were pinging State about two American Interpol agents named Nicholas Stafford and Drake Martignetti." He stepped around the front of the desk, moving closer to Walker. "Turns out Stafford and Martignetti each have a very authentic-looking file. One problem: not a single person at American Interpol has ever heard of them."

The smirk abruptly vanished and Cartwright glared at Walker, pointing an accusing finger at his chest, millimeters from his pressed green shirt. "Here's what I think, Colonel. I think those are your men, not Interpol's. I think you're running your own covert war out there, and civilians are getting killed in the crossfire." He backed up and narrowed his eyes. "Your friend at the FBI can only stonewall me for so long. The Intelligence Oversight Committee *will* be conducting an investigation into these attacks, and we *will* be looking into Romeo Seven."

"Romeo Seven isn't under your committee," said Walker, matching the senator's scowl with his own. "You don't have the authority."

Cartwright nodded. "We'll see, Colonel. We'll see." He sat down on the edge of his desk again and the phony smile returned. "In the meantime I've had Interpol deactivate the Stafford and Martignetti files. I guess those two boys are on their own."

CHAPTER 40

The Brits were disappointingly unimaginative with their interrogation room. A folding table surrounded by sickly yellow walls—one with a large two-way mirror— and an obvious microphone suspended from the ceiling. Nick had hoped for more from Scotland Yard. He had ordered Scott to mute the earpiece signals to avoid any chance of the Brits detecting them. Now that he saw the unsophisticated facilities, he realized that measure probably wasn't necessary. A uniformed bobby led him around the table, sat him down on a stool, and then took up a position at his shoulder, silently staring at the door.

"So, what are you in for?" asked Nick, glancing up.

The bobby said nothing. He kept his eyes level.

"You used to work the gate at Buckingham Palace, right? I almost didn't recognize you without the fuzzy hat."

Still nothing.

"Were you born without a personality, or did you have it surgically removed when you joined the force?"

The bobby finally reacted, looking down at Nick and pursing his lips. Then his eyes returned to the door.

While Nick was searching for some other way to harass the uniform, his interrogator entered the room, the same plainclothes superbobby from the square. He carried a file packed with papers.

"You clubbed me over the head and then drugged me," said Nick. "Do you know how dangerous that was?"

The plainclothesman shut the door. "You stole my service weapon and fired it in a public square. Do you know how dangerous *that* was?"

Nick's eyes narrowed. "You might want to start collecting job ads, Constable."

"It's Detective Sergeant, actually. Detective Sergeant Thomas Mercer, SO15, and you are?"

"Wasting time, here. Release me so I can find the people responsible for Paternoster Square."

Mercer shook his head. "No, mate, you got your lines all wrong. This is the part where you say 'Nick Stafford, Interpol,' and then I say 'No, you're not,' and then you say 'How do you know?' and then I slap this down in front of you." The detective pulled a thin stack of papers from his folder and tossed them onto the table.

Nick recognized his phony Interpol file. Large block letters printed across the top said SUSPENDED. He had nothing to say to that. He tried to redirect, throw the detective a bone. "Why don't you go look into a financial firm called Kingdom Ventures Incorporated?" He needed this guy to see him as an ally.

Mercer gave him an unexpected nod. "That is a very good idea. In fact, we already have." He pulled another packet from his file and slapped it down on the table.

Nick had expected the Interpol file, but this one hit him like a punch in the gut. The top page was the CEO profile for KVI. Nick had seen the file before—Molly sent it to him on his way to the square—but Molly's file had not come with a photo. Mercer's did. Nick stared down at his own face beneath the heading MOHAMMED AJAM. It was the same picture that CJ found on the suicide bomber, and it must have been added to the digital record after the Second Sign strike, a clear setup.

Nick looked from the file back up to the grinning detective. "Don't be an idiot. Do I look like a Mohammed?"

"Mohammed," said Mercer, leaning forward and placing his hands on the table, "a common name taken by converts to Islam. The spelling is changed out of respect for the prophet." He tapped the file with his index finger. "Ajam—meaning 'foreigner'—also commonly taken by converts, particularly white guys who join fundamentalist organizations."

This was going in exactly the opposite direction that Nick had anticipated. He switched to a different vein of evidence. "What about Dr. Maharani? He's the scientist they're using to build the weapon."

"Dr. Nashak Maharani?"

Nick nodded. "You met his daughter. She told you he was kidnapped."

"Oh yes, I talked to the Indian bird. She was all worked up. Then I called old dad's mobile and guess what? He picked right up. He told me he didn't want to see her. I gave her the phone, and he told her the same thing. Big alligator tears. Very tragic." He shrugged. "Not my problem."

Nick stared down at the table, searching his mind for a way forward. Mercer was no ally. Kattan had covered his bases. Finally, he looked up at the detective again. "I'll tell you what. You've got me. I'll give you everything, but I want to write it with my own hand so it can't be distorted. Get me a pen and paper."

The detective straightened. "You're offering me a signed confession? All of a sudden it's that easy?"

"You have enough to bury me. Consider it a professional courtesy."

"A professional courtesy from a fake Interpol agent. That's rich." The Brit hesitated for a few seconds, studying Nick's expression. Then he reached back and beckoned to someone behind the two-way mirror. "Okay, mate. I'll bite."

A moment later, another uniform appeared and placed a confession form and a pen on the table. Nick did not move. He stared up at the detective and coughed pointedly.

"Oh, right." The detective nodded to the bobby behind Nick, indicating he should cut the flex-cuffs. As the man bent down, Mercer held out a warning hand. "Oi, Bob. Mind your gun."

Nick did not fight. Once his hands were free, he took a few moments to twirl his fists and flex his blue fingers. When their color returned he removed the cap from the pen and started writing. He filled out all the personal information blocks with his Nick Stafford cover data and then stopped to stretch and twirl his wrists again. This time, when he continued writing, his left hand went to his lap. He wrote a few lines of text, replaced the pen cap, and pushed the pen and paper across the table.

Mercer glared down at the form for a few seconds and then read the lines out loud with utter disdain. "'I am not a terrorist. I did not plant those bombs. I did not attack the London Stock Exchange.'" He frowned at the bobby. "Cuff him up and get him out of here. Let's see how funny he is after a few more hours in the tank."

———

The flex-cuffs were not as tight as before, partly because Nick was conscious when they were put on this time, able to flare his wrists a little, and partly because it was the uniform who cuffed him instead of a vengeful Mercer.

As the escorting bobby marched him to the elevators, Nick carefully oriented a metal shiv and pressed it into one of the two locks on the plastic cuffs. His simplistic confession in the interrogation room had nothing to do with making a statement of innocence and everything to do with removing the clip from the pen cap he held in his lap. He could have written *War and Peace*, and would have, if it had taken that long to work the little metal stick free.

Once Nick got the shiv between the teeth and the catches inside the lock, one cuff would slide right out. Unfortunately, the clip was too wide. He had to wiggle it back and forth to grind through the plastic. If he couldn't make it work before the bobby got him back to his cell, there would be no point. He needed to stall.

When the bell rang and the elevator door opened, Nick suddenly squatted down and then thrust up and back with his shoulder, hitting the bobby in the chest and knocking him to the floor. By the time the constable regained his feet, the doors had closed and the elevator had moved on.

The bobby gave a frustrated huff. He punched the button again and then turned to face Nick, shaking a Taser at him. "Listen, mate. I like you. That Mercer is a total git, and you get under his skin nicely, but don't think for a second that I won't use this." The bell rang and the doors opened a second time. The bobby roughly pushed Nick inside. "Now, let's you and me go nice and quiet the rest of the way, shall we?"

The stall tactic worked. Four floors later, as the elevator doors opened onto the cell level, Nick's shiv slid home. His right cuff went loose.

The constable never saw it coming. As they passed the restrooms, Nick shot an elbow up under the man's chin, snapping his head back and throwing him off balance. Then he stepped behind and wrapped an arm around his neck for a rear choke. The poor man let out a long, pitiful rasp as Nick dragged him through the men's room door. Then he went limp.

Checking over his shoulder, Nick saw an open janitor's

closet at the back of the restroom, with a utility basin and faucet. "You're in luck, Constable . . . Gale," he said, reading the bobby's name tag. "I don't have to give you a concussion."

After stripping off Constable Gale's jacket and gear, Nick sat him in the basin and secured his ankles and wrists to the faucet with flex-cuffs. Then he glanced down at the constable's worn loafers and grimaced. Next came the unpleasant part.

The smell was pungent, a little cheesy. Nick scrunched his nose as he pulled off the bobby's sock. "There are powders and sprays for this sort of thing," he said, admonishing the unconscious policeman. "You should try them." Then he stuffed the sock into Gale's mouth until only the double-stitched toe remained.

Nick was cinching down a belt to keep the sock in place when Gale finally woke up. He let out a low moan and bobbled his head. Then his eyes zeroed in on Nick and flared wide. He drew in a breath to shout out and started to choke.

"Settle down! Breathe through your nose," Nick ordered, grabbing the man by the lapels and giving him a shake. "Do it, or you're going to suck down that sock and die."

The constable started breathing again. Fear gave way to anger. He struggled, but he could hardly move with all his limbs secured to the faucet. Nick lightly smacked him on the cheek. "Hey! Quit it! Pay attention. Number one: I'm sorry about the sock. It couldn't be helped." He paused and checked the light at the base of the bathroom door before continuing. No signs of movement outside. That wouldn't last forever. "Number two: you *have* to keep quiet. If you try to scream, you'll work that sock deeper until it blocks your nasal airway. Do that and you'll die."

The bobby stopped struggling and gave Nick an accusatory glare. Nick winced. "I know, you don't deserve this," he said as he gathered up Gale's gear. "I promise I'll make it up to you someday." Then he backed out of the closet and closed the door.

CHAPTER 41

Nick came out of the restroom wearing Constable Gale's black coat and his nylon utility belt with all its gear. As he placed a CLOSED FOR CLEANING sign outside the door, he spied the bobby's checkered wheel hat, still lying where it had fallen during the struggle. He dusted it off, seated it on his head, and reactivated his comm piece. "Nightmare Four, I'm loose in the building. Where's Two?"

If the engineer was surprised to hear Nick on comms, he didn't show it. "Stand by, let me call up his tracker."

Nick suddenly slowed his pace. Another uniform had come around the corner from the cell block. Both nodded curtly as they passed each other. Then, two steps later, both stopped cold.

"Nightmare Four, I found him." Nick reversed course

and looked up at Drake's usual grin, shadowed beneath a checkered wheel hat that matched his own. The name on the police coat read MCCORMICK. "Pen clip?" he asked the big operative, starting back toward the elevators.

Drake fell in step beside him. "You'd think Scotland Yard would know that trick by now. Where'd you stash your guard?"

"Janitor's closet in the men's room. You?"

"In my cell, against the front wall in the camera's blind spot. Someone is going to find these guys. We need to get out of here."

Nick stopped at the elevators and pressed the down button, instead of up for the street level. "Not yet. There's one more stop I want to make."

———

According to Scott, the New Scotland Yard evidence lockup was on the third sublevel, two floors down from the holding cells. "The design looks like a pass-through system. That means nothing but an examining table and a wall of two-way lockers with a clerk behind bulletproof glass. It's totally secure. The clerk puts the evidence in the locker and closes and locks the door on his side and then unlocks the door on your side so you can take it to the examining table."

Nick shook his head. "That kind of setup will have a digital ID sign-out system too, and we don't look anything like Constables McCormick and Gale. Can you hack their ID files?"

"Negative. Scotland Yard's security system is completely internal, unhackable from off-site."

"Maybe we should cut our losses, boss," said Drake as the elevator jerked to a stop.

The doors opened and Nick stepped out into an empty hall. "No. I want my stuff back."

Nick's key fob got them into the evidence receiving room. It was exactly as Scott predicted, with one small difference: the clerk behind bulletproof glass was a she, not a he. She was a brunette, midthirties, slightly plump but not fat by any stretch—and she was reading a romance novel.

"Things are looking up," whispered Drake.

Seconds later, the big operative was leaning on the short counter below the window, wearing his most charming smile. The clerk never saw it. Her eyes went straight from the book to the computer as she clicked it to life. "Depositing or checking out?"

Drake's charming smile faded. "Uh . . . checking out," he said, his accent a deflated Sean Connery.

Nick kept his face out of view behind Drake's broad shoulders. He gauged the distance to the exit.

The clerk pecked at her keyboard for a few seconds and then, with her eyes still focused on the monitor, gestured to a gray interrogator pad on the counter. "Identification, please."

If Drake scanned his key fob, a picture of the real Constable McCormick would come up on her screen. Nick took a step toward the door, but Drake grabbed his sleeve and held him fast. He winked.

Instead of swiping the fob across the pad, Drake unhooked it from his jacket, fumbled it, and dropped it into the receipt slot at the base of the window. "What a klutz," he said. "I'm terribly sorry." His Sean Connery showed renewed confidence.

When the clerk pushed the device back through, her fingers grazed his. She suddenly looked up and blinked. "Oh! That's . . . quite all right."

The charming smile returned full force and Drake kept her mesmerized while he smoothly ran his fob across the pad, motioning behind his back for Nick to quickly follow. Before the brunette could tear herself from his gaze, the ID photo from Nick's stolen fob had replaced Drake's. Nick turned and walked to the evidence table, sitting down with his back to the girl. Between his cap and the collar of his jacket, only the nape of his neck was visible.

The clerk checked her screen again. "What's up with Constable Gale?" she whispered.

"Oh, he's all right. He's self-conscious about his complexion." Drake circled a finger in front of his face. "Sudden hormonal imbalance. Very disturbing."

While Nick played the part of Constable Gale's back, Drake convinced his newest feminine fan to locate the Paternoster Square evidence boxes for them. "This is Detective Sergeant Mercer's case," she said as the file data replaced the ID picture on her screen. "Are you two working for him?"

Drake hesitated and Nick realized his teammate had not been formally introduced to their captor. He coughed an affirmative.

"Uh . . . Yes," said Drake. "Yes, we are."

"You poor dears." The clerk stood up to retrieve the evidence. "That man is a total git."

There were three file boxes. The first contained their empty satchels and overcoats. The second held their phones, fake ID wallets, cash, and all the equipment taken from the coats and satchels—everything tagged and bagged in ziplocks. Nick checked over his shoulder. The clerk had returned to her romance novel. He nodded to Drake and they quietly emptied the bags and pocketed what they could.

The third box contained only one item—a blackened thumb drive, also bagged and tagged. The tag, filled out by Mercer himself, noted that the drive had been recovered from the rubble in the exchange server room. Mercer had added a statement postulating that it was the source of the computer virus.

"Where are the weapons?" Drake turned the last box over as if he expected their Berettas and MP7s to fall onto the table.

"They must have a separate lockup for firearms."

Drake glanced back at the clerk. She looked up from her book and waved to him, wiggling her fingers. He waved back, wiggling his own. "I can get them. No problem."

"If there's a second lockup, she doesn't run it, chucklehead. No, we've already pushed the envelope too far." Nick stuffed the thumb drive into his jacket pocket, bag and all. "It's time to go."

He waited in the hall while Drake returned the boxes to the lockers and checked out with the clerk. On the way to the elevators, the big operative handed him a slip of paper. "She gave me this."

The block print showed the names McCormick and Gale, the evidence file numbers, and the in-and-out times. "It's just a receipt," said Nick.

Drake gave him a sly grin. "Flip it over."

On the back was a cell-phone number, circled with a heart. Nick slapped the paper into Drake's chest. "You sicken me."

As they reached the bank of elevators, one of the cars opened and a man in a black overcoat started out. He looked up from the smartphone in his hand and froze, staring at the two Americans. "You!"

Detective Sergeant Mercer reached for his Glock but he never got the chance to draw. Nick grabbed his wrist and clapped a hand over his mouth, heaving him back into the car until his head slammed against the rear wall. The detective slumped to the floor.

Nick pressed the button for the lobby and then snapped his fingers, holding out an open palm that Drake promptly filled with a CO_2 injector he had recovered from their satchels. Nick jammed it into Mercer's neck and released the charge. Then he pulled the detective's Glock from its holster and tucked it into his own waistband.

A few seconds later, the elevator bell rang, and the doors opened to a view of New Scotland Yard's gray marble lobby and the freedom of the London night beyond. "I guess that makes you even," said Drake, glancing back at the drooling detective as he stepped out of the car.

Nick hit the out-of-service button, smashed the detective's phone under his heel, and squeezed out through the closing doors. He looked up at his teammate with a thin smile. "He had it coming. That man is a total git."

CHAPTER 42

Nick's good mood was short-lived.

He and Drake moved quickly through the barrier outside Scotland Yard and crossed the street, turning toward an Underground station less than a half block away. They had only gone a few paces when Chaya Maharani stepped out from the dark doorway of a closed café and blocked their path.

"It's about time you two got out of there."

When Drake tried to step around her, she sidestepped with him and pressed in closer. She traced a finger down the black lapel of his police jacket. "This is new, but isn't it sort of a demotion from that whole Interpol thing?"

The pointedly indiscreet level of her voice caught the attention of a patrolman walking the beat outside police headquarters. He looked the three of them over as he passed.

Drake gave the bobby a nod and tipped his cap, but Nick's eyes dropped to the radio on the man's belt. For now, it remained silent. That wouldn't last. It could be seconds, or it could be an hour before one of the three stricken cops was found and the manhunt began. Murphy favored the first one.

Once the patrolman was out of sight, Nick grabbed Chaya by the back of the arm and spun her around. "Keep quiet and walk," he hissed, propelling her toward the Underground station.

"Oh, no. Not more trains," exclaimed the lawyer in a breathless, singsong voice. "My wardrobe can't take it."

Nick tightened his grip on her arm. "I said keep quiet."

The evening commuter traffic had long since faded. Only a small pack of teens haunted the station, and none of them wanted anything to do with a pair of Met policemen. They avoided eye contact with Nick and Drake and drifted out into the street. Nick sat Chaya down on a bench next to the ticket machines. "How did you find us?"

"You were arrested by SO15. Where else would you be?"

"He means how did you find us at the square," said Drake.

"She knows what I meant." Nick sat down next to her. She tried to scoot away, but he gripped her arm and jerked her back, jabbing the barrel of Mercer's Glock into her side.

The lawyer's glib demeanor fell away. "What are you doing? You're hurting me."

"Save it. I'm tired of your games. You and your father are both working for the Hashashin."

Chaya clenched her fists and glared back at him. "That's not true. I got lucky, okay? I'm a solicitor. My firm is in the financial district."

"So?"

"So I work less than a block from Paternoster Square, you idiot. After you dumped coffee all over me, I went home to change and then headed for my office to see what I could dig up on you. On my way there, I saw you in front of St. Paul's."

Drake folded his arms. "And you called the cops?"

"Wouldn't you?"

An automated voice from the tracks below announced that the next train was about to arrive. "We're leaving," said Nick, releasing the lawyer and standing up. Chaya tried to stand up with him but he shoved her back down by the shoulder. "Not you. You're staying here." He went over to the ticket machine and bought two zonal passes, using cash. There was no guard watching the turnstiles here, but there would be down the line at Cannon Street, a much larger station. When they left the Tube, he and Drake would need to slip through without drawing attention to themselves.

"You need me," Chaya called after them as they headed for the turnstile barrier.

Nick ignored her and passed through, but Drake hesitated. "Why?"

"While you were locked up, I went back to my father's

house. I found a file hidden under a false bottom in his desk drawer."

The train arrived below. Nick kept walking toward the stairs. "I don't believe her. Come on. We have to catch this one. We need to make the switch at Cannon Street before they find those cops."

Drake still lingered. "What was in the file?"

"Names, dates, formulas. Most of it made no sense to me. My flat isn't far. I'll drive."

"Drake, let's go."

Chaya stood. "The name on the cover was Kattan, Masih Kattan."

Nick stopped at the top of the stairs. Down at the tracks, the automated voice warned the nonexistent passengers to "please, mind the gap." Then it advised them that the train doors were closing. He pounded the wall with his fist and let it go.

"I left the file at my flat," said Chaya as Nick returned to the turnstiles. "You two could go through it with me."

Drake met his teammate at the barrier. He lowered his voice. "Do we trust her?"

Nick shook his head. "We have to get this thumb drive to Scott. That's our best lead."

"But a hidden file with the name of one of our prime suspects is a good lead too. We have to cover all our bases."

Nick knew Drake was right. But to cover those bases, they would have to split up. He winced. "I can't believe I'm saying this, but I want you to take the pretty girl back to her apartment and get a look at her file."

"Twist my arm."

Before his teammate turned to go, Nick pushed Mercer's Glock into his hands. "Be careful. If they have our biochemist, then chances are, they know where his daughter lives."

CHAPTER 43

The call went out just before Nick reached Cannon Street Station. From the flurry of activity on his stolen radio, he gathered that McCormick—the bobby in Drake's cell—had been discovered and that Detective Mercer could not be found. There was no mention of Gale.

Cannon Street was a major interchange, connecting multiple Tube lines with the National Railway lines above. One of those National Railway trains could take Nick straight to Greenwich, Scott, and the safety of the apartment, but with the bobbies now alerted and converging, it might as well be a hundred miles away. Just getting out of the Tube and up into the main rail station was going to be a trick. Getting through the platform turnstiles and onto the train itself—if not utterly impossible—would be like slapping the cuffs on his own wrists. The bobbies would pick him up at the next station down.

As the train pulled into the underground station, Nick spotted two bobbies on the platform between the east and west lines. They loitered near the stairwell to the street outside, blocking his quickest exit. Stepping off the train, he put his radio to his ear to cover his face and turned the other way, heading for the long escalator up to the main station.

Halfway up, Nick lowered the radio and turned to look back. He waited, expecting to see the two cops running up the rising stairs after him. They never came. That was a victory, but Nick was still a far cry from being out of the woods. He kept the radio in his hand, ready to use it for cover again at the exit turnstiles at the top of the escalator. Once again, though, his fear proved unfounded.

As the escalator reached the crest of its climb, Nick found himself completely alone. There were no cops, no other passengers, even the Lexan shack that usually housed the turnstile monitor was empty, its narrow door cracked open. Nick stepped through the barrier and snorted to himself. If this was the extent of the manhunt at the Cannon Street interchange, then maybe he still had a shot at getting out of the station.

Maybe not.

Nick walked down a short hallway and had just started up a small flight of stairs to the main station promenade when he heard an explosion of radio chatter—not on his own radio, but on at least a dozen radios near the top of the stairs. He hugged the left wall, crept to the top, and snuck a peek around the corner. His heart sank. A crowd of bobbies, most in yellow high-visibility jackets, huddled for a meeting near the main exit to the street. One of the attendees was the Tube monitor, which explained why her booth was empty. Another was the monitor for the train-station turnstiles. The two leading the assembly were SO15, easily distinguished because they were better dressed than all the others, with black ball caps, body armor, and G-36 submachine guns slung at their sides. Again, Nick's path to freedom was blocked. He retreated back down the hallway to the Tube turnstiles.

All aluminum and steel and ticket machines, no subway station had ever seemed so barren to Nick, not until now, when he needed options. Then his eyes fell on a lone rack of free magazines, the kind no one ever seemed to pick up. His fingers tickled the bobby's Taser on his stolen utility belt. It might work. It had to. There was no time to conjure up something better.

Nick dragged the whole rack—magazines and all—into the turnstile monitor's Lexan booth. He needed the enclosed space to contain the smoke, at least until he was well clear. He started ripping up magazines, working fever-ishly, fearing that the monitor might return at any moment, or a civilian might rise up from the station below.

The magazine rack served as his frame. He stuffed the lower section with loosely crumpled pages and then spread apart the magazines lined up on the top section, making sure there would be room for oxygen to flow. Then, for good measure, he pushed the monitor's rolling chair up against the loaded rack and set her mesh trash can on the seat.

That should do it.

Unwilling to push his luck any further, Nick stood sideways in the narrow doorway, aimed his Taser at the crumpled pages on the bottom of his pile, and fired, holding down the trigger to pump as much juice into the electric barbs as possible. The pages caught. He dropped the Taser and raced down the hallway.

Nick slowed as he topped the stairs, entering the promenade at an easy stroll. As anticipated, he did not make it far before one of the gathered bobbies spotted him.

"Oi! Mate! Over here!" It was one of the SO15 men. When Nick kept walking, the superbobby tried again, leaving the group and following after him. "Oi! Bob! I haven't given you your search ord—"

The superbobby's call was interrupted by an ear-splitting bell from the Tube station. Curls of thick smoke wafted up the stairs. The bobbies at the exit—as well as the superbobby who had started after Nick—turned their attention to this new excitement.

A few yellow jackets remained at their posts, still blocking the exit, but their attention was focused on the rest of the mob, rushing down the stairs to the Tube line. With both monitors equally occupied, no one was watching the long line of turnstiles in front of the train platforms. Nick reached the turnstiles, checked his six, and then vaulted over.

Seven tracks, each with their own platform, led straight out of the station beneath a wide arched roof and out across a bridge over the Thames. Nick hurried toward the bridge, keeping close to a long wall of restrooms and utility stations that separated the two central platforms. Fifty meters down, he crossed through a short passage to the platform on the other side, taking him completely out of view of anyone on the promenade.

Drake's voice sounded in his earpiece. "You okay, boss? I'm hearing a lot of radio traffic. They say they've cornered one of us."

"Just about," huffed Nick, jogging beside a waiting train. "They had a big contingent at Cannon Street, and I had to improvise to get past them. You can add arson to our list of offenses now."

"Nice. I'm on my way."

"Negative. Stay put. This area is too hot. Wait for my call and we'll set up a rendezvous."

An automated voice from inside the train announced that it was preparing to leave. Without breaking stride, Nick stripped off his jacket, hat, and utility belt and tossed them into one of the cars. If the SO15 man who called after him earlier was worth his badge, he wouldn't take long to put two and two together. He would have the trains leaving this station searched at their next stop. The stolen uniform gave him something to find, something to push the bulk of their search miles away from here.

Shortly before he ran out of concrete platform, Nick felt icy particles pelting his face. He was out in the open, out from under the broad station roof, and it was sleeting. Even

London's weather had turned against him. Maybe ditching the police jacket wasn't such a good idea. Two huge bell towers rose up on either side, and the roof and its fluorescent lights fell behind. The dark of the long railway bridge enveloped him. He could still hear the shouts of the yellow jackets back in the station, but they were distant, no longer threatening.

The train pulled out of the station and clacked across the bridge, covering the crunch of his boots on the gravel between the tracks until he was a good hundred meters from the station. At two hundred meters, he had reached the other shore. An old brown brick building with a high-pitched roof was pressed up against the left abutment of the bridge. Nick lowered himself over the side, dropped to the roof, and slid on his backside down the icy shingles until his heels hit a black half-pipe gutter. He had just started climbing down a thick four-story drainpipe when Scott came up on the comm link.

"Nightmare One, come in."

Nick paused in his climb to flex his frozen fingers. "I'm up. Go ahead."

"I have Lighthouse on the line for you. It's the colonel."

That didn't bode well. Walker rarely spoke to his people via earpiece comms these days, not with the team's ability to telecom almost anywhere. The colonel preferred face-to-face communication so he could scowl at his operators. Nick wiped his free hand on his pants and continued descending to the street. "Has there been a development?"

"A couple," Scott replied. "And neither of them is good."

CHAPTER 44

"'m worried about Nick," said Drake as Chaya opened the door to her flat. His police radio continued to buzz with calls about the fire at Cannon Street, and he had not heard anything on his SATCOM piece since Nick ordered him to stand by.

Chaya motioned him inside. "I am worried, too, but there is nothing you can do for him." She took the radio from Drake's hand and turned it off. "If I have learned anything about your friend, it is that he can take care of himself."

Chaya's apartment was not what Drake expected. He had pictured cold colors and spartan contemporary furniture—the flat of a smart, ambitious young business-woman who slept there but lived at the office. Instead, the colors here were warm and earthy. She patted the back of a low couch upholstered in silky burnt orange and gold. "Sit down and relax. And please, take off that ridiculous hat and jacket. They are too small for you anyway." She cracked open the door to her bedroom. "I'll be right back."

Drake laid the bobby's gear on a table near the kitchen bar and sank down onto the couch, resting his head back on the soft cushions. He breathed deep and detected a trace of some dark, intoxicating aroma. Maybe Chaya had lit a candle in the other room.

In the comfortable setting, the temptation to close his eyes and drift off was strong. After all, Nick had told him to sit and wait. This was an opportunity for some much-needed rest. Then again, Drake had grown accustomed to ignoring Nick's orders.

He shook off his exhaustion and sat up, activating the SATCOM feature on his phone rather than using his earpiece with Chaya so close. "Nightmare One, say your status."

Nick did not respond.

"Nightmare Four, are you up?"

Nothing from Scott either. He checked the phone. No signal.

"I hope you don't mind." Chaya emerged from the bedroom wearing maroon silk pajamas that hung from her slender frame. "This might take a while, and I couldn't bear to spend another minute in that suit."

"Uh . . . No, that's fine." Drake stumbled over the words as he slipped the phone back into his pocket. "If I had brought my jammies, I'd be wearing them too."

She laughed, slipping into her tiny kitchen. "I am certain you would be."

Drake heard the *clink* of glasses and the splash of pouring liquid. While he watched Chaya work, he noticed a set of three pictures, hanging one above the other on the narrow column of wall at the end of the bar. Each depicted a chess game in abstract perspective from the level of the board, and each featured the queen in the foreground. From the bottom picture to the top, the queen moved closer to the viewer, each time with more pieces lying on their sides behind her.

"I like these chess paintings. Do you play?"

Chaya returned with two glasses of wine. "I dabble." She pressed a glass into Drake's hand and sat down cross-legged at the end of the couch. "And you?"

"It's not really my game." He set the glass down on the coffee table. "Too much thinking."

She giggled in the midst of a sip, nearly spilling her wine, and raised a delicate hand to the corner of her mouth to catch a wayward drop. "You're too funny." She locked his eyes and touched the red liquid to her parted lips, gently sucking it in. "And too modest. My instincts tell me you are quite the chess player."

With that, Chaya set her glass on the table. She stretched and ran her fingers through her hair, arching her back so that the silk shirt lifted, exposing her flat stomach and small naval. "The game of chess is not always played on a board," she said, bringing her hands to her lap again. "It is a way of life—making your moves, anticipating your opponent's. I think you understand that more than you let on." She extended a leg and playfully pushed at Drake's thigh with the sole of her bare foot.

"You strike me as a man who enjoys the thrill of the hunt even more than the taste of the kill."

The vibe that Chaya was sending out left little room for interpretation. And she was right, this was Drake's form of chess. He loved the hunt, bandying flirtations back and forth, inching closer to the prize. Maybe that was why he kept pushing Amanda away, so he could start the game all over again, but how long would she keep coming back to the board?

At the thought of his girlfriend, Drake shifted uncomfortably. Chaya slowly pulled her foot back and tucked it underneath her thigh. She glanced down at his glass and folded her arms, pouting. "You're not drinking your wine. Is something wrong?"

Drake patted the cell phone in his pocket. "Nick could call at any moment. I need to stay alert." Then he glanced around the room. "So . . . can you show me that file?"

Chaya relaxed her defensive posture and rocked forward onto her knees, resting a hand on his shoulder. She pushed him back into the cushions. "There's no rush. If we're going to crack this case, we need to get out of our own heads for a few minutes."

One knee at a time, the lawyer crossed over his lap, her scented hair grazing the top of his head, her fingers lightly tracing the line of his collarbone as she passed. On the other side, she sat back on her heels and gently pushed him into a half turn. She dug the heel of her palm into his back and slowly ran it down to his waistline.

"Is that incense?" The trace Drake had noticed before had grown to fill the room.

"That is Nag Champa. I burn it when I want to loosen my brain cells and refocus. Do you like it?"

"It's . . . um . . . nice." He leaned back into her hands and closed his eyes. "I don't know that it's helping me focus, though."

She rose up on her knees and pressed herself against him. Her lips brushed his ear. "You might be right about that."

The powerful incense and the sultry purr of Chaya's whisper took Drake deeper into a relaxed state, deeper into his semiconscious mind. But the face he found there amid swirling oranges and reds was not Chaya's. It was Amanda's.

And she did not look happy.

His eyes popped open and he jerked upright, bumping the coffee table with his knee and nearly toppling the wineglasses. "Nope. Focus is back. Let's have a look at that file."

In the instant his knee hit the table, Drake could swear he saw a wisp of powder spiral up from the bottom of his glass, but the flicker of pink dissolved as quickly as it had arisen. He stared at the sloshing red liquid, trying to clear his mind. The thought occurred to him that he had really seen nothing at all, just a trick of the light playing in the wine.

"Shhh." Chaya's grip tightened on his neck and she pulled him back in to her. She rested her cheek against his and slid her hand down the front of his Lycra shirt. Her fingernails raked his chest. "You must learn to relax, Drake Merigold. Close your eyes."

Her words caught in his clouded brain. Merigold? Shouldn't she have said Martignetti? He fought her command, keeping his eyes open, fixed on the distorted, double reflection in the wineglasses. There he saw a twisted vision of the lawyer raising something above her head. It gleamed in the lamplight.

Drake shot to his feet, grabbing both Chaya's wrists and throwing her to the couch as he spun away. She immediately lunged, slashing at him with a gold-handled dagger. The blade was black, made of the same alloy as the Hashashin knife dropped by the Istanbul sniper. As Drake stumbled backward the tip sliced through his shirt, missing his abdomen by the breadth of a hair.

He kept backing away, rubbing his eyes. "What are you doing?"

"Come back to the couch, Drake. Drink your wine. Fall asleep in my arms with my lips pressed to yours." She rotated the knife to point downward, raised it high, and advanced a step. "Isn't that a better death than this?"

The incense had become a choking, pungent haze. Drake's eyes watered. He rubbed them, trying to bring her back into focus.

"A little fuzzy?" asked Chaya, circling him on the balls of her feet, her little toes spread into the thick fibers of the yellow rug. "I might have added a few extra ingredients to the Nag Champa. I am well used to them. You are not."

Drake steadied himself by placing a hand on a stool next to her bar. He pressed a hand to his ear. "Nightmare One," he gasped. "Nick, come in."

"Oh, do not worry about your friend. Nick Baron is likely already dead. You will join him, but it doesn't have to hurt. Please, Drake, sit down. Don't you find me desirable?" She took another step toward him.

Drake lifted the stool and held it out in front of him like a drunken lion tamer. "Stay away from me, lady. You're not my type."

"Fine. Have it your way." Chaya grabbed a leg of the stool and pulled with alarming strength, yanking Drake closer and swiping at his arm with the knife. He let go and jerked away in time to avoid the tip. Where was that gun?

He had no time to search. Chaya stepped in and swung the stool, breaking it across his shoulder and knocking him into the bar before lunging with the knife again.

Despite the opiates in his system, Drake was beginning to learn her rhythm. His left hand had fallen on a silver bowl and he pushed himself off the bar and swung it hard, connecting with her face. She reeled back with an angry scream, her hand over her nose. When she pulled the hand away, her face was bloody, her nose gashed and twisted sideways.

"Ugh," said Drake, wobbling forward and dropping the bowl. "You weren't my type before, but now you're ugly too."

"*Ooh!*" Chaya rushed at him, slashing the knife back and forth in an X pattern.

The bobby's gear lay on a table within arm's reach. Drake snatched up the utility belt and flung it at her head. It hardly slowed her at all, but the move was just a distraction. As the belt left his hand, Drake drew the baton from its holster.

He met her slash with an upward swing, whacking her hard across the forearm. There was a sickening *crack* of breaking bone.

Chaya cried out in pain, but she held on to her knife. As Drake wheeled her damaged arm farther upward with the baton, she pirouetted to his left and switched her weapon to her good hand, swinging the blade down and back at his kidney.

It was a gorgeous move, but he saw it coming. He caught her forearm with an iron grip and slashed down at her ankles with the baton. There was another horrible *crack*. Chaya cried out again and both of them fell to the floor, wrapped like lovers in a spoon. He held her tight while she struggled against him for another second. Then she was still.

After several moments, Drake cautiously let go with one hand and placed two fingers on Chaya's neck. She had no pulse. He struggled to his feet, leaving her lying on her side, and stumbled over to a window to push it open wide. The toxic incense that filled the room began to clear.

The knife remained embedded in Chaya's abdomen and seeping blood darkened her silk pajamas, but a wound that low on her torso should not have killed her. Then Drake recalled something he once read about the ancient Hashashin. They favored poison blades. He glanced down at the hole in his shirt. How many times during the fight had she almost nicked him?

After a few more breaths of fresh air, he knelt down to get a closer look at the body, searching for a Hashashin tattoo. Her forearms were clean, her palms as well. Then he noticed a black mark at the back of her neck. He gently brushed her hair aside. There it was, a small circle like Kattan's and Ashaq's. The symbol inside was a horizontal crescent moon.

Someone pounded on the door and Drake jerked his head up. His eyes darted around the room. Broken furniture, wine and blood staining the carpet, a dead woman lying on the floor as delicate and defenseless as a broken rose. This didn't look like self-defense.

The intruder pounded again. "Miss Maharani? Open up! We received a tip that you may be in danger from the escaped terrorists."

CHAPTER 45

"Baron!"

Walker's booming intrusion on the comm link nearly cost Nick his grip on the drainpipe. He winced and tucked his body closer to the cold metal. "Yes, sir?"

"I've been tracking you since you left Scotland Yard. What are you doing?"

Nick glanced down at the cobblestones twenty feet below. "You know . . . just . . . hanging around."

"Well, quit it. Gather your team and get out of Dodge. You're done."

"Say again?"

"This is no longer a covert fight. It's gone public—very public."

"You mean the incident in Paternoster Square?" asked Nick, sliding down the last section of pipe. He backed into a doorway to get out of the freezing sleet.

"Worse. I mean Senator Cartwright. One of his people bullied his way into CJ's files. Before she cut him off, he found out that the D.C. bomber called himself the first sign. He called a press conference and broadcast that information on live TV, linking the two attacks. He told the public that more signs are on their way."

"Can't CJ lock him up for releasing classified information?" As he asked the question, Nick turned and peered through the glass pane of the door he had backed into. The place looked like a pastry shop. It was closed and dark, but he saw a coatrack behind the register with a sweatshirt and a wool cap.

"Nothing's illegal for our national politicians," grumbled Walker. "You should know that by now."

Nick gritted his teeth and smashed the pane with his bare elbow.

"Did I hear glass breaking?"

"No." Nick reached through and unlocked the door. "You can't pull my team, sir. I'm the only one with a direct line to Kattan. We just need a little more time."

"Your direct line has been cut, Baron. Or haven't you noticed?"

"I don't follow."

"The stakeout at the café in D.C. paid off. CJ found Kattan's phone. No henchman, just the phone. It was buried in the bushes outside the café, transmitting the moves on its own."

Nick pulled the sweatshirt over his head. It was far too big—the owner must weigh four hundred pounds—but it was better than freezing. "You mean Kattan used it to retransmit the moves?"

"Negative. The receiver was disabled. There was no active connection to Kattan." The colonel went on to explain that the phone had simply transmitted a list of moves at predetermined times. Kattan had laid out the game in advance, predicting every move Nick made.

"He's not that good," argued Nick. "No one is."

"My evidence says different."

"What you're saying is impossible, sir. I've still got him on the line. Earlier today he put me in check with his queen. During the ride to Cannon Street, I took her out with my remaining knight. I'm waiting for his response."

"You won't *get* a response. CJ has the phone. There were no more moves in the hopper. That's it. Game over."

No. Nick suddenly felt an urgent need to pick up his pace. He grabbed the wool cap off the rack, pulling it down over his ears as he rushed out from behind the register. "Kattan had me in check, not checkmate. I escaped. I can still get to him." He yanked open the door to the street.

"Nick, stop."

At the colonel's use of his first name, Nick froze. His hand fell away from the handle. The door swung closed again.

"This chase is over." Walker's voice carried a trace of unusual sympathy. "There are no more moves in the sequence. You were never meant to finish the game. Kattan presented you with a grand gambit, and you walked right in. We all did."

Nick pinched the bridge of his nose in a long wince. His head was pounding, the pain that results from coming in out of the cold. "It can't all have been for nothing."

"Oh, it wasn't for nothing." Walker's tone hardened again. "Kattan designed this whole charade to bury the Triple Seven Chase, to keep us out of the way for whatever he has planned next. And he succeeded. The president is putting us on the bench and giving the search for the bioweapon over to the big agencies." Walker sighed into the comm link. "Come home, Nightmare One. Lighthouse out."

CHAPTER 46

Nick pressed his hands into the pockets of his oversized sweatshirt and stepped out once more into the night and the freezing sleet. To the right of the pastry shop, a dark tunnel passed beneath the solid foundation of the railway bridge. To the left, the cobblestone street stretched away until it curved into shadow. Iron lamps hung at sparse intervals from looming three- and four-story Victorian houses on either side, their copper-brick faces pressed together to form a long, unbroken passage. Nick felt as if he had dropped onto one of the darker pages of Dickens.

"Nightmare Two," he called, plodding forward through the puddles of orange lamplight.

Drake did not respond.

"Two, come in. I shook off the cops. I need you and Chaya to pick me up."

"I can't raise him either," complained Scott, still listening on the link. "You sent him home with a beautiful woman. You do the math."

"Fine. Come pick me up, and then we'll get Casanova and head straight to the airport. Ditch what you can and pack up the weapons and electronics. Leave out only what you need to do a little software analysis on the plane."

"Exactly what kind of analysis?"

"We took a thumb drive from Scotland Yard that may contain the Second Sign Virus. I want you to identify the creator or the source code and forward it to CJ. Our job now is to help the FBI."

"Can't do it," said the engineer flatly.

"You *can* and you *will*," growled Nick, starting to boil. "This is the only lead we have left."

"I mean I can't do it on the plane. You're talking about a monster virus, the likes of which the world has never seen. You don't just shove that into a SATCOM-capable laptop in the field. Things start going bad very quickly. I have to get the drive back to Romeo Seven if I'm going to exploit it."

Nick relented. He knew the engineer was right. "Then we'll have to fly fast."

"Where do I meet you?"

"You have a map. You tell me."

"Okay. Uh . . . there's a ship—the *Golden Hinde*—two blocks east. A boat in a square, you can't miss it."

The whine of a motorcycle interrupted the conversation, echoing through the brickwork canyon. Nick tarried between islands of lamplight and listened.

"Did you copy, Nightmare One?"

"Yeah. Got it. The *Golden Hinde*." The engine noise grew louder. The motorcycle was heading Nick's way.

"I have to go off-line while I transfer SATCOM control to Romeo Seven and pack up," continued the engineer.

Nick nodded slowly, as though Scott could see him, but his attention was fixed on the light from the motorcycle's headlamp, growing around the bend. An icy chill swept through him, despite the protection of his stolen sweatshirt.

"Four?"

"Yes?"

"Hurry up."

CHAPTER 47

A few seconds after Scott signed off, the motorcycle appeared, the rider dressed all in black. As he sped past, he turned his head and locked his gaze on Nick. Then he gunned the motor, continuing into the tunnel beneath the bridge.

Nick let out a long breath, but then he heard tires skidding to a stop. The engine idled on the other side of the tunnel for half a beat and then revved up again. Nick broke into a run.

The long brick canyon was a perfect kill zone, with few exits left or right. A side street broke off to the left thirty meters ahead, but Nick would never make it that far. The motorcycle was closing too fast.

Closer, only a few paces away, he saw a narrow archway blocked by an iron gate. He committed, twisting around to face the attacker and pressing his shoulder through the iron bars up to his chest. They had looked wide enough.

They were not.

The big sweatshirt caught and bunched up, making Nick too fat to squeeze through. He pushed with everything he had and the fabric started to give, but at an agonizingly slow rate. He looked up. The rider steadied his bike and took one hand off the handlebar to raise a suppressed submachine gun.

A fraction of a second later, Nick fell through the bars amid a ripple of clangs and a shower of sparks. He scrambled forward into the gloom, smacked into a brick wall, and turned. Then he smacked into another wall and turned again. He had stumbled into a maze of passages between the two-hundred-year-old buildings of London's wharf prison district. New structures had been constructed over the top, roofing in the alleyways and leaving them in total darkness.

Another round of clangs sounded from the gate, followed by a heavy crash as the rider broke through. The throbbing buzz of the motorcycle bounced off the brick walls, and Nick could not tell which direction it was coming from. He pressed his back against a wall at a T-intersection and looked from side to side until he saw a faint white light grow and then fade in the alley straight ahead. Almost instantly it grew and faded again in an intersecting alley to the left, and then—though it seemed impossible—again on the opposite side. The third time it kept growing until the rider appeared at the corner. The black helmet turned. The visor was up. The assassin's eyes fixed on Nick.

As the rider steered into the alley and fired, Nick dove down the passage straight ahead. A stream of bullets whizzed by, the shots muted down to a series of clacks by the weapon's compact suppressor. But this series ended in a premature *click*.

Nick spun back into the T-intersection and rushed the oncoming headlight.

The rider accepted the challenge. He let his empty weapon hang at his side and bore down on the accelerator, racing toward Nick in a lopsided game of chicken. At the last millisecond, Nick reached his goal, a small alcove between them. He sprang left into the doorway and twisted, throwing all his body weight behind a left hook to the side of the rider's helmet as he passed.

The assassin's head bounced off the brick wall. His bike wobbled with increasing oscillation until the front tire cranked ninety degrees and he went flying over the bars, tumbling into a heap. The bike stayed wedged between the walls with the cracked headlight still on, reflecting off the copper-colored brick.

Nick climbed over the bike, trying to get to the assassin before he reloaded his gun, but the rider didn't bother. He jumped to his feet, tore off his helmet, and squared off, drawing a long, curving knife from a sheath at his back.

Nick hesitated. Then he remembered the Hashashin knife he had carried since Istanbul. As soon as his feet hit the ground on the other side of the bike, he pulled it from his pocket and palmed the hilt. The two blades sang as they shot out. The Hashashin glanced down at the knife and then grinned. With a gloved hand, he beckoned Nick forward.

CHAPTER 48

At Nick's first step, the wall beside him erupted in a cloud of dust and brick fragments, forcing him back into the broken bike. Blinding light shone from the alley to his right. Another engine revved.

There was a second assassin.

He let his blades retract and half-fell, half-clambered backward over the bike. In the scramble, he saw that the first rider had dropped his weapon. A Kriss Vector submachine gun hung from the handle bars. He snatched it up. The gun was empty, but there was no point in leaving it there for the assassin to recover.

Nick dodged left at an L-intersection and paused to get his bearings. The illumination from the headlamp of the broken bike became his reference point. What seemed an endless maze in the dark now proved to be just a few intersecting corridors, bounded on four sides by two short passages and two long. Somewhere along those border passages was the way out.

As he rounded the corner to the next long passage, Nick saw a flash of steel. The unhorsed assassin slashed at his head while the other rider approached at increasing speed from behind him. Nick ducked the knife and struck out with his own, unleashing the spring-loaded blades as he slashed at his attacker's midsection. His knife cut easily through the leather riding jacket, but it scraped against something the tip could not penetrate. Kevlar. The assassin reversed his swing, slicing back down at Nick's head, and Nick countered with an upward thrust of his own. He embedded his blade in the assassin's forearm. No Kevlar there.

He jerked the blade, ripping muscle and nerves and forcing the assassin to drop his knife. With his other hand, Nick grabbed the man's belt, and before the assassin could push away, he found what he needed—a pair of magazines. There was a shout from behind. The wounded assassin ducked. Nick spun back around the corner as more rounds pelted the wall behind him.

He backed down the short passage that capped the end of the maze. There were only two approaches to this position, from the main passages to the north and south. The faded light from the fallen bike illuminated the passage to the north. The bright light and the revving motor of the other filled the passage to the south.

"Nightmare One, you up?"

Nick couldn't believe the timing. "Two? Where have you been?"

"You know. Wine, incense, beautiful Hashashin queen with a poison knife and a powerful comm jammer. Chaya tried to kill me."

"Was she in her underwear when it went down?"

"Close."

"Figures."

"So what's up with you?"

The other assassin kept revving his engine, but he did not breach the corner. Nick heard low voices in the same Turkic dialect he had heard in the catacombs. He wished he could understand the words. Then the voices stopped. "Two not-very-pretty and fully clothed assassins are trying to carve me up with knives and Vector submachine guns," he told Drake. "At least there's no incense. Can you get to me?"

"I was going to ask you the same thing. I'm pinned down in Chaya's neighborhood. Scotland Yard stormed the flat, and I had to bolt through the window. I might need a hot pickup."

Nick heard the scuff of a boot from the intersection behind him. He turned and fired to the north and the attacker retreated. At the same time, he sensed a shift in the light from the south. One of the assassins had passed in front of the headlight of the other bike. He tensed. The move to the north was a distraction, meant to turn him away from the real threat, and it had worked.

He twisted and fell flat backward as a line of rounds passed above him. The first bullet parted his hair. In midfall, he zeroed in on the shooter and pulled the trigger.

The rider's visor was probably Lexan—bullet-resistant—but he had lifted it to see better in the dark corridors. Nick put two rounds through his right eye. Then his back hit the ground, knocking the wind from his lungs.

The light wavered in the corridor with the stuck bike. The motor revved up. The other assassin had worked it free. The sound and the light retreated from the alley.

"You still there, Two?"

"Yeah."

"I'm clear."

"Great. Come and get me."

"It'll take a while. Find a good hiding spot and hunker down." Nick struggled to his feet and kicked the dead assassin, just to make sure. Then he dragged him into an alcove and propped him up, working in the light from the remaining motorcycle. The man's sleeve had crept up his forearm, revealing a tattoo. Nick recognized the design from the catacombs and from Drake's chess pictures—one triangle overlapping another within a circle, a Hashashin knight.

"Lighthouse says we've been played," said Nick, dropping the arm and unzipping the assassin's jacket. "We're at square one and Kattan is done with us. I'd say recent events support his theory. We're vacating London before this gets any worse."

"That's why Chaya tried to kill me. Kattan used us, and now he's tying up loose ends."

Tying up loose ends. Nick stopped rifling through the assassin's jacket and stood up. "Two, was Chaya standing there when I told you about Rami?"

Drake took a while to consider the question, then answered slowly, "Yeah, I think she was."

"Then you're going to have to wait a little longer." Nick walked around the corner and gazed down at the idling motorcycle. "I have to go to Cambridge."

CHAPTER 49

Nick sped past the *Golden Hinde* on the assassin's motorcycle and kept on going. He wore the assassin's gear—helmet, jacket, and gloves—to protect himself from the still-falling sleet. "Four, change of plan," he said over the SATCOM.

Scott did not reply. Molly came up instead, from her station at Romeo Seven. "Nightmare One, this is Lighthouse. Four is off-line. We have the comms now. No changes. Your orders are to get to the airport."

"Molly. Good. I need a phone patch." Nick swerved around a pedestrian pylon, nearly losing control on the slick pavement and sending his helmet askew. He growled as he straightened the bike and then jerked the helmet back into position. He had discarded the helmet liner in the alley because it was sticky with the Hashashin's blood and brains. Without it, the helmet didn't sit right.

"Nightmare One, we lost the GPS feeds in the transfer. Please state your position and the nature of the change."

"Who are you? OnStar? Just give me that phone patch." Nick settled out heading north on the London Bridge and punched the gas, weaving through the late-night traffic.

"Fine. What's the number?"

It only took Molly a few seconds to run the patch, but the line went straight to voice mail. "Rami, get out of the house," said Nick, hoping the scream of his engine wouldn't drown out the message. "The Hashashin are coming for you. Get somewhere safe. I'm on my way."

"You can't be *on your way* to Professor Fuad's," said Molly as soon as she cut the patch. "No delays. The Brits are preparing to shut down noncommercial departures from the airports. You have forty-five minutes before the Gulfstream is grounded. The pilots have been instructed to take off, with or without you."

"Then leave me behind. Tell the others to get out of here."

"No good." Drake's voice came up on the link, almost a whisper. Nick could hardly hear him over the whine of his engine. "I'm on the other side of the city, surrounded by cops. Four will never get to me in time to make the plane. If you're staying, so am I."

A plan started to form in Nick's mind. As he slowed to pass a blue-and-yellow police car, he reached down to check that the thumb drive was still safe in his pocket. He started looking for an appropriate spot to stash it. "That leaves Four only one pickup to make before he leaves. Molly, get him up on comms. Drake, stand by."

A short distance off the road, Nick saw what he was searching for. With the cop safely out of view behind him, he hopped a curb and slid to a stop in a small open square. After dismounting and checking the area, he bent down and feigned tying his boot, using the move to shove the plastic evidence bag into a crevice underneath a wooden crate. Then he jumped back on the bike and returned to his northeast course. "Nightmare Four, you up?"

"I'm here. Currently at the *Golden Hinde* and following the situation. Looks like I'm going home alone."

"Correct, but first you need to grab the thumb drive. Come north over the London Bridge to Brushfield Street. I left the package for you under the goat."

"Did you say you left it under the *goat*?"

"Yes."

Silence. Then, "What if the goat moves?"

Nick grinned despite the circumstance. "We're talking about a statue, a goat on top of some crates. Somehow it's art. Whatever. The drive is in a plastic bag underneath the crates."

"A goat."

"A *statue* of a goat."

"Lighthouse copies the plan," said Molly impatiently. "Goat and all. The colonel isn't going to like this. You two have no way out of the country."

"We'll figure something out," grunted Nick, fighting to keep control as he took a half right onto the A1208. He straightened out and gunned the engine, accelerating toward Cambridge. "We always do."

CHAPTER 50

The sleet stopped near the end of the ride. That was something. But it left a freezing remnant hanging in the air that chilled Nick to the core. He fought back shivers as he hung his helmet on the handlebars and then crawled over the low stone wall next to Latham Road, on the southern end of the university grounds.

Nick had stayed with Rami before, and he knew the property well. The professor's two-story cottage stood well back from the road, surrounded by an ancient circle of elms and chestnuts. A long gravel drive led straight from the road to the front door, but Nick stayed away from it, moving in a wide arc and keeping to the edge of the trees. His black gear kept him well hidden in the shadows.

He approached the house from behind Rami's one-car garage—little more than a brick shed at the edge of the drive—and when he reached the heavy oak front door, he found it cracked slightly open. He saw a wet glint on the frame, catching the faint light reflecting off the overcast above. He looked closer. Blood.

Nick raised the Vector to his shoulder and pushed the door inward with the suppressor. It creaked and then thumped against something soft on the floor.

A young woman—eighteen, maybe twenty—lay in Rami's entry, her blood spreading in a wide pool beneath her, seeping into the herringbone pattern of the old brick floor. Nick winced and gently shunted her aside with the door until he had enough room to slip through. He did not bend down to check the girl's pulse. No need. Her throat was slashed, her eyes open and lifeless, staring at the thick beams above.

There were no sounds in the house. No sounds at all. If Nick remembered correctly, the kitchen and the dining room were to the right, the study and the sitting room with its spiral staircase to the left. At this hour, the professor—a notorious insomniac—should be in his study, poring over the plans of a pyramid or the writings of Champollion.

Nick tried to block out the mental image of Rami, facedown and bleeding all over an ancient text, as he crept toward the study entry at the back of the hall. The sliding wood door was wide open. He cleared the corner, slicing the pie with the Vector still up and ready.

Empty. No dead professor.

Nick let out a short breath.

A heavy book lay open on the desk, next to an eggshell

teacup and saucer. Rami's beautiful lapis lazuli globe was on the floor, broken in three pieces. Nick removed a glove and dipped a finger into the cup. The tea was warm.

A floorboard creaked above. Nick set the glove next to the saucer and moved toward the open portal that led to the sitting room. He placed each step with a slight roll of his foot, silent. Then, as he crossed into the room beneath the spiral staircase, a shadow appeared at the bottom step.

"Hands up, now!" ordered Nick, uncertain if the figure was friend or foe. The shadow gave no hint of surrender. It turned to face him and raised a matching Vector.

Nick fired a burst on full auto and the intruder quivered with the impacts, staggering back into the front window, a black silhouette against the luminescent curtain. But the Hashashin did not fall. He was wearing armor like the others. And like the others, he had an uncanny ability to absorb pain.

Suddenly a panel in the oak wall to Nick's right opened. Rami darted out of a hidden space beneath the stairs and raced across the room between Nick and the intruder.

The Hashashin took full advantage of the distraction and sprayed rounds at Nick's head, forcing him to dive back into the study. Bullets dug into the woodwork and thudded against the books on the shelves.

Lying prone on the floor, Nick rolled back into the open and emptied his clip at the shadow's head.

The curtain fluttered. Glass shattered. But if Nick so much as grazed the Hashashin, his enemy didn't show it, and now he had no more bullets, and nowhere to go.

The assassin dropped his smoking silencer ten degrees, adjusting for the lower target.

Before he could squeeze the trigger, a deafening report obliterated the quiet of the covert battle. The intruder's head exploded, spraying deep red across the glowing white curtain behind. The silhouette slowly sank to the foot of the window and melted into the inky black beneath the frame.

CHAPTER 51

Nick flipped on a standing lamp next to Rami's antique couch, and found the professor standing by the end table a few feet away, a fat, snub-nosed Colt revolver hanging loose from his fingers.

The assassin had crumpled into a bleeding heap below the window. This one wore a black balaclava over his face, but his leathers matched those of the riders Nick had encountered earlier. He guessed that the Hashashin's motorcycle was somewhere in the woods near the gate.

"I ran," said Rami quietly. "There was nothing I could do."

Nick crossed in front of the couch, took the .357 from the professor's hand and laid it on the table. "No, Rami. You didn't run. You turned and fought and you saved my life."

Rami looked over at Nick. Tears welled up in his eyes,

betraying the sorrow behind the steady calm of his voice. "Not you. Her. Myra. The life saved does not redeem the one lost."

He lowered himself onto the couch. "I never heard him come in. I never heard a thing. I told her to go to bed, call it a night, but she insisted on making me a sandwich. He was standing over her body when I came out of the study. He saw me. I ran."

"Who was she?" asked Nick, returning to the stairs and inspecting the open panel in the wall. It concealed a priest hole—a hidden room used to hide priests during England's anti-Catholic period. Rami had never shown it to him.

"I have to tell her mother."

Nick closed the panel and knelt next to the dead assassin. He pulled the sleeve up the left forearm. This one bore the double crescent-moon tattoo, the same as the sniper from Istanbul—a Hashashin bishop. "Rami, who was she?" he repeated, adding some command to his voice.

"A no one. A Copt, like me." Rami put his head into his hands. "One less in the world for the Islamists to hunt. Her mother is a friend. Myra lived here and worked as my aide. In exchange I paid her tuition."

The assassin's pockets offered Nick no more clues than the others. He carried only a knife and a burner phone with no records of calls made or received. Nick had to assume they checked in periodically. More Hashashin might already be on their way. Not to mention the cops. He tossed the phone on the dead man's lap and stood up. "Someone will have heard that shot. We have to get out of here."

"What about Myra?" asked Rami, lifting his head.

"The police will take care of her." Nick dragged the professor up from the couch by the arm. "Come on. We have to leave."

Rami pulled his arm away and headed into the study. "Wait. There's a book we must bring with us."

Nick and Rami left Cambridge in the professor's '65 MGB hardtop. The little green MG coupe had some pickup with a V8 under the hood, but there was no shoulder room. The claustrophobia Nick experienced in the team's rented Peugeot was nothing compared to this. "How do you drive this thing?" he asked, breaking a long silence. "I keep banging my knee with the gearshift."

"Jokes are not going to help."

"I'm sorry about Myra. I'm sorry I brought you into this."

Rami stared out his window at the empty fields passing by. "You did not slit her throat. She was killed by an extremist deceived by a false religion, and she will not be the last." The professor was quiet for another long stretch. Then he straightened in his seat and folded his arms. He smiled wanly. "I know the MG is small, but I like how she corners. Besides, not many cars will fit in my garage."

Drake was in and out of contact throughout the drive. Partly because he was keeping quiet as he evaded the police, and partly because he was moving in and out of the dead zone caused by Chaya's still active jammer. The good news was that the jammer also affected police communications in the area.

By the time they arrived in West Central London, Nick had not heard from his teammate for a good twenty minutes. At his last communication, he was near Warwick Square, a tiny park west of the flat, just beyond the police boundary. Nick planned to drive right in and grab him.

That proved easier said than done.

When he finally rolled to a stop next to the park, after a number of backtracks and reroutes thanks to the heightened police presence, he saw no sign of his teammate. Across the street, a single bobby walked along a line of three-story row houses, heading away from them, shining his flashlight on doorsteps and down into window wells. Ahead and slightly left, blue and yellow lights flashed through the park's trees. They could not wait here long.

"Stay here," said Nick, watching the bobby round the corner at the end of the block. "If anyone questions you, tell them you were my hostage."

"That hardly seems plausible." Rami pulled the front of his jacket aside, exposing the revolver tucked into his waistband.

Nick frowned. "Shove that in the glove box . . . if it will fit."

At that moment a pair of large hands slapped the passenger window, and the startled professor jerked the revolver out of his waistband. Nick grabbed Rami's wrist to steady him as Drake's face appeared outside the glass.

"We need to go," said the big operative, crawling

awkwardly into the back, his effort to squeeze into the tiny car pressing the professor up against the dash. As soon as he was in, Rami dropped his seat heavily back into position and slammed the door. "I almost shot you, young man."

Drake ignored him. "We need to go, now!"

Even as he spoke, a pair of high beams flashed on behind them.

CHAPTER 52

Nick cranked the engine and shoved the gearshift into first, his tires squealing as the MG lurched forward. Ahead, a police Saab raced backward into view with its lights flashing and screeched to a halt in the intersection, blocking their path. Nick kept his foot on the gas and tightened his grip on the steering wheel.

"You might want to fasten your seat belt, Professor," said Drake, though he could not do the same. He had to sit sideways in the tiny backseat.

Nick accelerated for another fraction of a second and then muscled the wheel hard over, counting on the MG's low center of gravity and the slick road to keep him from tipping over. His foot never came fully off the gas.

The little car reversed course nicely, and as soon as the tires found their grip again, Nick accelerated straight past the vehicle that had crept up behind them. "This is your town, Professor," he shouted over the blare of the sirens behind them. "What's the best way out of it?"

"Take Kings Road."

Nick squinted through the windshield, searching for street signs that were not there. "And that would be . . ."

"West! Head west as soon as you can!"

A cross street was coming up, but a pair of police motorcycles approached from the west, blocking Nick's intended path. He turned the other way.

"East it is," exclaimed Drake, gripping the seats as Nick fishtailed through the ninety-degree turn.

Nick's route was chosen for him at every turn as more police vehicles appeared at each intersection. He jinked right and left to avoid a pair of oncoming bikes, turned onto a straightaway, and ended up staring into the headlamps of a civilian Fiat. The driver beeped a puny horn and slammed on his brakes.

Rami pressed himself back into his seat rest. "Left side! We drive on the left side in this country!"

"Dumb rule," grunted Nick, swerving around the hatchback and pressing the accelerator to the floor. "Makes no sense at all."

"Nightmare One, this is Lighthouse," said Molly, coming up on the SATCOM. "I thought you might like to know the police intentionally steered you onto that straightaway. They laid down a spike strip."

A faint strip of black stretched across the road ahead. Without Molly's warning, Nick would have never seen it.

"Thanks."

He hit the brakes and skidded onto the only side street

available, a narrow road next to a redbrick cathedral. The closest of the three police Saabs on his tail shot by and hit the spikes. It slipped sideways out of control and crashed into a parked SUV. The other two made the turn, along with a pair of motorcycles.

At the other end of the church, the road took a sharp turn to the right, but Nick saw an opportunity. He cut left instead, taking advantage of the MG's sixty-inch width to squeeze between a set of barrier pylons and onto a small plaza, dotted with iron lampposts. The two Saabs skidded to a stop at the barriers, unable to squeeze through, but the motorcycles kept coming. They followed nimbly as Nick zigzagged through the pools of light beneath the lampposts and then shot through another set of pylons back onto the road.

The new street gently curved to the west. More flashing lights approached dead ahead, once again blocking Nick's intended path. As they drew closer, he saw that the new arrivals were BMW armed-response vehicles. That meant guns. He jerked the MG into another 180-degree turn, forcing one of the bikes off the road, and turned north up the first street he came to. The BMWs followed and closed the distance, outmatching the older car for speed and acceleration.

This new street opened ahead into a large square with a huge fountain at the center. White marble angels surrounded a pillar topped with two more angels of gleaming gold. Nick had to crank the wheel left to avoid crashing into it. At the moment of his abrupt turn, one of the armed pursuers opened fire. A marble wing cracked and slid off one of the angels, splashing into the fountain below.

"He's going to regret that," said Drake.

"Why does this look so familiar?" asked Nick, putting the MG into a drift around the fountain.

Drake tapped the left window. "Nine o'clock, moving to six."

Still fighting to maintain control, Nick shot a glance at the mirror and saw the massive stone edifice of Buckingham Palace looming behind them. "Oh. Right."

Undaunted by his previous destruction of history, the cop in the lead BMW fired again. Bullets plinked off the MG's bumper.

"Gotta get those beamers off our six, boss," said Drake, ducking below the leather.

"On it." On the other side of the fountain, Nick fishtailed out of his drift and took a low ramp up onto a pedestrian sidewalk into St. James Park. Again, the wider cars couldn't follow through the barriers—only the motorcycles, and those had trouble maneuvering around their skidding comrades.

Nick followed the sidewalk around the western end of the park's narrow lake and onto a long stretch through the trees along its southern shore. The speedometer topped 120. Rami dug his fingers into the two-tone leather seat, but the old Egyptian was smiling. "I knew these cars raced at Monte Carlo. I never thought I'd experience it firsthand."

The motorcycles appeared to their right, tracking across a long grassy field on the other side of the trees.

Nick ignored them. Thanks to the Brits' restrictive fire-arms policies, even for their police forces, the riders could do nothing but try and keep pace.

Halfway through the park, the sidewalk broadened into a wide pedestrian thoroughfare. Nick recognized his surroundings from a previous trip to London. "I know this area. This route leads straight out of the park onto King Charles. We can take Westminster Bridge south out of town. We can still make it."

"Don't count on it," said Molly through the SATCOM. "The Brits are blocking off the park exits right now. These guys are not idiots."

"Suggestions?"

"I have none. I can't see a way out."

As soon as the exit to King Charles came into view, Nick saw that Molly was right. The Brits had walled it off with water-filled Rhino barriers. Floodlights kicked on. A cop with a megaphone shouted for him to stop. He ignored the command, if only because of the pretentious accent.

Nick pulled left, cut through the grass, and overran a decorative wire fence to get onto the main walkway that surrounded the park. More blue and yellow lights appeared a hundred yards in front of them, more BMWs with armed bobbies.

Ahead and to the right was the sandy parade ground of London's famous horse guards, blocked off from the park by tightly spaced two-foot pylons. Bleachers were set up to the north and south for their Christmas demonstrations.

A spray of rounds plinked the hardtop right above Nick's head. Instinctively, he jerked the wheel right—too far to stay on the path. The MG broke through a free-standing aluminum fence and thundered up the wooden wheelchair ramp of the southern bleachers. It bounced over a bumper stop at the top and flew another fifteen meters before crashing down onto the sandy parade ground. All three men in the car let out a stunned *oof* as they bounced in their seats. To Nick's surprise, the MG kept going. He put it into a wide arcing drift, kicking up dust and searching for a way out. "I take back what I said, Rami. I love this car."

Rami was ghost white. "It's yours!"

Behind them, a motorcycle tried to follow. The rider held it together through the jump, but he was thrown from the bike as soon as it smacked down in the sand.

As Nick started his second loop, the cops on the thoroughfare spilled out of their BMWs and rested machine guns on the roofs.

"Incoming fire!" warned Drake.

The bobbies shot indiscriminately into the cloud surrounding the vehicle. Bullets slammed into the MG's hood and ricocheted off the top.

Through the rising dust, Nick scanned the castlelike stables on the other side of the grounds. They blocked the entire eastern side, from one set of bleachers to the other.

Drake lifted his head and peered out the window at the same problem. "No exit," he shouted.

"Then we'll have to make one."

Nick came out of his drift heading straight for the arch that bisected the stables, a passage forbidden to any vehicles but those bearing the monarch of Britain. A heavy iron gate blocked the exit to the street on the far side. He had no choice but to give it a shot.

He hit the gate square and centered, gritting his teeth through the jarring impact. The iron bars smashed the headlamps and fractured the windshield into a hundred spidery cracks, but the lock gave way and the MG made it through.

On the other side, Nick punched the gas, jumping the median and heading downhill toward the street that paralleled the Thames. Beyond a short stone barrier, the neon-blue reflection of the huge Millennium Wheel stretched across the calm black surface of the river. "They didn't see that coming," said Nick, chuckling. "The bridge is two blocks south. We're—"

He stopped in midsentence. His foot was on the brake, trying to slow for the ninety-degree turn at the riverbank. With each pump, the pedal went straight to the floor.

"Look out!" shouted Rami, but there was nothing Nick could do.

The MG jumped the curb, smashed through the stone fence, and pitched down into the muddy Thames.

PART THREE

ENDGAME

CHAPTER 53

"Nick!"

Katy called to him.

Her voice was muddled, distant. He saw her atop a shining limestone wall, spotted with tufts of green rock plant and studded with tiny prayer scrolls.

Jerusalem.

Katy was in Jerusalem. That was right, wasn't it? Nick had sent her there with his father. To keep her safe.

Suddenly Masih Kattan appeared next to her, holding Luke in his arms and smiling triumphantly. Katy's face twisted with fear as a wall of flame rose up before them. Nick's face burned from the heat. She screamed his name from beyond the fire.

"Nick!"

Nick awoke, staring at streams of water pouring in through cracks in the MG's windshield. His chest ached, a consequence of having it slammed into the seat belt when they hit the water. Gravity pulled him forward. The MG was vertical, heading for the bottom of the river. To his right, Rami was struggling with his seat belt.

Strong hands shook Nick by the shoulders. "Nick! Wake up!"

"I'm awake. Help Rami," he said to Drake, his voice weak at first but gaining strength.

While Nick fought with his own seat belt, he felt the jarring impact of the MG hitting the bottom of the Thames—twenty, maybe twenty-five feet down. The winter current carried the tail of the car sideways and it hung at a steep angle, dragging its crushed nose slowly through the silt.

Thanks to gravity, the murky brown water filled the front of the car first. It had already reached Nick's chest. "Rami, I need your revolver," said Nick.

"No, you don't," countered Drake. He held up the bobby's baton. "Whenever you're ready, boss."

Nick's seat belt finally came free. "Go," he ordered. "I've got the professor."

Drake smashed the butt of the baton into the window and the river took care of the rest, caving the whole thing into the backseat and gushing into the car. As the water passed his neck, Nick fished out the Hashashin knife. He pushed Rami's hands away from the belt and cut him free. "Come on!"

"One moment!" countered the Egyptian, his face up against the roof. To Nick's astonishment, the professor ducked down beneath the seat, hunting for something on the floorboards. He came up hugging a thick text, blinking in the murky water. The car was completely full.

Drake was already gone, and Nick pushed Rami out next. The professor's tenured academic midsection barely fit through, but he made it. Once outside the car, Nick could see blue and yellow police lights flashing above, their colors muted by the green-brown water. He held on to Rami's jacket from below, keeping the professor from surfacing, letting the current carry them away from the police. When the professor batted desperately at his hand, indicating that he couldn't hold his breath any longer, Nick counted another ten seconds and then let him go.

They surfaced near a small dock on the southeast side of the river, a good bit south of the flashing lights on the opposite shore. Nick tried to grab Rami under the arms and pull him toward the dock, but the Egyptian pushed him away. "I am not an invalid, Nicholas," he sputtered. "I can manage."

They found Drake lying on the dock in a prone position, his arms over the side ready to catch them. He pulled the professor up onto the composite planks first and then helped Nick. All the while, Rami held on to his prize. Dripping, he lay on his back, hugging the book to his chest.

"Must be a really good story," said Drake.

"You will be glad I brought it. For now though, we need shelter and warmth. And I know just the place." The Egyptian struggled to his feet and ran to the end of the dock, crouching like a professional operator.

Nick and Drake exchanged a look. Nick shrugged. "I guess we follow him."

Rami led them several blocks away from the river until they came to a nondescript glass-and-aluminum door in a row of joined office buildings—distinguished from the other doors in the row only by the small bronze plaque beside it. One-inch block lettering read COPTIC CHURCH OF SOUTH LONDON.

Rami reached out with a shivering hand and pressed a white button below the plaque. "Our resident priest Youssef is a heavy sleeper. I hope he hears the bell."

———

A half hour later, Nick peeled back a yellowed shower curtain in the church bathroom and found a stack of clothes on the counter next to his towel—worn khaki slacks, a blue button-down shirt, boxers and socks, even a pair of Adidas. When he finished dressing, he stepped out into a narrow hallway lit with the warm wash of yellow incandescent fixtures. Drake was seated on a folding chair outside the door, wearing a blue and white Hawaiian shirt and tweed slacks.

"The church has a clothing-and-food mission for the poor," he said. "Rami and Youssef raided the shelves to find clothes for us." He kicked his feet out from under the chair, displaying a pair of shiny, patent leather shoes.

"Those are nice," said Nick.

"They had a little trouble finding something in my size."

"We can't stay here. We have to get home. If CJ is

taking over this chase, she's going to need our help behind the scenes."

"And where will you go at one o'clock in the morning?" asked Rami, stepping out from a doorframe a short distance down the hall. "The police are at every corner, and they will be for the rest of the night." He handed each of them a steaming bowl of soup. It looked like porridge, but it smelled divine.

"Eat. Sleep. Regroup. You have chased the Hashashin nonstop for three days, and they are always two steps ahead. Perhaps you need to slow down in order to get out in front."

Nick was too exhausted to argue with his old professor. He could play along now and get moving again once he checked in with Romeo Seven.

The two operatives followed Rami to a room with several cots and sat down to eat their soup while the Egyptian disappeared to talk to Youssef. The soup tasted as good as it smelled—lentil bean with rosemary and thyme, and something sweet Nick could not identify.

While they ate, they let thoughts of Kattan and the bioweapon rest. They caught each other up on the events of the night, recalling the better parts of their fights and chases as if they were already faded memories.

By the time his bowl was empty, Nick no longer had the desire to race back out into the cold. He wanted sleep and nothing else. He laid out a pad on his cot, and the moment his head hit the vinyl cushion, the room faded into darkness.

CHAPTER 54

When Nick awoke, he found Rami and Drake in the room next door, poring over the professor's old book, still wet from its dunk in the river. He leaned against the doorframe and yawned. "How long have I been out?"

"Five hours," said Drake, glancing at the screen of his smartphone. "It's seven A.M."

Nick's eyes widened. He had intended to sleep for an hour, ninety minutes at the most.

Rami removed his spectacles and gave him a knowing smile. "How do you feel? Rested?"

"Woozy. What did you put in that soup besides beans?"

The professor waved his glasses in the air. "Oh, this and that. A few spices, some poppy-seed oil."

"Poppy seed. You drugged us?"

"I helped you get the rest you needed. I gave you the

same soup I eat to help with my insomnia. Poppy-seed oil is a common ingredient in Egyptian culinary arts."

"Opium?" Drake looked from Nick to the professor and back again. He pointed at his teammate. "If Walker has us do a urine test in the next two weeks, remind me to borrow a bottle of Molly's."

Nick closed his eyes and shook his head. "What are you two doing with that old book?"

The professor put his glasses back on and folded his hands together, tilting his knuckles toward his former student. "Don't take this the wrong way, Nicholas, but you have approached your entire mission the wrong way."

"Oh, here we go," said Nick, stepping deeper into the room. "Always grading my work. You and my father."

Rami shrugged. "What good is a teacher who doesn't teach or a father who doesn't parent?" He opened his hands and smiled. "You are dealing with the Hashashin, not al-Qaeda. The two organizations have overlapping ideology, but they are separated by nearly a millennium."

"So?"

"So you are an expert at combating *modern* terrorists. You depend on a decade of experience and success, but in reality you have never faced, much less defeated, a threat like the Hashashin." Rami patted the soggy pages of the text in front of him. "I propose that you consult the one man who has."

"Hulegu."

"You remember!" The professor clapped his hands together. "That is why you were always my favorite."

Nick shook his head. "Hulegu employed overwhelming

force. He stormed the Hashashin stronghold at Alamut with a hundred thousand Mongol warriors." He gestured at Drake with an open hand, tracking down from the worn Hawaiian shirt to the patent leather shoes. "All I have is him, and even if we could send in the Marines, we don't know where to send them."

"Ah." Rami raised a finger. "You are forgetting that Hulegu foiled multiple assassination attempts *before* he destroyed the Hashashin at Alamut. No one, not even the Sultan of Rum had stopped their assassinations before."

The professor motioned Nick closer, his movements quick, energized by academic discovery. "Look here. It is difficult to find amid the rabid self-glorification, but I believe Hulegu gives us the true key to his success." Rami placed a finger on the page and read in the voice of a pompous Mongol khan.

Having inherited the divine foresight of the eagles, I sent my informants into their houses of worship. For I had discerned by the wisdom granted to me by heaven that the Mohammedans do not separate their worship from their war. Rather, they worship through war, by what they call jihad. Within the domed shrines frequented by the Ismailis, my informants discovered a network of Hashashin outposts with tunnels, secret rooms, and armories. There they learned of the plots against my brother the Great Khan Möngke and my adviser Kitbuka. Thus I laid in wait for my enemies and by my own hand met them with divine retribution for their sins.

"The mosques?" offered Drake.

"Yes. Yes!" said Rami, slapping him on the back. "Unlike the crusaders, Hulegu understood the value of infiltrating the mosques rather than burning them, at least in the early stages. And unlike today's intelligence agencies, he did not concern himself with the political consequences of having a spy discovered in a mosque."

Nick nodded, staring down at the page. "Eight centuries ago Hulegu discovered the heart of Islamic insurgency. 'The Mohammedans do not separate their worship from their war,'" he read. " 'Rather, they worship through war.' Nothing has changed. Today's generals are just too politically correct to say it." He tapped the illustration of the mosque. "This should have been my starting point. Instead, I let Kattan lead me around by the nose."

Youssef entered from the hallway, interrupting their conversation. "It is time," he said solemnly.

The academic smile on Rami's lips faded. "You must excuse me for a while," he said, standing up and patting Nick on the shoulder. Then he and Youssef silently walked out of the room.

Nick's phone chimed. He checked the screen. A black box with ivory text told him *The Emissary has taken your rook. Your move.*

He frowned at the screen. The game was supposed to be over. CJ had captured the phone that sent Kattan's moves. Was one of her techs playing with the program? Before Nick could fully process the ramifications, the box disappeared, replaced by an incoming call—one of the secure hard lines at Romeo Seven. He checked his watch: two A.M., D.C. time. Not a good sign. He pressed the green square and put the phone to his ear. "I swear I didn't shoot the wing off that angel."

"Nick?" The voice was Doc Heldner's. "We've been trying to reach you on SATCOM."

"We had to shut down the earpieces and let them dry. Long story, but—"

"Nick, Romeo Seven has been penetrated," interrupted Heldner. "We're in lockdown."

CHAPTER 55

Nick turned on the phone's speaker and set it down on the damp pages of Hulegu's text. "Clarify."

Dr. Heldner's explanation was urgent, hurried. "Scott is back, but he's hurt. We don't know how, but someone or something got to him while he was at his workstation. When he arrived, I came in to give him the standard postmission workup. He was healthy, but he was agitated. He wanted to get to work on an assignment you gave him."

Nick nodded at the phone. "Cracking the Second Sign Virus."

"That's it. I told him to go home and rest, but he blew me off and went straight to a workstation in the command center. I went up to the Ivory Tower to talk to Dick. A few minutes later, Scott cried out as if something hit him. We looked down in time to see him crash to the floor.

Dick hit the panic button and put the bunker in lock-down."

"Intruders?" asked Nick.

"None. None that security could find, anyway. By the time I got to Scott, he was unresponsive. His eyes are open, staring. His symptoms present like a neurotoxin."

Drake shook his head. "No way. There's no way the Hashashin got past base security and got into Romeo Seven. Maybe they hit him with a dart or something before he got to the airport."

"A delayed response?" asked Heldner. "Not by seven hours. That's not how neurotoxins work. There has to be another solution. Scott is fading fast. He may already be losing brain function. Without knowing the specific poison, I can't administer an antidote. Nick, I'm going to lose him."

Nick squeezed his eyes shut. The game was on again, and Kattan had taken another piece—Scott. But how? None of them ever gave away the location of the apartment, not even to Chaya. The Hashashin had no way to poison Scott before or after he escaped London.

Unless one of Nick's own team had done it for them.

Unless he had done it himself.

"The thumb drive," he exclaimed through his teeth. "I gave him a thumb drive that Scotland Yard found at the site of the second terrorist attack."

On the speaker, they could hear the sound of Heldner rushing through Romeo Seven on her way from the clinic to the command center.

Nick bent closer to the phone, placing his hands on

either side of the book. "Look for a partially burned thumb drive at Scott's workstation, but be careful."

When she reached the workstation, Heldner found the thumb drive already plugged in to one of Scott's computers. She described micro-needles protruding from the top and bottom. "It's not a drive at all. It's a CO_2 injector. The electricity from the USB receptacle must have activated the charge. It hit him as soon as he plugged it in."

"Can you save him?" asked Drake.

"Maybe. If there's enough residual toxin for me to make a positive ID, I might find a suitable antidote." She paused and then added, "But at this point, I don't know if there's much of him left to save."

After the doctor hung up, Nick and Drake stared at the blank phone for several moments. Then Nick opened up the message from his chess application and showed it to Drake.

The big operative gave him a wary look. "May I assume we're not going home as ordered?"

"Can't," said Nick, pocketing the phone. "The game isn't over yet."

"But the thumb drive was supposed to be our next break. It's a bust. How do we chase him now?"

"We don't chase him. We head him off." Nick smoothed out the wet pages of Rami's book, tracing his fingers over the illustration of the ancient mosque. "We go to the one place we know Kattan will appear."

CHAPTER 56

In a small rental in Hillcrest Heights, south of the beltway, a young woman with big brown eyes and a sullen disposition was dragged out of bed by a phone call from her boss. Molly had only been off for a few hours, but Colonel Walker had reopened the chase.

The colonel declared this massive course reversal only minutes before, announcing his defiance of presidential orders from the top of his wrought-iron staircase with his most officious scowl in place. In attendance were two security guards and a SATCOM tech, the only three people on the command center floor at two o'clock in the morning. There would have been four, but the third security guard had gone to get coffee.

By way of justification, Walker cited self-defense. A longstanding American tradition held that military units always had the right to defend themselves when attacked, and one of Walker's people was just struck down within these very walls. Unacceptable. Whether the commander in chief liked it or not, the Triple Seven was back in. The colonel had walked thinner lines to circumvent more well-founded orders in the past. Besides, he had never liked this president anyway.

Fueled by the twenty-ounce nonfat mocha that met her at the door, pale skin glowing in the light of her four monitors, Molly set about the task of finding Kattan's mosque.

Immediately, she encountered the first barrier. There were more than 2,200 mosques, worship centers, Islamic institutes, and prayer rooms in the British Isles. The task of narrowing the field looked insurmountable.

"Confine your search to greater London," said Nick. Both operatives still stood at the desk with Rami's book, watching a transmission of Molly's screen on their phones.

The analyst followed Nick's command and her map zoomed in from all of Great Britain to London alone. Red dots appeared all over the city. "Three hundred fifty-four remaining, Nick. What else?"

"The Hashashin are an Ismaili sect. Eliminate all potentials without Ismaili affiliations."

Molly complied, and the red dots rapidly dropped away until only four remained. Suddenly the problem looked manageable.

She started digging. The largest of the four mosques—the Ismaili Center of London in Cromwell Gardens, dated back less than thirty years to 1985. The Ismaili Community Center in Croydon was founded in 1979, and the Institute of Ismaili Studies on Euston in 1977. The Ismaili Jamat-khana on Fleet Street—a stone's throw from the ancient Templar stronghold at Temple Church—dated back only a few years to 1990.

Drake frowned at his screen. "None of these are old enough. They're nothing like the thirteenth-century catacombs we saw in Ankara."

"Great Britain wasn't always the bastion of religious freedom it is today," said Nick, glancing up at his teammate. "We won't see any religious records for a mosque dating back more than a century, but it doesn't mean they weren't there. Molly, focus on the history of the structures themselves."

Their shared feed flickered through Molly's data searches. "The buildings at Cromwell Gardens and Croydon both were built on empty lots," said the analyst. "Prior to that, one lot was a park and the other was a square."

That left Euston and Fleet streets, and both appeared to have changed hands several times over the centuries. Prior to the great fire in the 1600s, the address on Fleet Street belonged to a shipping company, dealing exclusively in goods from the Ottoman Empire.

"Bingo," said Drake.

"Circumstantial," countered Nick. "If we keep digging, I'm sure we could find a Middle Eastern owner for the property on Euston at some time in its history." He sighed. "One of these two buildings was a mosque long before mosques were all the rage in London. We have no way to tell which."

"Oh! I do." Molly sputtered the proclamation, like she was halfway through a sip of coffee when she made it.

Nick's screen flashed, and the subterranean-utility plans for both structures appeared side by side. On top of these, Molly laid in the city utilities—electric on top of gas on top of sewage—and then she rendered them all in 3D. Finally, she reversed the image, eliminating everything but the dead space to produce a ghost footprint.

"Oh, she's good," said Nick, smiling at Drake. By seeking dead space, Molly had just produced a map of the earliest stone foundations for each structure.

The stonework beneath the Euston mosque was shaped like a simple unadorned wedge, slightly askew from the current building. The Jamatkhana on Fleet Street, however, still matched its original footprint, down to a bulbous protrusion on the southeast corner of the building.

"That's it. The *mihrab* is still there in the ancient footprint." Nick tapped the picture of the protrusion, centering all their screens on that section of the structure. The mihrab was a niche that pointed the way to Mecca, a telltale sign of a mosque.

"If my footprint is correct," said Molly, "this building on Fleet Street was serving as a mosque for several centuries before it was officially declared a Jamatkhana. I think we found London's Hashashin stronghold."

———

They had no weapons, save for Nick's Hashashin knife. Rami's .357 and the Vector submachine gun were both at the bottom of the Thames, and Walker had no way to smuggle guns to them within any reasonable time frame.

On the bright side, their clothes had dried, and Nick was happy to return the hand-me-downs to the church clothing bank. Drake opted to keep the blue and white Hawaiian shirt. He called it a one-in-a-million find and promised Nick that he would send Youssef a check that more than covered it.

The plan was to hot-wire a car, but neither wanted to set out without first saying good-bye to Rami and offering their thanks to Youssef. They walked the narrow hall until they came to the church's small sanctuary. Here, the flooring between the two stories had been removed to make space for a traditional arched ceiling and a ten-foot-tall stained-glass window. The bright light of the rising sun shone through a depiction of Christ suffering on the cross, casting multicolored beams down on the mournful trio at the altar below.

Rami and a frail woman of the same age knelt on stools facing each other, heads bowed. Tears flowed freely down from eyes closed in prayer. Youssef stood over them, a hand on each of their shoulders, his eyes lifted to heaven and his mouth moving in quiet supplication. After a few moments, the priest lowered his head and whispered some unheard encouragement. Then he stood and raised them to their feet.

The woman left the altar first. Nick knew who she was—the mother of the girl he had left in a pool of blood in Rami's hall, the girl whose body he had shunted aside with Rami's door out of cold tactical necessity. He suddenly had the urge to fall at the mother's feet, to beg her forgiveness for letting her daughter pay the price for the father he had killed, but his knees wouldn't bend.

She stopped when she reached him and looked up, and in her swollen eyes, he saw the forgiveness he had not found the strength to ask for. She clasped his hands, patting them softly, and offered a brokenhearted smile. She did the same for Drake. Then she walked deliberately, step by step, into the hall.

Rami waited until she had gone and then turned to the two operatives. "You found it?" he asked, wiping his eyes with a handkerchief. "The stronghold you were looking for?"

Nick nodded. "The Jamatkhana on Fleet Street. It's very close to Paternoster Square, an ideal staging point."

"Then I'm coming with you."

"Out of the question."

"You've already done enough," added Drake.

The professor pursed his lips. "I see. I suppose that means you plan to sit outside the mosque and wait for Kattan to appear, because you must realize that two big white men will not get past the front door."

"And you can?"

Rami nodded.

Drake cocked his head. "This doesn't have anything to do with a plot to avenge the girl, does it?"

"That is in the past now," the professor assured him, slowly shaking his head.

Nick glanced down. His skin still remembered the soft press of that frail woman's hands, hands that would never hold her daughter again. He looked back up at Rami. "Maybe for you."

CHAPTER 57

Israel
The Hebrew University of Jerusalem

The applause wasn't exactly thunderous, but at least they were still awake.

As the lights came up, Dr. Kurt Baron smiled and gave a modest nod to the clapping students, scattered among the rising rows of seats like scrub dotting a rocky mountainside.

Avi Bendayan applauded too as he strode out onto the stage. "One moment," he called, beckoning to the students who were heading for the doors. "One moment, please. As this is the last installment of Dr. Baron's series, we must take a few extra minutes to bid him farewell."

The Israeli professor produced a plaque from under his arm and presented it to Kurt—the usual fare, a shining blue aluminum plate set on a piece of cherrywood, laser-etched with the school emblem and a word of thanks. There was also a scripture from the Talmud—Bemidbar

6:24–26. The two shook hands amid a final smattering of applause.

"Any chance of getting some brunch together?" asked Kurt, shutting down his laptop as the students filed out.

Avi sat down on a stool next to the lectern. "That would be nice, wouldn't it? But I'm afraid I have a class next hour, and I'm booked solid for the rest of the day. What about dinner?"

"Can't. My daughter-in-law got us reservations for a dinner theater for our final night in Jerusalem. Comedy with a Hasidic Jew or something."

"Ah, yes," said Avi. "You brought young Nick's wife along. How is she working out?"

Kurt slid his laptop into his leather portfolio and smiled. "This is the most time we've spent together since the two of them were married. She's grown strong, Avi. Much stronger than I would have guessed."

"As do they all once they have weathered a few of life's storms." Avi lightly slapped his knees and stood. "Well. This is it, my old friend. You are here, and then you are gone. You'd think we would have remembered to schedule a dinner together."

Kurt followed Avi down the stairs from the stage. "We're old men now. We're lucky if we remember our keys when we leave the house." He stopped at the base of the steps. "Speaking of forgetting. I never thanked you for bringing me out here."

"You're most welcome." Avi patted him on the shoulder. "I must apologize for taking so long to extend the invitation. It was long overdue. Had it not been for the hint in your last letter, I might never have realized my oversight."

Confusion clouded the older Baron's face. "My hint?" He and Avi maintained a tradition of writing pen-and-paper letters to each other every few months. But Kurt would never dream of dropping a hint that he wanted to come speak at the university. His sense of propriety forbade it.

His hesitation caused the smile to slowly fade from Avi's face.

Then again, Kurt decided, maybe his subconscious desires had overcome his sense of propriety. "Of course," he said, playing down his confusion. "My hint. Well, we absentminded professors need to help each other along sometimes." He winked at his old friend. "What was it the old rabbi said would be the first sign of old age?"

Avi hesitated a moment and then grinned and winked back. "I don't remember."

They laughed as they climbed the carpeted steps between the rows of seats. At the top, they stepped through double doors into a sunlit hallway. "You know," said Avi. "Your flight is not until the afternoon. How about an early breakfast in the courtyard at the American Colony, just like when we were students? The sunrise, a little scripture. For once we could both forget that we're old men, rather than forgetting our keys. Say, six thirty?"

Kurt smiled. "Six thirty it is."

Out on the university plaza, a young man in black jeans and a faded black T-shirt left the shade of a bushy olive tree and fell in step behind the American professor. The kid placed one earbud of his iPhone headset in his right ear and bobbed his head, moving his lips as if singing along to the music. He spoke so softly that none of the students passing him could hear. Even if they had, they could not have understood the unique conglomeration of Turkish and Farsi that he spoke.

"Position Two, we are on our way. Target is ten meters ahead of me, west side."

"Position Two copies. Leaving now," replied a voice in his earbud.

The American entered a narrow walkway, shielded from the desert sun by more olive trees and thin towering cypress. Ahead of him, another young man came into view, strolling in the opposite direction. This one, bearded and wearing a yarmulke, had his head buried in a thick black book. He seemed so absorbed in his studies that he did not notice his path drifting toward the oncoming professor.

The two collided, not hard enough to knock the American off the walkway and into the trees, but enough to give him a good jolt and knock the student's book from his hands. The kid apologized in Hebrew as he scooped up the book, keeping his eyes low and patting the professor's arm. The professor assured him he was all right, also in Hebrew, though his pupils drifted slightly up and right as he searched for the proper words. The student patted his arm once more and then continued on his way.

The professor paused and smiled, watching the young man go. As he did, the kid in the black jeans passed in front of him and kept walking along his original path, still bobbing his head to the imaginary music. He continued in this manner down a sidewalk until he reached a beat-up green Mazda RX-7. The moment he plopped into the driver's seat, his cell phone rang.

"Is it done?"

"Yes, Emissary. We planted the device in his portfolio, the one that never leaves his side."

"Excellent. His son will try to call him soon, but from this moment on, Dr. Baron will only receive and transmit the communications that we allow."

"Emissary," said the young man, his tone cautious, "the battery will not last much longer than twenty-four hours."

"Do not worry, young one. I have seen Armageddon, and it will come much sooner than that."

CHAPTER 58

Youssef offered up the use of his car, a white VW Golf from the early nineties. Nick protested, warned him he might never get it back, but the priest gave it anyway.

The drive across the Thames to Fleet Street was uneventful. The bobbies were still out in good numbers, but there were no checkpoints blocking the roads. Nick anticipated as much. A big city in a free society could not sustain checkpoints through rush hour. That could be a blessing or a curse, depending on which side you were playing for on a given day. This morning it was a blessing.

"The Jamatkhana is on the southeast corner of White-friars and Fleet," said Drake, hanging over the seats between Nick and Rami and flicking his finger across his phone. "Satellite photos show a courtyard behind the building, blocked in by the surrounding structures. Exits from the courtyard are to the north and west, with additional escape routes through the buildings on each side." He spread his fingers on the screen, zooming in. "I can see only one door from the mosque to the courtyard. Blocking that will effectively plug all those leaks."

"Plug away. You watch the back door. Rami and I will go in through the front."

They parked two blocks south and a block east in a garage off Victoria Embankment. The Hashashin would have lookouts who knew their faces, and Nick did not want to spook Kattan. But when the three of them turned the corner onto Whitefriars on foot, Nick got the feeling that lookouts didn't matter anymore. Up ahead, men in white *taqiyah* skullcaps poured by ones and twos out of the western entrance to the mosque's hidden courtyard.

"Uh-oh," said Drake.

Nick quickened his pace. Then a gunshot rang out. He started running. "We're too late! Come on!"

As they raced up to the archway, Nick motioned Drake and Rami to head around front, and then he fought his way through the fleeing crowd. The courtyard was divided into two sections by a low fence that ran right up to the double glass doors of the inner mosque. A smaller group of women in colorful *hijab* head scarves fled through the northern archway on the other side of the fence. Men still trapped in the courtyard by the bottleneck on their side jumped the fence and knocked some of the women down to get at the less crowded exit.

Once Nick was in the courtyard, getting through the glass doors into the mosque presented no problem. The interior had already cleared and nobody else wanted to get inside. As soon as Nick burst through the door, a short man in a suit and a gold-and-white *taqiyah* charged him, wagging his finger and chattering in a familiar but unintelligible Turkic dialect. Nick brushed past him, searching for the source of the gunshots.

Aside from a lectern near the rounded protrusion of the mihrab, most of the interior prayer room was wide-open space—green and gray carpet beneath a low ceiling, lit by six octagonal skylights that cut through the three floors above. Nick saw no sign of the shooter, and no cover where he might be hiding. He thought the room was empty except for the chattering imam, until he saw the shooter's victim lying on the floor.

A sporadic trail of dark spots led from a door in the western wall to the center of the room, where Dr. Maharani lay at the intersection of two circles of sunlight, bleeding out into the cheap industrial carpet.

"Kattan was here," said Nick as Drake and Rami appeared. "He fled the scene. Find him!"

The big operative turned back toward the front door. "On it!"

The imam stayed right at Nick's shoulder as he crossed the room to Maharani, still chattering away. Nick pushed him away, shouting, "Call an ambulance!" But the little man kept coming. With the imam ranting in one ear and Drake calling for satellite support in the other, Nick crouched over the fallen scientist. "Where is it?" he demanded, grabbing Maharani by his bloody shirt. "Where is the bioweapon?"

Maharani stared up at him with wild eyes. "Smallpox," he gasped. "Hemorrhagic. Resilient form."

Nick raised him off the floor by his shirt. "Listen to my question! *Where* is it?"

"Gone. Courier came . . . last night. My daughter . . . in danger."

Maharani didn't know his daughter had worked for the Hashashin. "Your daughter is safe," Nick lied, softening his tone. "Where is Kattan?"

Maharani's lips were turning blue. "He kept me here to make a vaccine. He . . . took it with him. Formula . . . on the computer . . . downstairs."

"Stay with him. I'll get it," said Rami.

"Delivery method!" demanded Nick, trying to get anything he could out of the doctor before he faded completely.

Maharani's eyes fluttered closed, "My . . . daughter . . . "

"I told you. Your daughter is fine," said Nick, slapping the biochemist's cheek to wake him up.

The doctor's eyes opened. "D . . . C . . . " Then his pupils lost their focus. With his last desperate breaths he made W sounds, trying to form a word that never came.

Drake reported in. "We've got nothing on satellite or the street cams. Kattan is gone."

Nick laid the lifeless Maharani down on the carpet. Then he turned on the chattering imam. "I know you speak English, you little—"

A blast ripped through the mosque. Smoke billowed out from the stairwell where Rami had descended.

Forgetting the babbling imam, Nick rushed into the choking cloud. "Rami! Rami, where are you?"

The carnage that greeted him when he reached the base of the stairs was too much for Nick to take. His eyes burned, but forcing them open, he saw that the blast in the confined space had been devastating. There was no broken body, no graceful, silent form like the girl the night before. There was nothing left of his friend and mentor but small, half-recognizable pieces.

Nick trudged back up the stairs, numb. Halfway to the top, his phone chimed. With a shaking hand, he checked the screen. The ivory letters in the black box taunted him.

The Emissary has taken your bishop. Your move.

CHAPTER 59

Nick emerged from the stairwell in a trance, the walking dead. Visual and auditory cues could not make it through the wall barring the way to his conscious mind.

The little imam met him at the top of the steps and resumed his barrage of unintelligible chatter. He fell in step, right at Nick's shoulder, completely oblivious to his own peril.

In his semiconscious state, Nick could not hear the grating buzz of the imam's chatter nor see the constant wagging of his finger. He might not have noticed him at all, despite the little man's complete disregard for the sanctity of personal space, but then the imam took hold of his arm.

The reaction was instantaneous and supremely violent. Nick came out of his trance with an angry roar, lifting the imam off the carpet by the lapels of his jacket and slamming him into the wall so hard that his shoulder blades broke through the drywall. The *taqiyah* skullcap fell to the floor. "You permitted this!" Nick shouted. "You hid the devil in your church, and now you're going to pay!"

The shock at Nick's sudden outburst quickly wore off, and the imam's surprised expression melted into a sneer. "The signs of the Mahdi are preordained," he said in perfect English. "You cannot stop his coming." Then he spat in Nick's face.

Nick let out another roar and hauled back his fist, but a strong hand caught his arm before he let the punch fly.

"We have to get out of here," said Drake.

The sound of sirens and screeching tires close at hand broke through the wall in Nick's senses, but he refused to let go of the imam. He dragged him across the prayer room by his collar instead. A growing crowd of bobbies pounded on the front door. Drake had thrown the dead bolts to keep them at bay.

"Leave him!" called Drake holding the courtyard door open.

"No! He's one of them!"

The little imp screamed and flailed and dug his heels into the carpet like a stubborn child. Then he gained his feet and managed to turn and bite Nick's wrist, digging his teeth deep into his flesh. Nick let out a guttural cry and let go. The imam ran toward the door and the policemen. Drake grabbed Nick's arm and pulled him out the opposite side.

The next sixty seconds were a blur. Nick saw little besides Drake's broad back ahead of him—an iron gate kicked in, flashes of cobblestone and pavement, a narrow street and a honking horn. There was a short tunnel of gray stone and then sunlight again and a crumbling cherub above a pair of tall oak doors, cracked and weathered. One of the doors opened and Drake pulled him onward, until he dragged him down a set of worn stone steps into darkness.

The two of them stood panting side by side in the gloom for a few seconds, and then Nick exploded.

"Get away from me!" He shoved Drake backward into the shadows beyond the foot of the stairs. The big operative fell against the opposite wall and something shifted in the dark. Stone ground against stone.

Drake recovered his balance, pushing off the object and holding out his palms. "Take it easy, boss."

Nick did not heed the warning. "I said, get away!" He lunged at his teammate, throwing a right hook at the face he could barely see.

Drake raised his forearms to block the right as well as the left that followed. Then he wrapped Nick in a clinch and held him fast, his big hands pressing down on the back of Nick's skull.

Nick struggled to free himself, driving uppercuts into Drake's ribs, but his teammate only grunted and tightened his iron grip.

"He's gone, boss," wheezed Drake, clearly pained by the blows. "Come on. Pull it together."

After a few seconds, Nick stopped swinging and Drake relaxed his grip. Nick jerked himself free. He let out an angry scream that echoed in the chamber. "Don't you get it? I can't beat him. This game ends with me dead. There's no other outcome, and anyone who stands with me is a target." He pressed his phone into Drake's face to show him the list of messages from the chess app. "First Quinn, then Scott, and now Rami. Kattan has anticipated every move." He shook his head. "No, he's shaping the moves, working me like a puppet. This whole thing is just another game of chess to him, and he's picking off my pieces one by one."

Nick sat down on the steps and hung his head, lowering his voice. "Go home. Or go see your cousins in California, I don't care. Just get away from me. If you don't, you *will* be the next piece to fall, and there's nothing I can do to stop it."

Drake sat down next to his teammate. He leaned back and rested his elbows on the steps. "You done?"

Nick breathed heavily for a few moments and then leaned back too, tilting his head back into the light that tumbled down the stairs from the church above. "Yeah, I'm done."

During their few minutes in the subterranean chamber, Nick's eyes had grown accustomed to the dark. He glanced around. Long shelves were carved out of the far wall and the wall to their right, and each shelf held a stone coffin. This was a crypt beneath an old church in the heart of London. A coffin on the far wall had shifted when

Drake bumped into it, likely the only action the corpse had seen for centuries.

"How did he do it?" asked Drake, staring up at the ceiling. "I mean, I get that he used the knife to get us to Ankara, and he lured us to Paternoster Square with the security cams, but the mosque was our idea. How did he know we were going to be there?"

Nick didn't answer for a few seconds. Then he turned and looked at his friend. "You ever hear of Dynamic Evaluation Lookahead?"

Drake shook his head. "Sounds complicated."

"It's not. We all use it. DEL is our ability to predict outcomes, anything from catching a pop fly to knowing it's a bad idea to tell a girl that her butt looks big in those jeans."

Drake smiled to see Nick's sense of humor returning. "And chess," he offered.

Nick sat up and let out a long breath. "Right. Chess. That's the most common example. People with a natural ability to see outcomes tend to be good at chess. A grand master may be one person in every five million. Then you've got your top quarterbacks and your superinvestors. Now we're talking one person in a hundred million. The top day traders in that group can see complex outcomes hours in advance."

"Hours?" said Drake. "Kattan had our moves laid out *days* in advance. How many people can do that?"

Nick closed his eyes. "One person in a billion—one in two billion. Something like this has never been documented. I think Masih Kattan can predict outcomes on a level the world has never seen."

"So you really can't beat him."

"No, I can't." Nick settled back and looked up into the light again. "But I still have to try."

CHAPTER 60

Canada, 20 miles south of Montreal

Samir Abbas slowed his aging Chevy delivery truck to a stop on a snow-packed side road, hidden in the trees off Canadian Route 15. He let the motor idle, kept the doors locked, and did not turn off the headlights. This seemed an especially creepy spot to meet his cargo, but under the circumstances he could see why it was necessary.

Sammy's Vegetables—that's what it said on the side of the truck—usually dealt in peppers, tomatoes, and squash of several types. Usually. On this trip up to Montreal, Samir had already delivered his cargo of fresh produce to the small groceries on his docket. At this point he would normally return to his greenhouse in Warrensburg, New York, with an empty truck, but not today. On this trip, Samir would bring something back across the border.

The imam had made it clear that this favor constituted

a holy deed of charity—a valuable commodity for an imperfect Muslim. At sixty-one, Samir had never made the hajj, and he could not fathom how he would meet this obligation before he died. How many vegetable farmers could afford to go all the way to Mecca? Without the hajj, and with a less-than-ideal record of *jum'ah* prayer at the mosque, where did that leave him on Allah's scales? Certainly, helping a young student at the behest of his imam might tip the balance in his favor.

Samir jumped at the startling sound of a fist pounding on his passenger door. He clutched his chest and leaned over to peer out the window. The face that stared back at him through the glass looked innocent enough, and young. The kid could not have been more than twenty, wearing a parka that dwarfed his stick-figure neck and blue jeans that hung from his waist like curtains.

Samir pushed open the door and smiled. "You must be Mahmoud." He held out a hand to help the young man climb into the cab. "And you must be freezing."

"Shukran jazilan," said Mahmoud, climbing up and setting his backpack on the floor. He pulled the passenger door closed and rubbed his hands together in front of the heating vent. "Before this trip, I had never left Egypt. I never imagined such a cold."

Samir glanced over at Mahmoud's bare hands and down at his soaked tennis shoes. He suddenly worried that this cargo might not survive the journey south. He pulled off his gloves and pressed them into the young man's hands. "You are underdressed. You will need these. I would give you my boots but I must get out at the border, and how would that look? Me in my socks?" He tilted his head back toward the box trailer. "You must make the trip back there. The border guards that work the grave-yard shift know me well, and they no longer bother to ask me for identification, but they would certainly ask for yours."

After Mahmoud thawed out a bit, Samir led him to the back. He eyed the backpack slung over Mahmoud's shoulder. "Is that all you've brought for a new life in America?"

"I have family in New York. They will provide all that I need. *Insha'Allah*."

"*Insha'Allah*," agreed Samir.

Mahmoud shifted his feet on the packed snow as Samir unlocked the roller door. "What if the border guards ask to look in the back?"

"They won't." Samir raised the door halfway and shined a flashlight into the cargo space. There was a stack of blue plastic crates at the front end. "If they do, just hide behind those. There are blankets as well. Wrap your-self up." He shined the flashlight on Mahmoud's feet and chuckled. "And when you are settled, take off those shoes. Better to wrap your feet in a blanket than leave them soaking in ice water."

As Mahmoud climbed into the back, his parka rode up, exposing the black grip of a compact automatic tucked into his waistband.

Samir's heart skipped a beat. He saw the officers who manned the border station more often than he saw his cousins in Albany. They were practically family. What fool had given this child a gun? "Please," he said, trying not to let on that he had seen the weapon. "Stay calm when we reach the border. As I said, they will not check in here."

Mahmoud turned to face him and set his bag down behind the crates. In the half light at the edge of the flashlight's beam, the boy's face looked much older than it had before. *"Insha'Allah,"* he said.

Samir nodded, lowering the flashlight for fear that Mahmoud would see his hand shaking. "Yes. *Insha'Allah*."

CHAPTER 61

United Kingdom
Farnborough Airfield

Nick picked his way through the network of airport roads toward the back of the airfield. The colonel had come through with an exfiltration plan using a fly-by-night CIA cargo operation. Nick didn't relish riding on today's version of Air America, but at this point, he was grateful for anything that would get him out of England.

On the way to Farnborough he had briefed Walker, going over every detail of the failure at the mosque and Kattan's disappearance with the vaccine. He also got an update from Heldner on his stricken team members.

Scott was stable, but in a medically induced coma. The doctor would not know the extent of the damage to his brain and nervous system until she brought him out of it and, for the moment, she was unwilling to do so. Quinn, on the other hand, had become the bane of her existence.

Forty-eight hours after having his stomach ripped open and his guts jumbled around in the back of a cargo jet, he thought he was ready to get back in the game. While Drake chuckled in the background, Nick advised Heldner to take the kid off his morphine. Removing Quinn's pain medication was a sure way to temper his youthful delusions of invincibility.

There were two nondescript cars in the gravel lot next to the CIA hangar. The once-white walls were stained red and brown with rust. Peeling white lettering on the glass door to the office read AIRDROP INC., WORLDWIDE CARGO SERVICES.

"Only slightly less obvious than Air America," said Drake, shaking his head.

The full-length blinds on the other side of the door were drawn. The window blinds were drawn as well, bent and dusty, with cobwebs and bugs pressed up against the tinted glass. Nick pushed the yellowed button on the doorbell. "Doesn't exactly inspire confidence, does it?"

They heard no sound, but a few seconds later, a thumb and forefinger spread the blinds apart at eye level, held them for a moment, and then disappeared. A dead bolt clicked back and the door cracked open. "Name?"

"Art Vandelay," said Drake without missing a beat.

The door cracked slightly wider and a long suppressor jutted out.

Nick frowned at his teammate. "Fryers," he said, using the name Walker had given him. "Eddie Fryers."

The blinds banged uncomfortably against the door as

a sandy-haired CIA agent with leathery features pushed it open and nodded for Nick and Drake to enter.

The office was mostly faux-wood paneling and dingy Formica countertops, dimly lit by a single incandescent bulb with no shade. This place had probably been in the Agency's hands since the eighties, and it appeared they had never redecorated. Or dusted. Nick wondered if the spooks put the same level of care into the aircraft that was about to carry him across the Atlantic.

An old cathode-ray-tube TV sat on the counter, tuned to the local news. The impish imam from Fleet Street stood in front of his damaged mosque with a reporter. There was a picture of Rami in the corner of the screen and a headline across the top that declared COPTIC RADICAL DIES IN SUICIDE ATTACK. The imam looked deeply saddened. "This man shot one of my congregation and blew himself up in our place of worship," he told the reporter. "I do not know what could have motivated his attack other than irrational hatred of Islam."

Nick angrily punched off the set, nearly knocking it off the counter.

"Easy, tiger," said the agent. "That's an antique. And we like to keep it on . . . for the ambiance." He pulled the switch out, turning it on again, but the coverage had moved on to the impending total eclipse in Israel.

The group turned to a beat-up metal door, and the agent shifted a gun to his back to punch a code into its cipher lock. "We don't normally take in strays," he said. "Especially strays wanted by Scotland Yard, but my boss owes your boss a favor." He pulled the door open. "Let me show you gentlemen to your ride."

The agent motioned Nick to go ahead, and he stepped over the threshold into a completely different world—stark white walls lit by powerful induction lights, a spotless gloss floor studded with an in-floor fire suppression system. Apparently the money saved on office furniture and cleaning supplies had been invested in the hangar.

Their ride, as the agent put it, took up most of the floor space. She was a C-27 Spartan, a miniaturized version of a C-130 Hercules with only two propellers instead of four. The whole aircraft was painted slate gray with no tail flash or lettering.

Drake surveyed the cargo plane with a skeptical eye. "A trash hauler? That's our exfiltration plan?"

"Oh, she's a little more complex than your run-of-the-mill trash hauler," said the agent, pulling the door closed behind them.

Nick winced. He was in a hurry, and this cargo plane didn't exactly scream speed. "How long will your prop job take to get us back to D.C.? Does it have the legs, or do we have to stop for gas in Iceland?"

The agent looked at him sideways. "D.C.? My orders are to take you to Cairo."

————

As the Spartan climbed through ten thousand feet, the sandy-haired agent nodded to his copilot and got up from his seat. He passed between Nick and Drake, motioning for the two of them to unstrap from their webbed seats and follow him to the next bulkhead. "Like I told you," he said, pausing at the door and raising his voice over the pulsating thrum of the huge propellors outside, "this baby is a little more complex than your average trash hauler."

They passed through into what should have been the cargo bay. Instead, they found a high-tech command center. The walls were baffled with black foam, so that the din of the engines faded to a low hum as soon as the agent closed the bulkhead door behind them. A ninety-four-inch screen, convex like an IMAX, dominated the right wall, and two short rows of black leather seats were set in front of it, each with a trackball and data-entry panel on one arm.

"Welcome to the EACC," said the agent. "The CIA's European Airborne Command Center. We can communicate with Langley from anywhere, and we have extra fuel bladders in the back for extended range and loiter time. At this point, I should remind you that you never saw any of this . . . or me. Of course, I never saw you either, so I guess we're even."

"You guys play Call of Duty on that screen, don't you?" asked Drake, nudging the agent. "Come on, you can tell me."

Nick took a seat in the center chair and eyed the controls. "How do we connect to our headquarters in D.C.?"

"Already done." The agent pressed a green button on a wall pad, and the huge monitor flickered to life. Walker's crew-cut head filled the screen from top to bottom. He was turned to the side, scowling at some unfortunate tech offscreen. "Are they up yet?" There was a muffled response, and then the colonel's right eye, big as a cantaloupe, shifted toward the monitor. The scowl turned to follow.

"Baron!"

Drake jumped at the greeting. Then he bent down close to Nick's ear. "Now I know why the cowardly lion ran away."

"I heard that, Merigold."

"Sir, why are we going to Cairo?" asked Nick.

Walker mercifully backed away from the monitor. "I'll let Molly explain."

The analyst rolled into the shot on a desk chair, clutching a large coffee cup in her small hand. "Do you recognize this man?" she asked, clicking the keyboard.

A head shot appeared on the left side of the screen, an older Middle Eastern man sporting a Hitler-esque mustache and a slicked-back dome of white hair.

Nick nodded. "Ahmad Kushal Wahish. The Pakistani death merchant. He's a physicist, used by Pakistani ISI to pass nuclear-weapons technology to rogue nations."

"Wahish is wanted by international agencies for proliferation crimes," added Drake. "He can't leave Pakistan."

"Except, he *did* leave Pakistan," said Molly.

Another picture flashed up on the right side of the big screen. It was shot from a distance. Wahish was standing at the foot of an old watchtower, next to a younger man with a shaved head. The younger man's face was less distinct, but it was clear enough.

"Kattan," said Nick, spitting out the name.

Molly bobbled her head. "Most likely, but not definite. We have a seventy-percent match. This was taken in Cairo two days ago by the GIS, the Egyptian General Intelligence Service."

"Is the GIS cooperating with us?" asked Drake.

"Not exactly." Walker bent down over Molly's shoulder to look into the camera. "A CIA infiltration bot stole that picture from their classified network. It was uploaded less than an hour ago with a surveillance file. It looks like the GIS has been tracking Wahish but staying out of his way. He hasn't left that location in forty-eight hours."

"So we know Wahish is there," mused Nick, "but Kattan can't—"

"There's more," interrupted Molly. "CJ went back over the evidence like you asked, searching for a link to the fourth sign—the rising smoke and the sky of molten brass. She learned that lithium-six has another use. It acts as a multiplier in a nuclear package." Molly took a nervous sip of her coffee and set the cup down offscreen. "We're talking a massive expansion of nuclear yield, the difference between a suitcase nuke and Hiroshima. Such a modification takes serious expertise, but Wahish is a serious expert."

Walker bent down into the screen again, his scowl as dark as ever. "The pieces fit, gentlemen. We may not know where Kattan is, but we know his nuclear weapon is in Cairo."

CHAPTER 62

The C-27 Spartan droned across northern France at 23,000 feet. On the screen in its small command center, Colonel Walker was adamant. "I have CJ and her task force to help me chase down the virus. You boys need to find that nuke in Cairo before Kattan decides to take out the pyramids."

Nick was staring at the floor, his features compressed in concentration. Suddenly he slapped the armrests and stood up, shaking his head. "No. It's too easy."

"Baron . . ." said Walker with a warning tone.

Nick gestured at the picture of Wahish and Kattan. "Sir, Kattan wanted us to see this, and he wanted us to see it at this exact moment. He's doing it again, shaping our moves, keeping us a step behind." He shook his head again. "No. I'm not doing it. We have to break the cycle, jump ahead to the target."

"And how do we know where that is?" asked Drake.

Nick glanced over his shoulder at his teammate. "The Hashashin already told us, the early Hashashin, the ones who etched those inscriptions in the catacombs eight hundred years ago." He pointed through the screen at the analyst. "Molly, bring up the translation of the prophecies."

The stanzas that Nick found in the catacombs replaced the picture of Wahish on the left side of the screen. "There," he said, gesturing to the first half of the fourth stanza. " 'A great smoke will rise up from the center of the world.' Kattan's legitimacy with this group depends on his staying true to their ancient prophecies. All we have to do is figure out where the early Hashashin thought the center of the world was."

The colonel's scowl took on a scornful twist. "Right. All we have to do is read the minds of the dead assassins."

"Mecca," offered Drake. "That's the center of the Muslim world."

Nick furrowed his brow. "I don't think Mecca is the target. Of all the hadiths about the end times that I've heard, none of them mentions Allah's judgment against Muslims. It's always the unbelievers and the Jews—"

He stopped, looked up at the screen. "The Jews. Of course. The target is Jerusalem."

The colonel responded, but Nick did not hear him. His legs gave way and he sank into his chair. Suddenly it all made sense.

The sun will be blotted out. Not from the smoke but from an eclipse, like the one coming up in Jerusalem. And then . . .

Armageddon.

His family.

It could not be a coincidence that after all these years Nick's father suddenly got an invitation to speak in Jerusalem, and Nick had stupidly sent his wife and child along. The terrorist's revenge would be complete. Kattan planned to kill his entire family in a nuclear blast.

Nick looked up at the screen where Walker's larger-than-life mouth was still moving, repeating a single word. It slowly came into focus.

"Baron!"

He finally snapped out of his trance. "We have to go to Jerusalem."

"And . . . he's back," said Walker. "I was trying to agree with you, but you checked out on me." He glanced down at the analyst. "Molly, what kind of death toll are we talking about if the target is Jerusalem?"

Molly shifted to another workstation in the background and worked the keyboard. "Given the lithium-six boost and the added tourist traffic from the eclipse—"

She stopped typing and stared wide-eyed at the colonel. "A hundred thousand from the blast alone. Two or three times that from the radiation effects."

"And the time of the eclipse?" asked Nick.

Molly returned to her keyboard. "Tomorrow morning. Full occultation at seven fifty-two A.M."

The sandy-haired CIA agent had been watching the conversation silently from the back of the command center. He suddenly pushed off the wall and held up a time-out sign. "Whoa, everybody. Egypt is one thing. Israel is another. The Holy Land is not on Airdrop Incorporated's list of destinations. That's the most heavily defended strip of land on the planet. If we even make it to the coast, it will be in a ball of flames." He shrugged. "The best I can do is our refueling base in Cyprus. That will get you close."

Nick shook his head. "Not close enough."

"Ahem." Walker cleared his throat. His scowl was contemplative. "Maybe it is." His gaze fixed at infinity for a heartbeat and then he nodded, more to himself than to the others. "Yes. This will work. You boys get to Cyprus. Let me take care of the rest."

CHAPTER 63

New York
U.S./Canadian Border

Markus. That was the name of the border patrol officer who waved Samir onto the scales at the Champlain border crossing. Markus Johnson. He looked like he could have played for the NFL if he wanted to. He had two kids, both of them girls. Markus was the crew manager for the early shift. He once told Samir that the quieter hours suited him and that midmorning release allowed him to spend more time with his family.

Samir could hardly count the number of conversations he and Markus had shared while his truck sat on these scales. They talked about vegetables, about family, sometimes they even talked about Islam. On most days, Samir was happy to sit and chat for a while. Today he prayed their conversation would be short.

It wasn't.

"I'm gonna have to look in the back, Sammy," said

Markus as Samir stepped down from the truck and handed over his freight papers.

The farmer's heart rate ramped up a notch. "Why? Is there a problem with the weight?"

"Oh no, nothing like that. It's just that Homeland Security raised the threat level. No explanation yet, but the new level means we have to check every vehicle." Markus sighed as he flipped through Samir's papers. "Standard bureaucratic baloney. Don't know what I'm looking for or why I'm looking"—he tilted his head and waived his clipboard—"but I gotta check a box that says I looked."

The image of the gun in Mahmoud's waistband flashed in Samir's mind. He scrambled to find an excuse to avert the confrontation. Then an idea emerged, and he let his shoulders sag. "Must you really?" he asked, feigning a yawn. "I did not sleep well last night, and I'd like to get back to Warrensburg before I'm too tired to drive."

Markus lowered his clipboard, his face registering genuine concern. He gestured over his shoulder with his pen, pointing at the guardhouse. "You know, we just made a fresh pot. And we have those foam cups—the big ones. I'll have Tom get you one while I check in the back. Follow me." He turned toward the facility.

The speed at which his excuse had backfired staggered Samir. "I . . . uh . . . No, thank you. I don't drink coffee."

Markus stopped and turned back, dropping his eyes and fiddling with his papers. "What was I thinking? That's a Muslim thing, isn't it?"

"Yes," Samir lied. Then he quickly followed with, "For

my mosque, anyway. Look, I'm fine. I just want to get going."

The border patrol officer raised the clipboard in the air and started leading Samir to the back of the vegetable truck. "And you will, Sammy. As soon as I get a look in the back."

As Samir followed behind Markus, he ran his hand along the side of the truck and slapped it a couple of times, trying to make it look like a natural, casual thing to do.

Markus stopped at the corner of the box and turned. His free hand came to rest on the grip of his gun. "You sure you're okay, Sammy?"

Samir's heart now raced so that he could hear its pounding in his head. He wondered if Markus could hear it too. Sweat formed at his hairline, icy cold in the northern air. He swallowed. "Yes. Of course."

At the back of the truck, Markus courteously held a flashlight on Samir's shaking hands while the farmer searched for the right key. "Where're your gloves, Sammy?"

The phone in the guardhouse rang.

Samir stopped. "Do you need to get that?"

"No. Tom'll get it. Go ahead."

"Of course."

As Samir pushed the key into the padlock, Tom appeared at the guardhouse door, shouting toward the scales. "Phone, boss!"

Markus sighed and shook his head. Then he straightened up and shouted back. "Take a message!"

"Can't! It's headquarters, the division chief. Something about the new threat level. He wants to talk to the shift manager. Stat!"

In the midst of their conversation, Samir had a flash of brilliance. He jiggled the key and then huffed dramatically. "It's stuck. Probably frozen. Happens all the time. Wait here, I have some lock deicer in the cab."

Markus looked back and forth between Samir and Tom, who was still waving the phone. He shoved the flashlight under his arm, checked a box on the paperwork, and then pulled the documents off the clipboard and handed them to Samir. "We're good, Sammy. See you tomorrow."

Five minutes later, Samir's heart was still pounding. He took a sip of coffee with a shaking hand as he passed a blue-and-white road sign that read WELCOME TO THE UNITED STATES OF AMERICA.

CHAPTER 64

The sun had risen high above a white overcast sky by the time Samir stopped his truck again. They were in a small parking lot lined with bare oaks, a parking lot that Mahmoud had directed him to. The student was in the passenger seat, digging in his backpack, and Samir hoped that it was not for some form of payment. This was supposed to be a charitable act. His eternity depended on it.

Samir watched with worried eyes as Mahmoud paused his searching to stifle a coughing fit. This was not the first. Mahmoud had grown increasingly ill throughout the journey. Samir patted him on the back. "Are you sure you're going to be okay?"

Mahmoud looked up from his bag and offered a weak smile. "I am fine, just worn out from the journey across the ocean."

At that moment Samir was overcome by a coughing fit of his own. He suddenly felt very tired. "Perhaps we are both coming down with something," he said, wiping his mouth with his sleeve, but when he looked up, Mahmoud was pointing the handgun at him. It now had a suppressor fixed to the barrel.

"Perhaps we are," said Mahmoud, and fired two shots into Samir's chest.

Samir could not speak for the pain and shock. He felt like his heart and lungs had exploded. His vision turned gray. Mahmoud faded from sight. From beyond the veil, he heard the young man speaking to him softly, gently.

"You have served Allah well, my friend. So I have spared you the suffering you would have endured before the end. I, however, must bear it a little while longer."

Then even the gray turned to darkness. Samir knew no more.

———

Mahmoud laid the driver back in his seat and brushed a hand across his face to close his eyes. Then he pulled the man's parka closed and zipped it up to hide the bullet wounds. He shut off the engine and lights and tucked the keys into the glove compartment, along with the gun and silencer. He would not need a weapon anymore.

The snow crunched beneath Mahmoud's feet as he walked toward the wide tangled oaks at the western edge of the lot, only stopping once for another fit of coughing. He would have to bring that under control, he thought, at least for a few more hours. Red spots of blood stained the snow at his feet. Mahmoud kicked and stirred the white powder to cover them up.

He found a short paved path through the trees and emerged on a little two-lane road that separated him from another parking lot and a long brick building. As he crossed the street, backpack slung over his shoulder, he gazed up at the building's tall octagonal clock tower and smiled. It reminded him of the minarets at home. At its base, next to the arched entrance, was a plaque that read ALBANY-RENSSELAER STATION, AMTRAK, DEPARTURES TO BOSTON, WASHINGTON D.C.

CHAPTER 65

D r. Patricia Heldner sat hunched in a black rolling chair in Romeo Seven's otherwise stark-white medical facility. Her back ached. Her head pounded. She had been there for hours, slowly bringing Scott out of his drug-induced coma.

From the tests she conducted along the way, it appeared the engineer had not lost any cognitive function, though she could not be certain until he was fully awake. There had been clear damage to the nervous system, however. Significant damage. Dr. Scott Stone would likely never walk again.

Moments after Heldner injected the last dose of stimulant into his IV, Scott's eyes fluttered open. His irises shifted around the room, but his head remained fixed to the pillow, and Heldner wondered if the paralysis was even worse than she thought. "Take it easy, Scott. You're in the clinic. You're okay."

Scott stared at the ceiling. His words were slurred by the drugs and the inevitable cotton mouth of long-term sedation. "The computer virus. I've got to tell the team."

"Yes," said Heldner, patting his forehead with a cloth. "You were working on the Second Sign Virus, but you need to let that go, now." She hesitated. "Scott, there's something I have to—"

Scott's head came off the pillow and he grabbed her arm. His eyes were wide, urgent, his jaw clenched. "No! I mean Grendel's virus, the one we all forgot about."

———

Just off the National Mall, in a dark room on the ground floor of Health and Human Services, a rack of servers labeled D.C. WATER whirred to life. An alien program that had lain dormant on the system for the last three days awakened and transmitted an executable file, which flashed at the speed of light through five miles of fiber-optic cable to a computer at D.C. Water's Blue Plains control station.

Once resident on the target computer, the file executed, running two subroutines in quick succession. The first presented a set of phony user commands to the Windows-based program that manages D.C. Water's analog industrial-control system. It initiated a cascading shutdown of every pump in the network, opening the fail-safe valves and linking the whole system for gravity feed from the highest pump station at Salem Park. The second subroutine destroyed the management program, locking D.C. Water's maintenance personnel out of the system.

At 4:25 P.M. Eastern Standard Time, the first D.C. Water technician discovered the change in pump status. At 4:34, after realizing he was permanently locked out of the system, he contacted his supervisor. Thus, by 4:52, when Agent Celine Jameson called on behalf of the FBI to suggest the possibility of an attack on the city's water supply, D.C. Water's chief of maintenance had a wide-open mind.

Scott had put it all together during his flight back from London. The fragments of code he found on Grendel's servers were not the type of code that would have crashed the London Stock Exchange. Grendel's code was a Stuxnet knockoff, designed to attack an industrial system like a power grid or a pump network. The engineer realized that was why Kattan had appeared at the site of the suicide bombing, dressed as a first responder. The front door security at Health and Human Services had been decimated by the attack, and Kattan used the opening to access D.C. Water's unhackable servers directly, the same trick he used at Paternoster Square to access the stock exchange.

Never one to present a theory without hard data, Scott wanted to compare the Second Sign Virus with Grendel's code before briefing the team. Then the neurotoxin hit him and he never got the chance.

As the sun dipped down into the Potomac, CJ and seven members of the FBI's Hostage Rescue Team raced across the treetops in a dark blue Bell 412 helicopter, heading for the Salem Park pump station. All of them, including CJ, were dressed in black tactical gear and helmets. Walker and Heldner were en route as well, with a CDC hazmat van, but they would take at least forty minutes to reach the site.

CJ checked the smartscreen integrated into the sleeve of her tactical jacket. Infrared satellite imagery showed a single individual kneeling next to the chain-link fence that separated the pump station from the high school baseball field to the south. He appeared to be cutting through the wire. She unstrapped from her seat and stepped up between the pilots. "Step it up, gentlemen! This is about to be a wasted trip!"

As the pump-house tower appeared on the darkening northern horizon, the figure in the infrared video broke through the fence. CJ tapped the Hostage Rescue Team sharpshooter on the shoulder and pointed to a steel-tube bench mounted on the helicopter skid outside the door. "Get ready!"

The pump station came up fast. As they passed the fence, the pilot turned and slid the chopper sideways while the copilot activated the powerful spotlight mounted on a turret under the nose. The blue-white beam fell on a scrawny individual in a parka and blue jeans. He carried a black backpack and walked at a plodding pace toward the station's huge open reservoir. He paused in midstep when the light came on. Then he kept going.

CJ grabbed the microphone for the chopper's PA system. "Stop where you are and lay down on the ground."

The individual ignored the command, now only twenty

meters from the reservoir, a short sprint away. He kept walking.

"Stop!" CJ repeated. "Lay down on the ground. If you do not comply, we will open fire."

When the man still continued, CJ turned to the sharp-shooter. He was seated on the helicopter floor with his feet on the external bench and his Remington M40 up and ready. "Can you take him down without hitting the backpack?"

"Yes, ma'am."

"Then do it."

"Ma'am, if I shoot now, I'll be shooting him in the back," argued the HRT man.

"His back is to us because he's about to dump a bio-weapon in that reservoir. Take the shot!"

An earsplitting crack rang out over the steady chop of the rotor blades. The terrorist went down, face first in the grass less than ten meters from the low concrete rise of the southern reservoir wall.

"Let's go!" shouted CJ.

Unable to land because of the fence line, the chopper pilot hovered twenty feet off the grass. The HRT men unfurled three black ropes from each side, and six of them fast-roped down while CJ and the sharpshooter covered the unmoving terrorist. Once the rest were down and covering the suspect with their MP5s, the other two fol-lowed. On the ground, CJ signaled the sharpshooter and another team member to follow her. The rest of the team spread out to look for additional threats.

The suspect was alive, groaning, groping for the backpack

lying in front of him. CJ nudged it away with her boot. When she did, the backpack felt light, empty. She picked it up with a gloved hand and pulled open the pockets one by one. There was no canister of virus, not even a glass vial. When she turned the bag upside down, nothing fell out but a worn Quran.

"Ma'am?" The sharpshooter's face was stricken with guilt—worry that he had just shot a civilian who had done nothing but cut through a fence.

Refusing to accept that, CJ knelt over the suspect and rolled him over. For the first time, she got a good look at him. His face and arms were covered in boils, his eyes sunken and bloodshot. While she stared at him in shock, he gripped her arm with a cold hand and pulled himself up to a sitting position, closer to her face. "I am the third and final sign," he said with a malevolent grin. "Now comes the Mahdi." Then his body convulsed and a spout of blood erupted from his lips.

CHAPTER 66

S ee anything?"

"Not yet."

Nick and Drake stood on an empty white beach a hundred meters south of the CIA refueling point, scanning the black waves for their transport to Israel. They had been on Cyprus for hours. The wait was maddening.

Unlike Farnborough, the Agency hangar on Cyprus was as rusty and dilapidated on the inside as it was on the outside, nothing but four corrugated steel walls, a big rubber fuel bladder, and a drywall bathroom with a reeking, stopped-up toilet. When they first arrived, Nick had found a quiet corner of the hangar—as far from the bathroom as possible—and made several calls. He tried to contact his family, but his efforts were futile. Katy had no phone. The older Baron was not answering his cell. Why should he, after the way Nick had left things?

Nick left messages on his dad's phone, at both hotel rooms, and the front desk. Never once did he get an actual human being on the line.

After his attempts at direct contact failed, Nick tried another tack. He called Walker and convinced him to try his contact at the Mossad. The result was disappointing. The colonel refused to tell the Israeli that a nuke was entering his country. Such a warning, if incorrect, had massive consequences, and the Triple Seven's evidence was merely circumstantial. Instead, Walker told the Mossad agent that a bomb was headed for Jerusalem. The contact actually laughed. There was always a bomb headed for Jerusalem. The man thanked Walker for his call and told him that with the usual daily threats and with the massive influx of tourists for the eclipse, the Mossad did not have time to hunt down a dotard American professor and his daughter-in-law.

Later Walker had informed Nick that he and CJ had a lead on the virus. Scott had figured it out. Nick was relieved that the engineer had recovered, but he sensed that Walker was holding something back. When he asked about it, the colonel cut him off. Heldner's CDC team was ready to roll. He had to go. That was the last Nick had heard from headquarters, more than an hour earlier. Now, standing on the beach in his bare feet with Drake, his phone rang again, but this was a call he expected, and it was not from Romeo Seven.

"Go."

"Nightmare One, this is Rawhide Two. Light your firefly."

Nick kept the phone to his ear and removed a clear,

one-inch-by-one-inch acrylic cube from his pocket, sliding a little black switch on the side forward with his thumb. The electronics within began to tick, once per second.

"Rawhide Two is visual. Cover."

Nick slipped the cube into his pocket. The fabric of his canvas pants partially muted the infrared flash it gave off with each tick, otherwise the powerful little beacon would block out half the coastline on Rawhide's night-vision goggles.

Drake raised his own night-vision monocle, holding it with two hands like a pirate with a spyglass. "I don't see him." The big operative panned the monocle from the left all the way to his right until he was looking down at Nick. "Your pants are flashing, though. Very hip."

"You're hilarious."

"Nightmare One, Rawhide Two is padlocked on your position. Stop firefly."

"Nightmare copies. Firefly off."

Even with the monocle, Drake was not able to pick up the SEAL raiding craft until it was fifty yards from the beach. Nick did not see it until it was half that distance. The Navy man drove the black dinghy right up onto the beach and then jumped out to hold it still in the sloshing tide. No one spoke. Nick and Drake ran to him, helped him push it back out into the waves, and hopped in.

White spray kicked over the side as they built up speed. Despite its power, the outboard motor was quiet, and when their squat, stocky coxswain finally spoke, he barely raised his voice above a conversational tone. "Gentlemen. My name is Chief Morales."

Nick could not see much of his face in the moonless dark, only the silver droplets of saltwater glistening on his bushy black mustache.

"I'm not supposed to ask who you are," continued the SEAL, "but you must have some serious connections to drag us all the way out here." He flipped his NVGs down in front of his eyes and adjusted the boat's course to the east. "Rawhide One is thirty meters off the bow and already under way. We're going to join up hot, so you'll want to keep your heads down."

Nick and Drake bent forward, but Morales shook his head. "I mean way down."

With his chin behind the bow rail, Nick could see little on the dark horizon. It didn't help that he had to keep wiping the sea spray from his eyes. Then a silhouette formed ahead, racing to meet them—a black trapezoid rising just above the water's surface. Nick dropped his head below the rubber hull and braced for impact.

The starlit floor of the dinghy went completely dark as it slid into the small rear bay of its mother ship. As soon as the bay doors closed behind them, Nick felt the larger craft rise up and rapidly accelerate, bouncing on the choppy sea. Dim blue lights flashed on, and the water in the bay drained out, allowing the dinghy to settle onto rubber rails, giving them all a little more headroom. Nick glanced around at the angular gray walls. He allowed himself a smile. He had just caught a unicorn—or at least, it had caught him.

The M80C Dagger was the Sasquatch of the maritime community—rumored to exist, occasionally sighted, only seen in grainy videos shot from a great distance. The stealth boat was sleek and thin, with a faceted structure and an M-shaped hull that rose out of the water at speed and sank at idle so that it could hide amid the waves. If anything could get them into Israel undetected, the Dagger could.

The chief led them forward through a corridor barely wide enough for one man. While the two Triple Seven operatives steadied themselves against the walls, the squat SEAL walked unaided, despite the pitch and roll of the boat. He led them up to the cockpit where the boat commander sat at controls, his face illuminated by the white glow of a wide forward screen. He was big, almost as big as Drake, with a square jaw and dark features, as if he had some Native American in the nearer branches of his family tree.

"Lieutenant Jonathan Lighthart," said the SEAL, his voice also carrying a Native American flavor. "Welcome aboard and thanks for ruining my day off." Lighthart's eyes never left the forward screen. At the speed it was cutting through the waves, the Dagger could not be left to an autopilot.

"Happy to be aboard," said Nick.

"Always a pleasure to ruin a Navy man's day," added Drake.

Like the Triple Seven's M-2 Wraith, the Dagger had no windows. Sensors embedded in the hull fed the forward screen. A grayscale, enhanced-infrared image showed them a clear picture of the waves ahead. Across the bottom, a six-inch-tall strip displayed close-in sonar returns. Flecks of blue and purple appeared and disappeared as the system found contacts and quickly dismissed them as small biologicals.

Drake pointed to a pair of small blue boxes floating on the horizon. "What are those, Lieutenant?"

"Radar tracks." Lighthart used his trackball to move crosshairs over one of the contacts. All of its data appeared on the screen, including its type—a container ship—and its name and destination. "We use position data and ship size to correlate targets with a real-time database. If she can see a boat, the Dagger can tell you who it is." He glanced back. "So? What do you boys think of her?"

Nick patted the gray wall. "She's a real beauty."

"All except the callsign," said Drake. "Rawhide? Couldn't you come up with something a little less land-locked?"

Lighthart returned his eyes to the screen. "Dolphin or Sea Lion would be too obvious."

"Have you considered Sea Monkey?"

As Nick slapped his teammate's arm with the back of his hand, his phone chimed. He had come to dread that sound. He fished the device out of a wet pocket, praying the alert meant a text from his dad, knowing, fearing, that it was something else. His fear proved justified.

The black box with the ivory letters waited for him on the screen. *The Emissary has taken your queen. Your move.*

An icy hand gripped Nick's chest. His queen. *Katy.*

On cue, the phone rang—just like with Scott.

He put the phone to his ear and turned toward the seclusion of the aft bay. "What happened? Is Katy okay?"

"Hey there, Nick Baron." The voice was CJ's. She

sounded weak. "Don't know about Katy, but I'm feeling a little peaked, myself. You might not have to buy me an expensive dinner after all."

Slowly, and with effort, the FBI agent explained what had happened at the pump station. Her team stopped the Hashashin from infecting the water supply, but the terrorist had already injected himself with the virus. He had planned to throw himself into the reservoir. The blood he coughed up infected her instead.

Nick steadied himself against the corridor wall, partly because of the bounce and roll of the Dagger, but mostly because of the flood of neurochemicals assaulting his system. The revelation that the lost queen was not Katy, the guilt of his relief, and the impotence of knowing that Kattan had wounded, perhaps killed, another friend while he had yet to even touch the man all combined and conflicted, weakening him to the edge of collapse.

"CJ, I—"

"Don't blame yourself, Nick. This is part of the job. Every agent knows it."

Nick pounded the wall with his fist. "This was *not* your job. It was a game, Kattan's stupid chess game. You were the queen, a piece to be taken. Somehow he knew you would be at the pump station."

"The queen. I like the sound of that." Her voice was fading. "Nick, I'm tired. I'm going to transfer the line to the doc."

"CJ, wait—" But the line clicked over.

"Nick? It's Pat."

Nick closed his eyes. "How long does she have?"

Dr. Heldner was cold, analytical. "Twenty-four hours. Maybe less. This bug is an accelerated version of the black pox, the hemorrhagic form of smallpox. It will kill her too quickly for us to synthesize a vaccine in time." She paused. "The infected Hashashin called himself the third and final sign, Nick. The *final* sign. What if this nuke is a wild-goose chase to keep you off Kattan's trail until he disappears for good?"

"You want me to abandon the search for the nuke. Go after Kattan directly to get the vaccine he's carrying."

"It would shorten our timeline from days to hours."

Nick processed the idea for a moment and then rejected it. "No. Whatever that guy said, the nuke is real. Going after it is our best hope on all fronts. Kattan wants revenge, a very personal revenge against me. He'll be there in Jerusalem, and he'll have the vaccine with him."

"You'd better hope so," said Heldner. "Because CJ and the pump station weren't the only targets for this virus."

CHAPTER 67

Washington, D.C.

A t nine P.M., after much deliberation with his advisers and six minutes after the seven-hundredth case of the black pox was diagnosed, the president of the United States held a press conference to declare a federal state of emergency. Before he finished eloquently delivering what CNN declared a presidency-defining speech of hope and comfort, fifty-two more cases appeared. The spread of the virus was accelerating. The FEMA disaster area encompassed half of the eastern seaboard, from Virginia to Vermont.

Helicopters flew over the capital, their spotlights searching for looters. The National Guard patrolled the streets in Humvees and hazmat gear. On the great green lawn of the Washington Mall stood a glowing white tent that rivaled Barnum and Bailey. The eastern wing housed the CDC's main conference room.

Dr. Heldner paused in a narrow hallway formed from undulating white laminate. She needed a moment to gather her wits before jumping into the shark tank. She took a deep breath, squared her shoulders, and then pushed through the plastic flap.

A barrage of questions hit her the moment she stepped into the room. A few of the voices sounded angry, all of them sounded scared. As Heldner stepped up to a free-standing smartboard, she held up her hands for silence. "Ladies and gentlemen, please. I'll answer your questions *after* I complete my briefing." She picked up a remote from the smartboard's tray and pointed it at the screen. Nothing happened. She scowled at a tech standing at the back of the room. "Could we?"

While the kid hunted for the source of the problem, Heldner scanned the worried faces at the long folding table—doctors, generals, politicians. Several wore latex gloves. Two of them, including Senator Cartwright, wore surgical masks over their faces.

She snorted. "This bug isn't airborne, Senator. You don't have to wear a mask."

The senator's cheeks rose beneath the blue covering, in what Heldner presumed was a smile. "I find this mask very comfortable, Doctor," he said in his Virginia drawl. "I think I'll keep it for a while."

The kid in the back found the problem, and the smartboard lit up, showing Heldner's first slide. There were gasps all around the room, a reaction to the massive numbers on the screen. She held up her hands again. "Take it easy. This is the might-have-been. I wanted you to see it because I want to stress the lethality of the weapon these terrorists have produced." She used the laser pointer in the remote to highlight her figures. "Had they succeeded in getting this virus into the D.C. water supply, a half million people would have died within the first forty-eight hours. And there is little we could have done to save them. Even if we had had a vaccine, we could not have reproduced it fast enough on that scale. Consequently, another one and a half to two million would have died before we got control of the outbreak."

"We don't need the might-have-beens, Doctor. We need the here and now," said Cartwright.

Heldner directed a frown at the politician and then continued. "By stopping the terrorist at the pump station, our tactical response blocked a major portion of the attack. However, they were smart. There was an additional means of distribution for the virus."

The doctor flipped to a new slide, a map of Washington, D.C. Dozens of red dots populated the screen, showing diagnosed cases. The spidery branches were clearly centered on Union Station, twelve hundred meters from the very tent they were meeting in. One branch leading away from the station was thicker than the others. Heldner pressed her remote and a map of the D.C. Metro system overlaid the first. The heavier branch of smallpox cases coincided with the Metro line running from Union Station up to a stop near Salem Park.

"He used the rail system, and that wasn't just for lack of a car. Look." Heldner expanded the map until it showed the upper East Coast. There were now hundreds of tiny red dots, and their branches centered on the train stations along the line from Albany to New York City to Washington, D.C.

"We found a spent vial on the train the terrorist took from New York City to Union Station. CDC doctors are using the remains to synthesize a cure, but that cure is seventy-two hours away, at best. It may be ninety-six, and every hour we lose has an exponential consequence." Heldner pressed her remote again, and the red dots grew outward at an exponential rate until the spidery arms stretched as far south as the Carolinas and as far west as the Mississippi.

"Is that your worst case, Doctor?" asked Cartwright.

Heldner shook her head. "This is our best case. Even if we have a working vaccine in three days, reproduction and dissemination will still be a nightmare. Many won't respond to treatment. There will be riots that slow us down. Within a week, twelve thousand Americans will die. Within two weeks, twenty thousand."

CHAPTER 68

In the narrow crew locker between the Dagger's aft bay and its cockpit, Nick and Drake found the equipment Walker had ordered for them. Two green waterproof duffels lay on the floor in front of a long bench. There was also a rubber submersible crate, four feet square and three feet tall, propped against the bulkhead behind it. Molly came up on SATCOM to brief them.

"We sent you FN-303 nonlethal dispensers," said the analyst as each man pulled a black polymer rifle out of his duffel.

Nick checked the seal on the air canister fixed to the side of the weapon and then eyed the large red rounds in the drum magazine. "What kind of grenades are these?"

"Eighteen-millimeter nanosecond electric pulse."

"You're kidding." He pulled out one of the rounds to examine it. NEP grenades were far superior to conventional Tasers and stun grenades, but they weren't supposed to be fielded yet. "I thought these were developmental only."

"So did I," said Molly. "But when Lighthart heard you were going to Israel, he offered them up. Those are a gift from his unit."

"Ouch," said Drake, clutching his chest like he'd been wounded.

Nick glanced at his teammate and nodded his agreement. Apparently Lighthart had access to ops technology that the Triple Seven Chase didn't. He was jealous.

The bags also contained a change of clothes, modified Sig Sauer P290 micro-compact pistols with suppressors, and various other mission necessities. Molly struggled through the rest of the list; it was clear she was reading off her computer, unfamiliar with the actual gear.

"Scott usually handles equipment checks," said Nick, sensing her discomfort. "Why the switch? I thought he was back with us."

Silence on the line. Then, "Scott's resting. That's all."

Nick touched his earpiece and switched to an isolated line. "Don't lie to me, Molly."

More silence.

"Molly . . ."

"He's paralyzed, Nick." After holding it in so long, she just blurted out the revelation. "Doc Heldner says he'll never walk again."

Nick could not respond. He had suspected something like this, but now that he knew it to be true, he could not speak. Quinn was down, Rami was dead and CJ close to it, and now Scott's life was changed forever, not to mention the dozens who died at Paternoster Square and the thousands who would die in America and Israel if he did not find Kattan. All this collateral damage from a single five-hundred-pound bomb that he called down on a tiny mud house nine years ago. How much more could he take? How much more could the world take? He gazed over at his teammate for several seconds.

Drake looked up from his inventory. "What?"

Chief Morales knocked on the wall next to the open portal. "Gentlemen, the L-T wants you up front. We're approaching the coast."

———

From three miles out, little could be seen of the shoreline besides the lights of Tel Aviv, blazing on the northern edge of the infrared display. The two blue boxes Drake had identified when they left Cyprus had multiplied into several, marking a variety of civilian ships near the coast. By two miles, the small stretch of beach that was Nick's target materialized in dull gray, dark and empty. On either side of it, green diamonds and red octagons appeared one by one, and kept appearing until there was a long line of them fixed to the shore, rising and falling with the motion of the Dagger. Each shape had a small stack of data next to it, identifying it as a piece of the extensive Israeli shore defense network—radars and optical trackers and the like. Stealth boat or not, this was not going to be easy.

Several minutes later, just inside one mile from the shore, Lighthart slowed the Dagger to a drift. Morales abruptly stood and offered his hand to his two guests. "Good luck, gentlemen, whatever your mission may be." The chief's phrasing sounded oddly final.

Drake stared at the distant shoreline as he cautiously shook the chief's hand. "Am I missing something?"

"Didn't you see the dry suits and rebreathers hanging in the locker?"

"SEAL boat," said Drake, gesturing all around. "We figured they were just part of the decor."

Lighthart glanced over his shoulder. "Do you see this display?" Then he turned back to the screen and pointed to the shapes on either side of the target beach, reading off each label in turn. "Surface radar, surface radar, passive sonar. This one is an infrared motion detector designed to break out anything that isn't a fish or a wave. The Dagger is invisible to radar but not to infrared." Even as he spoke, a new blue box entered the display from the right. The SEAL lieutenant captured the box with his crosshairs and expanded it, zooming in on a long patrol boat cutting across the waves. "And then we have these guys."

"And they are?" asked Nick, leaning in to get a closer look at the Israeli boat. He could see turret-mounted weapons fore and aft.

"You're looking at a Super Dvora Mark Three interceptor," said Morales, as if reciting it from a manual. "There are several guarding the Israeli coast, and every boat is packing an optically guided twenty-five-millimeter cannon and the naval variant of Hellfire missiles."

Lighthart looked back at Nick and raised his eyebrows. "I don't care who called in this favor. I'm not taking my

boat any closer to that briar patch than I have to." Then
his eyes returned to his control panel. "Nice working with
you. Now suit up. You're going for a swim."

————

"That was rude." Drake's voice sounded muted and tinny
through the comm link in their full-face dive masks.
"Don't you think that was rude?"

The two of them kicked toward the shore at a steady
pace, dragging their waterproof bags and pushing the big
submersible crate ahead of them. Thanks to the infrared
motion detectors and the patrol boats, Nick had to set the
crate's buoyancy for five meters below the surface, making
it all the harder to push through the water. The SEALs had
warned them not to break the surface outside a hundred
meters from the beach.

"Lighthart did what he had to. Now pipe down. We
don't know how good their passive sonar is."

Halfway to the beach, Nick heard an undulating hum
in his ear. At first he thought it was the comm link, then
he realized that it was engine noise. He checked to his
right and left, but he didn't see the lights or the disturbance of a Dvora on the surface.

"You hear that?" asked Drake.

They brought the crate to a stop and hovered in the
water, listening as the hum grew louder until it became
a throbbing metallic pound. Suddenly a twenty-foot-tall
leviathan materialized out of the murk to their left.
"Move!" Nick yelled into his mask.

Nick and Drake pushed together, kicking with

everything they had to get the crate out of the submarine's way. It passed so close behind them that Drake's fin smacked the dive plane. Even then, they didn't slow down. Neither of them had any desire to get tumbled by the black beast's monstrous prop wash.

Despite the slap from Drake's fin, the sub continued south on its patrol. As far as Nick could tell, the two swimmers and their rubber crate had been dismissed as a biological by its sonar filters.

They surfaced fifty meters out from the beach and removed their dive masks. Dawn was still more than an hour away, but a quick scan with a night-vision monocle told Nick the three-mile stretch of sand wasn't as empty as he hoped. "Two-man foot patrol," he whispered. "Eleven o'clock."

Drake nodded, silently lifting his FN-303 out of the water. He paused to dip the fat barrel and let the seawater spill out, and then raised the holographic sight to his eye and fired a single NEP grenade with a resounding *foomp*. The two Israelis stopped and looked out across the water, searching for the source of the sound. They never saw it.

Activated by a proximity sensor, the grenade opened a few meters from the foot patrol and released a net of ten barbs, all connected to its power source by micro-thin wires.

Nick heard two surprised yelps from the beach and watched the Israelis drop like stones. The high-voltage pulse instantly knocked them out. Conventional Tasers were painful, exposing targets to long-duration shock and only immobilizing them for a few seconds. The NEP grenade pulses lasted a billionth of a second, but they carried much higher voltage. The effect was significantly less damage and significantly higher downtime.

"How long will it last?" whispered Drake.

Nick stared at his teammate for a moment and then turned to look at the Israelis lying on the beach. "I have no idea."

The final stretch took them less than a minute; they were kicking hard and pushing the crate along the surface through the waves. Nick kept raising his head to make sure the patrol was still down. When they reached the shore, he ran over to the unconscious Israelis and carefully dosed each one with a sedative.

"We should take their uniforms," grunted Drake, dragging the crate onto the beach. "They might come in handy down the road."

Nick surveyed his victims. "That'll work for me, but I don't think you can squeeze into the other one's pants."

"Is he short?"

"He's a she. And I doubt she weighs more than a buck fifteen with her boots on."

Nick found the Israeli's pickup parked on an overgrown asphalt pad a short distance away. He and Drake loaded up the equipment and the unconscious patrol and followed a gravel road inland until they found a long low concrete bunker half-buried in the weeds. They laid the patrol inside and bound them hand and foot. Nick took the male's uniform, but they left the girl dressed, taking only her boots and socks to limit her mobility.

When Drake stripped out of his dry suit, he was already

wearing a set of khaki pants, but his chest was bare. He dug in his duffel for a few seconds and emerged with the blue and white Hawaiian shirt from the Coptic church.

"You can't be serious," said Nick.

Drake slipped the shirt over his head. "No time to argue. We've got a nuke to find."

The big operative started for the bunker door, but Nick stopped him with a hand to his chest. "I don't want you to come."

"Look, boss, the shirt stays. Deal with it."

Nick shook his head. "No. You don't understand. You got me this far. Now I go it alone. As far as Kattan is concerned, you're just another chess piece." He pointed to the east. "Somewhere out there is a bullet with your name on it, for no other reason than to torture me. If I let you come, I'm giving Kattan exactly what he wants."

Drake frowned at his teammate. "Don't be ridiculous. *This* is what he wants. He wants you isolated. Alone." He pushed by Nick and headed for the truck, calling to him over his shoulder. "And as long as I'm still breathing, boss, that's not going to happen."

CHAPTER 69

The Israeli Defense Forces pickup had a light bar and a siren, and Nick used them both liberally to cut through the traffic as he sped southeast through Jerusalem, doing his best to beat the rising sun. The most likely targets for the nuke were those within the walls of the Old City—more than a dozen churches, synagogues, and biblical sites that would make definitive spiritual and political statements as epicenters for the final blast—but when Nick came to a sign that said OLD CITY: DAMASCUS GATE with an arrow pointing due south, he took the road southwest instead.

"Wrong way, boss," said Drake, turning to watch the sign pass behind them.

Nick flipped on the lights again and swerved around the car ahead of them. "Got to make a stop first. We have to get my family."

"No. Not a good tactical plan."

"Says the guy in the gaudy Hawaiian shirt."

Drake's voice grew deadly serious. "Listen. I know your family comes before everyone else, but we don't have time. It won't do your dad or your wife and kid any good if you find them the moment the nuke goes off."

"Who's driving the truck?"

Drake frowned. "You are."

"Are you planning on Tasing me or shooting me or something?"

"No. Of course not."

"Then shut up."

A few minutes later, Nick parked the truck on the street outside the King David Hotel. He looked ahead at the bumper-to-bumper traffic on the road east toward the Old City. "Have Molly order me a cab for three to Ben Gurion International," he said, jumping out of the driver's seat. "Then get the equipment ready. We walk from here."

Inside the hotel, Nick raced across gold and purple marble tiles to the back of the lobby. He bypassed the elevators and took the stairs two and three at a time up to the fourth floor. Finally, breathing hard, he banged on the door to his wife's room. "Katy!"

There was no response.

He tried one more time, but as he pounded, Katy stuck her head out of the room next door. "Nick?"

Nick checked the room numbers. "I thought you were—"

Katy waved her hand and shook her head. "Your dad and

I switched rooms. The hotel put the crib in the wrong one. What are you doing here?"

He pushed past her, heading straight for the phone by the bed. "Don't you and Dad check your messages?"

The little orange light on the phone wasn't blinking. He picked up the receiver and pressed the retrieve button.

"You have no messages," declared a cheerful recorded voice, and then it repeated the statement in Hebrew and French. It appeared Kattan had tampered with the lines to head off Nick's warnings, which meant he had these rooms under surveillance.

Nick slammed the handset into its cradle. "We have to get you out of here." He went to the drawers beneath the TV and started pulling out clothes, throwing them at her suitcase a few feet away. "You and Dad are leaving Jerusalem. Now. Get Luke ready."

When Katy started to argue, Nick lost what calm he had left. He whipped around with a shirt and a pair of her jeans clenched in his fists. "Just do as I say for once!"

That was enough to subdue her, although the look in Katy's eyes told Nick he would pay for the outburst later. He hoped so. He hoped they would have a later. When he finished, he zipped up her rolling suitcase and yanked it off the rack. "You have cash?"

"Plenty."

Nick snapped his fingers and motioned with an open palm. "Give me a fifty. Where's Dad?"

"He had an early meeting with Avi."

"Did he say where?"

"Only that it was one of their old haunts, something about a garden."

By the time they reached the shaded drive out front, the cab was waiting. Nick hurried Katy into the back, tossed the child seat in beside her, and set Luke in her lap. "You have to go."

"Luke isn't buckled in."

"Buckle him in on the way. Get the next flight out, even if you have to pay for a whole new ticket." He kissed her hard and then kissed his son's hand. Luke giggled and smiled at his daddy.

Katy stared up at him, fighting back tears. "Nick, what is going on? What is this about?"

Nick didn't answer. He closed her door and tossed the fifty through the front window. "That's the first half of your tip," he told the cabby. "She'll give you the rest when you get there." He pounded the top of the car. "Tel Aviv. Ben Gurion Airport. Go!"

———

Kurt Baron sat alone in the lush courtyard at the American Colony Hotel, sipping a cup of English tea and listening to the water trickling down from a jade fountain. He pulled his fleece jacket close around him. The garden was still chilly and dark, the varied greens of its vines all muted gray by the shadows.

This hotel had offered visitors and expats a refuge from the turmoil of Jerusalem for more than a century, since the days of the British protectorate. Kurt remembered sitting here during his postgraduate studies, waiting for the first golden rays of morning to break over the eastern wall and spread across the bleached flagstone, bit by bit revealing the glory of this small Eden. In those days, he usually shared the experience with his fellow student, Avi. He had expected to share it with his old friend once more, but Avi had not yet arrived.

Kurt jumped as his phone buzzed with a text message. The thing hadn't made a peep since the day before. He checked the screen. Avi made his apologies. The Israeli professor had been called to an early faculty meeting. He suggested rescheduling tea for an hour and a half later on the Temple Mount Plaza, another one of their favorite spots from the old days. *I'LL BRING THE TEA*, said the text. *YOU BRING THE PASTRIES.*

Kurt smiled at the notion of the pastries. These days, Avi's wife placed very stringent restrictions on his diet. She did not allow him such pleasures. Kurt started typing his response.

———

On a dead-end street, a block away from the American Colony, Avi Bendayan sat behind the wheel of his car. Masih Kattan sat next to him.

When Kurt Baron's response came through, Kattan picked up the phone and patted Avi on the arm, causing the dead professor's head to slump to one side, stretching out the deep, bloody gash in his throat.

Kattan checked the message. *AVI, I'LL BE THERE WITH THE PASTRIES. WHAT PANINA DOESN'T KNOW WON'T HURT HER.*

The terrorist smiled. What a silly thing to say.

CHAPTER 70

Amran Jazar, the Hashashin lieutenant who had dutifully delivered the lithium-6 three days before in Cairo, parked a yellow taxi at the edge of the Palestinian village of Ras Al-Amud, east of Jerusalem. The crescent-topped spire of the town mosque on the hilltop above cast a long shadow westward across the deep Kidron Valley. That valley separated the Mount of Olives from the Noble Sanctuary—the Temple Mount, as it was known to the infidels—and many scholars and prophets claimed that it would one day be soaked with the blood of Armageddon. So, thought Amran, it would.

Amran's journey to Jerusalem had taken nearly fifteen hours, beginning the moment Dr. Wahish finished his work. More precisely, it began the moment Amran slit the physicist's throat—the same way he slit the throat of the Syrian who had brought them the virus. The Emissary had been clear. There was to be no trail, no witnesses that could be captured and questioned to jeopardize the final goal. Amran had carried the device away in an unobtrusive gray backpack, leaving nothing behind in the old watchtower but a white-haired Pakistani, facedown in a sticky black pool of his own blood.

From Cairo, Amran had carried the weapon to Ismailia, on the edge of the Sinai, and then, at dusk, continued on into the desert. He crossed the Egyptian portion on an ATV; the Israeli portion on foot. Abandoning the vehicle cost him time, but taking a noisy ATV across the border would have been suicide.

When he finally reached the frontier city of Beersheba early that morning, Amran had simply hailed a cab—one with the yellow license plates that allowed service vehicles easy passage through West Bank checkpoints. The cab driver had stayed behind, bleeding out in a ditch north of town.

Now Amran climbed out of the vehicle with his backpack and tossed the keys on the floorboard. He did not bother to wipe clean the cab's interior, not even the bloodstain on the driver's door. This age of the world was ending. No one was ever going to trace this vehicle to him or to the Hashashin. At this range, the cab would not survive the hour anyway.

———

"I didn't see your dad in that taxi." Drake was standing in the back of the pickup with the crate's lid open against the cab.

Nick pulled open the driver's-side door. "He wasn't there. Hop down and get in. I think I know where to find him. A place called the American Colony."

Drake didn't move. He folded his arms defiantly.

"Drake, come on!"

"We can't, boss. We don't have time to play hunches."

Nick stood there with the door open another moment. His gaze shifted to the east, toward a thin line of low clouds, burned orange by the rising sun. The eclipse was coming. Drake was right. He hung his head in frustration. Then he reached into the cab, pulled out an M4 rifle he had taken from the patrol, and slammed the door shut again.

"Good choice," said Drake, unfolding his arms. "Now get up here and tell me what I'm dealing with."

Nick climbed into the back. Inside the crate were four miniature UAVs, each drone two feet square with four enclosed rotors, all stacked on a short pole launcher. Titanium plates reinforced the flattened corners of their rugged, olive-drab frames. "This UAV system is called SWARM," said Nick, removing a mini-tablet computer from the foam wall of the case. "Synchronized wireless aerial reconnaissance machines. They are multipurpose, but this set is fitted out to complement a helicopter-borne radiation detector. At best, a chopper system can narrow the search for a radiation source down to a city block. SWARM is the next step. Once the helicopter finds the area, three of these UAVs work in concert to triangulate the exact position."

Drake rapped a knuckle on the side of the top drone. "And the fourth? The payload looks different."

"That one has a high-def camera. It hovers over the target for real-time video." Nick toyed with the tablet screen as he spoke. A green LED lit up on each drone, indicating linkup with the controller. "Unfortunately, we don't have the helicopter to find the general area. These UAVs were designed to search one city block. Our search area is equivalent to a hundred."

Drake lifted a hand to shield his eyes and looked out toward the Old City. "So we're hunting for the proverbial needle in a haystack."

"A needle that will go off in"—Nick checked his watch—"fifty-two minutes." He flipped a switch on each UAV. The rotors hummed to life, and the little aircraft hovered on the pole, separated by a couple of inches each.

He handed the mini-tablet to Drake. "You have control. Use the green toggle to—"

The UAVs shot up into the air, almost knocking Nick out of the truck.

Drake laughed. "I think I can figure it out."

"Right." Nick glowered at his teammate. "Let's get moving."

They entered the worn stone streets of Old Jerusalem at the Jaffa gate, looking like an Israeli guard and an American tourist. Despite his bravado, Drake had a little trouble walking and controlling the SWARM at the same time. He bumped into several people in the crowd, none of whom noticed the quiet formation of four remote-control aircraft hovering two hundred feet over their heads.

After the big operative nearly ran down a small but very loud French woman, Nick took the tablet away. He locked a set of crosshairs onto his teammate. The central bird, the one with the high-def camera, took up a position directly above them. "There," he said, handing it back. "Now they will follow wherever you go. We can release them when they get a whiff of the radiation."

Drake looked down at his own image under the crosshairs. "Creepy."

When they reached an open square inside the gates, Nick activated his SATCOM earpiece. "Lighthouse, any help?"

Molly was ready for him, but she didn't have good news. "Sorry, Nightmare. We couldn't get satellite coverage over Israel, not under State's nose. However, based on your previous encounters with the Hashashin, you can expect two or three hostiles. One will have the bomb, plus one or two outriggers armed with knives and machine guns. Watch the top floors and the crowds."

Drake turned in a slow circle, searching the rooftops for snipers. "I hate these guys."

"And the target?" asked Nick.

"Unknown. Too many potentials in the area. I'd start with the most famous crusader church in town."

Drake's Catholic upbringing rose to the surface. "The Church of St. Anne."

"Correct," said Molly.

Nick nodded. "I'll buy that. Big crusader church. It

definitely makes a statement. We can scan east from the Church of the Holy Sepulchre on the way."

"How much time?" asked Drake, squinting up at the drones hovering high above.

Nick checked his watch. The eclipse had already started. "If we're right about the bomb, every man, woman and child in this crowded city has less than forty-five minutes to live."

CHAPTER 71

Over the next twelve minutes, Nick and Drake used the SWARM to scan seven holy sites, working northeast from the Church of the Holy Sepulchre to the Church of St. Anne.

The UAVs found nothing.

The small plaza in front of St. Anne's was nearly empty. There, the outer wall of the Old City rose high above the street, blocking the view of the eastern sky. The tourists had moved elsewhere to see the sun. "We're running out of time," said Drake, slumping into a plastic chair at an open-air café.

Nick sat down across the table and waved the waiter away. "We haven't scanned a tenth of the city. This isn't working. We have too much ground to cover."

"Maybe Dr. Heldner was right," offered Molly through the SATCOM. "Maybe there's no nuke at all."

Nick shook his head. "False hope. Everything we know points to a bomb, right here in Jerusalem, but there has to be something we're missing. Read me the final stanza of the prophecy."

"We're wasting time," protested Drake.

Nick held up a warning hand. "Read it, Molly."

As the analyst carried out his order, Nick closed his eyes, letting the words sink into his consciousness, seeing them as three-dimensional structures and letting them float freely on their own. Somewhere in the open spaces between them was the answer he needed.

Then the sun will be blotted out and my servant will open the gate. A great smoke will rise up from the center of the world. The sky will burn like molten brass, and from the high place there will sound a deafening noise, as trumpets, announcing the entrance of the Mahdi.

Almost of their own accord, two small pieces of the whole separated and rose above the rest.

. . . my servant will open the gate.

. . . announcing the entrance of the Mahdi.

Nick's eyes blinked open. "I know what the target is." He stood up and left the café at a run.

———

As Drake rushed after his team lead, the SWARM stayed right above him, following like a flock of loyal geese. "Are you gonna share your thoughts with the rest of the class?"

"My servant will open the gate!" Nick shouted over his shoulder, heading west down the slanted Via Dolorosa, still well ahead of his friend. "The nuke isn't a sign. It's a key!"

Molly was unconvinced. "I'm showing a long list of gates surrounding the Old City of Jerusalem. Which one?"

"The one you don't see." Nick turned south from the empty street into a long corridor crowded with tourists and vendors. He started weaving his way through knots of well-dressed pilgrims buying crosses and eclipse glasses from kids in soiled clothes and *taqiyah* skullcaps. "There's a flat stone here," he said as Drake finally caught up. "The Muslims think it's the rock where Muhammad ascended into heaven. Some Jews and Christians believe it's the place where heavenly fire burned up the offerings of King David." He paused to dodge a rack of leather sandals and then turned sideways to scoot through a group of chattering schoolkids and into a narrow tunnel. "Either way, a lot of mystics think it's a gateway between worlds."

Nick emerged from the tunnel into a wide plaza and jogged to a halt amid a throng of eclipse-watchers. To the east rose a shining limestone wall, spotted with tufts of green rock plant. A crowd of worshippers at its base stuffed tiny prayer scrolls into the cracks between the stones. At the top, in the same place where Katy had stood and the fire had risen up in his vision at the bottom of the Thames, he saw the flaming golden dome of the Qubbat As-Sakhrah, the Dome of the Rock, brilliant in the light of the morning sun.

"The mosque?" asked Drake, following his gaze.

"Not the dome itself," said Nick, panting to catch his breath, "the flat stone inside. The Hashashin believe that rock is a portal, and I think they're planning to blow it wide open."

CHAPTER 72

A dense mass of tourists threatened to overwhelm the spindly ramp leading up to the metal detectors at the Moors Gate, the only access to the Temple Mount open to non-Muslims. Nick had run through the market toward that gate on memory and instinct. Now he realized they could not get through, not even by fighting their way through the line. The ramp was too narrow and the crowd too thick.

"The SWARM still has nothing," said Drake, looking down at the tablet.

Nick shielded his eyes to gaze up at the drones. "Release them. Send them east. We're confined to one gate, but Muslims can use the gates to the north and east. We've already covered the north."

Drake did as commanded, and as soon as the SWARM flew over the wall, an alarm sounded from the tablet. The southernmost drone picked up a radiation signature. The formation automatically shifted southeast to compensate, with the eastern bird picking up the signature next, and then the northern one. In half a minute, they had centered over a radiation source in the archaeological park south of the Temple Mount. There, under the crosshairs, was a man dressed in loose-fitting desert garb—a long tan shirt and olive trousers—with a black-and-tan *shemagh* around his neck. He carried a large gray backpack slung over one shoulder.

"Bingo," said Drake, and the two of them started cutting through the crowd toward the southern exit from the plaza.

"Is it Kattan?" asked Molly, over the SATCOM.

"Unknown," said Nick, as he and Drake stutter-stepped through the crowd. "We couldn't see his face." He shot a glance at the screen in Drake's hands. The target continued to work his way north and west through the labyrinth of walkways and stairwells of the archaeological park, entering the sparse ruins of a seventh-century Arabian palace that once stood against the Temple Mount wall. He seemed completely unaware of the drones. "He's heading for the middle of the south wall, Lighthouse. Where is he going? There's no gate there."

After a long moment of silence on the SATCOM, Molly came back with her answer. "My guess is he's heading for the southern access to your plaza, west of the temple. From there, he'll make for the Cotton Merchants gate, two hundred yards north. You're on a course to intercept now."

Seconds later, Nick and Drake popped out of the crowd near the southern access Molly had described. The drones were still southeast of them.

"We've got him," said Drake, slowing to check his tablet.

Nick clicked off the safety of the M4 rifle and checked the video as well, but the man with the backpack did not continue toward their position. He turned due north and disappeared beneath the sand-colored ruins of an archway that jutted out from the southern wall of the Temple Mount. The SWARM continued north for a moment, turned east, turned north again, and then hovered there, making tiny adjustments in all directions.

Nick's world grew a shade darker. The eclipse was more than halfway through. He stared at the tablet in disbelief. "He's gone."

Drake grabbed his arm and pulled him toward the plaza exit. "No. Look at the drones." He pointed to the sky where the SWARM still hovered. Occasionally the UAVs jerked one way or another in a synchronized dance that kept them centered on the radiation source. "They still have him. He's gone down a hole, probably planting the bomb right now."

The two operatives hopped the turnstile that separated the plaza from the archaeological park and raced toward the ruins.

Nick was the first to reach the area where the terrorist had disappeared. In the shadow of the crumbling archway, he found a set of steps leading down. "There's a tunnel here," he said in a low voice, depending on the SATCOM for Drake to hear.

The steps dropped only a short distance, but they turned east into a tunnel completely shaded from the half-eclipsed sun. Nick lit the flashlight on the rail of the Israeli M4, lifted the weapon to his shoulder, and moved cautiously forward. "What are the drones doing?" he whispered.

Drake had his pistol in his right hand and the tablet in his left. He raised the screen to his eyes. "Still hovering. The center point of the radiation is twelve meters ahead and ten meters left."

"Left?" Nick put a hand against the stone wall next to him. "Left is solid rock."

"That's what it says."

On a hunch, Nick let his fingers drag along the wall. The vines and weedy rock plants in the cracks grew increasingly thicker until he came to a point where his fingers lost contact with the stone. He stopped, pressed his hand deeper, and only found more plants. "There's a passage here."

Nick backed up and held his light on the vines while Drake tried to pull them away, but they were too thick to manage. They pushed through instead, with Nick in the lead, flashlight off, trying not to wonder what kinds of insects made their homes in the dark hollows of the tangled greenery sliding across his neck and poking into his ears.

A few feet in, the stones beneath Nick's feet dropped. Another set of stairs. There were just a few, and soon he emerged from the hanging foliage into open darkness. He raised his weapon to his shoulder and flipped on the light, turning in a slow circle. They had discovered a small chamber inside the Temple Mount wall. After Drake came through, the vegetation fell back into place behind him, closing up the portal like a natural seal. More vines and rock plants spread out from the stairway, covering the walls and ceiling of the chamber with matted green.

"Where is he, Drake?"

Other than the foliage, the chamber was empty.

CHAPTER 73

"Typical Hashashin trick," said Drake, lowering his pistol. "Vanishing into thin air."

Nick pursed his lips, slowly scanning the walls with the flashlight on his rifle. "With a nuclear weapon? Check the drones."

Drake did as commanded, and then shook his head. "The radiation signature is here, right on top of us. He should be here."

Nick could see enough of the stone walls through the vegetation to see that there was no other passage besides the one they came through. The rear wall was different, though, set with a tile mosaic. Crescents and stars in blue and white peeked out from behind the dark green vines. "Help me out," he said, lowering the weapon and stepping over to the wall.

The two of them started yanking vines away from the

tiles. Some fell to the floor. Others stubbornly clung to the ceiling and formed a living curtain behind them. When enough had been cleared away to get a good look, Nick saw that there were several rows of larger round tiles set amid the square mosaic pieces—five rows of twenty, to be exact. Each large white tile, maybe ten inches in diameter, was painted with a word in blue Arabic calligraphy and with blue horizontal crescent moons at the top and bottom.

"Is this that Persian-Turkish mix again?" asked Drake, rubbing dirt off one of the tiles with his thumb.

Nick pulled another vine away and scrutinized the script. "No. These are the ninety-nine traditional names of Allah. They're always written in Quranic Arabic."

"Well, they'd better tell you something. Our nuke is on the move again, look." Drake showed Nick the tablet. The SWARM crosshairs drifted along the roof of the Al-Aqsa Mosque on the Temple Mount directly above them. Then the terrorist emerged from beneath the stone awning at the entrance, as if he had simply taken an elevator up a few floors and continued on his way. He started pressing his way through the thick crowd of eclipse-watchers, all staring east through cheap square glasses of paper and black film.

Nick returned his focus to the tiles. "The answer has to be here."

"Why ninety-nine names?" asked Drake. "Why not a hundred?"

Nick snapped his fingers and slapped Drake in the arm with the back of his hand. "You're a genius. There are ninety-nine traditional names, but there are one hundred tiles. One of these serves another purpose." He started reading the names in English, looking for one that didn't fit. "The Mighty, The Judge, The Reckoner, The Humiliator—"

"The Humiliator," Drake repeated with a chuckle. "Nice."

Nick kept going, reading faster. "The Watchful, The Causer of Death, The—" He paused. He couldn't read the next tile. He stared at it for a few seconds and then tilted his head to one side.

Drake tilted his head as well, and kept it tilted as he stepped closer, examining the tile with Nick. After another heartbeat, he whispered, "Why are we sideways?"

"This one is upside down." Nick ran his fingers across the tile. The blue crescent across the bottom had a small bump in the center. "The Key," he said out loud, reading the inverted words. On a hunch, he pressed the crescent inward. It gave way and then sprang back.

Suddenly the answer hit him. Nick pulled the Hashashin knife from his pocket. The calligraphy on the hilt was not Turkic, like the Hashashin prophecy. It was Arabic, just like this wall. He muttered the phrase as he pressed the knife into the tile. "I am the key."

The bump activated the springs in the hilt and the blades shot out, a perfect fit inside the crescent-shaped indentation, but still nothing happened. Tentatively, Nick tried turning the tile with the knife in place. It worked. The tile rotated with a soft scraping sound.

Nick kept going until the crescents above and below had switched positions and the word was right side up.

There was a heavy *thump* and the sound of stone sliding across stone. Nick removed the knife. The blades retracted. The chamber was still again.

Drake panned his light around the room. "What just happened?"

The walls had not changed. There were no new passages, no stairwells leading up into the mosque above. At a loss, Nick looked up at his partner, and caught a hint of rose-colored light pouring down through a space between the ceiling vines. He motioned to Drake and shined his light on the area, revealing a vertical passage that had opened above them.

Drake didn't hesitate. He bent down and threaded his fingers together for Nick. "Going up?"

Before taking the boost from his teammate, Nick pulled the sling of his M4 over his head and laid it on the ground. Guns weren't permitted on the Temple Mount, even for the IDF, and there was no way he could conceal a rifle that size.

With Drake's help, Nick was able to get his hands on a stone jutting out from the interior of the octagonal well. Similar stones studded the well on either side, all the way up, forming a ladder. Nick pulled himself up, hand over hand, until he was high enough to get a foot on the lowest stone. Then the climb was easier.

Moments later, Nick emerged in the Al-Aqsa Mosque, into a narrow space between the mosque's rounded southern wall and a tall partition of solid red-and-white marble. A wide dome spread out above him, painted with elaborate patterns in gold and burgundy and illuminated by a ring of red and purple stained-glass windows. The sunlight shining through was dim, like on an overcast day.

Nick could see little to his left and right. At either end, the marble partition curved closer to the rounded wall, leaving only a narrow gap, but the partition itself was cut all the way through with intricate arabesque patterns, so that he could peer out through the carvings into the mosque's expansive prayer room. He did not like what he saw.

Nick had hoped that everyone would be outside, watching the celestial event. Instead, he saw scores of men reclining in circled groups on the carpet, many wearing the black-and-white *keffiyeh* headdress of Palestinian nationalists, either on their heads or around their necks. Several of these would be Al-Aqsa Brigade terrorists, here to protect their territory during the tourist hysteria of the eclipse.

"This is it," said Drake, shouldering up beside Nick. With his greater height, he had made it up through the well on his own.

"This is what?" asked Nick.

"This is the death Kattan had planned for me all along."

CHAPTER 74

Kurt Baron sat alone on a weathered bench amid a grove of olives on the northwest corner of the Temple Mount. If not for the timeless etchings in the other stone benches, he would not have recognized this spot. The trees here were tall and full, adolescents nearing their prime, but he remembered them as saplings. Had it been so long?

A paper bag with four pastries from the American Colony sat next to him, as did a set of eclipse glasses he had purchased from a vendor near the Jaffa gate. He picked up the glasses and peered through the black film to see how the sun fared. The orange disc was now two-thirds shrouded by the black silhouette of the moon. Soon the occultation would be complete, and the whole of Jerusalem would be covered in darkness despite the early hour of the day. Avi was going to miss it all.

Kurt put the glasses down and checked his phone for the seventh time in the last ten minutes. In the time since he had arrived at their old spot, he had sent his friend three additional text messages asking where he was and if he was coming. The texts appeared to have gone through, but he could never tell with these over-complicated smartphones. Either way, Avi had not replied.

He resisted the urge to break into a cheese-filled Danish and lifted the eclipse glasses to his eyes again. After a few seconds of watching the shadow creep across the sun, the image was suddenly blocked. Kurt lowered the glasses to find a young Israeli policeman standing in front of him.

"Dr. Baron, I presume?"

"Yes."

"Dr. Baron, Professor Avi Bendayan asked that I come and collect you."

"I'm afraid I don't understand."

The policeman shifted his feet uncomfortably and scanned the area behind the professor, adjusting the sub-machine gun slung over his shoulder as he turned. Kurt vaguely remembered that guns were not allowed up here, but the thought was pushed out of his mind when he noticed the hand with which the young man held the weapon. It was mechanical, a prosthetic designed to hold a machine gun and pull the trigger. He wondered if the kid had lost the appendage in a suicide bombing or a rocket attack.

"Sir, Professor Bendayan has arranged for you to take your tea in the Kipat Hasela," said the young man, using the Jewish name for the Dome of the Rock.

Again, Kurt was confused. He glanced southeast toward the central platform where the great mosque stood. "Non-Muslims are not allowed in there."

The policeman pursed his lips. "That is not entirely true. Some are. In particular, archaeologists are permitted to enter the Kipat Hasela for research or in special circumstances. Please, Dr. Baron. Professor Bendayan is waiting."

Kurt did not need much convincing. A total eclipse and a look at the Holy of Holies in the same day was a blessing you did not argue with. Anyway, as the kid said, Avi was waiting for him. He tossed the eclipse glasses into the bag with the pastries and got up to follow the policeman.

―――――――

"This is where we part ways, boss," whispered Drake, looking out through the partition at the Palestinians lounging on the carpet. "I said I wouldn't leave you, but that's the only way you're getting out of here in one piece."

"No. There has to be another way." But Nick didn't see one. The Al-Aqsa Mosque was expressly forbidden to non-Muslims. Jews had been stoned just for opening a copy of the Torah on the plaza outside, and those events were on good days, when the mosque was full of regular worshippers. There was no way a guy in an IDF uniform and a big American in a loud Hawaiian shirt were going to survive the seventy-meter gauntlet of Palestinian nationalists between their current position and the front door.

"I have to do this. We don't have a choice," argued Drake. He held the tablet up between them. The man with the backpack had already made it to the cypress grove at the edge of the Dome of the Rock platform. He stood there, leaning against a tree.

Nick watched him for a few seconds. The terrorist kept his eyes on the Dome, but showed no sign of continuing toward it. "What is he waiting for?"

Drake shrugged. "Maybe he's savoring his last moments on earth. It doesn't matter. What matters is, you've got to get a move on and catch him before he decides to finish the job he came here to do."

"If you step out there, there's going to be a riot."

Drake grinned. "I know. A riot is exactly what you need."

The big operative suddenly pressed his pistol and the tablet into Nick's hands and squeezed out into the open. The closest Palestinians were a good fifteen meters away. At first, none of them saw him. He glanced back through the gap and whispered, "Godspeed, boss." Then he strode out into the prayer room with his arms open wide, shouting, "Shalom, everybody!"

At first there was confusion. Heads jerked in Drake's direction. A Palestinian shouted. Then several more began shouting angrily from different parts of the wide prayer room. Those first sparks ignited the fuel of hatred that is always waiting at Al-Aqsa, and the crowd rippled to its feet like spreading flame. Drake's dubious plan worked. The men all rushed to attack as he led them to one side of the mosque. He belted the first challenger across the chin and threw the next into the wall behind him. Then he disappeared behind the flood, just like a character in one of his late-night zombie movies.

Ahead of Nick, the bloodred carpet of the Al-Aqsa prayer room was clear, all the way to the door.

"What are you waiting for?" grunted Drake through the SATCOM.

Nick didn't argue. He made one last, unsuccessful attempt to catch a glimpse of his best friend through the mob, and then bolted for the door.

CHAPTER 75

Four more Palestinians pushed through the tall green doors of the mosque right before Nick reached them. One of them took a swing. Nick ducked left and came up throwing a hook. He dropped the man to the floor in one punch. He took the next one down with an elbow to the temple and then ducked the other two and made it into open air.

Confusion was settling in. The crowd was beginning to notice the disturbance. Palestinians filtered out from the tourists and headed for the mosque. Nick was surrounded, but the group was thin, nothing like what Drake was facing inside.

Nick also had help.

Long experience had prepared the Israelis for trouble on the Temple Mount during a big event like the eclipse.

They were ready. Police in riot gear rushed out of a tent to Nick's left. He fought his way toward them. One Palestinian made the mistake of bear-hugging Nick from behind, trying to throw him down. He bought himself a head butt to the nose and a quick trip to the stone beneath the feet of his friends. Two more quickly followed, grabbing at Nick's IDF uniform. He pulled one man's head to his knee and heard the nasty *crack* of a jaw breaking. The other one got an arm around Nick's throat, but then a black baton flashed over Nick's head. There was an ugly *thock* and the arm went slack. The Israelis pulled Nick past the riot line to safety. Several patted him on the shoulders as he stumbled through, assuming he was one of the regular Temple Mount police group. Nick shouted that there was an American tourist trapped inside and kept going.

Unfortunately, the troops would not likely be much help to Drake. In the crazy world of the Temple Mount, the Israeli police were not permitted inside the mosques. Their few breaches of this protocol in the past had created massive riots all over the West Bank. The police could only set up a perimeter on the outside to protect the civilians on the plaza. In that capacity, always with unnatural patience and discipline, they had often faced rocks and Molotov cocktails thrown from the entrance of the mosque.

As he left the police line, Nick searched for the target, but a wall of sun-watchers crowding north to get away from the riot blocked his view. He could see the SWARM above them, though. The drones were drifting north. The Hashashin was on the move again.

Nick saw two men in green uniforms pushing toward him through the crowd, and he suddenly realized what the terrorist had been waiting for. The riot had lured the Islamic Waqf Authority guards away from their post in front of the Dome of the Rock. They would have stopped the target at the entrance to search his big backpack. Now they were out of the way, heading south for their customary harassment of the Israelis forming around Al-Aqsa. Nick winced. Once again, his team had become one of the dominoes in Kattan's string of outcomes. Unbelievable.

In his earpiece, he could still hear Drake being pummeled, grunting with pain and occasionally making a snide remark that his attackers couldn't understand.

"Hurry!" pleaded Molly. Nick could hear the tears in her voice. "Get the nuke so you can help him!"

"Working on it." Nick shouldered his way north through the crowd and slid into the narrow cypress grove that bordered the Dome of the Rock platform. He finally saw the Hashashin again, almost to the unguarded entrance of the mosque. In the cover of the trees, he drew his suppressed Sig Sauer pistol. He could end this right now and go back to save Drake. He lined the Hashashin up in his sights.

The moment Nick pulled the trigger, a group of civilians passed between him and the terrorist. He jerked the weapon up but it still spit out a round. A puff of dust erupted from the side of the mosque as the bullet obliterated a patch of five-hundred-year-old ceramic tile. With the noise of the riot, no one noticed.

By the time the tourists passed, the target had disappeared again. The SWARM hovered over the great gold dome.

There was a terrible *crack* in Nick's earpiece. Drake let out a pained cry and then his SATCOM went totally dead.

"Drake? Molly?"

No response from either.

Nick's phone chimed. He risked a glance at the screen.

The Emissary has taken your second knight and put you in check. Your move.

Nick growled as he put the phone away. He vaulted up onto the platform. This game was over.

A paper sign irreverently duct-taped to the mosque's great wooden door said CLOSED FOR CELESTIAL EVENT BY ORDER OF THE WAQF AUTHORITY in three languages. Nick held his pistol tight against his chest, pulled open the heavy door, and slipped inside. Blood stained the rich green carpet just beyond the marble entrance. A third Waqf Authority guard listed to one side in his chair, a bullet hole in his head.

Nick quietly pressed deeper into the octagonal mosque. Two circles of gray-and-white columns interspersed with five-foot-long partitions formed a maze of marble around the sacred Foundation Stone at the center. They offered a good deal of cover, but they obscured his line of sight to the Hashashin.

The great rock itself jutted four feet above the floor and was surrounded by a four-foot-tall wood-and-marble fence. Above it rose the massive dome, inlaid with dizzying floral patterns in green and blue and thousands of pounds of pure gold, barely lit by a few chandeliers and the darkening sunlight seeping through blue stained-glass windows.

Creeping up behind one of the rounded partitions, Nick got eyes on the terrorist, kneeling on the Foundation Stone with a semiautomatic in his left hand. A metal suitcase lay open in front of him.

To Nick's surprise, it was not Kattan. No matter. This guy had the nuke. Nick could find Kattan and the vaccine later. He leveled his weapon and was about to fire when he noticed a remote trigger in the terrorist's right hand—a black oval with a red trigger underneath, no bigger than a presentation remote. Nick lowered the Sig. In the throes of death, the Hashashin might still trigger the bomb.

Nick stuffed his gun behind his back and rushed forward from the inner ring, his footsteps muted by the thick carpet. He ran in a crouch, planning to spring up and knock the trigger away.

The Hashashin stood and turned just as Nick's feet left the carpet. Nick knocked the remote from his hand, but the terrorist caught his shoulders and threw him down on the rock. He let out a pained *"Oof!"* as the air left his lungs. The remote skipped across the carpet, coming to rest at the base of a marble column.

Nick took too long to recover from the fall. The Hashashin lifted him off the rock by his lapels, and before he got his hands up, the terrorist landed a cruel punch straight to his teeth.

"Infidel!" he shouted. "You cannot stop this. The signs have been cast. The Emissary has spoken."

"Your Emissary is a con man," retorted Nick, spitting out blood with the words. He rolled onto his side and kicked his top leg, sweeping the Hashashin's feet out from underneath him, bringing him crashing down onto the Foundation Stone. Then he scrambled on top and landed a counterblow to the man's face, bloodying the terrorist's lip to match his own.

The Hashashin swung up with a right, but Nick caught his arm and swept it across his body, sprawling his knees back and pressing down with all his weight to pin both of the terrorist's arms to his chest. Their bloodied faces were inches apart. Nick slowly raked his forearm across the man's jugular. The Hashashin coughed. His eyes bulged and he started to turn purple.

Nick put even more weight on the forearm. "You're not going to detonate any nukes today. Now, where's your boss?"

Out of the corner of his eye, Nick saw a man in an Israeli police uniform approaching. He leveled a subma-chine gun at them both.

"Don't!" Nick shouted, but the policeman pulled the trigger. Nick jerked up and shielded his face as the Israeli riddled his captive with bullets.

The light beneath the dome grew another shade darker.

The Hashashin coughed and gurgled and then went silent, staring sightlessly up at the rich gold above.

Nick slowly stood, raising his hands. "Easy, buddy, I'm not your enemy."

"How can you say that?" asked the policeman. Then he pulled the trigger again.

CHAPTER 76

The policeman fired a burst of three bullets. Two slammed into Nick's vest and one caught him in the right clavicle just above it, sending him reeling backward. He tripped over the barrier surrounding the Foundation Stone and fell to the floor.

"Tsk, tsk, tsk," muttered the policeman, walking around the stone. He kept the weapon leveled.

Tendrils of wicked pain radiated outward from the wound, lighting Nick's neck and chest on fire. He could sense loose bone fragments floating around as he struggled to his feet. "The case," he breathed, holding his hands up to keep from getting shot again. "It's a nuclear bomb. Get a team in here to contain it. And tell the men outside to breach the Al-Aqsa mosque. I have a man in there."

"I have a man in there too. Yours is dead," said the

policeman. The man's accent was hard to peg, New England maybe, with a trace of Gulf Arab. He backed up to the first ring of marble columns, keeping his weapon trained on Nick while he knelt down and picked up the remote trigger. "That is your problem, Nick Baron. You are completely unwilling to sacrifice your pieces." The man nodded at the corpse still bleeding out on the sacred rock. "Me? I don't suffer that deficiency. I treat my pieces the way they were meant to be treated—disposable."

"Your pieces?" Nick muttered. He tried to focus through the pain, squinting at the face in the shadow of the police cap. In the dim light of the mosque he had not recognized his primary target. "Kattan."

The young man took off his police cap and tossed it aside. "Good. Very good. You remember. That means you remember taking my father from me." Kattan abruptly stepped to one of the marble partitions and dragged Kurt Baron into view, bound and gagged. "And now I will take yours."

Nick lurched forward, but Kattan shot a burst at the carpet in front of him, sending ricochets into the sacred stone and forcing him back. His father tried to shout through his gag, but the effort only resulted in a fit of coughing.

The terrorist approached, motioning Nick aside with the weapon, and the two circled each other until Kattan reached the Foundation Stone. He pulled his bound captive up onto the rock and stood over the nuke and the dead Hashashin.

"You played well, Nick Baron," he said with a gracious

smile. "But you played exactly as I steered you." He raised his eyebrows. "Did you really think that you would out-smart me by not going to Cairo? I didn't *want* you there. I wanted you here, with me at the very end. And here you are." He spread his arms—gun, remote nuclear trigger, and all—and bowed.

"If you wanted me here," said Nick, stalling for time, "then why did your men try to kill me in London?"

"Kill you?" Kattan rocked back with laughter. "To steal a line from Hollywood, if I had wanted to kill you, you'd be dead. Those little distractions were just meant to keep you in the game, and they did, at least until a few minutes ago." He shook the gun at Nick with his severed arm. "You are a poor sport. Like a petulant child upending the board, you refused to make your last move in our little game."

"I was never in this for the game."

"Liar!" shouted Kattan, his voice echoing beneath the dome. "I have seen your life, Nick Baron! I have studied you for *years*! Whether by guns or planes or little wooden pieces, you *live* to play the game, and *I* kept you in it! I allowed you to survive this long and you repaid me by quitting the board." He turned the machine gun toward Nick's dad. "I sent you a move a few minutes ago after my man killed your partner. Pull out your phone, now. Make your countermove. Finish the game."

"No. This is absurd."

Nick's response infuriated the terrorist. He shoved the machine gun into Kurt's chest. "Do it!"

"Okay, okay." Nick held out his hands to settle Kattan down. "Take it easy." He pulled out his phone and opened the chess app. Kattan had only left him one move to get out of check, taking a rook with his king, exposing his own bishop. He pressed enter and then pocketed his phone once more.

They stared at each other in silence for several seconds, Kattan's weapon still pressed into Kurt's chest, until a chime sounded from the terrorist's pocket. The move had been received. He did not bother to pull out the phone. He lifted his eyes blissfully to the ceiling and quietly breathed, "Thank you," and then pulled the machine gun's trigger.

Nick's dad grunted through his gag and dropped to his knees.

"Dad!" In a rage, Nick drew the Sig from behind his back, ignoring the pain in his shoulder, but Kattan pivoted and fired again. One bullet seared Nick's finger below the trigger guard. Another sparked off the suppressor, knocking the weapon away. It clumped onto the floor behind him. Nick growled and pulled his stinging hand to his chest.

"The same abilities that allow me to dominate you on the chess board also give me superior reflexes, Nick. It's all part of the same package. You cannot outthink me, and you cannot outshoot me. Stand down."

The natural light in the lattice windows was almost gone. Kattan looked up at the dome, watching the shadow inside it grow. "I will let you observe your father's final

Kurt's eyes pleaded with his son as he collapsed onto his side next to the dead Hashashin. He had taken three rounds to the right side of his chest. Blood soaked his shirt and trickled down onto the Foundation Stone.

"At least let me go to him," said Nick, taking a step forward.

Kattan thrust his gun out. "Ah, ah, ah. I have been more than generous already. Stay where you are."

Nick kept his distance, but he circled, looking for an opportunity. "You have your revenge. You can kill us and walk away. Why D.C.? Why Jerusalem? You're not one of these Hashashin fanatics."

"Hashashin fanatics? Really?" Kattan chuckled. "You are the one racing around the world, killing, destroying lives, all in the name of a fallen power that still believes it governs the world by divine right. Who are you to call *them* fanatics?"

"A hundred thousand Israelis and tourists, ten thousand Americans," said Nick, still circling. He shot a glance at his dad. Kurt was propped up on his left elbow, following his son with his eyes, but they were losing focus. He was fading. His pooling blood mixed with the blood of the Hashashin to form a dark red river that snaked through the contours of the Foundation Stone. Nick looked back up at Kattan. "Do you really believe that killing them and blowing up that rock you're standing on will bring your Mahdi and some kind of paradise?"

"Stop!" shouted Kattan, raising the remote trigger.

Nick froze.

The terrorist's voice calmed again and he tilted his head. "Pardon the outburst, but your attempt to off-balance me is both obvious and annoying. I bid you stand still."

Nick nodded slowly and lifted his hands again.

"Messiah, Mahdi, they are all the same," continued the terrorist. "Archaic nonsense that has cost the lives of millions and plagued our world with constant conflict. Don't you see, Nick? There is no God, no paradise." He stamped the sacred stone with his boot. "This is just a rock. But the world . . . wants . . . Armageddon." He shook the bomb trigger to emphasize each word and then dropped it to his side and looked up into the dome. "I will give it to them. And when the smoke clears and the sun emerges from the shadow of the black moon, you and I and a hundred thousand others will be dead, and then what?" He shrugged. "The world will go on. But they will go on in the realization that Armageddon has passed and no messiah and no Mahdi came to save them from their miserable existence."

Kattan took a deep breath through his nostrils and smiled as if the air were suddenly clean. "The delusions that pollute this world will collapse and all will see that every religion is false. The crusades and the jihads will finally end."

Nick shook his head. "When the smoke clears, the world will rebuild their churches. The masses will keep watching for the messiah. You can't destroy faith that easily."

Kurt moaned and Nick's eyes dropped to his father in time to watch his head droop back. His elbow slipped from under him and he collapsed onto the Foundation Stone. Nick rushed forward but Kattan stamped his foot again, shouting, "No! I already told you, no!"

Nick stopped, closer than before but still too far to strike.

"Let me explain how the endgame has gone," said Kattan, calming himself. "Your last knight is dead, taken by my man in the mosque, and your final move exposed your last bishop." He viciously kicked Kurt's unmoving form. "And so, I have taken him too."

Nick's phone gave its dreadful chime, announcing its receipt of the final move of the game.

Above them, the last trace of sunlight vanished from the lattice windows. Kattan looked up and nodded his approval at the completeness of the shadow that filled the dome. He smiled down at Nick. "You have a message. Go ahead. See what it says."

As Nick pulled out his device and tilted up the screen, the terrorist raised the remote above his head. He wrapped his index finger around its red trigger. "Our game is over, Nick Baron. Checkmate."

CHAPTER 78

The instant that Kattan said *checkmate*, four of the windows encircling the dome exploded inward, showering the inner mosque with splintered latticework and tinted glass. The SWARM crashed its way into the chamber and hovered over the terrorist in a tight formation.

Kattan took his finger off the trigger as he ducked in surprise, shielding his face against the debris with his good arm.

The drones did not surprise Nick at all. He had called them. After the chime from the chess app, he had pulled out the SWARM control tablet instead of his phone. With a sweep of his thumb he had brought them in through the windows.

When the drones crashed in, Nick's left hand was already at his back, wrapped around the grip of a second Sig Sauer—the one Drake had pressed into his hands before braving the mob. His efforts to close the distance had brought him in range for a shot he could not afford to miss.

Nick whipped the gun around to his front and fired two rapid shots, obliterating the remote trigger and taking a large chunk out of Kattan's good hand.

The terrorist tried to return fire, but Nick dove out of the way, rolled to one knee, and turned his Sig on the mechanical hand holding the submachine gun, firing three more times. The weapon fell to the floor with a piece of Kattan's prosthetic still attached.

The terrorist rushed him, screaming with fury, and Nick shifted his aim to Kattan's head, but found that he could not pull the trigger, despite everything he had done. The person running toward him now was just an adolescent boy, enraged by the loss of his father.

Nick rose from his knee, rotated the pistol sideways in his hand, and struck the young man across the temple. Kattan stumbled past and collapsed onto the carpet, out cold.

A moan came from the Foundation Stone. Kurt Baron's eyes were open.

"Dad!" Ignoring his own pains, Nick leapt onto the rock and knelt at the older Baron's side. He tore away the gag and cradled his father's head in his hands. "Dad, you're alive."

"Sorry, Son . . . Had to play dead . . . Jerk was never going to shut up if I didn't."

"Try not to speak, Dad." Nick gently laid his father's head down again. "I'm going to get you some help."

Nick started to get up, but Kurt weakly grabbed his arm.

"The bomb, Son. It beeped while your friend was ranting. I think . . . it's active."

Nick cautiously removed the aluminum cover from the device and found a five-inch touch screen. Ivory-white numbers counted down on a black field. There were twenty-five seconds remaining. Kattan must have activated a timer as a contingency. A square in the bottom right corner read ABORT.

"He left himself a way out, a fail-safe in case I didn't show." Nick pressed the button, but the numbers didn't stop. They shrank to the top center and a gray keyboard and white entry window appeared. A cursor flashed, waiting for the password. Nick glanced over at Kattan. He had just knocked out the only man who could stop the bomb.

The keyboard looked strange. Some letters were missing. Other keys bore letter-number combinations. With sixteen seconds left on the clock, Nick realized he was looking at chess notation. "Checkmate," he said out loud.

He pulled out his phone and checked Kattan's last move. He had taken Nick's bishop with a pawn, *but which pawn was it when the game began?*

Nick had no choice but to take his best guess. He typed in the move WKPxBKB#, white king's pawn takes black king's bishop for checkmate.

He pressed enter.

The numbers kept going, less than ten seconds now. Nick winced.

Then green text appeared below the countdown, announcing access granted. Another button appeared next to it. DISABLE?

Nick quickly pressed it. The timer froze. The white numbers read 07.77.

"We did it, Dad." Nick turned back to his father and smiled, but the older Baron had closed his eyes again. There was an immense amount of blood on the Foundation Stone. Kurt's lips were blue. He wasn't moving.

EPILOGUE

Nick."

Katy called to him.

Her voice was muddled, distant like before. He was afraid to look, afraid he'd see her up on the Temple Mount wall with Kattan again, fire blazing up between them.

"Nick, wake up."

Nick reluctantly opened his eyes. Katy was not standing on a wall. She was standing right next to him. As his eyes focused, the look of concern on her face brightened into a beautiful smile. A tear rolled down her cheek. She sniffed. "There you are."

She was holding his hand. With effort, he turned his palm so that their fingers intertwined. "It's you" was all he could muster.

She nodded and wiped the tear away. "Yes, it's me."

Nick gradually took in the room. He was in a hospital bed, half-reclined, a rack of monitors on one side of it, Katy on the other. This was a private room. Luke sat on a little brown couch playing with his favorite car, a Corvette Nick's dad had given him.

Dad.

Nick tried to sit up. Pain shot through his neck and shoulder, bringing clarity—flashes of memory. He saw IDF soldiers storming the Dome of the Rock. He saw white stones rolling beneath a gurney, a red helicopter up ahead. He heard his own voice shouting that Kattan was dangerous and that he might be carrying a vaccine that could save thousands. He watched them leading the terrorist away in handcuffs, one of the soldiers holding up a clear vial, its contents sparkling in the emerging sun.

Another flash and Nick saw his dad cold and lifeless on the helicopter floor, the Temple Mount drifting away below them, a medic running a tube between their arms, sending Nick's blood to his dad. Then he saw a surgery room and a doctor holding a syringe to his IV port. He protested, but the doctor plunged it in anyway.

After that, there was only darkness.

Nick's head fell back onto his pillow.

"Slow down, baby, you're okay," said Katy, placing a soft hand on his forehead.

"Where?" he asked.

"You're at Hadassah Medical Center."

"I'm still in Jerusalem?"

She nodded.

"And my dad?"

"He's going to be okay. Better than that, he has several admirers now."

Nick struggled to push the fog of sedatives to the edge of his mind. "Admirers? I'm not following."

Katy pulled up a rolling stool and sat down next to her husband. She took his hand again, this time with both of hers, massaging his fingers. "There's a guy here, I think he's Mossad—"

"Walker's contact," interrupted Nick.

Katy nodded. "I think so. He's trying to keep people from talking about what happened up there. He's making everybody sign papers, but there's one story he can't stop."

"It's hard to stop Dad when he gets going," said Nick in a flat tone. "He's claiming he singlehandedly disarmed the nuke, isn't he?"

She sniffed and giggled, squeezing his hand. "Your dad's not even conscious yet, silly. The medics who pulled you out of the mosque are the ones telling the story." Then she leaned closer, lowering her voice as if sharing a secret. "They say your dad and a terrorist both bled buckets on the Foundation Stone. They say the blood trails joined as they descended the stone, but then the terrorist's blood turned and poured onto the floor. He bled out and died. Your dad's trail continued into the Well of Souls, the hole that used to capture the blood of Jewish sacrifices at the bottom of the stone."

There were voices in the hall, shadows outside the door. Katy glanced up and waited for them to move off before she continued. "The medics say the blood trail thinned right there, that your dad stopped bleeding when his blood reached the Well of Souls. The surgeon agrees. He should have bled out, but he didn't. The doctors are calling it a miracle. Word is spreading around the hospital like wildfire."

Nick let out a painful chuckle.

"What's so funny?"

"Faith. It's contagious. Kattan tried to destroy it, but all he did was fuel the fire. The joke's on him. Drake would have loved it."

"You should tell him. He's dying to see you."

Nick abruptly sat up, but the pain knocked him back again. "He's what?"

"He's dying to see you." Katy pointed toward the opposite wall. "Drake is two doors down. He can't talk very well, though. He's all beat up. The IDF found him in the ruins south of the Temple Mount, limping on a broken leg and dragging a dead man with him. He said the guy was a terrorist that tried to stab him with a poison knife."

"He's supposed to be dead." Nick glowered at the wall. "I'm gonna kill him." Then he turned to Katy. The fog of the medication was now completely gone. "And you, you're supposed to be on a flight to Washington. Why are you here?"

Katy straightened and scrunched up her nose. "You think I was going to leave you in Israel just because you told me to?"

"You and Luke could have been killed."

She relaxed, leaned into him again. "Not with you on the job."

Nick reached up and pulled his wife to him, kissing her deeply. Not to be left out, Luke toddled over, and Katy scooped him up and set him on the bed with his father. The boy took his daddy's hand and played with his fingers. Nick looked up into Katy's hazel eyes. "Do you think maybe one day you can learn to do as you're told?"

"No," she said, and kissed him again. "No, I don't."

Find out what happened to the imam
from the Jamatkhana, Detective Sergeant Mercer,
Constable Gale, and others.

Get the free Stealth Ops app for your smart device.